ATLANTIS
FALLEN

Also by CE Murphy

The Heartstrike Chronicles
ATLANTIS FALLEN
PROMETHEUS BOUND (*forthcoming*)
AVALON RISING (*forthcoming*)

The Austen Chronicles
MAGIC & MANNERS
SORCERY & SOCIETY (*forthcoming*)

The Walker Papers
URBAN SHAMAN • WINTER MOON • THUNDERBIRD FALLS
COYOTE DREAMS • WALKING DEAD • DEMON HUNTS
SPIRIT DANCES • RAVEN CALLS • NO DOMINION
MOUNTAIN ECHOES • SHAMAN RISES

& with Faith Hunter
EASY PICKINGS
A Walker Papers/Skinwalker crossover novella

The Old Races Universe
HEART OF STONE • HOUSE OF CARDS • HANDS OF FLAME

BABA YAGA'S DAUGHTER

The Worldwalker Duology
TRUTHSEEKER • WAYFINDER

The Inheritors' Cycle
THE QUEEN'S BASTARD • THE PRETENDER'S CROWN

STONE'S THROE
A Spirit of the Century Novel

For Deb!

ATLANTIS FALLEN

The Heartstrike Chronicles: Book One

Thank you for introducing people to my books!

C.E. MURPHY

a miz kit production

ATLANTIS FALLEN

ISBN: 978-1-61317-129-5

Book design: The Barbarienne's Den
Cover art & design: Tara O'Shea / fringe-element.net
Copy editor: Stephanie Mowrey

mostly for Peter, of course

1

Eventually her hair would fill the room.

Hip-length when she was captured, she could only guess at its length now. Folding it from her feet to her head told her it was at least a dozen times her body's height. It made her frantic, being unable to escape the tendrils, no matter where she dove in the room. They followed her, invisible spiders whose subtle brush were the only contact she had with anything living.

She had broken it off at first, tearing great handsful apart and letting them go in the little prison. It hadn't taken long to realize the folly of the tactic: at least while attached to her head, she had some control over the impossibly long strands. Those torn free twisted themselves around her legs and arms, constricting her movements.

Those broken lengths were what made her realize that someday the room would fill with her hair. The thought terrified her. Captivity for eternity was bad enough. Captivity wound motionlessly in a secondary prison of her own making was enough to set her screaming.

The sound carried to the walls of her prison, bouncing harmlessly back to her, distorted with water. Only exhaustion made her stop, hours or perhaps days later. Time's passage could not be counted here. Neither light nor tide passed into the deeps, leaving her with no idea how long she had been trapped. Only the first few hours were clear.

She'd wakened with a surge of pain, screaming air into her lungs, thrashing wildly in salt water. In absolute dark she fumbled for the door, finally diving in search of it. The floor lay several feet below her, and her blind searching found no exit. Shoving back to the surface, she realized there was barely two feet between the ceiling and the water level. Pounding wildly on the ceiling, she screamed. Screamed for her gods, for her mother, for her lover, for anyone to save her. Silence answered, and the patient lapping of the water as she caused it to slosh back and forth in the free space in the chamber.

"Please, please, please." It became a rhythmic sob, growing more frantic as the water level rose. Soon the air would be gone and she would drown with the rest of Atlantis.

The water level was rising!

Somewhere, there had to be a fracture, a break in the stone that let the water in. Again, she dove, running her hands over the stone, looking for the flaw. Time and again she floundered to the surface, gasping for air, only to drive herself back under the water, determined to find the passage where the water flowed in.

It proved fruitless. The water rose, slow and terrible and inexorable. The break allowing it to seep in could only be a hairline fracture, too small for panicked fingers to find, too narrow to break further apart for escape. As she shoved her way to the thin layer of air, despairing, she tasted the air going stale. Fighting tears, she lay on her back in the cool water, trying to breathe shallowly. How long she lay there she couldn't say, fading in and out of consciousness as the air thinned further.

Panic regrouped when her nose bumped the ceiling. A scream tore her throat, the faint metallic taste of blood pooling at the back of her mouth. She smashed her hands blindly on the ceiling, wasting the little air that was left. Then, in the barest moment of time, the water closed over her head entirely.

Sinking into the quiet tomb, she held her breath, desperately trying to extend her life just a few more seconds. The physical desire to simply open her mouth, to breathe deeply, was nearly impossible to resist. She fought it, pale stars dancing behind her eyes in the blackness, and then the conscious decision to hold her breath failed before the instinctive reflex to breathe.

A fit of coughing, the attempt to dislodge water from her lungs doubled her over, sobbing in the darkness. Not until it had passed, and she lay floating in the water, curled in a fetal position, did it slowly dawn on her that she did not need to breathe.

It took longer yet before the implications of that set in. That she, like Aroz, was immortal. *Timeless.*

Like Lorhen.

She would live here until she escaped. If she could not escape, the room would be her prison, but never her grave.

The thought jarred her from her fetal floating. Unfolding, kicking toward a wall, she began working over every centimeter of the room with frantic, blind fingers.

It was no longer shaped like it once had been. The walls were melted smooth, a uniformity to them that the architects could only have dreamed of. There were no cracks, no imperfections that might be exploited.

The door was simply gone. She could not locate where it might once have been, no hollows or changes in texture in the stone to hint at a way out.

Only in two places did the texture change at all. The stone turned to metal slag, short rough spots on the floor. Desperately, she scrabbled at them until her fingers bled, trying to gain some purchase in the two small flaws. That she failed each time she tried did not stop her. What else was there to do?

Nearly five thousand years passed.

2

Dawn wasn't even a promise on the horizon when a staccato knock sounded at the door. Not even the apartment door: the one downstairs that opened into the vintage club—known locally as The Vin—and which sat directly beneath the window beside Emma Hickman's bed. Emma pulled a pillow over her head, willing the knocker—probably a drunk hoping for an after-hours drink—away.

A second rapid knock sounded, sharper and clearer than drunks usually managed. Emma folded the pillow around her head, promising herself, as she always did when a long night meant using the over-club apartment, that she would never again convince herself that she was too tired to manage the five blocks home to her house. She was on her feet by the third knock, flinging the window open to snarl, "Do you know what time it is?"

A lanky, dark-haired white man with sharp features and a duffel bag slung over his shoulder rocked back on his heels to look up at her. "About three. Good morning, Emma."

"For Christ's sake, Logan." Emma closed the window and sat on the edge of her bed, allowing herself to imagine, for a moment, that she wasn't going to let him in. Then, swearing under her breath, she rose again, pulled on a robe, and stalked barefoot to the door that stood as the sole occupant of a narrow hall cut between a rattletrap freight elevator and the wall. The door opened outward onto a grate staircase that shone black with new rain and dully reflected the streetlights just up the road. Logan Adams was taking the stairs two at a time, most of the way to the landing already when she pushed the door open. "Go away. I'm mad at you."

"You wouldn't have opened the door if you were that angry." Logan—*Lorhen*, Emma reminded herself—slid past her, making some small effort to keep his duffel bag from crashing against her as he came in, and knocked a light switch on with his elbow as he made his way down the hall. Emma leaned her forehead against the door frame, then sighed and pulled the door closed before following Lorhen back into the apartment.

Speakers, lights and other equipment from the club downstairs extended the doorway hall another third of the way into the apartment and left only an aisle to navigate into the lift through. Emma had long since given up imagining the equipment was less than a permanent feature, even if its details changed, and had put a leather couch up against it on its innermost side, making the equipment the de facto apartment wall. A glass-topped coffee table and two armchairs faced the couch; past them on the elevator's end of the apartment lay a kitchenette with a free-standing counter, and the bedroom—all part of the same open space—sat at the far end of the room. Years ago it had been a perfect space for a single woman just out of the military, right above the business she was building; now it was a useful crash space not only for Emma but for the singers and bands who played The Vin on their tours.

And, apparently, for men of her acquaintance who turned out to be Timeless, the immortal warriors whom Emma had helped to watch and keep records of since leaving the military almost seventeen years earlier. Not just Timeless, either: Logan Adams, whom Emma had known for a decade, who was himself a Keeper, whose job within the Keepers was heading up a tiny band of researchers investigating the oldest and most legendary of the Timeless…was the oldest and most legendary of the Timeless, a six thousand year old man called Lorhen.

Emma was fifty-four years old and, she would have thought, long past holding grudges. Why she would think that when she had Kept records for people ten, twenty, even thirty times her own age who themselves clearly held grudges was a question for another time; the point was that she had learned Lorhen's true identity by accident, when he'd been shot down in front of her and gotten up again, and then, enragingly, it had transpired that Emma's own charge, a Timeless named Cathal Devane with whom she had—illicitly—become friends, had already known Lorhen's secret, and neither of them had told her.

Outrage, it turned out, was remarkably invigorating. Emma had felt more satisfaction just in being pissed off at the two of them than she had in the last several years of being a Keeper.

Lorhen dropped first his duffel, then himself, into the couch, asking, "Did I wake you?" with a certain blithe airiness.

"What do you think?" Emma threw herself into one of the armchairs across from him.

A twitch or two rendered the ancient man comfortable on the couch before he folded his arms behind his head to inspect her as if it wasn't obvious she'd been awakened. After a good look, he opted to ignore the question. "I had an idea."

"I'm sure you did. I'm sure it could have waited until morning, too."

"It could have, but my plane just got in, and the cab ride out here took all my money, so I had nowhere else to stay. You realize it costs almost fifty dollars?"

"I realize it costs half that to get to Cathal's house, or that you could have stayed at a hotel next to the airport and called him in the morning."

"I hate airplane noise pollution, and besides, you know perfectly well that Cathal is in Chicago. Besides, I didn't want to stay with him. He snores."

"Lorhen." Emma pressed her fingertips against the inner corners of her eyes before looking up to tick points off on her fingers. "First, he doesn't snore. Second, even if he did, he doesn't snore loudly enough to hear him from Chicago. Third, and this is my duty as a Keeper, not prurient curiosity speaking, he has a three bedroom house. If you're sleeping close enough that his snoring bothers you, I'll be delighted to go make note of that in his records."

"It *is* prurient curiosity that makes me ask just how it is *you* know he doesn't snore." Lorhen flipped over on the couch, trying, to no avail, to make himself fit better: it was four inches shorter than he was even including the arms. He ended up on his back again, with his feet dangling over one end, with the long black coat he hadn't shed pooled halfway onto the floor. "Anyway, I don't have a key to his house so I came here."

"To wake me up in the middle of the night. How thoughtful of you, Logan. How did you even know I was here? I'm not usually."

"I know. I went to your house first."

Emma dropped her head against the back of the chair. "You're telling me there was no way I was going to avoid an uninvited house guest."

"That is, in fact, what I'm telling you." Even relaxed on the couch, Lorhen had a nervous energy about him that suggested a grad student functioning by the grace of caffeine alone, but his flickering gaze came to rest on Emma briefly, and his voice softened unexpectedly. "I wasn't actually sure you'd let me in."

Emma thinned her mouth, unwilling to soften in turn. "Well, I did. What do you want?"

"Mmm. All right, then." Lorhen ran a hand over his hair, making it spike and then settle over classical features and eyes that shifted from hazel to nearly black. He looked about thirty

and bookish, as good a disguise, Emma thought irritably, as a
Timeless of six-or-so thousand years could ask for. "You were
about to ask what this great idea of mine was," he said.

"I really wasn't."

"Well, you can't possibly be prepared to wait until morning.
I couldn't stand the idea of you lying there awake with suspense.
I'm doing you a favor."

Emma closed her eyes, muttered, "Next time, don't open
the door, Em," to herself, then opened her eyes and bared an
unpleasant smile at the ancient Timeless. "All right, Lorhen.
What's this great idea of yours."

"I'm so glad you asked," he said promptly. "I've been thinking
about the Keepers."

Emma turned her wrist up, rubbing her thumb over the tattoo she and Lorhen both shared: a circle encompassing a tilt-
waisted hourglass, and kept her voice deliberately flat. "What
about us."

"'Us'," Lorhen echoed, faintly surprised. "'Us', Emma?
Where are you drawing the distinction there, between you and
me or between you and me, and the rest of them? Because I
seem to remember things coming down to a pretty distinct 'us'
and 'them' back there, and you definitely weren't on the side of
'them'."

"Maybe I wasn't thinking clearly." Emma glanced away,
knuckles folded against her lips.

"Most people aren't when their friends get shot down in front
of them. Emma—"

"Lorhen, I am not prepared to talk about this. What about
the Keepers?"

Lorhen fell silent a moment. "All right. All right, Emma.
Look, the ones who found me out weren't exactly happy to learn
they'd been harboring a Timeless in their ranks all these years."

"*They* weren't?"

"You're the one who just said you didn't want to talk about

it, Em. Have you changed your mind in the last five seconds?"

"Dammit, Lorhen. No. I haven't. Fine. We weren't happy about it. *I* wasn't happy about it."

"But you chose me over them," Lorhen said, voice gone soft again. "Those two Keepers didn't turn on each other before I woke up, Em. And I wasn't the one with the gun, when I *did* wake up. I'm good, but not good enough to take out five armed people who knew how to kill me, not on my own."

"But you had a sword!" The accusation burst out, driving Emma to her feet in search of a drink. "You had a sword," she said again more quietly, once a generous tumbler of whiskey had been poured. "If you'd just been a new Timeless, Lorhen, but no, you had a goddamn *sword*."

There were factions inside the Keepers, had been for decades, probably centuries. Emma knew that, but discovering a group determined to find immortality for themselves had still come as a shock to her. They'd been after an artifact said to prolong life, and Lorhen—Logan, at the time—had gotten in their way. Up until the moment he'd risen from the dead and drawn a blade that he knew how to use, she had believed he was only a Keeper dedicated to their policy of neither interfering with Timeless lives, nor seeking immortality for themselves.

He'd fended the Keepers off, but it had only been later that Emma had realized he'd never so much as blooded one with his blade. She'd done the dirty work, shooting her fellow Keepers with a sniper's steadiness. In the aftermath, with the two of them standing in the darkness staring at one another, Logan Adams had said, with unexpected clarity, "I'm sorry, Emma. I didn't mean to drag you into this. My name is Lorhen, and I think we'd better run."

They had run, Lorhen back to his research position in the Keepers, and Emma to Cathal, where her hurt and anger at learning Lorhen's secret had been compounded by her big Irish charge already knowing it. The two men had, in their ways, been among her closest friends, and she'd barely spoken to either of them in the five months since.

"I had a sword," Lorhen said quietly, "and you didn't tell anyone. But it gave me an idea, Em. I need to die, really spectacularly."

Emma paused with her drink halfway to her lips, then turned to stare at Lorhen in genuine surprise. "You what?"

"Can I have some of that? In front of a lot of Keepers would be particularly good. I wake up befuddled. 'What? Me? A Timeless? After all this time studying them? It can't be!'"

"Lorhen, that's…depraved."

Lorhen sat up to lean forward. "No, listen, it'll work. It even explains why Devane's been hanging around me all this time. The Keepers know Timeless can sense the Awakening in potential Timeless, and it fits his pattern of befriending a potential Timeless to train him if he gets in an accident."

"The last thing he needs is another student, Lorhen. Look how well the last one turned out." Emma finished her drink in one swallow and poured herself another one, grudgingly bringing Lorhen one before she sat again.

"That wasn't his fault. Occasionally people are simply hopeless punks. Besides, I wouldn't exactly be an average student. It's just a cover story, and I need your help to pull it off. When we're through, I'm Logan Adams, died in the early years of a new millennium, age thirty-four."

"You're insane." Emma sat down, eyeing Lorhen. "You actually think it could work?"

"Sure. And think: I'd be the only Timeless with two records in the Keeper files."

"Oh, for the love of…you're hopelessly vain, Lorhen." Lorhen tilted an eyebrow in acknowledgment as she added, "And you're wrong, too. There are dozens of records of Timeless being misidentified as someone new."

"Those all get fixed eventually, though. Listen, I may be vain, but I'm also practical, Emma. They won't be looking for Lorhen in me if they see Logan Adams die the first time."

Emma thumped her head against the back of the chair and muttered, "I'll think about it," before glaring at Lorhen. "You can't live here."

Lorhen's eyes widened. "Would I impose on your hospitality like that?" The innocence didn't fade from his face as he added, "Can I have a blanket, by the way? The couch is comfortable, but it's chilly in here."

"What makes you think I'm not going to throw you out on the street?"

"You let me in in the first place."

Emma got to her feet, muttering, and looked for a blanket, asking, "What makes you think they'll assume it's the first death, anyway? That they—we—won't figure you've been pulling the wool over their eyes all this time?"

Lorhen stood to finally shed his overcoat. "Because I'm a very good actor, Emma. I can't afford a bad performance."

Emma balled up a blanket and threw it down the length of the room at Lorhen, hitting him in the back of the head. "None of you can." Two pillows followed the blanket, Lorhen turning to catch them neatly. "Go to sleep. I'll tell you all the flaws with your harebrained idea when I'm awake enough to think."

Lorhen shook the blanket out, grinning. "Good. We should have the whole thing done before that happens."

3

Earthquakes rolled through the water in peculiar, soft shocks. The dim rumbling and muted scraping of stone were the only sounds she could remember, aside from the distorted noise of her own screams. There was no way to mark how often either, screams or earthquakes, came to pass, in the timeless prison.

At junctures the quakes seemed to come often, sending the water quivering over her skin again and again in reverberating series. It wasn't a comfortable feeling, the concussions jarring through her bones and sending chills through her teeth. Goosebumps lifted on her skin, so rare an occasion she felt at them in wondering confusion. Any texture at all came as a fascinating alleviation to the endless litany of despair that was her only company.

The earthquakes provided rare moments of coherency, functionality in a mind that she could recognize as disturbed, if not shattered, in those cognitive minutes. Awareness was not welcome. It made the hopelessness of the situation more pressing. She could hear discordant thoughts shying away from comprehension, thoughts that seemed to belong to someone else entirely.

Nothing, nothing, nothing. Nothing in the world but us, our little black room and the water. Nothing but us, nothing to fear here, nothing to hide from, here is home, here is all. Don't think about outside, it's a bad place, it's not really there at all, nothing was ever really there but the dark room and our hair, oh our hair, play with it, keep it from tangling us. Ignore! Ignore the rumblings and the shakings! Nothing is outside! We are everything, all here, all one, all safe. Nothing surrounds us, nothing at all.

She shook her head, trying to clear the frightened little voice away. The water stilled again, leaving her drifting in smooth silence. *Escape,* another voice whispered. *Someday we will escape. We'll stay here until then, but someday, someday. We'll kill the one that did this to us, and then we'll make ourselves a home again, safe in Atlantis where the gods will favor us again. Patience. Patience is all we need. Nothing is forever. This is not forever.* Smooth and calm, the voice soothed her to sleep.

When she woke again, awareness had slid from her grasp once more. She swam back and forth across the room, followed endlessly by yards of hair, infinitely patient. It might be years before the frightened one emerged again. Decades could pass before she was given another taste of herself, another hour or two of discerning between the patient one and the terrified one, and time to reach for the woman she'd once been.

The patient one didn't mind.

The report of the wall shattering woke her from sleep, cracking into her bones and leaving her stunned, confused. She hung in the water, bewildered, unable to put a name to what had wakened her, but in only a few minutes she could feel the difference, fine grains of stone floating in water that had only been filled with strands of broken, dissolving hair in the past. For a time, she reveled in the new sensation, rubbing the grit between her fingertips and tasting it against her tongue.

Hours, perhaps even days or weeks, went by before an understanding settled into her. Fingertip by fingertip, she began to explore the familiar curves of the oubliette once more, unable to do so much as hope; that had been drained out of her long ago.

Then suddenly, for the first time in memory, there was pain from something beyond her own self-inflicted injuries. She doubled over, clutching her toes in shock, a hoarse curse roughing out of her throat. The pain subsided in seconds, and she unclenched her fingers, upending herself in the water, hair flowing around her like a cloak, to search for the unexpected obstacle that her toes had encountered.

Blind fingers found the stone: wedge-shaped, rough-edged, and as large as her head, it seemed to weigh a tremendous amount to her weak arms. Clutching it possessively against her belly, she kicked up, trailing her free hand along the wall to find where the stone had fallen from.

It began as a crack, almost indiscernible, even to fingertips long familiar with the smooth stone. In inches, though, it split wider, one side of it rising away from the other fractionally. Small as her hands were, she couldn't force her fingers deeply enough into the crack to find an outside edge. After a while she gave up, kicking higher, following the split until it reached a curve in the ceiling, and there lay a divot, a space her precious rock had broken loose from.

With a shout, she smashed her stone against the hole it left, kicking hard to keep herself aloft in the water. Soft clouds of dust broke free, washing over her face. Again and again, in the darkness, she brought the stone down. Smaller shards of rock splintered away. As her hands grew numb from the repeated shocks, a slightly larger chunk dropped, falling to connect with the top of her foot as she kicked. A moment later it clicked lightly against the floor, leaving a delicious ringing pain in her foot.

Eventually she noticed the dull thud of the stone cracking

against the wall was dimmed beneath a high-pitched giggling. It was longer still before she realized the sound was her own laughter, unheard for centuries, released by the prospect of escape. It would take time to break through the wall. It would take time to make a hole large enough for her to fit through.

Time is not a problem, the patient one whispered.

4

Intense sunlight spilled over the bed, too bright and warm for dawn. Emma threw her arm over her eyes, then sat up to squint first at the clear sky and bright light beyond the window, then at the silent heap of blankets and pillows on the couch. Lorhen might sleep until all hours, but even being awakened in the middle of the night didn't usually keep her from rising with the sun, a habit formed through twenty years of military service. "You're a bad influence, Lorhen." She swung out of bed and stretched, then padded past the couch to scowl at its unmoving contents as she put coffee on and sought her tablet for the morning's news.

Chaos sown by economic inequality, climate change, and war led the stories above the fold. Emma muttered and skipped to the lower half of the page, looking for lighter fare before a story caught her eye and, despite herself, she chuckled. "Somebody says they found Atlantis. I admit to wondering lately if you knew where they'd lost it. God," she said under her breath, "you sleep like the dead." Louder, she said, "Wake up, Lorhen. If I have to put up with you, you have to answer my questions."

The metal stairs outside rattled and a blast of cold air announced the door opening. Emma waited, eyebrows elevated, to watch a sweaty Lorhen come around the sound equipment and throw his T-shirt on the couch. There were no scars on the slim muscular lines of his torso, no physical reminders that he had survived hundreds—probably thousands—of sword fights over the centuries. The Timeless were all like that, unless they'd taken wounds before their first death; anything after that, save a killing blow, healed. In Lorhen's case, that unmarred skin left him looking like the youthful, soft-living researcher he played at being. "Mind if I jump in your shower?"

"You can't possibly have turned into a morning person, Logan, you were perpetually late for early meet…" She trailed off at his growing smile, then bared her teeth and looked across the kitchen. "Logan Adams isn't a morning person, but Lorhen the Ancient is," she said to the wall, voice gone sharp with frustration. "Is that it?"

"That's it, although Lorhen would like to never hear 'the Ancient' appended to his name again. And whichever man I am, I just went for a five mile run and need a shower." Lorhen pointed a thumb toward the bathroom at the far end of the room, his eyebrows lifting.

Emma rubbed a hand across her forehead. "Yeah. There are clean towels on the top shelf in there. You want coffee?"

"Please." Lorhen grabbed his duffel and went into the bathroom as Emma poured him a cup, emerging again, dressed but barefoot and with wet hair, after just long enough for the coffee to cool to a drinkable temperature. He had a sip, then made an effort to be a decent house guest by neatly folding the couch's blankets. "What's for breakfast?"

"Granola."

Lorhen looked up from folding blankets in visible dismay. "That sounds hideous."

Emma brightened. "You could mix it with plain yogurt."

"You have got to be kidding."

"Not at all. When did you take up running?"

"Me? I don't know. Probably the first time something chased me, about five and a half thousand years ago. As for Logan

Adams, he's always been a runner. He usually goes out late at night instead of in the morning, but I slept on the plane and thought I'd work the kinks out." Lorhen finished tidying the couch and came to watch Emma mixing the threatened cereal and yogurt. "You're not really going to eat that, are you?"

"I am. Some of us have to worry about our cardiovascular systems, you know. You sure you don't want some?"

Lorhen shuddered. "Positive. Do you have anything that's not good for you around here?"

"Eggs in the fridge. Maybe some frozen bacon. I don't live here, remember." Emma poured herself a second cup of coffee, then pulled a stool to the edge of the counter and sat down. "Did you see the news?"

Lorhen, with more easy familiarity in her kitchen than seemed warranted, dug around for a frying pan and rooted through the freezer until he found the bacon. "No, why?"

"Somebody's claiming to have found Atlantis." Emma nodded at the tablet. "Some Turkish archaeologist. I haven't finished the article yet."

"Seems unlikely. It sank a long time ago. What's his name?" Lorhen put the bacon in the microwave to thaw and started juggling the eggs, drawing Emma's half-astonished attention.

"I didn't know you could juggle."

"You don't know lots of things about me. What's his name?"

"Must you remind me?" Emma pulled the tablet toward herself, skimming the article. "'His' name is Mary Kostani, you sexist pig. 'The artifacts are carbon-dated at more than five thousand years old, and are of a superior workmanship than examples from other contemporary civilizations. The legends of Atlantis suggest a more advanced civilization than those surrounding it....' It goes on like that. There's bread in the freezer, too, if you want toast."

Lorhen put the eggs down in favor of finding the bread, took the bacon out of the microwave, and dropped it into the already-hot frying pan. Sizzles and rich scent made Emma reconsider her cereal. Lorhen caught the glum look, grinned, and dropped another half dozen pieces into the pan. "Is there a picture?"

"Of what? Atlantis?"

"No, the archaeologist." Lorhen dropped bread into the toaster, then made a face over his shoulder. "Yes, the ruins. Ow!" He shook bacon grease off his hand, glaring at the frying pan.

"One, of some of the pottery they've found. Here." Emma scooted the tablet toward the edge of the counter and stirred her yogurt again. "Don't get bacon grease on it. Sheff ghibbng a—"

"Didn't anyone ever tell you not to talk with your mouth full? Oh, she's giving a lecture in Chicago." Lorhen used his elbow to scroll the news story and read the end of the article. "I'm sure she didn't find Atlantis. That stuff could be from anywhere." He squinted at the pictures. "Well, anywhere with delicate five thousand year old pottery. That's pretty nice stuff."

"It'd be the find of the century. Even if it's not Atlantis, she'll get enormous publicity."

"Yeah, but she shouldn't have claimed it was Atlantis. It'll embarrass her department when she's wrong. I wish they'd published the location."

"Why?"

Lorhen shrugged, flipping eggs. "So I could see how close she was."

Emma put her spoon down. "You *do* know where Atlantis is."

The ancient man glanced at her, expression bored. "Doesn't everyone?"

"Lorhen, how can you keep that kind of knowledge secret? That's criminal!"

"It's surprisingly easy. All you have to do is not mention it."

Emma set her teeth together. "Is there anything about you that isn't going to constantly remind me that you're an arrogant, ancient Timeless?"

"Probably not, particularly since almost no one knows the truth and it's nice to be able to let my hair down a little." For a moment he looked up, cross-eyed, at his hair. Emma's gaze went to it, too: not quite brush-cut, enough length to be shaped, but nowhere near long enough to be let down. "Anyway, one of the advantages to being my age is you remember where all the great stuff that everyone else has forgotten about is."

"No one has forgotten Atlantis, Lorhen."

"Maybe they should." Lorhen slid bacon and eggs onto a plate. The toast popped, and he danced it on his fingertips while buttering it, chanting, "Hot hot hot!" under his breath, before pushing it all toward Emma. She stared first at it, then at Lorhen, in astonishment. He spread his hands. "Don't tell me it's not more appealing than yogurt-covered granola."

"I didn't even know you could cook, and now you're feeding me. Are y—you are. You're trying to butter me up."

"Is it working?"

"No." Emma sounded sincere, even to herself, but she couldn't fight off a rueful smile of appreciation as she looked at the plate of food again. "Maybe a little. Tell me about Atlantis."

Lorhen turned back to the stove, cracking more eggs into the bacon grease and dropping more bread into the toaster. "I should say no, and make you wonder."

"Old man, you may have six thousand years of mortal combat under your belt, but I have a pistol under this counter and I'm not afraid to use it. You wanted to die, right?"

"Only with an audience." Lorhen cast a glance over his shoulder, eyeing the counter. "Do you really? You probably do, don't you."

"If I've learned anything in sixteen years of being a Keeper it's not to hang out unarmed around Timeless, any more than you would. I can see the outline of your heartstrike knife under your shirt."

"You can see the outline of *one* of my heartstrike knives,"

Lorhen corrected. "And if you tell anybody I've got more than one I'll never cook for you again."

"It's bacon and eggs, Lorhen. You're going to have to do a lot better than that to bribe me. Atlantis?"

Lorhen finished getting his breakfast ready and sat to eat it. "All right, all right. Even if they did find it, it's not going to have all the wonderful knowledge they're looking for. They wrote on paper, Em. Really fine paper. It's been underwater for thousands of years. It'll all be dissolved. Even if it's not, nobody but me knows the language."

"They figured out the hieroglyphics," Emma pointed out.

Lorhen snorted. "Some of them. Occasionally I have to suppress the desire to tell them where they got it wrong. At any rate, some of the stories about Atlantis are dead on. It was a culture unlike anything else of its time. There was a ruling elite, but people moved in and out of it. More of a meritocracy than a democracy. The population was small and educated enough that it actually worked. Competence was the primary requirement for any sort of job, and that was it. They had a, what do we call it these days. A strong work-life balance, and gender largely wasn't an issue. Nurturing men and women both stayed home with children, less nurturing sorts all found work of some kind or another. There were a lot of good things about the place, but it's still a bag of ashes that shouldn't be stirred."

Emma spread her hands expectantly. Lorhen shrugged. "The immortality crystal our unfriendly neighborhood Keepers were after? The Atlanteans made that."

"What?" Emma lifted her hand, stopping Lorhen before he spoke again. "Wait. It was a crystal?"

"Yes, a big awkward hunk of rock that didn't work the way any of them thought it was going to. Keep up, Emma, that's not the point. The p—"

"Lorhen," Emma interrupted softly, "you are not nearly far enough into my good graces right now to be rude. I opened the door to you last night. Don't imagine I won't put you out it again."

Lorhen fell silent, lips pursed, then dropped his chin in a nod. "Sorry. I forget."

Emma's eyebrows lifted. "What, that you've been lying to me for a decade?"

"I'm always me underneath the name I choose or the role I play, Emma. Once someone knows—which doesn't happen often—it's easy to let myself forget who I'm 'supposed' to be. It's like taking a corset off."

"So you're saying Lorhen is considerably more of a jackass than Logan Adams."

A faint smile twisted Lorhen's mouth. "Probably." He hesitated. "Do you really think I'm a sexist pig?"

"What? Oh." Emma glanced at the tablet. "No. No, that isn't one of your faults. Have you worn corsets a lot?"

"Almost never. They haven't often been fashionable for men, and even then mostly only for fat men. I've always been slim."

Emma nodded. "All right. Your point about Atlantis, then?"

Another brief smile pulled at his lips. "The point was that the crystal was made in Atlantis, by Atlanteans, or at least, by their gods. The ones I knew certainly didn't know how, not anymore."

"Their gods?"

"That's what they called them. Somebody made them, anyway, and it might as well have been gods." Lorhen frowned at his last bite of toast, then shook his head. "I think I used to know more about it, but I don't anymore."

"Gods aren't real, Lorhen."

"Hah. Aren't they? The Timeless exist, and we can do what any reasonable person would consider magic. I carry a sword around a major metropolitan area in broad daylight every single day and nobody stops to comment, much less arrest me. That's ma—"

"I'd like to see it."

Lorhen's eyebrows shot upward. "My sword? Goodness, Emma, are you flirting with me?"

"Don't flatter yourself."

"Of course not." Lorhen still smiled as he left the remains of his breakfast and went to the couch to extract a hand-and-a-half sword from the folds of a coat which, to Emma's eyes, lay loose across the back of the couch, incapable of hiding anything rigid. He cast the scabbard aside easily and returned to offer the blade, hilt first, to Emma, who took it with a surge of surprise. She knew he had at least two knives on him, but Timeless didn't offer the blades that kept them alive up for inspection casually. He was trying, not subtly, to earn her trust again, and they both knew it.

Irritatingly, she could feel it working. More effectively than cooking for her, although she had to lower her eyes swiftly to examine the blade to hide amusement at the thought. He would probably read it anyway: the Timeless were exceptionally good at sensing the smallest shifts in emotion. As they should be, with decades or centuries—or in Lorhen's case, millennia—of practice.

The sword was about four feet long from pommel to tip, with the blade itself making up around three feet of it. There were no unnecessary decorations: the crossguard was broad enough to provide protection and the pommel looked like it could crack a skull effortlessly, but neither shone with jewels or even engravings. The leather wrapped around its hilt shone soft with use and fit her hands better than she would have expected. Both her hands: she'd seen Lorhen wield it one-handed easily, but her instinct was to wrap both hands around the hilt, snugged against one another. "It weighs less than I thought."

"Around three pounds. Even Timeless get tired. A lighter blade is less wearying, especially if you use it one-handed, and I like to keep one hand free if I can."

"For the heartstrike," Emma murmured. Anyone, Timeless

or not, would die if their head was taken, but to release the Blending, the magic that Timeless carried inside themselves, a blow to the heart had to be struck before the head was taken. Otherwise the Blending simply disappeared, returning to the ether. The Keepers theorized that new Timeless were made that way, somehow absorbing the free magic, but there was no way to know for certain.

"For the heartstrike," Lorhen agreed. "I never did go for the big swords. They're too slow, but these ones, what you mostly call bastard swords these days, are light and fast and still have enough hilt that you can use it two-handed if you really need the power. You hold it well."

"I've been a Keeper for sixteen years, Lorhen. I've learned a couple of things about swords in that time." She reversed the blade and offered it back to him, and he took it with a thoughtful look.

"But not how to use one. I've always thought that was an oversight on the Keepers' part. Not that I would go around saying so."

"Except to me?"

Lorhen gave her a half smile and went to put the sword away. Even watching, she couldn't see where it went: it simply faded into the folds of his coat, no longer visible even though she knew it had to be there. "It's magic," he said again. "And there are a lot of other legends that have nothing to do with us. Monsters, demons, gods, spirits, things that aren't Timeless-based stories at all. Elements of magic we can't explain. What made Atlantis special, and really, what makes it remembered, is that they were able to harness that power to a degree no one has ever duplicated. Christ's holy Grail, the sword they called Excalibur. They bred unicorns, Emma."

"Unicorns." Emma's eyebrows rose again.

"I know." Lorhen came back to the breakfast bar to mop up the last drips of yolk with a crust of toast. "They weren't horses, though. More like war-rhinos, except more delicate than rhinos. About that graceful, though, graceful the way killing machines are, not in fanciful light tripping fairy-like ways. The horns were only about—" He spread his hand wide, indicating the distance from pinky tip to thumb. "That long. Thick. Brutal. They were incredibly difficult to kill, but they drowned when Atlantis did." He looked up, eyes black. "I don't know if it was knowledge they had, or something about the island itself, but they were able to create artifacts of immense power, artifacts which have frequently taken on lives of their own. I don't know what else drowned with Atlantis, and frankly, I don't want to. There were too many things of power. I'd rather they stayed under the ocean." He finished the last of his juice. "Now. How are we going to kill me so that I can gain my immortality and hornswoggle the Keepers?"

"I don't know. How did you die the first time?"

"Don't remember."

"That must make you the only Timeless in the world who doesn't remember his first death." Emma got up to clear the dishes as Lorhen spun on his stool to watch her.

"I'm the only Timeless who was there before the pyramids were built, too. Coincidence, or conspiracy? The thing is, it's got to be public enough that a Keeper will see it, or hear about it soon, but not so much as to get the police involved."

Emma sighed. "The police usually get involved when there's a violent death, Lorhen. That's their job."

"I could get in a car wreck."

"In whose car!"

Lorhen grimaced. "Maybe not. I'm afraid Logan Adams is the sort to get mugged."

A slow, not particularly pleasant smile crept across Emma's face. Lorhen pointed an accusing finger at her. "You can't mug me, Emma. What would be your excuse?"

"It would be extremely satisfying."

"Emma." Lorhen managed to look injured. She huffed disbelievingly, and he pulled the tablet back toward himself. "Cathal's been in Chicago a while. We could go up to this lecture and see if he's met anybody who could mug me while we're there."

"We?"

"C'mon." Lorhen gave her a sly smile. "Don't tell me the Keeper in you wouldn't like to listen in on a lecture while a man who was really there whispers the truth into your ear."

Emma acknowledged the temptation with a wrinkle of her nose. "Who's going to pay for it?"

"We could expense it to the Keepers."

"There are dozens of Keepers in Chicago, Lorhen. Why would they pay for us to fly up instead of just having the locals go?"

"Because I'm the head researcher on ancient-world Timeless and it would be absurd to send anyone else."

"…that's a very good argument."

Lorhen, dryly, said, "I do have several thousand years of practice at getting my own way, Emma. Call Cathal, will you, and tell him to rent a bigger hotel room. The Keepers won't put us up in style."

5

She couldn't remember how thick the walls had been.

It doesn't matter, the patient one told her. *We have time.*

But I want *to remember!* she raged back. The patient one was right: it probably didn't really didn't matter. The texture of the walls had been changed utterly by the cataclysm that drowned the city; almost certainly the depth of the walls had been changed by the same events.

Never-the-less, as she scraped and tore away fragments of stone, she tried frantically remember. As deep as her forearm was long? Leaning in the door, did the stone stretch wider than the breadth of her shoulders, to encompass her safely in the carved structure? Had there been windows she could reach through?

Had there been windows at all? The wedge of stone slipped from her hands as she drifted in the water, trying to bring the memory of the original room to mind.

No doors! No windows! Always smooth, always safe, keeping us here inside! the frightened one insisted. *Always here.*

No. She shoved the voices away, trying desperately to focus. She curled on her side, catching her hair over an arm to prevent it from wrapping around her face. Had there been windows? The wide floor she could envision, from aeons of testing it with fingertips. The walls, she knew, had never been so smooth, but they had curved into the arched roof in the same essential structure of her prison.

The door had been deliberately simple, wide and carved with the symbols of the Houses. The memory slipped in and out, foggy, sometimes teasing her with the idea that the door had not been deep enough to outstretch her shoulders, other times insisting with an almost physical shock that she had fit neatly between the two sides.

It might be a childhood memory, she realized after hourless floating. Perhaps the door *had* surrounded her when she was smaller, but time had shifted her perception.

Time. She laughed into the faintly gritty water. How much time? How long had she been damned to the watery hell, already? How much longer would it be until she broke free?

It doesn't matter, the patient one whispered again. *What matters is freedom. We'll be free soon.*

She uncurled, angling toward the floor, to collect her hammer again. Stone chips lay scattered around the room, providing texture she reveled in. Small fingers lifted a sharp stone, and slid it across her cheek. The pain was thin, fading almost before she tasted the blood in the water. With a giggle, she let the piece go, and searched for her wedge.

Finding it, she pushed up again, feeling for the hole she drilled with mindless perseverance. She could fit her whole head in it now. Eventually she would break through to the other side. In time, she would break free.

In time, the patient one promised, *there will be revenge.*

6

Cathal Devane met them at the auditorium's front door, bending to kiss Emma's cheek before giving Lorhen a fond clap on the back. It was easy for him, Emma thought: charm came naturally to the big Irishman, more naturally than anything, perhaps, save sword fighting. Probably more naturally than that, though; he hadn't been born with a sword in his hand. "If I'd known ye's couldn't bear to be without me for three weeks I'd have invited ye's along in the first place."

"He's pulled out the 'ye's'," Lorhen announced airily. "We must be in trouble. If he starts in with the 'faiths' and the 'begorrahs', run."

"Ah sure and we say ye's even now so, but show me an Irish man or woman who after sayin' faith and begorrah with even a wee little bit of sincerity in the past hundred and fifty years and I'll eat me own hat," Cathal said with all the flourish he could manage, and for good measure took a bow. Emma laughed, miming applause, and he gave her one of his broad, easy smiles. She'd been his Keeper for almost the whole of her career, and watching him daily had largely inured her to his beauty. It always startled her to see him again after a break and to realize just how handsome he was. He wore dark brown hair shaggy, caught between fashions but making the most of light blue eyes and warm tones in his pale skin with a kind of artless vanity. He stood taller and broader than almost anyone of his generation should have—the Timeless often seemed to run tall and strong—and his features were so even and attractive that they looked like they'd been thought out beforehand. Lorhen's sharp, narrow face looked like it could have—and may *have*, Emma thought sourly—inspired a Roman emperor's bust; Cathal was the template for an Adonis.

Lorhen rolled his eyes and let Cathal hold the door for both of them, but stopped barely a handful of steps into the auditorium foyer to mutter, "I hate crowds. Are we late?"

Emma, under her breath, said, "Yes," while Cathal said it more loudly. Lorhen glared at them both and Emma shrugged. "I told you we needed to be at the airport two hours early, Logan. It's not my fault we missed the plane."

"I thought you were being irritatingly militaristic," Lorhen protested. "I remember when you could just walk in off the street and on to your plane without all that nonsense."

"Logan, anybody who's watched *Die Hard* remembers that, if they don't to begin with. At least we made it to the lecture."

"Nearly," Cathal said cheerfully into their bickering. "If we don't get into the auditorium you'll have flown eight hundred miles for the sake of my company."

"And fine company it is," Emma announced somewhat dourly before finishing with, "but let's move."

The lobby itself, despite Lorhen's complaints, wasn't too bad, but the auditorium doors led into a well-dressed cattle feed, gossips standing in the aisles while noisy students wrangled for seats and called to each other across the enormous room. Emma watched them for a moment, thinking how young they looked from her viewpoint as a mortal in her mid-fifties, and wondered if they all simply seemed impossibly unfinished to Lorhen and Cathal.

Lorhen edged his way around a small crowd of gossips and collapsed his ribs and shoulders inward, letting grey-haired dignitaries squish past him toward the stage but bumping into a woman behind him. She wobbled and yelped, and Lorhen, with a patently apologetic and utterly insincere smile, leaned forward again to let her pass. "Please tell me we have ticketed seats near an exit so we can escape easily."

"The University said it couldn't be a ticketed event. The Keepers got us reserved seats in the first five rows, but they're not assigned. We'll need to find three together." Emma pointed stage left, near the front of the auditorium. "Maybe down there. Go on, Lorhen, you've got long legs, make use of them."

"Cathal's two inches taller than I am." Still, Lorhen stepped into one of the rows, then, expediently, started stepping over each row, angling for empty spaces where people had not yet seated themselves, and got ahead of the crowd.

"You two patching it up, then?" Cathal asked the moment Lorhen was out of earshot. Emma gave him a flat look and slipped into a space too small for Cathal to fit, then smiled at the man who begrudgingly let Cathal follow her. "Right, so," Cathal breathed as he caught up. "Are you and I patching it up? I've barely seen you for months, Em, and I know you haven't had me reassigned."

"Do you."

The confidence in Cathal's smile faltered. "You wouldn't. Not with as much as I know about the Keepers. You'd not compromise another Keeper's identity, risk me figuring out who was watching me now." He hesitated. "Would you?"

"I've known you—been friends with you—for almost five years, Cathal, and I've been working with Logan Adams for nearly a decade. I thought we were friends. All of us. I didn't think my friends would keep a secret like that from me."

"Says a woman whose job is to watch immortals commit murder and not tell anyone," Cathal said very softly indeed. "Emma, it wasn't my secret to tell, or I would have, and I truly don't believe Lorhen knows how to stop keeping that secret. Even Lisse— she knows he's Timeless, but she doesn't know who he is."

There was the faintest salve in Cathal's argument. Lisse Rousseau was, in no particular order, a liar, a charmer, a cheat and a thief, a renowned beauty, twelve hundred years old and capable of retaining a child's delight in finding and wallowing in trouble, and she had known Lorhen, under one name or another, for at least a century. Lorhen seemed genuinely fond of her, and she, unlike Emma, probably stood a reasonable chance of actually killing him for keeping secrets of that magnitude. She probably wouldn't, but she might be able to. And if she didn't, she could take centuries to get over being angry at him, a luxury Emma didn't have. "He told *you*."

"He *wanted* something from me." Cathal gallantly offered his elbow to guide Emma through a group of college students, and although she took it, she also said, "I can navigate a crowd, Cathal."

"I know, but far be it from me to fail to provide escort for a beautiful woman."

Amusement pulled the corner of her mouth up and she ended up laughing and shaking her head. "You're much more difficult to stay angry with than he is."

"Well, you're not as angry at me to begin with. He could have told you anything, you know, Em. He could have said he Awakened a few years ago and had been afraid to tell anyone. He didn't have to tell you he was Lorhen. Don't you think that says something?"

"That he's monumentally arrogant and couldn't resist the chance to rub it in." Emma flared her nostrils and flattened her mouth at the sideways glance Cathal gave her. "Yes, all right, fine. Maybe he was looking for an excuse. That doesn't make it any damn easier, Devane."

"Fair enough. Would it make it easier if I told you he comes by and mopes about you not talking to him?"

Emma eyed the tall Irishman. "Does he?"

"He does, as a matter of fact. Not that he'd ever confess to it, but he keeps dropping by to hang around in a desultory fashion and ask after you. He does a very good heartbroken teen act."

Emma gave a startled laugh. "Can you imagine what an awful teenager he must have been?"

"There were different expectations even when I was a teen, Em. I can't imagine what it was like when he was one."

"Probably brutal." Emma's tone became clipped and she slipped her hand free of Cathal's escort, working her way down the crowded aisle until they reached the row where Lorhen had secured their seats. The ancient Timeless stood so Cathal could pass him, then sat again, leaving Emma to sit on his other side. They were as close to an exit as Lorhen could get them, and she couldn't help smiling as she murmured, "I'd think you'd be used to crowds," and got herself settled.

Lorhen squirmed around, trying to get long legs comfortable in the narrow row. "Used to and enamored of are very different things. I always prefer to have an escape route."

Anyone who had combat experience did, Emma thought, but before she spoke, the auditorium lights dimmed, turning their attention to the stage. A rangy woman with an expensive haircut and a well-cut suit came out to smile beyond the lights at the audience. "Good evening, everyone. If you can just take your seats, we'll get started. It's nice to see a full house. I know we've got some sensational claims to talk about here tonight, but it's always good to know that archaeologists not named Jones can get everyone's attention every once in a while." A laugh rippled through the auditorium and she smiled. "I'm Dr. Michelle Powers, the head of the archeology department here at the University. I expect a lot of you are waiting impatiently to debunk the findings we've made claim to."

Lorhen snorted. Cathal and Emma both elbowed him and he acquired a look of put-upon offense as Powers continued, "But I think you'll be pleasantly surprised. This isn't the kind of announcement we'd make without being very sure. I have the honor of presenting to you tonight's speaker, Dr. Mary Kostani. Dr. Kostani has been an associate of the University for about five years, and is widely known in archaeological circles for her work in translating some of the more difficult Egyptian hieroglyphics. Like many of us, she's had a life-long passion, although hers was the outrageous goal of finding the legendary city of Atlantis. Unlike most of us, she seems to have achieved this, and in record time. Ladies and gentlemen, without further ado, Dr. Mary Kostani."

Polite applause echoed through the auditorium as Dr. Powers stepped back, beckoning Dr. Kostani onstage. Petite, with black hair cut at cheekbone length, Kostani had an expression of pleasant neutrality, approachable but firm, in the manner of a small woman accustomed to setting some immediate expectations of her audience. She came onstage with confidence, but paused as she approached Dr. Powers, looking past her and beyond the bright stage lights to scan the dark auditorium. Lorhen shrank down in his seat while Cathal straightened as if stung, and Emma, long familiar with both reactions, shot a startled look at them. "She's one of you?"

Dr. Kostani continued across the stage with only the slightest hesitation, her smile still warm, if not quite reaching her eyes any longer. She adjusted the microphone to her height—even standing on the raised podium the university provided, she was clearly not quite five feet tall—and inclined her head. "Good evening," she said, in faintly accented English. "Thank you for your welcome. I assure you, I have been looking forward to this day for a very long time."

Under the pleasantries opening Kostani's speech, Cathal

nodded. "She is, but I don't know her. I'd remember that face. Do you know her, Logan?"

"Yes," Lorhen said, almost voicelessly.

Pacing in sand did not lend itself to the dramatic strides Lorhen tried for. The ground had the unpleasant habit of shifting away underfoot, causing sudden unexpected lurches at best, and badly twisted ankles at worst. Eventually he quit pacing, and, lifting his hands to guard his eyes, squinted over the dunes. In the distance, the great Anapa, guardian of the dead and guide to the underworld, rose up in the foreground of Khufu's massive, nearly completed pyramid, blinding white with polished limestone reflecting the sun as brightly as a mirror. Anapa had guarded the land for centuries before Khufu began his monument to himself, and Lorhen half-remembered, at times, that even the god's dog head wasn't the first face the massive sculpture had sported. Nor would it be the last, most probably; gods changed faces as often as kings, but only the Timeless had any hope of remembering them all.

The wind-blown sands between himself and Anapa were no busier than the dunes he'd been climbing, and after a moment he turned away from the brilliant erections to rest his eyes on river-fed greenery where it began to fade into desert sands. Slave camps lay on that border, and a tent city along their edge, where merchants and travelers trade stories and goods beyond the regulated bazaars in the ruling city of Manf. All of it bore life and motion into the sand, but it felt remote, belonging to another world, or at least another people. Lorhen turned his back on it, preferring the deliberate solitude to unexpected melancholy. Finally a voice, thin in the heat, broke the air: a woman calling his name. Moments later she crested the edge of a sandy hill, waving to draw attention to herself. As if there was anything else worth watching nearby, Lorhen thought.

He slid down the loose earth to meet her in a small valley, lifting her easily into an embrace before setting her on her feet again and smiling down at her. No more a native of this country than he, Ghean looked the part more, with her bronzed skin and dark hair, but something else entirely set her apart from even her own people. He had met Timeless by the score, but only one or two, in his long life, who held the waiting potential of immortality in their blood. That untapped power waited to be triggered through violent death; nothing else he had ever encountered awakened Timelessness. He wished, at times, for her life to be gentle all the way through, and at others, that the magic might roar to life within her, so that an impossibly long future might be hers, as an impossibly long history was already his own.

Centuries fell away inside a heartbeat, back to the night he had made his first—so far as he recalled—heartstrike blow, and experienced the Blending for the first time. The memory was blurred, with a black sky and hard stars, and weapons in his hands. An ax in one, stone but with a keen edge and a short, thick haft, bound together with sinew rope. A knife in the other, hardly more than a hand in length, and more poorly made, but made well enough. He'd taken it from his opponent, and when the man rushed him to get it back, he'd skewered himself on the stone blade, a heart strike. Nothing at all, no vestigial memory, told Lorhen where he'd learned the skill to wield the ax as efficiently as he had then, or why, having slain him already with the knife to the chest, he then took the nameless man's head in a moment of panic.

Certainly nothing had prepared him for the storm that surged from the clear sky, or for the lightning that screamed through him, leaving him in the shaken aftershock of the Blending, shuddering from the intense electric pain, almost indistinguishable from pleasure, that rattled his body. When it occurred to him he was not dead, he'd staggered to his feet and limped away, leaving the body behind, but keeping the weapons clenched in his fists.

Before that night, before that foggy memory, there was nothing but a vague sense of many, many years passing.

Hairs rose on his arms despite the heat, and he cast the memories away, but not without wondering how much of a kindness immortality was, after all. It didn't matter: neither path would be decided for Ghean today, and she'd asked him to come out beyond the Anapa monument to talk, so he put on a faintly petulant look and demanded, "Where have you been? I've been out here sweltering in the heat half the day."

Ghean laughed. "I saw you leaving the edge of town not more than," she glanced at the sun, pursed her lips, and finished, "not *much* more than an hour ago. Mother wanted help with a seam. I don't understand how she can write so neatly and not sew a straight seam."

"She probably doesn't understand how you can sew straight seams and still have dreadful handwriting."

"Mmm." Ghean slipped an arm around Lorhen's waist, tugging him along with her. "True. Come, let's circle back around to town."

Lorhen smiled briefly. "I thought you wanted to talk out here in the gods-forsaken sand, instead of in town, in the shade, with sweet juice to drink."

"I wanted to talk to you without people overhearing, and that's impossible in town. You're looking awfully solemn, Lorhen." Ghean stopped to look up at him, and he felt, for a moment, very tall and very foreign beside her. He had browned as much as he could, but towered above even the tallest men. He usually did that in the cooler climates he remembered as being his first home, too, but almost everywhere along the inland sea, whether on its northern or southern shores, he seemed a pale giant.

"Mmm." He echoed her sound from earlier. "I was thinking, earlier, about the past, that's all. And the future."

Ghean held her breath. "Our future?"

Lorhen laughed. "You are never one to dance around the point, are you, Ghean? Yes. Our future. Tell me what it was you wanted to talk to me about." He nudged her into walking again.

"Mother is settled now, with all her papers and research, and she's ready to meet you. She only expects to be here a few weeks, Lorhen. She wants to return to Atlantis at the end of the flood season, and I want you to come with us. You will, won't you?"

"I'd have a hard time marrying you if I stayed in Kemet, wouldn't I?" Lorhen glanced toward the gleaming pyramid, thinking for a moment of the histories being recorded inside to be kept for all time. That was what had drawn him to Kemet initially, a fascination with how short-lived mortals marked the stories of their lives, but there was no need to stay; the monuments would last for centuries, even aeons, and he would have ample opportunity to return and see how those stories had played out in fact and in telling. "Of course I'll come to Atlantis. Only, you understand, because its reputation precedes it as a center for learning."

Ghean laughed. "Only. Of course. Mother will like you," she predicted. "You're cut from the same cloth she is, a scholar to the bones. I don't know why you've never been there, anyway. Why you haven't moved there already, instead of wandering around squinting at hieroglyphs. I know you can read, and we have more written knowledge than anywhere else in the world."

"I learned to read and write when I was—younger." He chuckled to cover the pause. "Obviously. It would be difficult to be able to do it, and have learned when I was older, wouldn't it?"

There were journals, secreted away, on clumsy clay tablets, rough notes sketched out in Sumerian pictographs and later, cuneiform. Writing had made him, in a very real way. Those tablets recorded history he could already no longer actively recall, though looking over them often wakened memories buried deep in his mind. Often, but not always: sometimes they read like a stranger's stories. Lorhen had wondered, from time to time, if those unfamiliar tales were in fact not his own memories at all, if they were taken from Blended minds, the strength and power of someone's loss or love so great that he had been moved to write it down even after the heartstrike's power had been subsumed into his own. In the end he always rejected the thought, believing his own strength of personality to be great enough to dominate the absorbed Blendings. Once or twice he'd met Timeless who lacked that sense of self, people who had become lost in their own minds, or who had taken a Blending so powerful it had altered their very being.

That had not, he believed, ever happened to him, but then, before the advent of writing, he wouldn't know. Written words gave him a persistent thread to follow, making him a whole person even when he shed memories in self-preservation. He wondered, often, how old he'd been when writing was invented, and how he'd come to be in the right place to learn it in its infancy. His easily-burned skin and his faintest, oldest memories said he'd come from more northerly climes, but somehow he'd been thousands of miles from his presumed homeland, waiting at the heart of civilization for writing to be born. Whoever he had been before he learned to write was long gone; the man known as Lorhen began with his journals, carefully preserved so he would lose no more time.

He was brought back to the present by Ghean saying, hopefully, "We'll settle there after the wedding. You could study." Black eyes searched his face, waiting for a reaction.

His heart lurched, though he smiled. How fair was it to wed her, when he would not grow old, and she would—or worse, when she might die accidentally, releasing her waiting immortality and extending her life down through the centuries, married to a man she'd met in her childhood? Not that he would hold her, or anyone, to such vows, but that the question was there at all disturbed him. "Settle? Perhaps," he answered. "You're the one eager to travel and study architecture. Return often? I should think so. But it isn't a decision we have to make now, or quickly. Tell me," he continued lightly, "did you have to escape Aroz?"

Entirely aside from Ghean's unrealized potential, Aroz was another problem. Employed as Ghean's mother's bodyguard, the man was clearly in love with Ghean herself, and her self-appointed guard dog. Above that, he was skilled with the heavy blade he carried, and Timeless to boot. And he obviously didn't trust Lorhen. There had not yet been cause or opportunity for a confrontation, but the peace would not hold.

Ghean rolled her eyes. "No. Mother sent him to get more ink, and so when I was done with the stitching I just slipped out. Lorhen." Her next words tumbled out in a rush. "You must come meet Mother, very soon. I've told her all about you, but I'm afraid she's planning to marry me off to Aroz. You have to convince her that we want to marry."

"Your mother plans to marry you off without your consent?" Lorhen asked incredulously. "Has she *met* you? And to Aroz, of all people? That would be a complication." He gnawed the inside of his lower lip, considering survival. Staying within the tent city's boundaries would be the easiest way to delay the apparently inevitable battle. No Timeless in their right mind would fight with mortal witnesses: they might live through being burned as a witch, but no one wanted to experience that.

"A complication! It's a lot more than a complication! It'd be awful! He's so stern and so—old!"

Lorhen couldn't stop the laugh, although he swallowed it and looked as apologetic as he could manage. Aroz certainly appeared older than he did, but Lorhen was absolutely certain he was not only the elder of the two, but very likely the elder by centuries. "He's certainly a better financial match than I am," he teased Ghean, but relented at the horror on her face. "All right. I'll come meet her. What will you do if she opposes the match?"

"Marry you anyway." Ghean frowned to hide the doubt in her eyes. "When will you talk to her?"

"Tomorrow," Lorhen promised. "Alone." He lifted a hand to ward off her protestations, and spoke as lightly as he could. "You've already told her all about me, and I don't think I can make a good impression on two women of your family at once."

Ghean's shoulders dropped. "All right. But you'll talk to her tomorrow? You promise?"

"I promise."

Cathal leaned toward Lorhen, speaking softly as the woman on stage began her lecture. "Well? Who is she?"

"Technically," Lorhen whispered, "I think she's my wife."

7

She could fit her shoulders into the hole she'd chipped away before she broke through to the outside: the ceiling was that thick, and she needed room to maneuver her wedge of stone, to keep bashing at the wall. The space she'd carved was triangular, widest at the base and narrowing rapidly up to the apex, hardly large enough to fit her head into, at the top. But her wedge fit, and she had just enough space to keep cracking away at the roof as she kicked and kicked, keeping herself aloft to continue her excavation.

The rock made a different sound when she snapped through the final layer, a thin report echoing into other waters than those that had held her captive for so long. A few more frantic blows gave her an opening large enough to stick her fingers through. She flailed them against the water outside, shouting at the top of her voice, as if someone would join her in the drowned city. How long she cried for help, she didn't know; it didn't matter. Withdrawing her hand from the hole brought fresher water into the room, a wash of salt much heavier than she was accustomed to after the long years. It tasted wonderful. With renewed energy, she swam for her wedge, and began again to pound at the rock.

It seemed to go faster now, with the greater circulation of water, and the taste of freedom. Stone cracked away, bigger pieces knocking out to fall on the opposite wall of her prison. Only hours went by before she could push her whole hand, up to her forearm, out into the water beyond. It seemed no time at all until she had a hole big enough for her head, then her head and one shoulder and, finally, both shoulders.

Only then did panic strike. She knew she would fit through the hole, though it was visible only to her impatiently seeking fingers. What was on the other side? *Nothing. Nothing. Nothing. Nothing is there, all is here, here is safe, here is where to stay.* She curled into a ball again, hair drifting around her, deadly as jellyfish tendrils.

What *was* on the other side? Drowned Atlantis, the shell of her home. The sea, and eventually sunlight. She remembered the idea of sunlight, the brightness that colored the world, but the world itself, those colors, were gone, lost in thousands of years of darkness. Would she be able to see at all, or had her eyes atrophied entirely, leaving her blind to the world she had once known?

Blind, the frightened one encouraged. *Blind, we'll be blind, stay here where the blackness can't hide anything from us. Stay. Stay. Stay. There's nothing left of the world we knew. Nothing's there. Just the sea, just the water, just blackness forever.*

The thin wail that escaped her was a sound unlike any she had made in hundreds of years. It vibrated through her, forcing tears from her eyes as she shivered, clutching her knees closer to her chest. *Changed, all changed utterly,* the frightened one chanted. *Nothing recognizable. Our people drowned, our language lost. No one to talk to, no one to understand our words. Stay in the safe place.*

She lay in the nest of her hair for days, images of a world she could not fathom holding her captive in the prison that was her home. *We didn't choose prison*, the patient one whispered eventually. *Sea and stones, captured forever, captured because of* his *actions,* his *inactions, not ours. Outside is different. Outside is frightening,* the patient one agreed. *Outside is freedom.*

Strands of hair drifted across her face, brushing her mouth and nose, and the patient one made her shake her head at the feeling. *Outside is better than being mummified by our hair. Languages can be learned. Give us the chance. If we stay, we accept his prison. If we stay, we can't make him pay.*

The wash of courage was tenuous at best. She twisted free of her hair, the strands unwinding in graceful slow motion. Foolishly, she dove again, and located her wedge of stone, dulled now to a much smaller size. Clutching it in one hand, she pushed up to the wall, and through the hole as quickly as she could, before her grasp of boldness eluded her again.

Several feet beyond the wall of her prison she stopped. Endless hair billowed out after her, clouding around her like a blanket of fog.

The blackness was still complete. She could not see even the ruins of the city. For a while she drifted in the darkness, and then, tentatively, she tilted her face up, and began to kick toward the surface.

Very gradually, she became aware of light. It stopped her where she was, hovering in the water, trying to define the nebulous changes in the sea around her. Only when a fish darted by her face, a shadow in the shadows, did she realize vision was beginning to return. A cry of delight broke free from her, and she began to kick upward again.

The next fish that swam by brought to mind a sudden, vicious hunger. For time unknown, she hadn't eaten. Further thought was delayed until she chased down one of the slippery animals and smashed its head in with her stone. Floating in the water, she gobbled it down, sucking the blood from her fingers before it had time to wash away.

For hours, she stayed at the faintly grey level, chasing more fish with wild shifts and twists in the water, snatching them by their tails and bashing her stone into their brains. While she ate she sat in a protective cross-legged position, her stone resting between her thighs.

Later, she suspected she'd stayed at that level of the sea for weeks, swimming after fish of all sizes and eating them raw, leaving only the bones for the water. Eventually, her body stopped demanding the food, and she was able to think again.

The nutrients in the water must have been bare, she realized, and long blank periods of time ending in pain were many deaths and rebirths. This Timeless body of hers must have taken what it could out of the waters, over years of time, recreating life out of death. Hunger was such a way of life that until food was directly presented to her, she had not recognized the sensation.

"Gods above," she whispered into the sea. "How long?" Waking memory was far too long. If immeasurable time had been spent dead, trying to eke life from the water...how long might it have been? Once more, she looked up through the murky water. There was only one way to learn how long it had been. She began swimming up again.

It took longer than she expected, partly due to convulsive hunger pangs that would send her after schools of fish. After a while she noticed fish would nibble on the long strands of her hair that drifted by. She started drawing them in that way, sitting silent in the water, her rock in her lap, waiting until she'd pulled her hair close enough to bash the fish's head in. It was more effective than chasing them. Once sated, she would begin the journey up again.

The light also slowed her. The slow increase never quite pained her eyes, and she realized abruptly that she could see herself when she glanced down. It was a young woman's body that she saw, painfully thin. She was relieved she hadn't seen herself before her gorging in the deeper seas, before her body was able to add and redistribute some of the weight that had wasted away over the years of captivity.

Her fingertips were scarred, which surprised her. Perhaps the healing skills of her Timeless body had their limits. Certainly the trauma of scrabbling at the stones in futile attempts to escape had left their mark. The bronze of her skin had faded to pasty white, emphasized by the dead-colored scars.

Even as the light grew brighter, she could not really see the end of her hair. It drifted too much, and seemed to fade into the water instead of stopping. The vague plan to sell it had formed in her mind. In Atlantis, wig-makers created wigs out of real human hair. Surely the world would not have changed so much that she could not find someone to buy the mass of endless hair that was her legacy of imprisonment.

It could *have changed so much*, the frightened one whispered. She thrust it away, kicking up.

Not until the sea began to glow blue with the sun's light did she suddenly appreciate the visual acuity immortality had granted her. She had no idea what depth Atlantis had descended to, but her vision had begun to return at a level she was sure no ordinary human would have been able to see in. To discern such detail in such complete darkness had been a marvel; what would full light bring? She looked up at the sun, a distorted ball of white fire that colored the ocean and her hair. Schools of fish flitted above her, shadows against the blue.

How long had it been?

She kicked upward. A moment later her head broke through the surface and she inhaled, fresh sea air, for the first time in centuries. Instinctively, she squinted her eyes shut against the light bouncing off small waves, wincing with small pain, but it wasn't as bad as she had feared. She could still see, the light coloring her vision crimson until she dared peek through lashes pushed almost all the way closed.

Wherever the currents had brought her, it wasn't close to land. Quiet, open sea filled all the horizons, brilliant white and vivid blue, the sky scarred with thin, idle clouds.

Nothing at all, the frightened one hissed. *Go home. Go back to Atlantis. It's safe there. Go back. There's nothing here.*

We're in the middle of the sea, the patient one said sourly. *Of course there's nothing here. Swim. We'll find land and people again. We'll rebuild a life and then we will find the one that did this to us and we will have revenge.*

Go back to Atlantis, the frightened one pled.

Revenge, she told them both, *and then Atlantis reborn. That will be the way of it.* She lifted her stone, her single legacy of her drowned home, out of the water to inspect it.

It was quite ordinary, white, wedge-shaped still, and scarred around the edges, much as her fingertips were. She hugged it to her, and then turned around in the water, tangling herself in her hair. No land was visible in any direction. With a glance at the sun, she judged which way land might be. Turning on her back, the stone protectively resting on her chest, she began to kick her way south.

A few hundred miles to the north, Europe fought a war they called the Great War, and the War to End All Wars, and, in time, World War One.

8

"Your what?!" The exclamation came in outraged stereo, slightly louder than was prudent for a quiet lecture hall. Heads turned irritably, and Emma and Cathal both sank deeper into their seats, ashamed but also staring openly at their companion.

"It's a little complicated," Lorhen muttered, without taking his eyes off Mary Kostani. "I think we should get out of here."

Emma shot a glance at the stage, then back at Lorhen. "We just got here. She's just starting her speech."

"You don't need to hear it," Lorhen growled. "She found Atlantis for them. I really think we need to go, Emma. Now."

"Don't you think it's bizarre to run out at the start of the lecture?" Emma whispered.

Lorhen shook his head. "I don't care. She shouldn't be alive. I had no idea she was alive. I'd rather have the whole audience stare at us as we leave than have her walk up to me at the end of the seminar. I need some time to think this through. She shouldn't," he repeated, with soft intensity, "be alive."

Cathal looked at Emma, who shrugged. "All right."

Lorhen lurched to his feet, offering a hand to Emma, who put her hand in his without thinking, then frowned at their joined hands. Lorhen pulled her past Cathal, tugging her toward the far end of the aisle. "Closest exit," he hissed. In a slow wave, everyone in the row stood, expressions ranging from mild exasperation to outright indignation. Lorhen kept his face averted from the stage as he climbed over expensively shod feet, and Emma cast apologetic glances at a few of the more offended people. Behind them, Cathal murmured, "Excuse us," and followed after.

On stage, Dr. Kostani arched her eyebrows at the disturbance. "I didn't think I was that boring," she said dryly. "Perhaps I should arrange a three-ring circus next time."

"Or a bull to sacrifice," Lorhen said, under the ripple of laughter that went through the crowd. Emma pushed the exit door open and the men followed her out, Cathal turning to catch it so it closed quietly. Emma squinted against the bright hall lights, then at Lorhen. "What the hell was that about?"

"Not here," Lorhen said flatly. "There must be a bar or a coffee shop nearby. Anything. Just not here."

Cathal and Emma exchanged glances again before Emma shook her head, but gestured down the hall toward the main doors. "This had better be good, Lorhen."

"Oh, it is." Lorhen's voice sounded thin. "Come on." He stalked out of the building, shoulders hunched, and walked silently for several blocks. Emma and Cathal trailed behind him, taking turns watching his tense walk and regarding each other from the corners of their eyes. Eventually Lorhen ducked into a bar labeled with a badly stenciled sign, the letters worn to illegibility.

Emma stopped beneath the guttering streetlight that lit the sign and glanced over the street. "Do you have any idea where we are?"

"No." Softly, the better to not give anyone any ideas, Cathal added, "You told me he was hoping to get himself killed."

"Looks like the right place for it. Are we going in?"

"Do you want to see what's the story?" Cathal held the door for her, then followed Emma inside.

Orange and olive glass light fixtures, decades out of fashion, barely lit individual booths, their small pools of light coloring one end of each table and leaving the far end dimmed. The scent of ancient cigarette smoke pervaded the place, although the air itself was clean enough. A few people sat at the bar, and a handful of others in the poorly-lit booths, and what little sound there was fell away as the trio entered.

Lorhen ignored the silence that flooded in front of him, and a hubbub picked up behind him as he pushed his way to the back corner of the bar. He stood a moment, hands shoved in his pockets, and scowled at the back wall. Two bathroom doors, both marked 'Men', hung slightly open, and around a corner, another door was nearly lost in grime. Emma and Cathal hung back, watching him, as he went down to the third door, twisted the knob, and pushed it open on a dank alley. He hesitated there, then turned back, closing the door and coming back to sit in a grungy booth, fingers steepled against his nose and his gaze locked on the pitted table. Emma exchanged one last glance with Cathal, then sat down with Lorhen to engage in a silence that lasted several minutes before Emma, impatiently, said, "Well?"

"Did you know," Lorhen said from behind his hands, "that they had coffee in Atlantis? I don't know who went down into Ethiopia to find it, but someone did. I didn't have coffee again for four thousand years. They guarded the plants jealously. No one knew where they'd come from. There are people who would argue that Western civilization wasn't, not until they rediscovered coffee."

"Lorhen," Cathal said deliberately. "What about the woman?"

"Who is she?" Emma asked on the tail of Cathal's question. "We don't have any records of a Mary Kostani."

"Her name is Ghean." Lorhen shook his head, not bothering to look up as Emma drew a protesting breath. "She won't be in the records, Em. She shouldn't be alive."

Emma, through her teeth, said, "I believe you mentioned

that," as Cathal, incredulously, said, "She's your wife?"

"Well, probably not any more. Even in Atlantean law a sep-aration of four and a half millennia probably constitutes an annulment." Lorhen flagged down the barman, muttering, "I'd better start at the beginning," as the man made his way over, then said, "A couple pitchers of whatever you've got with the highest alcohol content," to the man, and went silent again until the drinks arrived.

Heat seared down, thickening the air. Lorhen grinned at the woman clinging to his arm. "You'll have to let me go," he said. "I can't go talk to your mother while you have a death grip on my hand."

Ghean loosened her fingers. "I'm nervous."

"Why? You're not the one who has to go present a case to your mother why you should marry a penniless scholar she's never met instead of a well-employed bodyguard whom she's known for twenty years."

The worry faded from Ghean's face, turning to mock sever-ity. "You're making fun of me."

Lorhen grinned. "Maybe a little bit. I'm sure it'll be fine, Ghean. A kiss for luck?" He bowed his head, touching his lips to hers, and she smiled into the kiss. "I'll meet you in the market later, all right?"

Ghean nodded, and let his hand go, watching him turn into the sun, down between the sandy streets of the tent town. The borders of the town were not far apart, and a few minutes' walk brought Lorhen to Ghean's mother's tent. He bowed in greeting to the guard, who scowled benignly. "Would you tell the lady Minyah that the scholar Lorhen is here to see her?"

"Come in," a voice called from inside. "I can hear you quite well."

Lorhen's eyebrows lifted a bit, and he stepped inside, idly

glancing at the thickness of the cloth woven into the tent. It was not unusually thin; Minyah apparently had excellent hearing. He bowed a second time as the tent flap fell shut behind him and blinked to adjust his vision to the relative darkness inside. Minyah sat at a neatly crafted desk, surrounded by thin paper of unimaginable quality. Lorhen's eyes widened and he took an avaricious step forward before catching himself. With something of an effort, he looked up at Ghean's mother.

Taller than her daughter, but with the same smoky skin and dark hair, Minyah had none of Ghean's impetuosity; instead she gave the instant impression of contained serenity. Her eyes were hazel, almost gold, to Ghean's brown, giving her an aura that conveyed the impression she could look through someone in the first moment she met them. Lorhen shook his shoulders unconsciously, as if warding off that gaze. Minyah stood, brightly dyed and finely woven linens swirled around her, loosely cut to keep cool in the desert heat. A silver pendant shifted between her breasts, catching the light for a moment. "Ghean calls you her giant. I see why. Would you like water?"

Lorhen inclined his head. "Please. Thank you for seeing me."

"I could hardly wait," Minyah countered. "Ghean has been writing home about you for months. Even if I had not planned to visit Kemet, I would have been obliged to come and see her giant."

"Has it been that long?" Lorhen frowned as he accepted the water.

Minyah settled back down at her desk, comfortably, in a rustle of fabrics "It has." She considered him silently for a few minutes, her disconcerting hazel-gold eyes intent. He let her study him, faintly amused at the thin thread of nerves that made his shoulders rise higher than usual. He had been inspected by parents before, but somehow that never made it any easier. With a twitch of a smile, Minyah said, "You love her."

Lorhen's own smile brightened swiftly enough to make him

feel silly. "How could I not? She's so vibrant, so full of life."

"Are you really penniless?" Lorhen, startled, began to reply, but Minyah cut him off with a short gesture. "Never mind. I am almost certain you are not." For the second time, she slipped off her stool, coming around to frown deeply at him from a foot or two away. Lorhen returned the look, one eyebrow rising quizzically. Just as he was about to speak, Minyah murmured, "Ah."

"Ah?"

"You are like him, are you not? Like Aroz. You do not die."

Lorhen took a sharp step backward, hand closing on the knife he wore at his belt too instinctively to stop, though a wince ran through him at the action: nothing could have signaled how right she was more obviously. But no mortal had ever guessed that, and there was no sense of Timeless power about her, nothing at all out of the ordinary. "What are you talki—"

Minyah shook her head. "Do not try to dissemble. It is in your eyes. I have seen it in Aroz for a very long time, and I think it is stronger in you."

Lorhen stared down at her a long moment, astonishment and curiosity warring with caution. Curiosity won, and he slowly backed up until he found a seat among pillows piled on the floor. "...how did you know about Aroz?"

Minyah waved a hand dismissively. "He saved my life once. I wept over his body, and he rose up again. I thought the gods had answered my prayers, but he told me a different tale. I have seen it again since then, and I have come to believe the story he told me was true, and that he cannot die."

"He can," Lorhen said automatically. "But not unless someone takes his head."

"Ah!" Minyah clasped her hands together. "So he has said. I am right, then. That is always satisfying." She turned, collecting her own cup of water and lifting it to her lips. "Do you wish to marry her?"

Lorhen blinked, taken off guard by the return to subject and his own hesitations. Minyah, too observant, lifted her eyebrows. "You do, but there is some doubt in you. Tell me of it."

"Marriage is not lightly undertaken," Lorhen said slowly. "Not in any case. Especially for my kind. There is always the problem of...truth. Whether to confess what we are, or to keep it hidden away, to save our lovers pain. This time it's more difficult than most." He lifted dark eyes to the tent's ceiling, weighing his words, then spoke again. "Has Aroz told you that Ghean has the potential to become immortal, as we are?"

Minyah's eyes widened. Lorhen cast his gaze downward a moment. "I didn't think so. Minyah, your daughter is intelligent and beautiful, and if she were wholly mortal, I would wed her tomorrow. But she isn't, and I don't know what to do or say, to either you or her." He stood to pace uncomfortably, water cup in hand.

"If she were mortal, you would wed her, and love her for the rest of her life." The words were spoken almost to herself. "If she were immortal now—" Minyah looked up. "Would you marry her?"

"Probably not."

"Why?"

"If she were to become Timeless today, she would still be terribly young. I wouldn't want to marry an immortal in her childhood. I don't know that I would want to marry one of us at all."

Minyah's eyebrows quirked up. "Why?" Concern for the current state of affairs visibly faded from her face as a new piece of information swam into her grasp.

"Because I wouldn't ever want to find myself in a position where I had to take my own wife's head," Lorhen said flatly.

Goosebumps rose visibly on Minyah's arms, despite the heat of the room. She let the line of questioning go, pressing her lips together as she looked into her water cup. "When will she die?"

"That's not how it works. She could die of old age, or of illness, and never Awaken." He listened to himself speak with a faint sense of disbelief. In all his life, he could not remember telling a mortal these things, with the exception of a few wives. "We only become Timeless through violent or untimely death. But how can I marry her, knowing that she might die accidentally and then be married eternally to someone she expected a decade or two with?"

Minyah, without a hint of romance evident, said, "Lifematings dissolve. Very few people have the temperance to remain with one mate forever, whether words of ceremony have been said over them or not. Does she know the truth about you?"

"No."

"Perhaps you should tell her, both about herself and yourself, and let her choose."

"I can't. Or—we don't. It's—it's not exactly hard to talk about, save for why anyone would decide to believe us, but we don't interfere that way. We let nature take its course."

Minyah's eyebrows lifted. "Why?"

Lorhen stared at her a moment, then breathed a chuckle. "I don't know. Because we don't. Because everyone wants to grasp at immortality, but the reality is harsher. We kill each other, Minyah. We carry power inside ourselves, and we kill each other for it. It's almost a compulsion, and it's one of the prices that comes with immortality."

"What other prices are there?" Minyah circled her desk, not sitting. "The compulsion can be denied, yes? You and Aroz have not tried killing one another."

Lorhen muttered, "Not yet," then, more clearly, said, "It can be denied, yes, but it's often not. We can't have children, either, Minyah. Not once we've Awakened."

Minyah went quite still for a moment. "But before?"

"Until we Awaken we're just mortals. Most of us can, at least in theory, have children. And then if we Awaken, we outlive them. Watch them die. Watch their children die, if we're masochistic enough to do that to ourselves."

"Have you any?"

"Not that I know about. I don't remember being mortal."

Curiosity filtered over Minyah's features. "How long must it be, if you cannot remember?"

Lorhen sighed, putting his cup down on Minyah's desk, careful not to place it near any of the fine paper she was working with. "A very long time. A thousand years or more."

Minyah's eyes widened. "Thirty lifetimes," she breathed. "More."

Lorhen nodded, a tired motion. "A very long time," he repeated. "All of which has come down to now, and whether or not to marry your daughter."

"She will be angry, if you do not tell her the truth."

"If I tell her the truth, she'll fling herself off Anapa or the pyramid!"

Laughter sparked in Minyah's voice. "Would you not do the same?"

"Well…yes."

"Do you love her enough to grant her immortality?"

"I don't grant it. It's just the way she was born. I would prefer not to interfere. It's not how it's supposed to be done."

"And if I told her?"

The corner of Lorhen's mouth twisted. "You'd be betraying my trust."

"She is my only daughter. Would you not do anything you could for your child, to ensure she would live beyond a normal lifespan?"

"I just told you we can't have children."

Minyah, again, dismissed the words with a brush of her hand. "That is not what I asked, Lorhen. If you had a child, what would you do?"

He scowled at her, pained. "I don't know, Minyah. I'm a

scholar, and a very old one, at that. I walk around the world observing and writing down what I see. I try to stay out of the way, not to influence things, because I don't want to draw attention to myself. I don't have any children. I don't know what I would do."

Minyah looked over her shoulder at her paperwork, and at her fingers, stained with ink, the marks of a shared profession. Thoughtfully, she said, "You have my permission to marry, if it is the decision you ultimately reach. Go. Find her. Tell her."

Lorhen blinked, nonplussed. "Thank you. Why?"

Minyah chuckled. "Because my daughter loves you, and you are honest. Perhaps not reassuring, but honest. Go." She flapped her fingers at him impatiently, and circled back to sit on her stool.

Lorhen smiled faintly. "Thank you," he repeated, and pushed the tent flap aside to step out into the desert again.

Minyah watched the small clouds of sand settle as the door flap drifted shut before reaching for the thin pen and ink she wrote out the language of Atlantis in. In her free hand, she lifted her necklace, turning the pendant so she could see it right-side up. Neatly, in the upper right-hand corner of her parchment, she began to sketch a copy of the necklace, the ancient symbol of her House: the night sky's Hunter, the harbinger of winter and the aspect of death, whose brilliant three-star belt drew the eye and whose uplifted arms held the heart. She encompassed its seven points within a circle and left the ink to dry, then, in smooth print, began to write.

> *I am a Keeper. I alone know of a people who walk among us, men and women who cannot die. They are Timeless, and are compelled to fight among themselves for the power they carry within. It is my wish to observe and record the histories of these immortals, though not to interfere....*

9

Ten minutes after Ghean crawled onto shore, she dug up a razor-edged shell and chopped her hair off. She'd had to put down her wedge to gather up the mass of it. Without holding its length in her arms, she couldn't lift her head; she could barely even hold it in her arms. When she was done slicing it off, the ragged ends barely brushed her chin, but she could move her head.

Afterward, she thought she should have braided it, but couldn't figure out how she would have manipulated it all anyway. She laid it out on the beach, the still-wet, gleaming length of it, and walked from one end to the other. Walking itself was awkward, uncertain steps on feet no longer familiar with bearing weight. She lost her balance more than once, tripping to hands and knees on the shore.

There had to be more than fifty feet of hair. Ghean set her wedge down on one end of the length, and went back into the water. She came back out with strands of seaweed, and wrapped her hair up in it, twisting the seaweed rope around it to keep it close and still.

She was hungry again when she finished. With her stone, she returned to the water again, to dart after fish. It was easier without having her own hair to dodge.

The next weeks blurred, as much as the time under the water had. She stole clothes from the first town she found, under the cover of dark. Certain memories stood out: the first car that whisked by, and the first plane that flew overhead. She'd fallen to her knees, shrieking in fear, when the plane buzzed over. The sound seemed too much like the end of the world, to her untrained ears.

Even without the language, she was able to communicate that she wanted to sell her hair, and to do so. She had no idea if the price was fair, but neither could she bargain; she had to trust, and to ask, lifting the paper and coins that represented his offer, "Kemet? Ta-mehew?"

"Kemet." He echoed the word, blankly at first, then with a laugh. "Egypt?"

Egypt. Kemet was still there, then. Renamed, perhaps, but the names of everything changed, with time. With relief, she tried what few words she'd learned: "Egypt where? Go Egypt?" She lifted the fistful of money.

The wig-maker nodded again, pointing to the east. "Egypt is that way. There are buses."

"Buses." It meant nothing to her. "Buses where?"

He took pity on her, and brought her to a bus station, and arranged for her passage to a place called Cairo. A map, pinned to the station wall, seemed to tell her that Cairo stood where Manf had once been, that Manf had been swallowed up into the sprawl of a city that looked larger, on the map, than could be actually possible. She went to the bus rigidly, already knowing it would roar and rattle at unbearable speeds, but accepting that the journey to Cairo would be endless, and dangerous, on foot.

The bus terrified her anyway, and she distracted herself by struggling to speak with the people around her. The language was vastly different, but people were friendly, and she would ask and point, and they would give her the words for things. By the time the bus reached Egypt, she could make rudimentary sentences, and she had learned the year was 1915. It made no sense, to her own calendar.

In Cairo, there were camels that took people into the desert to see the pyramid and Anapa. Ghean rode the camel with the ease of muscle memory, idly stroking her wedge of stone as they loped along. The pyramid—pyramids!—came into sight first, looming on the horizon but strangely dull in the distance. Even so, as they came closer, the pyramids' yellowed, wind-wracked sides looked better than Anapa, whose elegant long head was terribly shrunken and flattened, no longer a god at all. Ghean let out a cry of dismay, turning to the guide and gesturing at her face. "Head! Face! No! Where Anapa?"

He laughed, white teeth bright in a dark face. "Anapa? It's the Sphinx, not a god. Its nose got shot off by Napoleon's cannon." None of the words made sense to her, and she stared at the great god's thick blocky shape in horror. It had been so beautiful when she left Egypt, and now it was so worn and old. Afraid, she turned back to the guide, pointing at the wreckage of Anapa again.

"How old?"

"Forty-five hundred, five thousand years old. About that."

Ghean stared at him blankly, trying to understand the numbers. She shook her head unhappily, and held up her hands, fingers spread. "How many?"

"What, fingers? Ten. Ten fingers."

"Ten," she repeated, and looked worriedly at the monument and the aged pyramids behind it. "How many tens?"

The guide hesitated, then slid down off his camel, encouraging her to do the same. She did, crouching in the sand next to him. He drew out ten marks in the sand. "Ten," he said, patiently, and drew a picture beside it: a stick with a circle following it. "Ten."

Ghean nodded, short hair brushing along her chin. Rapidly,

but neatly, the guide made nine more rows of ten marks. "Ten tens," he explained. "One hundred."

She nodded again, touching the numerals he'd drawn. "Ten. One hundred. Yes."

His smile blossomed momentarily. "Very good." He drew a third numeral, a line with three circles. "Ten one hundreds is one thousand. Do you understand?"

Ghean did, but lapsed into her own language to state her understanding. "Yes. Ten times one hundred is a thousand. I understand." She nodded, dark eyes on his face. "Ten one hundreds," she said carefully, in his words. "One thousand."

He grinned again. "Good. Yes." Then he pointed at Anapa. "Five," and he held up five fingers. "Five thousand years old."

Ghean's chin jerked up and she stared at the ruined lines of the Egyptian wolf-god. "Five thousand years?" The brilliant blue sky around Anapa dimmed and fogged, and blackness swept in to comfort her.

She woke slowly to a familiar scene, the desert left in darkness by the sun, and the crackle of a fire just beyond the edge of the tent. For a moment, she relaxed, smiling, wondering when her mother would come get her for the evening meal.

Firelight glinted on the metal post of the tent, and memory rushed home with an almost painful blow. Her mother had been dead five thousand years. A wordless sound of loss ripped out of her, shattering the quiet night. Camels, not very far away, bellowed in irritation at the unexpected sound. As she had done for so long, Ghean curled on her side, no longer floating free, but weighted by gravity on a scratchy bed pad. Panicked fingers reached out far enough to find her stone, and she drew it close to her.

The guide came running, kneeling at her side to check on

her. Ghean rocked gently, barely aware of him, as she tried to make her mind encompass the time that had passed. Still without noticing the guide, she climbed to her feet, and walked beyond the fire's perimeter, staring up at the sky.

She had looked at the sky for several nights, while she was in the water, but she had never *seen* it. The stars had wheeled in their cycle, no longer where they once belonged, rising in wholly different parts of the sky. Shaking, she picked out the Hunter, the sign of her House.

She was the last member of her House. "Mother," she whispered.

Leaving the guide behind, she began to walk toward Anapa. Methodically, in the cold desert night, she circled it, trailing her hand against the stone. It hadn't weathered the centuries well, the poor beast, and she couldn't bear to look beyond it at the ruins of Khufu's pyramid, which had once been so bright and beautiful. Long before dawn, she knelt between Anapa's paws, gazing up at him, no longer feeling the cold. No longer feeling fear or patience, either; it was, for this little while, as though those things had been burned out of her and nothing was left but a terrible silence.

When the sun rose, she stayed where she was, letting it bring scalded color to her pale flesh, as it had once done to Lorhen, hundreds of lifetimes ago.

She sat for hours, until men came to make her move, and then with a remote dignity that made the men fall away, she stood, and walked out of the desert to claim her destiny, five thousand years delayed.

10

Lorhen sat in the sand with a graceless thump, burying his toes in the hot grains and propping his arms on bent knees. Wind blew traces of sand into small heaps, and smoothed them out again. He watched without seeing, still considering the conversation with Minyah. It had probably been a mistake to tell her about Ghean, but there was no doubt it had also been something of a relief. All of it: not just Ghean, but his own immortality, which was a closely-enough held secret that he could count the number of mortals he'd shared it with, over the centuries. Minyah was a scholar, the kind—he hoped—who sought knowledge for its own sake, not to sell or trade it for her own benefit. No: he could be certain of that, if she'd known Aroz's secret for decades. So the unburdening of hidden truths was a relief, if not, exactly, the answer he'd been looking for.

The answer, he had to admit—finally, after a few hours of wandering the burning sands outside the tent city—the answer was that he'd more than half expected Minyah to forbid their marriage, thus relieving him of the burden of deciding whether to tell Ghean anything about her potential. Mortals never alleviated problems that obligingly, nor should he have expected Minyah to, not on any level. If he had a child—and if he did, it was long lost to time and memory, because no Timeless he knew of had ever become a parent after their first death, and few enough did before—but if he did, he would like to imagine he could allow that child to shape their own life, and perhaps even their own death.

A snort of amusement shook him and he stood again to slide down the dune into one of the endless valleys created by shifting sand. Noble thoughts from an ignoble man; the truth was that if he had a child he'd probably throw her off the pyramids himself. Time was such a gift. The pain of loss that every Timeless experienced balanced the gift, but the possibilities brought by time were too great to ignore. Mortal lives were so short. Some burned brighter for it, while others simply disappeared in a moment. Ghean burned bright with her black-eyed enthusiasm and love as intense as the desert sun for everything she encountered. Time might dull the edge of that enthusiasm some, but the gift would be greater than the loss. He didn't have to tell her now, but he would tell her before her youth was gone.

The rules they followed weren't set in stone, after all. They were more like guidelines, inspired by the whims of the magic within them, and any Timeless who had walked away from a fight knew the power could be denied, at least for a time.

Lorhen followed his tracks back toward the tent city. Another glance at the sun when he came to the town's borders told him he'd lost track of more time than he'd known. The sky hadn't yet begun to color with sunset, but it wouldn't be long now, and he'd left Ghean before noon. She would have paced a trench in the sand by now, probably deep enough to raise ground water, and she would drown him in it for making her wait. Well, it was one way to have the truth out, because she deserved, if nothing else, to know about *him* before they were married. Driven by a wry combination of determination and amusement, Lorhen made his way through the city, side-stepping merchants and failing, with deliberation, to see other wares on offer.

A chill, wholly at odds with the desert heat, swept him before he reached Ghean's tent. The Timeless almost couldn't help it, the brief stillness that came over them, the unintended glance for another of their kind. It made them stand out in a moving crowd, as Aroz did now; Lorhen, through long practice, kept moving easily, but his height made him easy to pick out of the masses regardless. Their eyes met, and while neither precisely relaxed, Aroz's gaze dropped and he continued on to beneath an open tent filled with tables and stools, taking a seat across from Ghean. He leaned in, speaking to her, and she craned her neck, peering around him. A smile blossomed, then faded into her best attempt at a scowl as she remembered Lorhen had abandoned her for the entire afternoon. With a careless gesture, she excused herself from Aroz and came darting around the crowd to glower at Lorhen.

"I've been looking for you all day. Where have you been? What did she say? Did she say no?"

"She said yes. We need to talk, Ghean."

Ghean's shriek of delight pulled Lorhen's attention from Aroz, though not before he saw the frown the other Timeless wore, or the black expression in his gaze that promised a reckoning later. Ghean's broad smile, though, wiped most of that away, and Lorhen laughed as she clapped her hands together. "She did! Oh, I knew she would!" She grabbed his hand and tugged him toward a nearby booth. "Come on, let's get betrothal bracelets now, Lorhen!"

The merchant behind the counter Ghean dragged Lorhen toward looked up with sharp interest. "Betrothal tokens!" he agreed loudly. "For the outlanders, a special price, mmm? Let me show you." He lifted a pair of glittering bracelets, gold and delicately jeweled, turning them to catch the evening sunlight.

Lorhen took one, looked at it without seeing, and handed it back. "Very nice," he said politely. "Ghean, later, for the bracelets, all right? We need to talk about some things."

"Like what?" She sighed, patting one of the bracelets.

"Later," she promised the merchant. "What's wrong, Lorhen? Did Mother say something awful?"

He laughed again, in spite of himself. "No," he said, "but she did make me think. Come back to my tent. We need some privacy."

Ghean's smile curved slowly across her face. "That sounds promising," she purred, an entirely different voice than the concerned one of a moment earlier.

Lorhen laughed a third time and curled her into his arms for a kiss before releasing her. She made him laugh: if there was anything more appealing in a woman, he hadn't found it in a thousand years. "That was *not* what I had in mind."

Ghean *tsk*ed, sliding her arm through Lorhen's as they walked. "I'm doing something wrong, then. What did you want to talk about?"

"The future," Lorhen said, not for the first time, and as he often did, couldn't help but tie it to the past. "Do you remember the first time I saw you, arguing with that poor old man over structural integrity?"

"Well, he was wrong," Ghean said with a sniff. "The Anapa designs were too thin at the neck. It never would have held the weight of his head, and can you imagine the Pharaoh's rage if his portal guardian's head fell off?"

Lorhen lifted his free hand equitably. "I can. You probably not only saved Anapa's head, but the lives of every unfortunate soul who worked on the thing. I was expecting someone much older to turn around, when you finally won."

Ghean wrinkled her nose dismissively. "Anyone with the slightest background in structural engineering could have seen that the design would fail, and I started studying architecture when I was practically a baby. My father designed several of the new House centers in Atlantis, and the new temple, so I grew up with it. I always wanted to build things. Mother still hopes I'll change my mind. Building is so physical," she said in an excellent mimicry of her mother's precise tones.

"She won't mind it when you design the greatest House on Atlantis for her." Lorhen stopped as they reached his tent, pushing the tent flap aside for Ghean. She ducked out of habit, though there was more than two feet of head space for her inside Lorhen's tent. There was nearly a foot of clearance for Lorhen himself, unlike any of the other tents in the traveling city. The extra yards of fabric had cost him, but it was worth the relief from the sense that the roof was balanced precariously on his head.

The single room was otherwise unimpressive. Sleeping mats lay piled to one side, over the thin carpets that kept the floor from being desert sand. A desk, not nearly so well crafted as Minyah's, but foldable and more portable than hers, took up a significant portion of the wall opposite the sleeping mats. It, in turn, was littered with sheets of papyrus, again not nearly as fine as Minyah's, but serviceable. A stool sat crookedly behind the desk. Inches from it, a short, fat blade leaned on the far side of the desk, nearly invisible when the tent was entered. Another stool, shorter but with a padded cushion, was piled with thick papyrus sheets. Lorhen removed them, and offered the seat to Ghean.

She remained standing, looking at the sheets as Lorhen stacked them neatly on his desk. "You're not as poor as you pretend to be, are you, Lorhen? I never thought about it, but papyrus isn't cheap, not even in Atlantis, and you've got a lot of it."

"I make it myself. It's not hard, just time consuming," which was true, but led away from the point. "You're right, though. Ghean, please, I have some things to tell you." He pulled the stool around the desk, began to sit, and then reconsidered, moving to shorter one.

Ghean, puzzled, took the bigger stool, then straightened with a look of amusement. "I'm taller than you." She folded one leg in front of herself, arms wrapped around it. "All right, Lorhen. What is it?"

Lorhen steepled his fingers, then dropped his head against them with a wry smile. Years of silence made an effective barrier on their own, even if that barrier had just been breached in the discussion with Minyah. "I'm not sure where to start. Ghean…"

She reached out to fold a small hand around his templed fingers. "It's all right. Tell me."

Lorhen lifted his head. "I'm going to tell you something that will sound utterly absurd. Bear with me, all right? Give me a chance to finish."

Her eyebrows crinkled. "All right."

Lorhen took a breath. "You asked me when I learned to read. I don't remember exactly, but it was around five hundred years ago, maybe a little more. My first memories are from about five hundred years before that, although I don't remember when or where I was born. It might have been around a thousand years ago. It could have been much longer. I don't know a great deal about my people," he went on more softly, watching Ghean's face. She hardly changed expression at all, little more than a trace of amusement in her features. "Where we come from, why we're so different…" He shrugged. "I do know that we don't die of old age. I know it's very hard to kill us. I know we don't have children, Ghean."

She stared another moment, then gave a short laugh. "For a moment, I almost believed you. Come on, Lorhen. What is it? You don't have to make up stories. Nothing can be as bad as you're making it."

"You should believe me," he said softly. "It's true. I'm immortal, Ghean. I'll heal from almost any wound. You have to believe me before we can seriously consider marriage."

What little humor she had drained away into a shiver. "Stop it, Lorhen. You're scaring me."

"I can't stop," he said, still softly. "I know how it sounds, love, and I wish—" A rough chuckle escaped him. "Most of the time I'm just as glad it is so unbelievable. Most of the time it's far better to rely on it being unbelievable than to make any attempt at explaining my reality. It's too alien, too frightening. But you do have to believe me, Ghean. In this case, you do, and the only way anybody ever really believes is if they see it. I'm going to have to show you. Please don't scream." He slid his belt knife from its sheath and laid his palm open with one swift movement.

Ghean pulled in air sharply, not quite a scream. "Lorhen! What are you—you'll need a physician!"

"Watch," he said. "I am not like you. I heal from any wound in moments. Watch."

He spread his hand, fingers splayed back, to display the cut. Tendons lay bared, crimson flowing back between his fingers to drip on the sandy floor. Dispassionately, he watched as both ends of the injury began to heal, eating inward to the deepest part of the cut. The newly released blood discolored and dried as the healing slowed, the severed tendons visibly knitting together, then the muscle reconstituting. The skin reformed in a smooth swirl, and Lorhen closed his hand into a fist. Looking up at Ghean, he opened his hand again, rust-colored flakes drifting down to the carpets.

Her eyes were locked on his hand, shock writing itself over her delicate features. "How did you do that?" she demanded, voice tinged with fear. "I saw the cut. It was deep." Her eyes snapped up to meet his.

"We call ourselves Timeless," Lorhen murmured. "That kind of injury is easiest to demonstrate with. I can do something more drastic, if you need me to."

"No!" Her voice rose. "It's not possible. It's some kind of trick. No one heals that fast. You've tricked me somehow. Why are you doing this, Lorhen? Why? It's not funny. Why are you doing this?" She scooted back on the stool, cringing away from him.

Lorhen took a deep breath. "Because you deserve to know who it is you might marry. What I am."

Ghean's eyes dropped to his palm, still extended, unscarred. "Are you a god? Have you come from the heavens to—" Her imagination failed her, and she broke off, fear setting itself more deeply in her face.

"No, not a god, Ghean. Just a man. A little different than most, but just a man. There are others like me. Please, Ghean. I don't mean to frighten you, but you had to know before we married." Carefully, he reached out to touch her shoulder.

She bolted back in a flurry of fabrics, knocking the stool over as she scrambled to her feet. Lorhen, startled, surged to his feet as well, his hand still open to her.

"No! Don't touch me! Don't—!" She ran for the door, all but stumbling over her robes as she rushed out.

Lorhen dropped to his knees, his hand falling, palm open, to smack quietly against the carpets as he gazed after his fleeing betrothed. "Well. That went well."

Across the town, Minyah straightened, reading over the words she had written.

> *I have met two of these Timeless that I know of. One is Aroz, my bodyguard, who has given his life to save mine more than once. The other calls himself Lorhen, and claims to be a thousand years old.*
>
> *Lorhen told me more, in a few unguarded moments, than Aroz has in the many years I have known him. It is a trust I think he does not often share; I wonder at his sharing it with me. The bonds between us are slim: my daughter, Ghean, and*

the scholarship we both follow. It seems little, but is apparently enough.

He calls the power that keeps the Timeless alive a kind of magic. A few mortals have it within them, this magic, but it can only be released through violent or untimely death. He tells me my daughter has this magic in her, and then he beseeches me to not interfere, to not tell her.

Lorhen and Aroz both spoke of a compulsion to battle other Timeless, that ends only when one Timeless takes the other's head. If I tell Ghean, I will force her into a life of war, unlike anything she has ever known. It seems cruel, but it seems more cruel to consign her to certain death: with her immortality released, there is always the chance she will live another day, and experience another thing which may never otherwise have come her way.

It seems right to force her into this immortality now, to insure that she remains young and strong, to make certain it does not somehow slip away. Aroz has not seemed to age while I have known him, and Lorhen carries his years only in his eyes. How do I judge Ghean's peak, and thus the time to best tell her of the secret she bears in herself?

Lorhen says the Timeless cannot have children, that he cannot father a child on her. Though there are few deaths from childbirth in Atlantis, it is no longer a relevant fear for her safety, for the eventual release of her potential, not if she marries this man, at least. Illness does not come so quickly that she could not be dispatched into death by a mortal blow before sickness took her, and any other death, violent or accidental, will trigger the magic and force her into immortality.

I will do as Lorhen asks, and not yet tell her of her potential. There is time, yet. If she has not met her first death through accident in five years, then, I think I shall tell her. It is little enough time, even for a mortal. For her, it will be as nothing.

> In the meantime, there are the Keepers to think of. I think
> it must be a group as unspoken as the Timeless themselves. As
> unlikely as a people who live forever is a society who records the
> lives of those Timeless, and both, I think, must remain separate
> from the rest of the world.
>
> There are those on Atlantis whom I think would belong in
> my little group of Keepers. So many of the relics belonging to
> the Houses are objects reputed to prolong life. It seems natural
> to approach those who bear them to participate in this project.
> Even my own House has its Hunter's Cloak, which legend
> claims will make its wearer invulnerable.
>
> Perhaps I shall test the cloak, at that. Carefully. I should
> hate to discover the legends were wrong after plunging a knife
> to my breast.

Minyah chuckled softly at herself. Reserved and intellectual, she was probably one of the least likely people she knew to rashly test a legend in such a fashion. She yawned, setting her pen down, and pushed her fingers into the small of her back, stretching.

The tent flap burst inward, sending soft sprays of sand over the carpets. Ghean tripped on the edge of the first carpet, crashing to the floor. Fabric ripped audibly, and the girl struggled to her feet, oblivious to the torn knee of her tunic. Tears tracked streaks through the dust on her face. "M-mother," she wailed. Despite having just climbed to her feet, she suddenly collapsed, knees giving way in a boneless rush, sending her to sit hard on the floor, face buried in her hands.

Minyah sat frozen at her desk a moment, her hands still pressed into the small of her back. Ghean's dark hair was disarrayed and sand-streaked, tumbling over her shoulders in tangles. Judging from other rents in her gold-colored silks, and sand crusted under her fingernails, the fall at the door had not been the first. Minyah cleared her throat, and stood. "I must gather you have seen Lorhen," she said, as delicately as she could.

Ghean lifted a face pale under the tears and dirt. "He's not human!" The last word came out in a burst of miserable confusion, a floodgate for more tears.

Minyah knelt before her daughter, resting a hand on her shoulder. "I know," she said. "I insisted he tell you."

"Tell me!" Ghean's voice rose. "You knew? He's not human, mother, he's a—a monster, or a god, of some kind, and you knew?" Her tone ranged between despair and outrage.

Minyah straightened her shoulders. "I deduced it. I believe he is as human as you or I, Ghean." A small wince distorted her features for a moment, as she thought about the implications of her words. Ghean, focused on her own misery, didn't see the expression, and after a brief hesitation, Minyah continued. "He is human. He is merely longer-lived than most."

Ghean sat upright, the better to project. "Longer lived! He says he's immor—!"

Minyah cut her off with a sharp gesture. "More quietly, daughter." The frown sketched lines into her forehead. "Such behavior does not become you."

Ghean scowled, sullen, but repeated herself more quietly. "He says he's immortal, Mother. Humans aren't immortal."

Minyah settled back on her knees. "Most are not," she agreed. "Think about your history, Ghean. Even on Atlantis we have legends and stories, and indeed, history, of people who lived longer than normal. Is it impossible that others could share that longevity?"

Ghean pushed strands of hair out of her face, leaving a few still sticking to drying tear paths, but her anxiety was fading into the pleasure of debate. "Those are with the artifacts of Atlantis, Mother. It's not the same at all."

"But if our artifacts exist, and have the power to grant longer life, why is it inconceivable that some other power, unknown to us, could grant it without an artifact to focus through?"

Ghean frowned. "You sound like you've thought about this for a long time. How long have you known Lorhen?"

"I only met him today."

"Then you know somebody else like him. Not even you think this fast."

Minyah debated briefly, then shrugged her eyebrows. Ghean would learn eventually. "Aroz is like Lorhen, Timeless. I have known since I was a little younger than you are."

Disbelieving anger wrote itself across Ghean's face. "Are you like them too? Am I the only normal person in the whole world?"

Minyah struggled to control her expression. "I am not Timeless," she promised. "I am, however, quite certain you are not the only normal person in the whole world." She reached out to touch her daughter's face with gentle fingers. "Lorhen has trusted you with something very deep and personal about himself, my daughter. He did not have to tell you, you know. Think, before you reject him. You ran from fear of the unknown. Determine if your fear is greater than your love. Then make your decision. But not before, Ghean. Do not be hasty. He, and you, have time to think, before you act."

11

The line was familiar, spoken by a fresh-faced young man trying to be politely flirtatious: "Where are you from? I can't place your accent."

Ghean smiled. Try as she might, she couldn't erase the faint traces of Atlantis from her voice. At first the fact had been a source of chagrin, but she'd come to be quietly amused at having a singularly unique accent in all the world. "I'm from the Mediterranean," she explained easily. "My family moved a great deal when I was a child."

The lie came easily after more than a decade of living in the twentieth century. At first she'd stuttered and mumbled useless explanations, certain her secret would be revealed. The frightened voice often resurfaced in those times, screaming out its horror of being found out. The other, infinitely patient, waited until the frightened one had yelled itself out before interfering.

They have no reason to suspect you, it said then. *Write out your new history and study it. Make it simple, and there will be no flaws. Be confident. They cannot possibly suspect us.*

And they didn't. Ghean knew the exact moment when she'd begun to think of mortals as 'they', as creatures different from herself. It had taken years, years in which she grew accustomed to the new world she was in. She learned languages, Egyptian first, from the young guide who'd told her how much time had passed. Two years with him was not enough to feel the difference between herself and mortals, nor were the following handful of years while she learned English and German from archaeologists robbing the magnificent temples and crypts the Egyptian pharaohs had left behind.

The illusion that she was the same as she had been, as mortal as those around her, ended with a car crash. Her English teacher, a skinny American, sped around a corner and into a cart pulled by oxen. He, the oxen, and two of the three in the cart died; Ghean jerked awake minutes after the crash, shattered skull stitching itself back together while a handful of terrified onlookers stared. A woman screamed, naming her a witch, and ran for the authorities.

The war has ended, the patient one advised then. *The gods are telling us it is time to leave Egypt and search for our enemy.* Ghean pulled herself from the wreck and sold the last of her stash of hair for passage on a boat going to America.

"I do not understand this Prohibition," she said now. "Nowhere that I have been would such a thing be thought of."

The boy next to her smiled, waving his hand. "Only in America," he agreed. "It doesn't work very well, does it?" Another wave of his hand encompassed the dark little tavern—*speakeasy*, Ghean reminded herself—where they, and dozens of others, were congregated.

Ghean shook her head, about to speak when a headache rocketed through the back of her head, the abrupt wash of pain hard enough to feel as though it would come out her eyes. As quickly as it came, it passed, and she was left gripping the edge of the bar. After a few seconds she lifted her head, frowning beyond the boy.

A tall woman, dark hair bobbed and curled in permanent waves, stood just inside the door, scanning the room with narrowed eyes. In a moment, her gaze fixed on Ghean and she nodded slightly before making her way to the other side of the bar. Ghean watched her sit, then excused herself to the boy, and followed the other woman, coming to a stop a few feet away from her table.

The woman looked up, eyebrows arched. "I'm not looking for a fight," she said without preamble. "If you aren't either, have a seat."

Ghean sat, tentatively. "You gave me that headache," she half asked.

The woman's eyebrows went up again, and sympathy suddenly washed across her face. "You don't know what you are, do you? I thought you would. You feel…heavy. Old."

Ghean hesitated. *Tell her no!* the patient one ordered. *We need to learn to fight. She may help us, but how would we explain knowing what the Timeless are, yet being unable to fight?* "No," she said slowly. "I was in an automobile accident in Egypt a few years ago and…."

The woman's mouth twisted in a smile of acknowledgment. "And you got up from a fatal injury." Her voice was soft. "Maybe it's happened again since then. Maybe not. It will, though." She lifted her head, catching the bartender's eye and lifting two fingers. He nodded, and a minute later a pretty young woman delivered two drinks to the table. "Thanks," the Timeless woman said, and paid, pushing one drink across the table to Ghean. After the waitress was gone, she said, "I'm guessing that was the first headache like that you've felt."

Ghean nodded, picking up the drink to taste it, and grimaced. "What is this?"

"Gin and tonic." The brunette laughed. "It's awful, but it's cheap." She sipped her own drink, then offered a hand, across the table. "I'm Caterina. I was born in Venice in the late sixteenth century. Have you ever used a sword?"

Surprise, largely heartfelt, flooded Ghean's face. She'd imagined Timeless would be much more secretive. She shook the other woman's hand slowly. "I'm Ghean. I—no, I've never used a sword."

"Funny, you look as though you're here. Maybe it's a case of here today, Ghean tomorrow." Caterina smiled as a pained look twisted Ghean's mouth. "Sorry. You probably get that a lot. Unusual name. Kind of pretty, though. You're going to need a teacher, Ghean. Finish your drink and we'll go to some nice little church and I'll tell you all about what you are."

"Why a church?" Ghean asked, surprised, and Caterina laughed.

"You *are* new. Because holy ground is our sanctuary. Not even humans fight on holy ground. Mostly, anyway." She shrugged. "Point is, it's meant to tell you I don't plan on taking your head while we talk."

Two days later Ghean went west with Caterina, to a cabin in remote mountain territory where the modern world hadn't yet invaded, nor seemed it ever could, and for three years, she studied under the Venetian woman's tutelage. Caterina towered over her, and most men would be at least the Venetian woman's height. "Use it to your advantage," Caterina said, and taught her the short sword, and the use of daggers first, because no Timeless should ever go anywhere without at least a short blade, for the heartstrike. Ghean came to love the elegance of the rapier, and drilled long hours even after practice had ended.

Caterina came out of the cabin early one morning to watch one such drill, arms folded. When Ghean eventually turned to her, the other woman came forward with an envelope. "There's not much more I can teach you, but there's a lot left for you to learn. There are fighting styles in the Orient that would suit your size and frame, but I can't teach them to you. This is a letter to a friend of mine, and cash for the journey. I'll bring you to California. I've already arranged passage for you, if you're willing to go. It'll help you keep your head."

Europe was racing toward war again by the time Ghean returned from the Orient to America. Only days after she landed, the thrill of warning shot through her as she walked a San Francisco street. The warning was accompanied by the nearby sound of swords clashing. Curious, she followed the sound, creeping forward down an alley to watch the battle. It lasted only minutes, two men silent with intent, the only sounds that of labored breathing and metal slamming against metal.

Ghean had taken no heads herself; the fury of lightning that rained from the sky was the closest she had ever been to a Blending. She stood rigid in the aftershock, hair blown astray and heart racing as the survivor walked away, down the other end of the alley. Ghean sank against a wall, eyes closed, only to shriek in surprise when someone put a hand on her shoulder. Years of drilling came into play before she thought, and she knocked the hand away, whipping around to drive the heel of her hand toward the lower chest of the man who'd touched her.

She stopped the blow just before it landed, but he jumped back anyway, both hands lifted in apology. "I'm sorry," he said. He was brown: brown eyes, brown hair, brown skin, altogether mild-looking. "You saw?" he asked, though he gave no indication what she might have seen.

Ghean pulled in a breath, about to deny having seen the battle as the man lowered his hands. For an instant she froze, reconstructing the image of his hands in the air. There was a mark on his inner wrist, impossibly familiar. "I—what was— he killed that man!" she blurted. "And the storm! Where did it come from?"

The brown man hesitated. "It would be best if you forgot what you saw," he suggested.

Ghean shook her head. "No. No, I want to know. What was

it? Who were they? You know, don't you?" She could hear her accent growing thicker, and calmed herself. "Please tell me."

Another hesitation, then the man gestured with his head. "Walk with me. Tell me about yourself. My name is Thomas Burns."

"Marion," she replied. "Marion Townsend." It was the name that had been on her traveling papers, the ones Caterina had provided for her. "I just came to San Francisco. I want to go to college. I want to learn history."

"Do you?" Thomas smiled. "I'm a historian, myself."

Ghean lifted her eyebrows. "I don't think I've ever seen a historian with a tattoo." She nodded at his wrist. "That's what's on your wrist, isn't it?"

He smiled again, and turned his wrist over, displaying a dark blue tattoo, an hourglass with a tilted waist. Ghean stared, feeling heat surge to her face.

It isn't possible, the frightened one insisted, and even the patient one seemed to agree. There was no detail within the hourglass, yet the curves were hauntingly familiar. The circle bordering the design had bullet points as familiar as the interior. Ghean swallowed, gazing at them, her heart pounding.

It has to be, she told the voices. *The Houses surrounding the Hunter, just as we used the symbols at home. It has to be. That's my House symbol!*

After five thousand years? the frightened one demanded. *It's impossible.*

It's improbable, Ghean corrected it, and slowly looked up at Thomas. "It's very interesting. What's it of? The only tattoos I've ever seen have been fantastic creatures or women's names, things like that."

Thomas shrugged, smiling again. "It's a symbol that caught my eye a long time ago."

Ghean glanced back down the street toward the alley where the battle had been. *It's impossible*, the frightened one whispered again. Aloud, she guessed, "It has something to do with the fight back there, doesn't it?"

Thomas stopped walking, frowning down at her. "You're very astute."

Ghean nearly stopped breathing. How? What did her family have to do with the Timeless? Who was this man? Why was he watching the Timeless? What did he know about them? She stopped the race of thoughts with effort, and said, "I think I would like you to tell me about it, if you would."

Eight months later, Ghean entered the Keeper Academy. She had taken no heads, and her Timeless existence had been quiet enough, evidently unnoticed by the Keepers; even her time with Caterina seemed to have gone unnoticed. She went into research as quickly as she could, and in a few years transferred to the European branch of the Keepers, unable to find what she was looking for within the American texts.

The Parisian vaults held no more answers regarding the use of her House signet than the American histories had. Paris did, however, have dozens of texts on the only Timeless she had any interest in finding. They were called the Lorhen Chronicles, and for nearly a thousand years, there had been no new entries. The final journal came from 1066, the Battle of Hastings; his Keeper had lost him, and no one since had been able to find him. There were a few sightings that might have been him, over the last ten centuries, but most of the writers seemed to agree that Lorhen was dead, if he'd ever really existed at all. More than one chronicler suggested 'Lorhen' had been a number of different Timeless over the centuries, laying claim to the name of a legend.

Ghean sat with the newest of the Chronicles a long time, turning pages without seeing them. It hadn't really occurred to her that he might be dead. Even looking at the scrawled handwriting that recorded his last verified sighting, she did not entirely believe it.

She had time. If her old lover was still alive, she would find him somehow. The Chronicles were a disappointment in that aspect. She decided to study them anyway, as much for the sake of learning history as reading about her beloved. The newer texts were fairly easy to decipher, written in Old English or German, but she spent years learning Greek and Latin. The latter was easier, and let her read back centuries; the former took more time, but the oldest texts about Lorhen were in that language.

The older the books, the more unwieldy they were. By the time she had learned enough Greek to read the very oldest books, the covers were nearly as thick as the paper between them. They were terribly fragile, three thousand years old, and Ghean turned the heavy covers and thick paper carefully, remembering the fine, thin paper her mother had used in Atlantis.

The next piece of paper was very nearly that thin, and Ghean's fingers slipped on it, crumbling an edge to dust. She'd hardly been reading the pages as she turned them, and gave the piece under her hand a startled glance.

My darling Ghean,

For a few seconds Ghean couldn't read beyond the first words, written in her mother's delicate hand, in her native tongue of Atlantean.

My darling Ghean,

I realize the chances of you finding this are so slim as to be nonexistent. Still, I write these words in the hopes that this letter will somehow survive the centuries and end up in your hands.

Your Lorhen saved my life. I find this ironic, as only weeks before I had chosen to make him and his kind my life's study. Had he not saved me when Atlantis fell, that study would have died with me, and the Keepers would not exist. Because he did,

I have this final chance to communicate with you, through the barrier of time.

He said that you died in the first moments of the panic. I have no reason to doubt him, other than the hopes of an aging mother. I know that you are, as he is, Timeless, or have that potential within you. It is a comfort to me to imagine that you somehow survived the destruction of Atlantis and live on, the last child of our House.

Sheer willpower prevented Ghean from crumbling the paper to dust. Her hands trembling, she stared down at the words. *I know that you are Timeless.* She was betrayed on all sides. Shaking, she took her hand away from the paper, to prevent herself from clenching her fist and taking her mother's last words to her away. In time, she was able to go on.

I do not imagine you will ever find this letter, but if you do, I do not know what the world will be like, how much it will have changed, where the Keeper's archives might be.

If you have found this at all, it is likely you have found the Keepers themselves. I chose the Hunter symbol as the marker for the Keepers before Atlantis fell; now I am glad I did so, for it is a sign you should be able to recognize, no matter how many years pass.

I thought to teach my students Atlantis' written language, for it is more elegant than any other writing yet known, but in the end it seemed a foolish pursuit, asking them to learn a drowned language. I can only imagine what language this letter might have been translated into by the time you find it. I only hope that in whatever form, it survives the years, and that you, too, have somehow survived, and will be able to read this.

If you do, share your history with the Keepers. Share our family with them, as they are a very real legacy of our House.

Tell them of Atlantis, and if there is some way in the new world that you live in to bring Atlantis back to the sun, I hope that you will try. I hope that its magic will be a part of the world again someday.

Remember that, for all time, I love you.

It was signed with the graceful scrawl of Minyah's name.

Ghean read the letter until she could see the words with her eyes closed, committing them to memory. Her mother had known, and hadn't told her. *We don't interfere*, the patient one reminded her, echoing Caterina's lessons.

"She was my *mother*!" Ghean shouted back. "She wasn't Timeless! She wasn't bound by the same rules! She should have told me!"

She began the Keepers, the patient one said, too rationally. *She made her own rules of non-interference. We couldn't have known Atlantis would fall. If we'd known, perhaps she'd have told us, to protect us. It's too late now. Let it go. Be glad there is anything of her at all, after all this time.*

Ghean's head dropped, and she nodded. "The letter," she murmured, in Atlantean, "the Keepers, and me. And someday, we'll bring back Atlantis for her." Feeling weary, she turned the letter over, trying to focus again on Lorhen's history.

A second piece of paper cracked free of the back of the letter, falling forward against the pages. For a handful of seconds she simply stared at the blank sheet. Picking it up took conscious effort. She could see the impressions from where pressure had sealed it to the back of her mother's letter, and wondered how long it had been since anyone had looked at Lorhen's chronicles. She turned the sheet over, carefully. It was old, but far less delicate than the ancient sheet her mother's letter had been written on. Seeing her name written again, in a different hand but in the same tongue, sent a dull sick thud through her, the feeling of a missed heartbeat.

Ghean,

This is the third time I've joined the Keepers to make certain your mother's letter was all right, and to hide something she left for you. It's funny, the things we do for our beloved dead. I can't imagine that you're alive, and still, here I am.

If you're reading this, you're in the Paris Headquarters. In the extremely impressive vault where they keep my chronicles, there's a safe, cut into the wall in the back bottom left-hand corner. I could fit under the stacks to cut it there, so I'm sure you can fit under it to open it up. There's no lock, just the stone set back into the wall. There's a box in there, one of those damned Atlantean things with the pressure points. Minyah left it for you when she died. I expect it's going to stay there for the rest of eternity, but here I am writing a note to someone forty-six centuries dead anyway.

I wish I could have saved you, Ghean. There was no time, and I don't believe anybody could have survived that cataclysm. I still think about you sometimes. I hope your rest has been a peaceful one.

There was no name, only a date, written out in longhand, in Atlantean: eighteen hundred and forty-five.

Ghean set the letter down gently, hands shaking. Only ninety years ago. He was alive. The conviction filled her.

Lorhen was alive.

12

Emma held her palm up. "Back up a little. What's the cloak you're talking about, and what sorts of other artifacts did these Houses have?"

Lorhen looked up from his beer. "The cloak was—well, it became—Jason's Fleece. The golden one."

"Logan." A note of exasperation, like she'd caught a five year old lying to her, came into Emma's voice. "That's mythology."

"So are people who live forever. Most myths have some basis in reality."

"Yes, but—back me up here, Cathal." Emma glanced at the Irishman, who studied his beer pensively.

"I don't know. It sounds preposterous, but then, what would you say if someone came up and told you about the Timeless?"

Emma leaned back in the bar bench, staring at Lorhen. "Then what else was there, besides the Fleece and the immortality crystal, if there were all these Houses?"

Lorhen lifted a hand, ticking points off on his fingers. "Fleece, Stone, Excalibur, Excalibur's scabbard, which was actually the better of the two icons, the Cauldron." He ran out of fingers, and began again. "The Grail. The Dragon's Teeth. The unicorns. A ring that did approximately the same thing the Lazarus Stone did, but was easier to carry."

Emma said, "The Laz—" but was overrun by Cathal's voice breaking like a teenage boy's as he echoed, "Unicorns?" They eyed one another a moment before Emma finished, "The Lazarus Stone?" in a near-whisper that underscored Cathal's break. "I never heard you call it that before."

"It's a bad name for it. It doesn't resurrect anyone, it just keeps them alive. But Methuselah Stone was taken, and I had to call it something."

Emma folded her knuckles in front of her mouth, not really trying to hide a frown. There had obviously been a faction of Keepers who had believed the fragmented immortality crystal, once pieced back together, would give them lives as long as their Timeless charges'. Even knowing about the Timeless, even in the midst of the fight over the damned crystal, she had written it off as wishful thinking. That Logan Adams believed had been one thing. That Lorhen, six thousand years old and counting, believed, was something else. That he had a *name* for it somehow brought it beyond dispute, drawing it into a kind of grim reality that cast too much light on who he was and what he had seen in his impossibly long life. Emma closed her eyes, pushing away the mens' conversation—Cathal was hissing, "But *unicorns?*" into her silence—and let herself wonder for a moment if she would be so resistant to mythology come to life if Cathal or even Lisse was the one presenting the arguments. Probably not, but she had always known who they really were.

Lorhen sighed. "Excalibur and the Grail are fine, you can handle that, but mention unicorns and you freak out. Why does nobody believe me about the unicorns?"

"Lorhen, come on. I was there when Polo came back from his expedition with his account of seeing a unicorn. It was obviously a rhinoceros. Rhinos, gazelles, whatever they were, they weren't unicorns. Everybody knows that. Nobody's ever found a unicorn skeleton."

"As a point of fact," Lorhen said acidly, "they have. Siberian unicorns, some merely tens of thousands of years old. Big, monstrous, furry rhinocer…i. I've wondered if the ancient Atlanteans had somehow bred their unicorns down from them. But even if they didn't, were they there?" Emma opened her eyes again to find Lorhen looking balefully at Cathal. "All these people who know there are no unicorns? Were they there? They haven't found any skeletons because the bloody things all drowned when Atlantis sank, Cathal. If Ghean manages to dig it up, you'll see." He sank into the booth, scowling at his beer.

"So it really did sink," Cathal said softly. "What happened?"

"Wonderful. You believe that Atlantis sank, that's fine, but unicorns are beyond the bounds of reason. I swear to God, you're as bad as mortals sometimes. What do you think happened? It all went to hell. Everything went straight to hell."

Ghean avoided him for days. Lorhen made it easy enough, keeping largely to his tent during the heat, venturing out at night to pace in the desert chill. He was less concerned with the betrayal of his secret—who would she tell? Who would believe her?—than he was with the probability that he'd lost his lover forever, but there was little he could do about that. The decision to stay away or return was hers alone, and he was left with a twisting regret, wondering if he should have told her of her own potential immortality at the same time. Seeking her out to tell her now seemed likely to add fuel to the fire of her fear and anger, and the fact that she'd run away before he could tell her everything about herself would hardly be an acceptable excuse.

Lorhen sat in the sand with a sigh, looking up at the star-littered sky. Sharp-edged in the desert's clear air, only a few shone with any color, faint traces of blues and reds. The rest were stark, white against black. Lorhen smiled thinly at them. *The universe presents itself as black and white, and we're offended when there are shades of grey in between.*

He didn't realize he'd spoken out loud until Ghean answered, from not far away. "It's a lot easier to see things in black and white. I thought you were all white, at first. A good scholar, a good man, someone to love." She slipped down the side of the dune, fingers trailing in the sand as she controlled the slide. "Then you told me what you were, and I thought you were all black. Something evil and unnatural, to be feared and hated."

Lorhen closed his eyes against the stars, lips pressed together to ensure no more damning commentary slipped free.

"I have been thinking," Ghean went on, "very hard, these last few days." She sat down in the sand beside him, spreading a cloak out around her. Her hair was long and loose, falling over the cloak to brush against the sand. "I'm not very old, and I've always seen everything in black and white, I think. But you aren't black or white, are you? You're grey. You belong to two different worlds, and that, if nothing else, makes you grey. You have to have different considerations. Do you try to do the right thing, Lorhen?"

"I try to stay alive." He sensed, more than saw, Ghean turning her head to look at him, and shook his head. "I don't know if I try to do the right thing. I thought telling you was the right thing, not for survival, but because I love you. I have done things you would not consider right, to survive."

Ghean nodded, and looked out over the desert again, quiet a while. "How old are you?"

"I don't know. A thousand years. Maybe more, maybe a little less. I don't remember much before I started keeping journals."

"When was that?"

Lorhen's mouth turned up in half a grin. "About ten minutes after they invented writing. Five hundred, eight hundred years ago."

"You've been married before."

Lorhen nodded. "Eight or nine times."

Ghean glanced at him. "How many of them knew?"

"Three," Lorhen said. "Two who saw me die and come back, and a third whom I chose to tell."

"Why did you tell me?"

Another half-smile curved his lips. "Atlanteans are long-lived, comparatively. It's easier than lying or acting out an old age I'm not actually achieving. You would have realized in a few years, ten or fifteen at the most, that something was wrong. You're too intelligent to accept lies, in the long run. I would have to tell you the truth eventually. It seemed better to do it now."

Ghean almost laughed, making a sharp sound. "I'm not sure if I'm flattered or insulted."

"Be flattered," Lorhen advised, adding, "It's not your age that makes you see things in black and white. Most people never learn to see the world any other way."

"Most people," Ghean said, "aren't in love with a thousand-year-old man. Tell me about being Timeless, Lorhen. It's hard to imagine. Everyone dreams of never dying, but what's it really like?"

You'll find out, he assured her silently, and wondered at his continuing reluctance to say it aloud, especially when he'd just been convincing himself he should. That was before it seemed she might forgive him, though. A self-deprecating breath escaped him, and he pushed the thought away to answer her question. "It's exhilarating. And difficult. Watching those you love age and die while you remain eternally the same never ceases to be painful."

Ghean shook her head. "I don't believe anyone can remain eternally the same. Haven't you changed, since you became immortal?" She shrugged a shoulder as he glanced at her. "Mother explained to me how your immortality works. That you live a normal life until you die violently, and then you can't die unless someone takes your head." She glanced back toward the town, and asked, "Will you and Aroz fight?"

"If he makes it necessary."

"Will you kill him?"

"If I can."

Ghean shuddered, drawing her cloak tightly around herself. "How many men have you killed?"

Lorhen shook his head. "I stopped counting. The only time I see their faces clearly are in dreams."

"You frighten me," Ghean admitted in a small voice.

Lorhen sighed. "I don't want to. In most respects, Ghean, I am what you thought I was. I'm a scholar. My interest is in watching history, not making it. All I want is to keep seeing it happen. My luck is in that I have more time than most to do that."

"And you'll really live forever."

Lorhen smiled with faint humor. "Or die trying."

Ghean looked at him, startled, and laughed. "I guess that's what we all do. How many others are there like you? Are they all as old as you?"

"I don't know, and no. New Timeless are Awakened every day, but I don't know how many. There were some who were almost as old as I was, but I don't think I've ever met anyone older."

"Were?"

Lorhen looked up at the stars again. "We fight," he said. "It's what we do. The few I've met so far who were close to my age are dead now. I'm not. That's all that's important."

"Were you the first?"

The image of the ax rising and falling, blood dull in the pale moonlight, danced in front of the stars. "I don't know," Lorhen said. "I don't think so." Had the man he'd killed been his teacher, or some chance Timeless, whose life crossed with Lorhen's, only to end in a rush of primitive instinct? Eyes closing, Lorhen tried to chase down the memories. The images faded again, to a grey blur that crystallized into surety only as the battle with the nameless stranger began. He shook his head, and repeated, "I don't think so."

Ghean nodded, drawing her knees up under her chin, silent again for a time. Eventually, just louder than the wind, she asked, "How can someone like you love me?"

Lorhen turned to face her, slipping his arm over her shoulders and pulling her against him. "How could I not?" he asked just as softly. "You're intelligent and brave enough to beard the lion in his den, even after I told you about myself. Your vivacity and love for life remind me of why life is worth living, even after the long years. Without someone like you, there's just history, and history is about death. In a way, I need you more than you need me." He let the words fade into the darkness, wondering how much of it was true. Enough for Ghean to sigh and snuggle against him. Lorhen smiled at the top of her head, relaxing.

The warning tingle of pain and nausea that flowed through him a moment later made him stiffen, straightening to search the shadowed dunes. Ghean sat up, blinking curiously as she pushed a strand of hair back from her face. "Lorhen? What is it?"

"Company," Lorhen growled, and scrambled to his feet, hand on the sword's hilt at his waist. Ghean remained where she was, seated in the sand, looking up at him in confusion. "Go. There's another Timeless nearby. Go back to the town. I'll meet you there later."

Her eyes widened in alarm, pupils swallowing the brown in the faint moon's light. "No."

A shadow separated itself from the night, easy strides across the sand marking Aroz's approach. He stood several inches shorter than Lorhen, but the inches he lost in height were made up in breadth. His face was sharp-edged, craggier than Lorhen's, with thin white scars under his cheekbones and on his chin standing out vividly against skin so black it veered toward blue. He stopped several feet from the pair, and bowed slightly to Ghean.

"There you are, my lady. Your mother asked me to find you and send you home." Aroz's voice was much lighter than expected from a man with a chest as broad and deep as his; a poet's voice, not a warrior's. He lifted his eyes from Ghean to Lorhen. "Lorhen and I have business to attend to."

Ghean shook her head, coming to her knees in the sand. "No. No, Aroz. Bring me back with you. I'll go back with you right now. With you." She climbed to her feet, hovering between the two men.

"Ghean," Lorhen said gently. "Go on. It's all right. I will see you," he repeated firmly, "in a few minutes." The bronze blade he drew made a whisper of a sound as it left the sheath. Aroz drew his own blade. Lorhen watched it glint dull silver in the moonlight, and whispered a curse under his breath. The bronze blade he had come by was hard won and had taken time to forge, but the color of Aroz's sword suggested it was of legendary Atlantean steel. "Ghean," Lorhen said more urgently, "go."

Ghean whimpered, and then ran, tripping over her cloak and pulling herself up the sandy hillside with hands and feet. In mere seconds the desert swallowed the sounds of her flight. Lorhen's shoulders loosened, and he turned his full attention to the other Timeless.

Aroz paced around him in a wide circle, sizing him up in a ritualistic fashion. Lorhen turned to watch him steadily, waiting for him to press the attack. Only when he had completed a full circuit around Lorhen did Aroz speak.

"You have the reach." His light voice was pitched to carry just to Lorhen, and no further. "But I have the better blade. Make this easier on both of us, and let me take you. I will tell Ghean you fought well."

"Thank you," Lorhen said, "but I'd prefer to carry my own tidings. Are you mad? We don't have to do this."

"We do," Aroz disagreed. "If for no other reason than it is what we do."

"Right," Lorhen grated. "The girl has nothing to do with it."

"She would make a fine prize, wouldn't she?" Aroz sprang

forward, the deadly steel blade whistling down toward Lorhen's weaker bronze blade. Lorhen danced backwards, withdrawing his sword just slowly enough that sparks darted along the edges of both blades as they clashed together. Lorhen winced, seeing threads of metal shard away from his sword. It would have to be a fast fight, or he'd be left without anything to fight *with*.

He spun away from another charge, stepping just outside Aroz's reach and whirling to drive a wide, circular blow toward Aroz's back. Aroz, misjudging the length of Lorhen's reach, turned back to the battle, and all but into the swing of Lorhen's blade. Skin tore in a wide rent along his ribs, and the younger Timeless staggered back with a startled gasp. Hardly defeated, he knocked the bronze sword aside, wrapping his free arm around his side to stem the blood flow while his Timeless healing knitted him back together.

Lorhen pressed the attack, unwilling to let the advantage go. Too tall to effectively step inside Aroz's reach and still leave himself room to maneuver, he met a strike or two with quick parries, watching nicks fly from the edges of his blade as the two swords met. A third blow he deflected badly, deliberately, and crashed to his knees, leaving himself open and vulnerable.

Aroz grinned in triumph, a flash of white against his pain-etched dark face. He took two running steps forward, sword lifted high for the final strike.

Lorhen flicked his free hand to his belt, whipping out the table knife he wore there, and shoved it into Aroz's abdomen, just above the pelvis. Aroz staggered, shocked, and Lorhen rolled out of danger's way, to his feet, the knife in his hand. While the other Timeless swayed, Lorhen smashed his blade against Aroz's wrist, severing tendons. The steel sword fell to the sand. Aroz followed it, crashing to his knees. Lorhen took a breath, then flicked his knife around in his hand again, preparing for the heartstrike blow.

"No!" Ghean's scream made both men jerk, looking up. Lorhen's knife stopped a breath from Aroz's heart. Ghean all but fell down the dune, sliding to a halt a few feet from Lorhen. "Lorhen, no, please, don't. Please. I've known him my whole life. I don't want him to die."

Lorhen rested his knife in the hollow of Aroz's throat, holding it steady and not taking his eyes off Aroz. "May I point out," he said, a little shortly, "that he was just trying to kill me?"

"He won't do it again. Will you, Aroz? Please? Please promise me. I don't want you to die. I don't want either of you to die. Promise you won't try to kill Lorhen. Please?"

For a long moment there was utter silence, broken by the harsh breathing of both warriors. Finally, Aroz inclined his head in agreement. Lorhen crouched and picked up the steel blade, leaving his own knife still at Aroz's throat.

"Spoils of war," he said thinly. "Care to argue?" He waited a few seconds, then straightened again, throwing his bronze sword to the sand. "Didn't think so." He stalked up the shifting sand dunes. Behind him, Ghean hesitated, looking at Aroz. Then she ran after Lorhen, catching up with him in a few steps.

"Lorhen?" she whispered.

"I told you to go back to the town," he snarled.

She flinched, but lifted her chin. "I couldn't. Not with the two of you fighting. I couldn't bear to lose either of you."

He shoved the steel blade into his belt and glared at her. "You shouldn't have interfered. It's what we do, Ghean. I told you that."

"I couldn't sit back and do nothing." Her eyes were angry in the reaching light of the town's fires.

Looking at her, Lorhen's own anger faded. He kept quiet until they'd reached his tent, and held the door flap aside for her. "I don't suppose you could have," he said then, tiredly. He sat down on the floor cross-legged, withdrawing the blade from his belt again. For a moment he tilted it, studying the workmanship, then found a cloth to rub over it, bringing more gleam to the metal. "But Ghean, you have to promise me. Next time, you can't interfere."

Ghean sat down across from him, pulling her hair over her shoulder and braiding it swiftly as she considered him. "No," she finally said. Lorhen looked up, surprised, and she shook her head. "I can't promise. I can't imagine letting you fight to your death if I could prevent it. So I won't promise."

Lorhen stared at her a moment, then laughed, setting the blade aside and placing his hands on either side of her face. Too late, he noticed the blood still staining his hand, from stabbing Aroz. Ghean noticed it as well, and Lorhen waited for her cringe.

Instead, she lifted her small hands to cover his, with a steady strength. "I love you," she said. "I can't promise not to interfere."

Lorhen couldn't stop the smile that worked its way across his face. "You are an impossible woman."

"I am." Ghean nudged the steel sword away with her toes, and reached for the knife Lorhen had put back in his belt. "Let's put these away for the night," she whispered, "and find a less murderous way to distract ourselves."

Lorhen's smile broadened. "As you wish."

13

The lecture hall lights came up slowly, giving the audience time to adjust. Ghean took the time to scan the auditorium, searching for the Timeless she had sensed when she came onstage. The crowd was shifting, most people collecting their coats and bags and preparing to leave, although a select number began threading their way down to the stage for a question-and-answer session. Ghean ignored them, focusing on the seats that had been abandoned at the beginning of the lecture. She tapped her thumb against pursed lips, building the glimpse she'd caught of the trio leaving into a more solid image.

Two men, and a woman, all dark haired, all tall, the patient one recounted. One of the three had to be the Timeless, but that wasn't much to go on.

Ghean beckoned to Michelle, encouraging her onstage. "Could you field the questions for me?" she asked quietly. "I think I caught sight of an old friend in the audience, and I'd like to look him up." Close enough; the Timeless who had left at least shared the brotherhood of Timelessness with her, and that could be stretched to friendship in a tight pinch.

Michelle smiled. "Of course. I keep telling you that you don't get out enough. Go take a look. Don't forget the flight leaves at eleven tomorrow morning."

"If I got out more, I wouldn't have dedicated my entire life to this dig and we wouldn't have found Atlantis yet." Ghean nodded. "I'll be there with bells on. Thanks, Mich." She hurried backstage to find her coat and to reluctantly switch from the heels she wore to flat black shoes. Even in Atlantis she hadn't been tall, but at least she hadn't stood a full six inches shorter than most of the women, never mind the men. No one took someone her size seriously. *Being small makes them underestimate us*, the patient one reminded her. *We can fight to compensate for it.*

I know, she answered irritably. *That doesn't mean I like it.* She pushed the backstage doors open, frowned at the hall, and went up to the main lobby. A bored young woman sat behind the ticket booth, her head tilted back as she contemplated the ceiling "Excuse me?"

The girl jerked upright, looking guilty. "Yes? Um, yes, ma'am? What can I do for you?"

Ghean tilted her head at the door. "Three people left just after the lecture began. Did you see them, by any chance?"

"Oh, yeah, I saw them. A black lady and a couple of white dudes. They were arguing about something."

Ghean nodded. "That's them. Did you happen to see which way they went?"

"Nah, they just headed out. The guy with the nose didn't look very happy. Hey, he said something about going to a bar or a coffee shop or something, does that help?"

Ghean's eyebrows quirked and she laughed. "The guy with the nose? Didn't they all have noses? And yes, it does help, thank you. Was one of them wearing a long coat, kind of like mine?" She moved her hands in her pockets, making the tails of her trench coat swing.

"Two of 'em," the girl said. "Both the guys. Hope you find them. Hey." She squinted at Ghean. "Did you really find Atlantis?"

Ghean paused again, smiling. "I really did."

"How do you know it's really Atlantis?"

Carefree, Ghean grinned. "I was born there." She dropped the girl a wink and crossed the lobby to walk out into the Chicago night. Wind knocked hair into her eyes instantly and she pushed it out of the way, leaving the University grounds. A steady drizzle began as cars pulled away with people leaving the lecture. *Whoever it was doesn't want to meet up with us*, the patient one said. *Perhaps he's young, and doesn't want to risk a battle.* Ghean pressed her elbow against the hilt of her sword, hidden beneath her coat.

"Maybe. But I don't want a fight, just to talk. I want to see why he left."

It could be dangerous! the frightened voice broke in.

Ghean shrugged, resorting to silent speech for her argument. *It could be, but I've had training, even taken a head or two. We'll be fine.* Admittedly, she had only taken a very few heads. The Keeper files had proved very useful, and Ghean didn't want to risk her ability to rejoin the society at some point if she needed their knowledge again. The only battles she'd fought had been after making absolutely sure her opponents had no Keepers nearby. Idly, she lifted a hand to touch the pendant of her necklace.

The vault the Lorhen Chronicles were kept in was dusty, not impressive. Ghean scowled at the lower left-hand corner, crouched to peer under the stacks. The shelving was far too deep to just reach back and feel for the crack that would indicate where the safe Lorhen had cut would be. Bringing a mop into the vault would be noticed. Ghean swore softly, and batted at the dust, then sighed and crawled under the shelving. Even with a flashlight, it took several minutes of squirming to find the edges where the stone had been cut. Ghean sneezed. *How the hell did he expect me to pull this out? There's no handholds, no grooves. I'm not as strong as he is.*

He didn't expect you to at all, the patient one pointed out. *He thinks you're dead.*

"Oh, shut up." Ghean gained a tiny purchase against the stone, pulling back without success. Her fingers slid off the sharp corner, skin tearing.

Trapped! the frightened one screamed. *Trapped again! Forever and ever in the darkness again! We should have stayed! Atlantis was safe, we knew Atlantis! Now we're trapped again!*

Ghean shuddered violently, biting back a scream as she flung her arms up, hiding her face. *Trapped!*

We are not trapped. For the first time, the patient voice sounded impatient. *Roll backward. We're safe. There are answers to mysteries behind that stone, but* we *are not behind that stone. We are safe. We won't ever be trapped again. Now try again. We're fine.* It subsided into a grumbling silence.

Ghean, trembling, unwound her arms, and tried a second time to pull the stone out. The struggle flew back and forth within her mind, practicality and fear shouting at each other until her own thoughts were all but drowned. When the stone abruptly came free, it shocked both voices into silence, and Ghean dropped her head against the floor in relief.

"Gods, you're loud," she muttered, then wiggled backwards to pull the stone further out. It came out smoothly, once there was enough to get a grip on. Ghean brushed dust out of her eyes, studying the stone for a few seconds.

Time had distorted her memories too far to be sure, but she was fairly certain the square of rock would have been too heavy for her mortal self to move, aeons ago. She had long since lost a sense of what was normal, but she didn't think a woman her size should have been able to move that stone.

Greater endurance, greater strength, more developed senses, the patient one said. *We are more than human. Not as great as a god, but greater than a mortal.*

Ghean rubbed a dirty hand over her face, picking up her flashlight, and crawled forward into the space left by the stone, breathing, "I know, but why? Maybe when I've found Atlantis and we've had our revenge I can become a doctor, study what makes us the way we are...." The gap went back about three feet, more area than the stone she'd dragged out took, though there was nothing visibly set into the space. She lowered the flashlight, running her fingers over the floor, setting her teeth to ignore the screaming frightened voice. Too familiar, the search for imperfections. Shivering, she almost missed the thin bump in the floor. In a moment, she was able to lever the box out of the floor, and back up with it, flashlight clutched in her other hand.

She shoved the stone back into its resting place as quickly as she could, then sat on the floor of the vault, running her fingers over the Atlantean box. It took several minutes to find the subtle depressions where pressure would open the box, and she held her breath as it quietly clicked open.

An envelope lay at the end of the box, and two delicate velvet bags lay atop it. Ghean picked up the larger, working it open uncertainly, and turning it to spill its contents into her palm.

A silver chain tumbled out, drawing with it a pendant painful in its familiarity. Minyah's pendant, the symbol of their House, was blackened with time, the silver uncleaned in at least a century, but even so Ghean was certain it was her mother's original necklace. She slipped it on, fingers clutching the pendant. Even the voices were silent as she clung to the necklace, trembling with memory.

Eventually she worked open the second bag. A gold ring, etched with the stamp of a lion, fell into her palm, and she smiled. What little had been saved from Atlantis, it seemed, was now hers. She slipped it on over her thumb, where it fit snugly.

Lorhen's handwriting spelled out her name on the outside of the envelope, written in Atlantean as the other note had been.

Ghean slowly lifted it, still hardly breathing. It cracked open, and she withdrew the note carefully. A key fell with it, and she caught it quickly, scanning the note.

> *The key is to a safe-deposit box at the Bank of England, in London. Minyah's Keeper papers are there, detailing the first fifty years of the Keepers. The family name they're under is Lazarus; I couldn't help myself. Someday my sense of humor is going to get me in trouble. There's a bank account associated with the name. I didn't put much money in it, but I made the deposit in 1720. I rather expect it's built up. I imagine I'll use it someday, since I've got the other key to the safe-deposit box, and you've been dead forty-six centuries.*
>
> *The things we do for old lovers.*

Again, there was no signature. It was dated the same year as the note Ghean had found in the book, 1845, only ninety years earlier. Ghean sat, re-reading the words, and finally let out a whispered, "Well. I hope all that money is still there. I'd like to be rich." She tucked the box under her arm, and stood, trying to brush some of the grime off her clothes as she left the vault.

Ghean turned the pendant again, splashing as she made her way down the street. *If we were running away to hide,* the patient one said, *we'd hide somewhere with a bolt-hole.*

"Our shy friend might not be that clever," she murmured, but nodded anyway, lifting a hand to tuck damp hair behind her ear. She crossed the street, examining the occasional open business and evaluating them as likely hideouts for an elusive Timeless. Most of them looked too well-kept and wholesome. She continued up the block, glancing up as a street lamp sputtered on and off above her with a faint electric hum, occasionally illuminating a bedraggled bar sign over a door that looked like it hadn't been opened in half a decade. Light crept out around its edges, though, and she put her hand on the doorknob, trying it.

A rush of nausea hit so hard she swayed, yanking her hand off the doorknob as though it had caused the sudden illness. She backed up, staring at the door, then stepped back to look both ways down the street. An alley, obscured by rain and dark, made a shadow in the building walls. Smiling, Ghean tucked the collar of her coat closer and went into the alley to lean against the wall just a few steps away from the bar's back door.

Lorhen broke off his story mid-word, intent assessment drawing his eyebrows down. Cathal's eyebrows rose and he leaned out of the booth, glancing through the dim bar in expectation. Emma groaned. "Another one?"

Lorhen swung out of the booth, pulling a fistful of cash from his pocket and throwing it on the table. "Come on."

"Life with him is never dull," Cathal murmured to Emma as they followed him through a crowd that had grown considerably since they'd arrived.

"Not if you like running away."

Lorhen pushed his way to the back door, using his elbows liberally to clear the path. "A very wise man once said there's no problem so big you can't run away from it, Emma."

"Yeah?" Emma asked. "Who?"

"His name was Trent." Lorhen opened the back door, gesturing Cathal and Emma through before him.

Ghean grinned again as the door swung open. *So I was right*, she thought, in her mother's often-used phrase. She pushed away from the wall, still smirking, head cocked to the side, to see whom it was she had trapped.

The first person out was the woman, handsome, dark-skinned, and in her fifties, with a military bearing that went beyond the short-cropped black hair that curled tightly against her head: dark eyes scanned the shadows and the street at the alley's mouth, though she didn't—perhaps couldn't—see Ghean in the darkness, any more than she might have seen the blade Ghean carried under her coat. Not that Ghean believed herself to actually be invisible, but there were moments when the Blending stirred inside her and mortals looked away. Most often it happened in the midst of battle, else there would be dozens of witnesses when Timeless fought in cities, but on occasion it seemed that the power responded to her need to go unnoticed.

Exasperation was settled into the lines of the woman's face as she stepped away from the door, waiting for her companions. Ghean recognized the next man from her years spent as a Keeper: Cathal Devane, a big Irishman she'd once thought might make a good teacher. Abruptly, the woman came into context: Emma Hickman, almost a renegade amongst the Keepers for her unsanctioned friendship with Devane. He hadn't seen Ghean yet either, turning to wait on the second man. Ghean stepped farther into the shadows, watching with interest.

Devane looked less exasperated and more amused than Hickman, an expression that sat well on unexpectedly handsome features. He'd looked rougher around the edges in the 1930s photographs the Keepers had had on him, and now that she saw him in the flesh, Ghean discarded the old idea of being his student. He was too pretty to take seriously as a teacher, even if his records proved he was a deadly warrior. She smiled at the thought as the third man stepped out.

Her heart gave a violent lurch, pain of the missed beat settling into her stomach as she stared, disbelieving, at the man she had not seen in five thousand years. His black hair was cropped short, now, but the sharp cheekbones and thin, expressive lips were the same. The ticket booth girl's words came back to her: *the guy with the nose.* Ghean had forgotten how sharp his nose was, how it dominated his features. In the darkness, his deep-set eyes would be black, uncomfortable, and the small light above the bar's back door made skin she'd last seen ruddy with sun look sallow. Ghean pressed up against the wall, steadying her breathing.

Lorhen turned to close the door with a solid thud, and leaned against it a moment, rubbing long hands over his face. "Let's find our hotel and hole up," the ancient Timeless muttered, loud enough to be heard over the rain. "I have had *just* a little too much fun tonight. I want a bottle of whiskey and no more surprises."

Cathal clapped him on the shoulder. "And then you'll tell us the rest of the story." Lorhen dropped his hands to give him a dirty look.

Ghean grinned so hard her teeth hurt from pressing them together. *One more surprise*, she thought gleefully, stepping out of the shadows. "One more surprise," she repeated, aloud, and flared a grin at the man she was going to kill. "Hello, Lorhen."

14

The rain increased from a drizzle to a more enthusiastic down-pour. Lorhen went utterly still, like a rabbit trying to avoid detection by a soaring eagle. After several seconds, water beaded and dripped off the end of his nose. Cathal and Emma stood nearly as motionless, gazing transfixed at Ghean.

They were all tall: even the woman stood eight or nine inches taller than Ghean, and wore heels that added to her height, but for the moment Ghean knew she unquestionably held the power in the equation, commanded it despite her diminutive size. She let them gape a moment longer, aware and pleased that her sharply bobbed straight hair took the rain water well and would still look good, and that with the distant streetlight her coloring would be warm in the rain. It would be best if this had been the very first time Lorhen had laid eyes on her in five millennia, rather than the brief glimpse on stage, but this was nearly perfect. Perfect enough that the violence of her grin felt likely to split her top lip.

When it appeared her very presence had created a stalemate, Ghean, without losing her grin, asked, "Are we going to stand here in the rain all night, or is there a more pleasant place for this little reunion?"

Lorhen flinched as though he'd been bitten. Cathal, casting a glance at his friend, struggled with and lost to a grin, not quite as profound as Ghean's. As he opened his mouth to speak, Lorhen cut him off, snapping, "How can you be alive?"

Ghean's humor fled. "No one's taken my head yet," she said flatly, as deliberately obvious an answer as Lorhen's question had been, without coming anywhere near what he wanted to hear. "Really, Lorhen, aren't you going to introduce me to your friends?" She stepped forward to offer her hand to Cathal. Lorhen took two steps back. Ghean lifted an eyebrow at him, and spoke to Cathal. "I would say he didn't used to be this careless, but I'm not sure it's true. I'm—"

"Ghean." Lorhen came forward again, clearly irritated with himself for the retreat. "I saw the t—"

Ghean cut him off with a quick gesture, tsking. "Don't spoil the punchline," she chided. "I'd guess you've been telling them all about us since you ran out of the auditorium."

"I did not run."

Cathal and Emma both said, "You ran," though Emma said it much more loudly, earning herself a bitter look from Lorhen as Cathal bowed over Ghean's hand. "Cathal Devane. It's a pleasure to meet you…Mary?"

Ghean smiled. "Ghean will do. Unlike my infamous husband here, nobody knows I exist." She glanced at Emma, judging her reaction to the word husband, and nodded. "So he'd gotten that far. I imagined he would have."

"That's 'legendary'," Lorhen muttered. "Not 'infamous'."

"Ghean, then," Cathal replied. "And this is Emma Hickman."

Emma stuck her hand out to shake Ghean's. "Nice to meet you."

"You too, Emma. Interesting company you keep."

"You have no ide—" Emma silenced herself, as it was manifestly obvious that Ghean had an excellent idea of just how interesting her companions were.

Ghean's smile broadened again. "I'm guessing we have no secrets here? You don't know Lorhen under another name?"

Emma gave Lorhen a brief, sour look. "I met him as Logan Adams, but no, I know his story. We go back a ways."

Ghean turned an incredulous, amused glance on Lorhen. "'Logan'? *Really*, Lorhen?"

"Please," Lorhen muttered. "You'd think it was obvious, but nobody in the Keepers pays attention to popular culture. They're all too far stuck in the past. Besides, it actually almost sounds like my name, and that's a nice change."

Emma, half-aloud, said, "Lorhen, Logan," a few times, testing them for similarity, and, after exchanging a glance with Cathal, shrugged it away. "I wouldn't have put it together."

"You weren't supposed to," Lorhen said testily. "Besides, you don't really say my name right. The 'rh' should be almost guttural. Go listen to a Scotsman say it a few times and you'll get the idea. Ghean, how are you alive?"

"Are you really offended enough to find me alive that you'd rather stay out here in the rain than go somewhere dry to discuss it? Maybe you are. Running the moment you laid eyes on me isn't exactly the most charming way to greet your wife, Lorhen."

"I did not run." Lorhen brushed water off his face, scowling. "Fine. Where are you staying, Ghean?"

"I live in an apartment on campus. We could go back there, I suppose. Or do we need to find a church somewhere? I'm guessing Emma's presence isn't going to dissuade you from a fight if you decide you're looking for one."

"Mine will." Cathal's voice dropped an octave, dry with warning. Lorhen shot him a filthy look, but only said, "Do you have any beer?" to Ghean.

"Yes, as a matter of fact."

"That'll do, then." Lorhen hunched his shoulders against the rain and walked down the alley, kicking puddles. Ghean watched him, not moving until he reached the end of the alley. Once there, he turned impatiently to look at her, clearly waiting for directions. Then she followed him up to the street, and took the lead, trying to remain outwardly composed, though she felt an almost unbearable smugness as Lorhen, his shoulders bunched, kept trying to pull ahead, then remembered he didn't know where he was going and fell back again. A childlike chant ran through her head: *I know something you don't know!*

More than one thing, in fact. She pressed her elbow against her rapier's hilt, smiling at its deadly presence. Her heartstrike knife lay at the small of her back, a presence so old and comforting she wouldn't know what to do without it, and the song ran through her mind again: *I know something you don't know!*

He knows things we don't know, too, the patient one reminded her. *We should be careful around him.*

"I will be," she murmured under her breath as she examined the man stalking past her again.

He had to know his whole body expressed outraged tension, but he just as clearly didn't care. Ghean supposed that in a way she couldn't blame him: even the Timeless usually stayed dead, once they were dead. No doubt they weren't supposed to crop up as archaeological experts, and no doubt dead wives were especially not supposed to turn up. Ghean's smile broadened again, enjoying Lorhen's offense. He dropped his shoulders suddenly, like he was trying to shake his anger off, and rain trickled down the neck of his coat. With a grunt, he hunched up again, forging over the curb and into the middle of the street as Ghean tilted her head at the other two and guided them up a side street. Several seconds passed before she heard Lorhen's footsteps alter and his pace quicken as he strove to catch up with them, and she took advantage of the time to grin even more violently at the wet street ahead of her. She probably wasn't being fair, enjoying his discomfort so much, since she'd been searching for him for decades while he'd had no idea she was alive at all.

Fair? the patient one said incredulously. *Fair?!* Ghean laughed and the voice subsided. She glanced back and caught

Cathal and Emma both watching her with open interest that, in Cathal's case, turned to faint guilt at getting caught. Emma, long since accustomed to spying on the Timeless, only lifted her eyebrows as if offering a faint challenge that Ghean chose not to accept. Lorhen, sulking along behind them, kept his gaze fixed on the wet concrete and missed all the byplay, but Ghean had no doubt the other Timeless and his Keeper were trying hard to communicate to each other without words, guessing at whatever story Lorhen hadn't yet divulged.

"Right here." Ghean turned abruptly to climb up a short flight of stairs and dig keys out of her pocket. The locks clicked open and she herded the others inside to drip on her carpet. "Towels, anyone?"

"Beer," Lorhen said, shedding his coat.

Ghean pursed her lips. "Perhaps it's just fond memory, but I'm sure I remember you being somewhat more polite."

"It was a long time ago," Lorhen said shortly.

Cathal frowned. "Lorhen. There's no need to be rude."

Ghean opened a coat closet, reaching up for a hanger. "Why, thank you, Cathal. Do you make a habit of rescuing damsels who may or may not be in distress?" She hung her coat up, handed Lorhen a hanger, and offered to take Emma's coat.

Cathal, reaching past her, got his own hanger, and smiled. "I'm afraid so. Lorhen thinks it's a character flaw, but most of the damsels don't seem to mind."

"I'm sure they don't. The beer is in the fridge, Lorhen. No one else wants a towel? You must, Emma. You've got rain beaded in your hair. The kitchen and living room are that way." Ghean pointed down the hall and gestured to the left. "I'll be out in a few minutes."

Ghean disappeared into a second door in the hall, her flats clicking on the hardwood floor. For a moment the other three stayed where they were, overcome by silence, but then Lorhen shrugged and went in the kitchen in search of beer. A moment later he returned, carrying four beers by the necks in his long fingers, to find Emma and Cathal at the door to the living room, looking guiltily at the rain water they were dripping on the rug. "For God's sake, she said to come in." Whether they intended to or not, he did, glancing around as he put three of the four beers on a glass-topped oak coffee table, and opened the fourth for himself.

The living room was elegantly decorated. Bookcases, the top shelves no more than five and a half feet from the ground, were stuffed with textbooks of histories and languages. Knickknacks were settled on top of the bookcases, one a photograph from the early twenties, obviously of Ghean, signed, 'Love, Grandma'. Tall lamps bounced light off the ceiling and cream-colored walls, their white light clashing with a warmer kitchen light at the other end of the room. A pale cream rug with splashes of crimson covered most of the floor.

"College professors must be getting paid better these days than I remember." Ignoring his squelching shoes, he crossed the rug to sit on an overstuffed loveseat several shades darker than the rug. Cathal came into the room barefoot, and looked disapprovingly at the rug. "You left footprints."

Lorhen tilted his beer back, shrugging his eyebrows. "You're very refined for a boglands barbarian, Devane. Water dries. Have a beer."

"You're always so free with other people's beer." Cathal sat on one end of a couch that matched the loveseat and reached for two of the beers, offering one to Emma as she came to sit on the couch as well. "Why are you being so unpleasant?"

"She should be dead, Cathal. The things that happened in Atlantis…nobody could have survived it. I don't like mysteries."

Cathal's eyebrows shot up. "You? You're the original mystery."

"Not mysteries like this one. It's too big. Too dangerous.

Mysteries like this end up with somebody dead, and I don't want it to be me." Lorhen shook his head, picking his beer up again.

"I can't believe we have no record of her," Emma said. "At least we have confirmed records of you, no matter how old the last ones are. I don't know how somebody could get by for five millennia without the Keepers noticing."

"My mother *did* begin the Keepers." Ghean came through the hall door, dressed in jeans and a black t-shirt, with her hair fluffy from being rubbed dry. She tossed a towel to Emma, who patted her hair with it. "Maybe she told me all about them, and how to avoid them. Or maybe I infiltrated them, learned how to avoid them myself, and then went on my merry way." She stopped in front of Emma, displaying the inside of her left wrist to her. The Keepers tattoo, greatly faded, was still visible against her olive skin.

As Emma gaped, Ghean curled up in the single chair left empty, a dark red recliner. "Or maybe someone there has known about me all along, and has kept the records very secret, at my request, because of this." She pulled a black cord with a silver pendant out from under her shirt, removed it, and handed it to Cathal with a nod toward Emma, then picked up a beer from the table as she settled back to watch the Keeper.

Emma gave the pendant a perfunctory glance, looking back at Ghean. Then her gaze returned to the necklace, sharply, and she straightened, staring at the symbol in her hand.

There could be little doubt that the Keepers' symbol had been derived from the necklace she held. Where the tattoo Emma shared with Ghean and Lorhen was rounded, the necklace was visibly the hourglass of the Hunter constellation, seven small, bright stones set into place at the four corners and across the belt. In the encircling silver surrounding the hourglass were thirteen studs, worn down with time but distinct all the same.

Emma turned her wrist up to study the differences between the necklace and tattoo, murmuring, "It's the belt. I always thought the tattoo's hourglass waist was angled because it represented sand that hadn't fallen, that would never fall, but it's Orion's belt." Cathal leaned over to examine them, too, looking back and forth. Lorhen, elbows on his knees and beer held in both hands, watched the pair of them.

"Or maybe," Ghean concluded, "it's none of those things at all. The necklace was my mother's."

Emma looked up at Ghean, the necklace still cradled protectively in her palm. "Why an hourglass? Or—Orion, why Orion? Do you have your mother's records? They would be invaluable."

"They would be unintelligible. I do have them, but I'm the only one who could translate them. How would you know if I was doing so accurately?"

Lorhen lifted an eyebrow at Ghean. Her lips pursed, and she inclined her head. "I stand corrected. There are two of us who could translate them. Orion—we called him the Hunter—was the symbol of my House. My mother considered the Keepers to be her children, as much as I was. In a way, by wearing that tattoo, you're part of the last House of Atlantis. It makes you my sister, by Atlantean law, as it makes family of all the Keepers."

Lorhen, silently and with a small quirked smile, slid his arm forward to display his inner left wrist. "Sister-wife," he said, somewhat drolly. "A custom I thought the Atlanteans had foregone."

Ghean's eyebrows elevated, and she looked at Cathal with amusement. "Well?"

Cathal grinned. "I'm afraid not. Just an ordinary Timeless. I don't belong to any other secret societies."

Emma reluctantly offered the necklace back to Ghean. "I would love to read your mother's files," she said wistfully. "I wonder why we don't have copies of them."

"Time, most likely," Ghean answered. "Really, Emma, the Keepers have done an astonishing job of maintaining the records. There are gaps, of course, but once I was done with the

Lorhen Chronicles—" She broke off as Lorhen straightened uncomfortably. "How else would I have found the necklace, Lorhen? I read everything the Keepers had on you. I had to learn new languages to do it." She shook her head, and added, "They're woefully incomplete, you know. There's very little about you prior to about thirty-five hundred years ago. Even Mother's records are sketchy, though you're the first Timeless she talks about. You began the Keepers, you know. Without you, they wouldn't exist."

Lorhen looked down at the beer in his hands, nodding. "I know. No more than they'd exist without Minyah. She was a remarkable woman. I've met very few people as dedicated to the preservation of history as she was."

Ghean smiled briefly, but turned her attention back to Emma. "I was in the Keepers during the second world war. I was astonished at how much information they'd managed to maintain over the centuries. The oldest records seemed to have been written about three thousand years ago, since they were in Greek, but many of them recorded events far older. I found nothing about Atlantis, nor my mother, so I suppose the copies I have are the only originals written in a drowned language. I suppose she would have written the rest of them in some other tongue."

Lorhen shook his head. "She kept hers in Atlantean. It was far more sophisticated than any other written language of the time, but her students, the Keepers, kept them in whatever language they wrote most fluently in. She did the translations, both of her own records and many of her students' work, into Greek not long before she died. I helped, some. The originals were in tatters."

"Greek," Ghean said in a soft, dangerous voice, "didn't come into existence for two thousand years after Atlantis drowned."

Lorhen shifted his shoulders. "The cloak worked. Your mother lived a very, very long time."

A sensation of ice coated Ghean's skin, much colder than the rain had been, and though her spine straightened she did all she could to remain expressionless, gazing at Lorhen. "How long?," she asked hoarsely. "How long did she live?"

Lorhen shrugged a shoulder. "About two thousand years."

Ghean shuddered. Betrayal upon betrayal. For nearly five thousand years she drowned and starved and Awakened, while her mother survived through the centuries. *There will be revenge*, the patient one promised. Aloud, Ghean managed, "I have only fifty years of records," in a barely-controlled voice. "And the Keeper archives, I've read all of the oldest records there. None of them were written by my mother. I'd know her style, even in another language. But you said you'd helped translate them."

Lorhen nodded. "I did."

Emma was staring at Lorhen. "The Keepers," she echoed in a tone much like Ghean's, "don't have her records. We have nothing by or about our founder."

"No." Lorhen almost smiled. "You don't."

Emma's voice went colder. "Where are they?"

"Safe. Hidden."

The chill in Emma's words exploded into heat, and venom. "Two thousand years of records, Lorhen! Two thousand years, all kept by one person? One viewpoint, one mortal experience, over that long? How could you? How *could* you?" Her hurt sounded very similar to the throb cutting through Ghean's every breath, a pain so sharp it silenced even the patient voice.

Cathal pulled a hand over his mouth and spoke so quietly it seemed he'd cast his voice away with the gesture. "You're a scholar, Lorhen. Why didn't you give the Keepers the Greek translations?"

A smile filtered across Lorhen's face without touching his eyes. "There was far too much information about me in them."

Emma crushed her eyes shut, a spasm of profound loathing distorting her features as Ghean's voice rose. "You kept all that information to protect *yourself*?"

"Of course he did." Emma spat the words. "Of course you did, you son of a bitch. Two millennia, Lorhen. We thought we didn't begin until Grecian times, that the stories written down about Gilgamesh and Methuselah—"

"Oh, Methuselah wasn't Timeless," Lorhen said with aggravating calm. "Gilgamesh, now, yes, but not Methuselah."

"—that they were hearsay, ancient stories recorded by Greeks who had traveled and collected tales about the Timeless, not that someone had been there, recorded it, and lost the records—!" Emma's rage was so clean and honest that Ghean's throat tightened on it, wishing she could release the same kind of anger so freely.

Patience, whispered the one voice, and *never, never*! whispered the other. *Don't be angry, don't feel, don't let them see if they see they'll know if they know they'll kill us we don't want to die, hush, hush, shh.*

Over their whispered advice, but beneath Emma's fury, Ghean asked, "How could you do that? How could you dishonor my mother that way?"

Lorhen made a moue. "Minyah was my friend, Ghean. She knew more about me than anyone else ever has, more, maybe, even than Timeless I've shared Blendings with. I can't afford that knowledge to be public, even to as select a public as the Keepers. I have worked very hard for a very long time to make myself an unknown quantity. Believe me, hiding some records is not a particular transgression on the list of things I've done. Overall, it's been extremely successful." He looked directly at Ghean. "In fact, the only person who's been more successful in hiding her existence for the last five millennia is you. How is it that you're alive, Ghean?"

Ghean closed her hands in the padded leather of her armchair, cords tense in her throat as she whispered, *patience, patience*, to herself until she no longer knew whether it was her own voice or the patient one guiding her. *There's time yet. Don't be hasty. Devane isn't going to let you kill him now anyway.* It seemed a long while, even to her distorted, immortal sense of time, before she trusted herself to speak, and when she did her voice was still tight and small. "How far in the story had you gotten?"

"You'd just forgiven me for being Timeless. Right after you stopped me from taking Aroz's head."

"Oh," Ghean whispered bitterly. "There's a lot left, then."

15

Atlantis rose out of the sea like a giant's long-forgotten castle. Jagged mountains swept down into the water, waves beating an endless tattoo against obsidian walls. Far above the edges of sheer stone that met the water, trees clustered along the mountains, rendering the sharp lines just faintly blurred with green soft-ness. Tiny ports circled the island, large enough for the fishing boats that provided Atlanteans with their staples of life. Villages scattered up through the mountains at each port, roads spider-ing in toward the main city, all but nestled in the clouds. Lorhen leaned on the railing of their vessel, hands clasped loosely over the water as he looked up at the legendary island. The ship's captain had announced his sighting of Atlantis at mid-morning, and since then, the slender Timeless had been on deck, watching the island as they sailed by. A glance at the sun told him it was mid-afternoon now. Ghean came up as he looked back toward Atlantis, and smiled at him.

"The main port is around the next curve," she assured him. "You won't have to wait much longer."

"How can you tell? One mountain looks the same as any other to me." He gestured at the craggy, weather-beaten stone a few hundred meters away.

"I've made this journey since I was a little girl. Before my father died, he used to test me on the different ports, to see if I could pick out details to distinguish them." Ghean leaned against the rail, pointing at a copse of trees that hung precariously out over the water, growing nearly parallel to the water below. "Those trees are how I know Atlantis is around the bend. It's the only place on the island they grow like that. Father used to tell me a story about them. He said that when Atlantis was young, it was a small flat island, without the mountains, good for farming. The waves touched shore gently, with hardly a ripple. A young boy who was very vain would watch himself in the water for days on end, while he was supposed to be keeping watch for enemy ships approaching.

"One day, the enemies came, and he didn't notice. Because Atlantis is favored by the gods, they saved us from certain destruction by lifting the land into mountains and difficult ports. To punish the boy for his carelessness, they changed him into that stand of trees, destined to always look into the waters and never be able to see his reflection again."

Ghean smiled up at the trees as the ship passed under them. "I always felt badly for the boy. I can't imagine Atlantis being as beautiful as it is, if it were flat land. I never thought it was very fair of the gods."

"Your people have kind gods," Lorhen said. "Most gods would have let the enemy overrun the island, to teach the boy a lesson by killing his family and leaving him the only survivor."

"Maybe it's because our gods are kind that we've created a civilization unlike anyone else's."

Lorhen smiled. "Possibly." The ship banked hard to starboard, and Lorhen glanced up. "Good gods."

The port itself was vastly larger than any they'd passed. Ships of varying sizes and shapes were docked or sailing free, some with a multitude of sails catching the wind. Lorhen stared at one of these with fascination as it swung closer to their own ship, watching a dozen sailors nimbly traversing the deck and masts to better use the wind. Masts, many masts, of varying heights, all littered with sails to catch the wind. Lorhen leaned further over the railing, squinting against the sunlight on the water to try to get a better glimpse yet. One sailor caught his intense observation and waved in greeting. Ghean waved back. Lorhen lifted a hand, but continued to study the vessel until it was past. Only then did he turn his attention to the rest of the port.

Sailing ships mingled with triremes, dozens of oars resting idle in the water in neat rows. Smaller vessels zipped between the larger ships, some piloted by children, who, laughing, would speed alongside their ship for a few moments, until outpaced. Whitecaps churned out of the water shone brilliantly against the glowing blue of the harbor. An area in the distance had been roped off. No ships sailed there, but a number of people, ranging from child-sized to adult, swam in the water there, their shouts of pleasure mingling with the general cacophony of the port itself.

The scent of fish was stronger here than it had been on the open water, as fishing boats offloaded their catches in another section of the port. Men and women both worked the boats, calling directions to each other. Lorhen took it in as rapidly as possible, glancing from one area to another. "I've never seen a port this clean."

Delight lit Ghean's face. "We work hard to keep it clean." She pointed to one of the smaller skiffs, captained by a young boy. "They clean up after the ships coming in from the sea. The sewage systems here don't drain into the water. There are natural chutes in the mountains that we drain waste into. About once a moon they're burned clean, to keep disease from coming up."

Lorhen looked down at her in admiration. "What the world couldn't learn from Atlantis," he breathed, and then, finally, looked beyond the harbor, up to the mountains.

Just beyond the docks lay an enormous set of gates, opened now, their doors swinging outward as if to encourage the world to enter. Traffic, both horse and foot, moved up and down a broad road cut into the stone. The rise was just shy of dauntingly steep, and even from the water it was possible to see rest areas carved out of the mountains. People and carts, small with distance, could be made out sitting or napping in the rest areas.

"The city is just on the other side of the pass," Ghean said. "We won't be able to see it at all until we're at the crest."

"Until then, I'll have to content myself with admiring you."

Ghean laughed. "You are not very good at extravagant compliments, Lorhen. You should practice more."

"I will," he promised. The hairs on the back of his neck stood up in a wash of warning, and he turned, wary, to scan the ships closest to their own. Not too far away, he watched a man straighten with the same familiar expression of caution on his face. For a moment the two locked gazes across the water. Then the second man inclined his head, in acknowledgment, and returned to his observation of the port. Lorhen watched him for another few seconds before his attention went back to Ghean. "I will," he repeated, trying to remember what he'd just promised.

"Are you all right?" she asked, worry creasing her forehead. He nodded, looking over his shoulder as a second tingle of nausea swept over him. Aroz came up from below deck, scowling curiously at the nearby ships, and less benignly at Lorhen himself. Lorhen tilted his head toward the ship with the other Timeless on it. Aroz grunted in reply, coming to stand a few feet away from Lorhen and Ghean, his hands planted at his waist. Lorhen's battered bronze sword hung from Aroz's hip. Lorhen absently touched the hilt of the steel sword he now carried, as he nodded at the pass through the mountains.

"How long does it take to reach the city?"

"Only an hour or two. The road looks worse than it is. Coming back down takes no time at all."

The ship banked again, to drift into dock. Ghean hovered impatiently at the gangplank, rushing down it and over the dock to the beach. Lorhen grinned, watching her spin wildly on the sand, and then went below to collect his journal, too precious to leave to the careless hands of ships-men. Minyah, engaged in the same task, smiled at him as he left his cabin. "Let me guess," she said. "My daughter is cavorting in the sand like a child released from captivity." She arranged a satchel over her shoulder, and accepted Lorhen's hand up the ladder leading to the deck. He nodded as she turned to wait for him, and the older woman smiled again. "She has done that on every journey since she could walk. I sometimes think she would outgrow it, were it not for my expectations of her antics."

Lorhen straightened, looking down at the sand where Ghean was engaged in animated conversation with a little boy. The child nodded eagerly and ran off, leaving Ghean to begin her dance on the beach again. "I don't know," Lorhen said. "The celebration seems very much in her nature. She might do it anyway."

Minyah paused at the gangplank, watching Ghean fall to lie on her back in the sand, smiling up at the sun. "I am glad you came to an understanding," Minyah said as she began making her way down to the dock. "I will be pleased to have you as a son."

"You just want to study me as a scientific anomaly," Lorhen accused.

"There is that," Minyah replied equitably. "You know these last two months she has come to repeat all the stories you have told her to me."

Lorhen laughed. "I would save everyone a lot of time if I simply told the stories to both of you at once."

Minyah blinked mildly at him. "An excellent suggestion." She left Lorhen at the end of the dock with the suspicion that he had just been had. Bemused, he followed her, stopping on the waterfront beside Ghean.

"We can't go up to the city yet," Ghean announced. "Ertros

is bringing us iced coffee and chocolates to fortify us for the trip up."

Lorhen shook his head at unfamiliar words. "Coffee? Chocolates? What are they?"

Minyah chuckled. "I am not certain they can be qualified as fortifications. They are derived from beans grown across the world, far away. I think neither is necessary for survival, although they are most pleasant, and the coffee is a reviving drink."

"Chocolate," Ghean said firmly, "is necessary for survival. I always bring some when we leave Atlantis," she went on, looking up from her seat at Lorhen, "and they never last the whole ship's journey to land."

Lorhen sat down beside her. "But what are they?"

"Small bitter treats, with sugar or milk added to soften them. Ertros is nearly as tall as I am, Mother. By next summer he'll have outgrown me."

Minyah looked at her diminutive daughter. "That is not a difficult task, Ghean."

"But I remember when he was born!" Ghean mock-wailed. "I'm getting old and decrepit!"

Lorhen felt Minyah's glance slide off him, and didn't meet her eyes. "You are the freshest blossom on a young and slender tree," he assured Ghean earnestly, then gave her a sly smile. "How was that?"

She clucked her tongue. "You can't smile. Smiling ruins the whole effect. Ertros!" She bounded to her feet again, waving at the boy who made his way across the sand.

Shaggy-haired and barefooted, he was about eleven, and only an inch shorter than Ghean. He carried a plate of mugs, heavy clay that would stand up to being dropped. There were eight chocolates, two for each cup. "You owe me," the boy said to Ghean severely. "It's hot, and I ran all the way up the beach to get this for you."

Ghean eyed the four mugs. "It looks to me like I paid you back by buying you some coffee."

"It'll do for starters," Ertros said smugly. He handed a mug to Ghean, then Minyah, and stopped before Lorhen, studying him suspiciously. "Who're you?" he demanded.

"My name is Lorhen."

"He's my betrothed, Ertros!" Ghean broke in. "We're to be married as soon as we can."

Ertros' expression slid from suspicion to outright dislike. "He's awfully tall," the boy said critically to Ghean. "And pale. What do you want to marry an outlander for?" *After all*, his tone said, *you've got* me. Lorhen ducked his head, grinning at the sand.

"Well, he's very nice," Ghean explained. "For an outlander."

Ertros looked dubious, but offered Lorhen a mug. "Welcome to Atlantis," he said with chilly precision.

Lorhen fought back another smile and nodded his head gravely in reply. "Thank you. I'm honored to meet a man of the island who is such a good friend of Ghean's." He accepted the mug, looking curiously at the chipped ice in the dark liquid. "I've never had coffee before," he confessed to Ertros.

The boy puffed up visibly. "Real Atlanteans drink it all the time," he said loftily, and took a swig from his own mug to prove it.

Lorhen took a more cautious sip, aware of the anticipatory eyes of all three Atlanteans on him. The chilled liquid was considerably more bitter than he'd anticipated, from the slightly sweet scent of it. After another two slightly tentative sips, he slowly nodded his approval. "I think I could get used to this coffee."

Ghean beamed, clearly pleased. "Now a chocolate," she proclaimed, and broke one of the pieces on the tray in half to pop it in Lorhen's mouth.

Bittersweet richness coated his tongue. For several seconds he didn't move, letting the bit of chocolate melt in his mouth.

Then, in sheer disbelief, he stared at the mug of coffee. "They're made from the same thing?" He took another sip of coffee, trying to discover a similarity in the flavors. Something about the sharp edge. Perhaps. If he used his imagination. And closed his eyes. "That's wonderful."

"Different beans," Minyah corrected. "Coffee is from far south of Egypt, and the chocolate, from a bean grown on a continent far to the west. I prefer the chocolate as a drink, myself, but the coffee seems to stimulate my thoughts."

"Which are quick enough as they are," Lorhen said. "A continent to the west? And what lies south of Egypt? I've traveled there, but never beyond the jungles that beget the Nile. I got lost," he admitted with chagrin, and Minyah laughed.

"Our explorers have taken expeditions all over the world, following seas to their nadir and then crossing the land as a team. There are records in Atlantis. I'm sure you'll have plenty of time to investigate them."

Lorhen, with genuine sincerity, said, "I look forward to it," and Ghean settled back with her drink and a smile. "I think he'll fit right in here, don't you, Ertros?"

Ertros scowled. "I guess."

Several minutes later, Minyah sighed with contented resignation. "We should begin the journey up to the city soon. A sunset over Atlantis would be an admirable way to introduce Lorhen to our home."

"Is that your way of saying you've finished your coffee?" Ghean teased. Minyah nodded, and Ghean, in a precise mimicry of her mother's tone, said, "Ah. So I was right. That is always satisfying."

Minyah laughed. "Insolent daughter. I will forbid your marriage and betroth you instead to a toothless old minstrel who must sing tales of woe to earn his daily meals."

Lorhen sucked his cheeks in, crumbling in on himself to appear smaller, and climbed to his feet to totter uncertainly toward

Minyah. "Will I do, madam?" he creaked. "For such a fair prize I will sing my best songs, though I fear my voice is not what it once was." He blinked near-sightedly at her with eyes suddenly gone rheumy and watery.

Minyah, unnerved, stepped back from the approaching Timeless, stilling herself after one pace. Her usual composure reasserted itself as she lifted one eyebrow. "How extraordinary," she murmured. "Despite the grain of your skin and the color in your hair, I see an old man."

Lorhen pushed himself up straighter, a hand at the small of his back to suggest stiffness. "Not so old!" he said in the same raspy tone. "Young enough to please that impertinent daughter of yours so she'll care for me in my old age!" He thumped an imaginary stick in the sand. Ertros jumped, then looked abashed, casting a glance to see if Ghean had noticed his slip.

She had not. Still sitting in the sand, Ghean clasped her coffee mug in loose hands, staring at Lorhen. Minyah laughed, and Lorhen shook the character off, unbending himself to stand at his full height. "You're spilling your coffee," he said gently to Ghean.

She flinched the mug upright. "Oh! Lorhen, that was—was that you?" With an uncertain frown, she climbed to her feet, setting her empty mug aside on the plate Ertros had brought.

"Of course it was." Lorhen extended a hand to her. "Come. You have a city to show me."

The trek up the mountains took a little over three hours. Lorhen was met with mildly curious stares as he walked, and the Atlanteans with him by delighted greetings and hugs. "I believe you'll have introduced me to the entire city by the time we reach the top," he commented softly to Ghean, after they'd been stopped for the fourth or fifth time.

She laughed. "Just wait. I predict that in the next week our House will be flooded with visitors wanting to see my outland scholar."

"I'm not that remarkable," Lorhen protested.

"Scholars in Atlantis are nothing new. Scholars from outside are a rarity. You'll be very popular. Close your eyes. The city is just over the next rise." Ghean took his hand to lead him forward as Lorhen closed his eyes, lips quirking with mirth.

Perhaps two minutes later, as the land changed from an incline to a decline, Ghean stopped. "All right," she decided. "You can open them now."

Lorhen did, looking first at Ghean. Her mouth curled in expectation as she watched him. Light from the setting sun gleamed red in her hair and warmed her skin. For a few moments he simply admired her, disregarding the images that were her backdrop. Then, because she was waiting, he looked up and beyond her, to the city.

Atlantis was the color of fire. Built of stone, it glowed like fading embers, the sun's dying rays reflected in soft-edged shadows that blended the city's edges into the mountains surrounding it. The road he stood on dropped sharply down to the gates. From his vantage, Lorhen could see the simple layout of the city, built around a central circle. Dominating the central circle was a temple, the roof a high dome that stood above any other building in the city. Streets webbed out from the temple circle, some major and innumerable minor. The smaller streets fell in ever-widening circles, details lost to the setting sun. It was a city that had been planned, not one that grew up in a random pattern. The symmetry was awe-striking.

"Gods above," Lorhen said quietly. "I've never seen anything like it, Ghean." He glanced at the black mountain beneath his feet, and back at Atlantis. "The stone," he half- asked. "It looks white." He gestured at the walls, their true color returning as the light dimmed.

"Legend says that the gods came down to look at the city our fathers built, and they were pleased," Ghean answered. "But it was not enough for the children of the gods, and so they struck it a thousand times with lightning. When the skies cleared, all the color had bleached from the stone, and so it has always been."

Lorhen nodded slowly, looking over the city again. "How old is Atlantis, Minyah?"

"Older than you," she replied, "and more enduring. Shall we go home?"

16

Ghean and Minyah had not been in error, when they'd predicted Lorhen would be a highly anticipated conversational partner amongst Atlantean scholars. After only a week in Atlantis, he had spoken in depth with more people than he usually did in a year. Most of it had been fascinating, stimulating, and he dared imagine he'd made a few friends out of the constant throng of well-wishers and critical intellectuals.

He did feel something like the prize bull at a market, though. A significant portion of the visitors had come simply to see what oddity Ghean had brought home from outside. An alarming number of those had returned later with their daughters. The daughters were evenly divided: either they were reluctant and refused to meet his eye, or he required constant motion to keep from being latched onto. Ghean sat through each display placidly only to crawl into bed late at night and giggle about it. Lorhen couldn't decide if he should be offended or relieved that the situation amused her. "What if I found one of them irresistible?" he demanded.

Ghean propped her chin on his shoulder, smiling. "I'd magnanimously allow you to wed your new beloved," she said cheerfully. "And then I'd sneak into your house and kill you. Right in front of her. And then I'd cart your body off the island and marry you anyway. And I'd hold it all over your head for the rest of my life."

"That's not fair," Lorhen said primly. A moment later, with admiration, he added, "You have a mean streak."

Ghean's grin turned smug. "I do. You'd better not find any of them irresistible, hm?"

"No one could ever be as stimulating as you are," he promised extravagantly, and pulled her over for a kiss.

"No one in this lifetime, at least," Ghean replied.

"You also have a morbid streak, wife."

Ghean sniffed. "Not yet," she corrected. "Three whole weeks until the ceremony."

"Doesn't Atlantean law provide that once a parent's blessing has been given to a betrothal, the couple are considered wedded?"

Ghean nodded. "Unless something happens before the ceremony and they decide to not have the words said over them. Then neither is considered to have ever been married." Her eyebrows went up. "Where did you learn so much about Atlantean law?"

"I spent some time at the library yesterday."

"When? We had visitors from daybreak to dusk."

"*You* had visitors," he said. "I snuck out while you were planning the ceremony." Lorhen grinned. "And here I was worried you'd be offended that I left."

"I am," Ghean had said. "Terribly. You'll have to make it up to me. Now."

Lorhen had laughed and pulled her on top of himself, glad to forget, for a while, about the parade of scholars and visitors filling his days, and the nearly-accusational commentary on his apparent youth that too many of the scholars felt obliged to make.

Another faintly offended scholar was making that same accusation now, under the mid-afternoon heat of the Atlantean sun. Lorhen wasn't sure, in fact, that this particular man hadn't come to see him for the express purpose of being offended; it seemed to him that in the past day or two scholars of that nature had begun turning up. This one was was in his middle fifties, slightly portly, called Ragar, and could very clearly not decide if he should be impressed with the Hunter House's new acquisition or resentful of it.

Lorhen suppressed a sigh, wondering for the thousandth time what this man would say if Lorhen told him the truth. "I have tried to keep an open mind and a wide base of studies," he said instead. "I find it's more practical, given my habit of traveling."

"You travel extensively?" A greater degree of irritation came into Ragar's voice.

Irritation, Lorhen thought, or perhaps envy. His evident youth, his knowledge, and his broad travels could be easily envied by someone who had ambition but not boldness, or who had lacked opportunity. "I've traveled ever since I can remember," he replied as politely as he could. Technically, it was true. "Studying the places and people I came in contact with seemed natural. I was lucky enough to learn to write, so I could keep notes on my studies."

Ragar shook his head. "How do you survive? Most people aren't interested in histories. Most people don't have enough history." He obviously excluded Atlantis from that group.

Lorhen spread a hand in deprecation. "Nearly everyone loves history. They just call them stories. It's how I survive, by telling stories. Most people are willing to offer a space by the fire and a bit of food in exchange for new stories, or even old ones. It's—" Lorhen broke off as goosebumps raised on his skin, prickles of caution alerting him to an approaching Timeless. His eyes on the door, he said to Ragar, "Please excuse me? There's someone coming that I need to talk to."

Ragar shot a puzzled look at the door. "Of course. Who—" He, too, broke off, as a shadow appeared in the door. "You must have excellent hearing," the mortal scholar said to Lorhen.

Lorhen twisted a small smile. "Yes," he agreed. "We'll talk more later, Ragar?"

Ragar nodded, stepping past the new arrival to make his way out of the grounds. Lorhen stood, examining the man as he entered the room. He was tall, nearly Lorhen's own height, and judging from his coloring, no more of Atlantis than Lorhen himself was. Fine, narrow features were dominated by lively green eyes that added an animated attraction to a face that fell a little short of handsome. Brown hair was held back in a long tail, falling past his shoulders. He wore the sword and long knife at his hips easily.

"Ah!" He bowed extravagantly. "The great scholar Lorhen. At last, we meet."

Lorhen's eyebrows lifted, amused but not relaxed. "You have the advantage over me."

The man straightened, stepping forward to offer a hand. "My name is Karem. I'm afraid I'm only a warrior, nothing to make a fuss about on this island of studies."

Lorhen clasped Karem's forearm briefly, then stepped back, still studying the other. "You're the one I saw on the ship last week."

"I am," Karem agreed. "Terribly rude of me to take so long to stop by and visit, but I've been awfully busy. Do you realize this island is teeming with Timeless?"

Lorhen inadvertently glanced through the door, as if expecting an army of Timeless to stand there. "I didn't. I haven't sensed any since I've been here." He gestured at a chair in invitation.

Karem sat in a loose, fluid movement. "No, you wouldn't have. They're not like us. Somehow these people have discovered how to make artifacts of immortality."

Lorhen regarded the other man skeptically. "How?"

Karem shook his head. "I have no idea. It seems to be common knowledge, but not bandied about. Each of the Houses apparently has one of these artifacts. That means if they're all in use, there are at least a dozen Timeless on this island, including you and me."

"More," Lorhen heard himself say. "A man and a young woman, like us." He sat down across from Karem, intrigued despite himself. "I've seen some of the wonders they've created. They've bred horned war-horses that are possibly the smartest animals I've ever seen. But immortality artifacts?"

"I was told about them by a man called Methuselah, years ago. He carried a stone, a giant crystal, and he said he'd been alive for nine hundred years. Can you imagine? A mortal, nine hundred years old? I tested him as best I could. If he wasn't older than I am, he was a brilliant liar."

Lorhen's eyebrows crinkled curiously. "Where is he now?"

"The islanders say he got tired of living, and gave the stone to his grandson. Apparently the grandson has been down in the harbor for weeks, building a boat. He says the gods have told him a disaster is coming and the only way to survive is to sail away from it."

Lorhen smiled faintly. "I see. It grants immortality at the price of lunacy?"

Karem shrugged. "The old man seemed perfectly sane."

"Why are you telling me this?"

"I want to learn how they're made. You're already an established scholar. They'll be more receptive to you than me." Karem leaned forward, eyes bright and eager. "Can you imagine, Lorhen? The ability to grant immortality to our loved ones? Never losing the people we care about?"

Thinking guiltily of Ghean, Lorhen murmured, "It's not our decision to make."

Karem spread his hands expressively. "Who better? We have experience at immortality. We can pick and choose those who would be best suited for it and bestow it upon them."

"A world full of Timeless," Lorhen retorted. "Do their artifacts, if they work, prevent children? How long until the births so far outnumbered the deaths that there was nowhere to live? How would you feed everyone?"

"The world's a big place, Lorhen! We wouldn't have to worry about it for generations."

Lorhen rubbed his eyes with the tips of his fingers. "You sound like them. Thinking of now instead of forever. You could live forever, Karem. How long do you think they'd let you live if they realized you were born to live eternally, while they had to depend on trinkets and toys?"

"If I gave them the toys, why would they be anything but grateful to me for sparing them from death?"

"Because men are remarkably dense, Karem. They will kill what they fear, and they fear that which is different. They'd kill you, and me, and any other Timeless like us they could find."

"So I'd choose my children carefully." Karem leaned forward again, strands of his ponytail falling over his shoulder with the movement. "It's what they'd be to us, Lorhen. Think of it. Children of our own."

"We can't have children," Lorhen said impatiently. "Not Timeless ones. At best any mortals would be disciples, students, to whom we'd be mentors. And sooner or later they'd turn on us."

"Not if we kept how to make the artifacts a secret."

Lorhen let out an explosive sigh. "Which gives you power over them, which they will resent, which will turn to fear and hatred, which will lead to your death, Karem! The pattern is the same, can't you see that? Besides, what has been discovered once will be again. If your old man was telling the truth, Atlantis has had the secret of immortality for nearly a thousand years. They've kept it secret, too. Take heed from their counsel, Karem. Let it die. Let *them* die."

Karem sat back, clearly unconvinced, yet unwilling to press the issue to a fight. "Bah! I'll convince you yet, but I've no wish for quarrel with you. Are we still at peace?"

"We are. Think abou—" He trailed off, lifting his eyes to the door as the chill of warning came over him for a second time in the afternoon. Karem turned to face the door, dropping his hand none-too-subtly to the hilt of his sword.

Seconds later, Aroz appeared in the door frame, expression as wary as both Lorhen's and Karem's were. Lorhen relaxed slightly, back into his chair, and gestured at the Timeless sitting across from him. "Karem, Aroz, bodyguard to the mistress of the Hunter's House. Aroz, this is Karem, an itinerant...trouble-maker, I think." Lorhen grinned apologetically as Karem shot him an amused, mock-offended glance.

Aroz looked over Karem with apparent disapproval. "A friend of yours?" he asked Lorhen.

Lorhen tilted his head. "Time will tell. I doubt you're here for my company, Aroz. What do you need?"

"Ghean is not here."

"Ghean is not," Lorhen agreed drolly. "I presume you didn't drop by to tell me that." Not actually eager to pick a fight, he relented at Aroz's darkening scowl, finishing. "When it became apparent I was going to spend the entire afternoon discussing obscure historical texts with Ragar, she went down to the market. Wait a moment," he said as Aroz turned to leave, his broad shoulders filling the doorway. "You've been a part of Atlantean society a while. Did you know a man named Methuselah?"

Aroz stopped, looking back over his shoulder. "He's dead now."

"But you knew him," Karem interjected. "Tell Lorhen about his crystal, his immortality stone."

Aroz cast a look down the walkway toward the distant market, and, sighing heavily, came back into the room to stand in a wide-legged stance, arms crossed over his chest. "I met Methuselah when I was very young," he admitted. "Nearly two hundred years ago."

"Hah!" Karem barked triumphantly. "You see, Lorhen? They do have the gift of immortality."

Lorhen ignored Karem, frowning studiously at Aroz. "Why doesn't everyone here have artifacts that extend their lives?"

"Don't they? What's the average mortal lifespan, Lorhen?"

Lorhen waved his hand. "Thirty, thirty-five years."

"Atlanteans live an average of sixty."

"Yes, I know. I assumed their lifestyle, their knowledge—"

"Maybe. Maybe not. I don't think they're sitting on a well of spring water that lets them live forever, but they live twice as long as the rest of the world, and some of them do have objects that appear to protect them from death."

"How?" Lorhen shook his head.

Aroz split an ugly grin. "I don't know. Maybe they're right, and the gods did favor them."

"Why only one for each House, then, if that's how it works? Why not for everyone?"

"There are at least two Houses whose artifacts aren't related to immortality, or not directly. The war-horses, though I'm told they don't age and I know they don't breed. They're a lot like us," Aroz said sourly. "They can die, but it takes a lot of effort to kill one. There's also a box of bones, which are supposed to transform into warriors when planted in the dirt."

"That seems unlikely," Karem said.

"So does Methuselah's crystal," Lorhen said. Karem conceded the point with a brief nod. "But why not one for everyone?" Lorhen repeated.

Aroz lifted a thick shoulder and let it fall. "Legend says that the final artifact was hundreds of times more powerful than any of the others, that the gods poured far more into its creation than any of the others. There was nothing left to make smaller gifts with."

"How careless of the gods," Lorhen murmured. "What was it?"

"A book."

"A *book*?"

Aroz nodded. "That's what they say. It was created and lost at the dawn of Atlantis' history."

"How can a book grant you immortality?" Lorhen demanded. At the same time, Karem asked, "What was in it?"

Aroz spread his hands. "Who knows? The secrets of alchemy, science, the Scorpion House's secret recipe for bread. It doesn't matter. It doesn't exist anymore."

"What if the book explains how to make the artifacts?" Karem's voice was eager.

"Then it's better off lost." Lorhen stood. "Enough of us handle immortality badly. Giving it to all mortals would be disastrous."

"Who are you to make that decision?" Karem snapped.

Lorhen paused at the door to slip his sword-belt on, looking back at the other two. After a moment he stepped through the door, heading for the market, letting his answer linger in the air behind him. "I am the oldest living Timeless."

Karem's eyebrows elevated slowly, and he looked at Aroz. "Is he?"

Aroz shrugged, standing to follow Lorhen. "Ghean says he claims to be a thousand years old. Do you know anyone that age?"

Karem shook his head as he, too, came to his feet. "No. Who's Ghean?"

Aroz's face shut down. "Lorhen's betrothed."

A thin smile spilled across Karem's face as he waved Aroz ahead of himself and they left Lorhen's suite. "I see that you love her. Perhaps she was intended for you, before he arrived?"

Aroz stopped at the head of the garden path, watching Lorhen as he grew smaller with distance. "No. Never through anything more than an unspoken hope between her mother and myself, at least."

"Why not just kill him?"

"I tried," Aroz answered without emotion. "I lost. Ghean stopped him from making the heartstrike."

"He has weaknesses, then. He can be swayed by her. Maybe that can be used against him to your advantage."

"Why my advantage, and not yours? A thousand years of power would make someone very strong."

Karem stepped down the path toward the city. "I want his influence with the scholars in Atlantis more than I want his power. Once I've obtained that, who knows?"

Aroz followed, letting out a sound of bitter amusement. "I won't wait if I have the chance for the heartstrike."

"She'll only die, you know. Is it worth it?"

"She's one of us," Aroz said, "or she will be. We could have eternity."

"Really," Karem breathed. "How very interesting. All that untapped potential. You'll have to introduce me to the girl. Does she know?"

"No. She knows we exist, but not that she's one of us."

Karem nodded. "What does she know about Atlantis' history?"

Aroz shook his head. "She's studied to be an architect, not a historian. Her mother, Minyah, is the one you'd want to talk to for history."

"Mmm. Let's find a drink at the marketplace, Aroz, and you can tell me about Minyah."

17

To Lorhen's surprise, the scholar Ragar did return the next day for another conversation, and then again the following day, until days turned into weeks and camaraderie grew between them. Lorhen, more intrigued by Karem's stories of immortality artifacts than he wanted to admit, guided Ragar into telling him the history of Atlantis, and into the topic of the artifacts. There were as many as there were Houses, and if they didn't all grant immortality, the tales certainly indicated they were all imbued with magic.

Ghean's House had a cloak, said to be from the Hunter himself, and, both fascinated and bemused at his own fascination, Lorhen asked Minyah if he could see it. She looked at him thoughtfully before bringing him into a small, unused room in the house. It was filled with wool cloaks, dyed through a spectrum of yellows, all hanging on small racks set into the walls. "Can you tell which one it is?"

Lorhen pursed his lips, walking around the room. His footsteps on the stone floor were muffled by the wool that virtually lined the walls. After several minutes, he returned to Minyah's side. "Not at all," he confessed. "I thought I would be able to."

She crossed the room unerringly, to select a mid-length cloak dyed pale gold. "This one." Folding it over her arm, she presented it to him.

He took it gingerly, half expecting some sort of backlash, but it looked, and felt, like a perfectly ordinary cloak. "You're sure?"

Minyah nodded. "Quite. It produces no special feeling, nothing like your sensation that warns of other Timeless?"

Lorhen shook his head, inspecting the cloak more carefully. "Nothing. I would never be able to choose it out of a room full of other cloaks."

"I thought not." Minyah sounded smug. "Our gifts of immortality are utterly unlike yours."

Lorhen looked up from the cloak. "Did you know Methuselah?"

Minyah nodded. "Certainly. In truth, I never thought to test our cloak, despite knowing his crystal worked. Many of us saw him as something closer to the gods than we are, a protector left from the early days of the island. That the gift could be passed on did not occur to me. Shall we test it?"

"Test it?" Lorhen looked skeptical. "How? It won't work for me. I'm already Timeless."

Minyah took the cloak back, slipping it over her shoulders. "It is supposed to protect the wearer from harm." She nodded at his sword. "Strike at me."

Lorhen's eyebrows went up in horror. "And if it doesn't work? I really don't want to explain to Ghean that I accidentally chopped her mother in half ten days before the wedding."

Minyah laughed, extending her hand. "Give me your knife, then. I will test it myself, in the same fashion that you showed Ghean your healing ability."

Reluctantly, Lorhen unsheathed the little blade and placed it in her palm. "Don't cut too deep," he warned. "If it doesn't work, I'd hate to see you crippled. A scholar needs her hands."

Minyah nodded, shifting her grip on the hilt, and considering her other palm. "I find this somewhat alarming," she announced, then took a quick breath and curved her fingers around the blade, pressing it into her skin. A sharp cry escaped her, and Lorhen caught her wrist to turn her palm toward him, flinching in anticipation.

Her palm was whole, not even creased by the blade's path. Shocked, Lorhen looked at the knife, which remained unbloodied. "Dear gods."

Minyah stared at her palm with as much surprise as Lorhen. "By the gods," she agreed softly. "So it is true. It protects the wearer."

"Minyah," Lorhen said slowly. "May I try it? Our power doesn't stop an injury from happening, it just heals it faster. It might work."

Minyah, still looking wide-eyed at her hand, pulled the cloak off and handed it to Lorhen. He swung it on and took his knife back from Ghean's mother. With less trepidation than she had shown, he drove the knife toward his palm.

Both mortal and Timeless startled violently at the sharp crack of the blade shattering. Lorhen lifted it to study the jagged pattern where the tip had broken off, then turned his hand up to gaze at the unbroken skin. *I could be invincible.* With a shiver, he pulled the cloak off again and handed it back to Minyah. "That is not for me," he said softly, intently. "Not for any of my kind. If it fell into the hands of the wrong Timeless, if he were the last one—destroy it, Minyah, before handing it to a Timeless again. Destroy it."

Minyah folded the cloak over her arm. "The last one," she repeated. "You battle to the death, but why?"

Lorhen turned away. "Put the cloak away," he asked quietly. "I don't want to watch you do it. I don't know why we fight," he said, answering to drown out the sound of her soft footsteps, to lessen the chance he might somehow accidentally learn where the cloak was placed. "Something in us compels us to. Not always, not constantly. It can be overcome. But the impulse is

there, any time we meet another of our kind. The desire to con-
quer and command their power." Despite his speech, he heard
her cross the room, shifting cloaks aside as she hung the artifact.
"Some of us believe that the last of us will become gods, or be
given the world to rule."

"Do you want that?" Minyah returned to stand before him,
her eyes calculating and thoughtful.

Lorhen spread his hands. "I really don't care about ruling the
world, or being a god. All I want, all I've ever wanted, is to live
another day." A faint smile creased his mouth. "Just like anyone
else. I just want to live."

I just want to live. The words, that simple inherent truth of his
being, echoed in his mind now, late at night and days after he
and Minyah had experimented with the Hunter's cloak. Moonlight's hard shadows mixed with the softer, flickering edges of
candlelight shadows as Lorhen sat with his head dropped, long
fingers pressed against his temples and forehead. The papers
spread over the table in front of him were written in Atlantean,
recognizable but painfully archaic. He hadn't moved in four
hours, other than turning pages and sipping coffee.

Lorhen rubbed his eyes again, before pushing his stool away
from the desk so he could stand. The Hunter's cloak was painfully tempting. More than once he'd found himself retracing the
route to the storage room, only to deliberately walk away when
he'd realized his goal. Such a device would encourage complacency, reliance on an outside resource, and that could be—*would*
be—his undoing. Survival was a solitary pursuit.

With a quiet sigh, Lorhen reassembled the papers he'd been
going through. After nearly two days of meticulous research, he
was certain that the histories would not provide him with the
details of how to create the artifacts, nor with the location of the

mythical Book of Atlantis. Still, he would finish reading them in the morning.

Barefooted, he padded into the bedroom, watching Ghean sleep for a few moments. Relaxed in the dim moonlight, her hair braided and dipping over the edge of the bed, she looked very young, though by most mortal standards she was more than middle-aged. With a smile, he slipped out again, hesitating briefly in the main room before blowing out the candles, picking up his blades, and making his way down toward the city.

The streets were deserted, taverns and markets all closed. Lorhen glanced at the moon and the position of the stars, judging it to be well past midnight, closer to the new dawn than last night's dusk. The city glowed, the white stone reflecting the moonlight with an eerie, unreal edge, as if lit from within. The shadows were blued, full darkness unwilling to encroach on the city's streets. It lent an aura of peace to the sleeping town, lulling Lorhen's walk into a slow and leisurely pace.

He had almost reached the temple at the city center before he realized it was his destination. He paused at the door, considering the blades he still carried, sheathed, in his hand. He knew of no mortal enemies on the island, and among the other compulsions of his kind was the aversion to fighting on consecrated ground: even the idea made his hands itch and cramp, as if he'd be forced to drop his weapons if he tried. Still, Atlantis had no tenets requiring temple-goers to abandon their weapons outside the sanctuary, and after a moment's debate, Lorhen stepped inside, sword still in hand.

The weeks in Atlantis had not afforded him more than a few minutes' visit in the temple. It had been enough to register the fine architecture and artwork, but little else. Now, he thought, the wait had been worthwhile. The circular building was domed, the roof set upon wide pillars at even intervals. Head tilted back to study them, Lorhen walked further into the temple, coming to the center of the room and placing fingertips on the altar that dominated the building.

The pillars were carved, each in its own distinct style, as if each of the thirteen had been commissioned by a different artist. The Houses of Atlantis were represented there, beasts and creatures from the stars rendered in white marble to hold up the dome of the sky. Some were stunningly lifelike, the effect added to by the shadows cast by the moon's bright light. Lorhen turned to find the Hunter, his arms lifted to support his section of the ceiling. With a self-mocking smile, Lorhen bowed to the sculpture, amused at the real respect he felt. Though his own gods, if he'd had any, were long dead, there was still a small degree of comfortable familiarity in acknowledging the gods of others.

Scattered cushions were the only seats in the temple. Atlantis' religion was more one of quiet contemplation than gathered masses, though the central altar saw monthly sacrifices from each House, as its constellation grew dominant. Faint, discolored traces of blood stained the stone, rendered innocent by the lighting.

Lorhen withdrew from the altar, fingers sliding off smooth, worn stone, and knelt on a nearby cushion, sword held loosely across his thighs as his eyes slowly drifted shut. Time slipped away, the meditative silence of the temple helping to loosen the restraints of memory.

His arrogant claim came back to him: *I am the oldest living Timeless.* The oldest he knew about, at least, though he couldn't imagine he was the first. Surely he would remember being that old, somehow.

Memories prompted by centuries of journal-keeping, remembered because they had been written down, surfaced. Heads he'd taken, ages of the Timeless who had died, whose power had Blended with his. None of them had been older than he. But what about the first one? With a heavy breath, Lorhen let all conscious thought slip away from him, giving himself up to the flickers of memory.

The first remembered heartstrike, the first Blending. The electric thrill still jolted his fingertips, raising hairs on his arms. Power was left, but the man whose head he'd taken was gone, memories of his life swept away on time's river as much as any mortal life might be lost. For an instant, the thick features came into focus: wide nose, heavy cheekbones and wild, wild hair, frantic eyes visible in flashes under it. Lorhen snatched at the image, trying to follow it to more knowledge, only to watch it dissolve. Hunger and fear, rage and despair, replaced it, the sensations remembered more in bone and muscle than in mind.

With thoughtless determination, Lorhen pursued even those shreds of memory, wading through the grey blur of time. On one level, he noticed the prickle at the back of his neck as he sat in the temple, noted the arrival of another Timeless. Beyond the awareness, he ignored the physical, falling deeper into memory in search of answers.

Nothing came forward. No faces, no teachers, nothing of the Timeless who had come before him. Briefly, the face of an old man, toothless with age and utterly bald, filled Lorhen's mind. With it came a dozen other glimpses of faces, men and women and children whose presence spoke faintly of family to the ancient Timeless. As quickly as they'd come, they were gone, leaving Lorhen with a small smile playing at his mouth. He spoke without intending to, voice quiet in the stone temple, and only truly heard the last word: *Nolan.*

Karem's voice broke him out of his reverie entirely. "What did you say?"

Lorhen opened his eyes to regard the man crouched on a cushion some feet away. The words were too awkward in his mouth, already faded in his mind; he couldn't form them again, and said, "It meant...'your memory is mine', roughly. It's something you say to someone who is dying or leaving, so they'll know they won't be forgotten."

"Who is Nolan, then?"

"He was…" Lorhen freed one of his hands from around the sword, lifting it to pinch the bridge of his nose. "A friend," he said finally. "A mortal."

"I didn't recognize the language."

Lorhen dropped his hand to look across the room again. "Neither did I," he said, with no particular humor. "What are you doing here?"

"I might ask you the same thing."

"I was meditating," Lorhen said dryly, "until you interrupted me."

"With a sword on your lap?"

Lorhen shrugged, unfolding himself from the cushion. "We live and die by the sword. Why not pray by it, too? You ask a lot of questions, Karem."

Karem smiled easily. "It's the best way to learn. Have you learned anything else about the immortality artifacts?"

"No." Half a dozen explanations and addendums leapt to mind, and Lorhen closed his mouth firmly on them. No need to let Karem know he'd actually been researching the artifacts. Better to let him think he'd dismissed the stories entirely.

Karem remained where he was, crouched over the cushion. "Have you looked?"

Lorhen showed half a smile, shaking his head. "No, again, I'm afraid. Maybe in twenty years when they're used to me."

"I want it now."

"Why?" Lorhen paused at the door, looking at the other Timeless. "Is someone dying, or are you anticipating a challenge you can't win without a crutch?"

Curious, Karem looked up. "Do you think they'd work for us?"

Lorhen shook his head. "Our immortality doesn't work that

way. What if it turned out to be catastrophic?" There had been no consequence for trying to stab himself, but he hadn't been engaged in battle with another Timeless. "I wonder if we would be repulsed by trying to use them in battle, like we are if we consider fighting on sacred ground."

Karem glanced around the temple. "What happens if we push through that repulsion, O Oldest Among Us? We're compelled to fight, too, but we don't suffer for not fighting."

Lorhen opened his hand as if releasing his knowledge. "I don't know. I've never tried. Good night, Karem." He stepped through the temple doors, letting them swing shut behind him, and walked until cresting a hill would take the temple out of his sight. There, he turned and looked back down the broad avenue he'd followed, gazing at the now-distant temple. He wondered, briefly, who Nolan had been; who *he* had been, to promise the dying mortal that he would be remembered. But whoever they had been were both lost to time. Lorhen shrugged the memories away, leaving the questions behind in the sanctuary of the Atlantean temple.

"What were you doing in the temple?"

Lorhen glanced down a side street, eyebrows elevated, to see Ghean's young friend, Ertros leaning against a wall. "What are you doing up this early?" he asked in return, then smiled. "Praying, I suppose. Something like it. Good morning, Ertros."

Ertros folded his arms across his chest suspiciously, squinting up at Lorhen. "Good morning," he said, without a great deal of courtesy. "My mother runs a tavern. I always start the fire just before dawn so the cooking can get done. Atlanteans," he accused, "don't pray in the middle of the night."

Lorhen lifted his eyebrows, crossing to lean against the alley wall opposite Ertros. "I'm not Atlantean," he pointed out. "Too tall and too pale, I think is what you said? Your mother must appreciate your help a great deal."

"So how come you're here, if you don't belong here?" the boy asked resentfully. "Coming from the outlands to marry Ghean. She should marry an Atlantean."

Lorhen slid down against the wall to make himself smaller than the boy. "I met her in Kemet," he said. "She went there to study how they were building the pyramids, and to see the Anapa monument."

Ertros nodded impatiently. "I know. I didn't want her to go away." He scowled at Lorhen. "What were you doing in Kemet?"

"Studying their language and the stories they have written down. I've been studying stories a long time. Ghean told me that you work in the library yourself."

Ertros straightened, clearly proud of himself. "They don't let most kids my age work there because they're not careful enough. I'm real careful."

Lorhen smiled. "You must be. Even I get nervous going through the old manuscripts. I suppose if you've been around them your whole life you're more confident with them."

The boy thawed visibly, almost smiling with pride. "If I keep doing well I'll be able to study the very oldest of the Atlantean histories when I'm grown up. I might even join a House, if I can." He glared at Lorhen suddenly. "I was gonna marry Ghean."

Lorhen half smiled. "She's almost eleven years older than you are, Ertros. You'll find someone closer to your own age, maybe someone who shares your love of history, too."

Ertros scowled again. "Maybe. That might be all right. Then I could tell our kids about Atlantis' history."

Lorhen grinned, nodding. "You've got a head start on Ghean and me. Ghean's studied architecture, not history, and me— well, I'm a newcomer to the island. I'm trying to find the oldest histories of Atlantis to read them now, but maybe outlanders don't get to read them. I can't find the very oldest. Y—"

"What," Ertros asked curiously, "like the Book of Atlantis?"

Lorhen broke off, blinking in surprise. "I've heard of that," he admitted, "but it doesn't seem to exist."

"I haven't seen it either," Ertros said, "but the kids say it's under the temple." He grinned. "We always look for it in the summer. A couple years ago I tried chopping a hole in the temple floor. I've never seen the priests so angry."

Lorhen laughed. "I can imagine." He glanced back up the street toward the temple, then at the horizon, greying with dawn. "Let me know if you ever find it," he said wryly. "Right now you'd better go start the hearth in your mother's tavern."

Ertros looked toward the horizon as well, nodded, then grinned again. "Maybe I should try chopping another hole in the middle of the night."

"The priests," Lorhen warned, "will be *very* angry."

Ertros laughed and headed down the street. "Not if they don't catch me!"

Lorhen laughed, stepping into the main street, looking back at the temple as the moonlight faded from it to leave it bleached colorless in the dull morning light, and wondering if there was really a room beneath it. Shaking his head, he turned away and made his way back up to the Hunter's House. Ghean sat up in bed, blinking at him through strands of hair that had escaped their containing braid. "Where have you been?"

"Setting old ghosts to rest," Lorhen murmured. "Or trying, at least. I didn't mean to wake you."

Ghean's smile was rueful. "I haven't been sleeping well. I wake up and wonder if it's the morning of the ceremony yet."

He chuckled. "Not for a few days."

Ghean pulled her knees up to her chest, wrapping her arms around them. "Mother says you've been studying about the House artifacts." Lorhen nodded and Ghean's expression turned wistful. "Do you suppose they might work? That I could live forever with you?"

A pang of guilt went through Lorhen. "You'll inherit the Hunter's cloak when your mother dies, Ghean. If it works, you'll find out then."

"I'll be old when she dies, gods keep her. I want to be young forever, like you are. I'm the last of my House, Lorhen, and we won't ever have children. I don't want my House to die out."

At a loss for words, Lorhen sat on the edge of the bed, wrapping his arm around Ghean's shoulders to pull her close to him. "Marry a mortal, then," he said softly. "There's no reason you can't have children, Ghean. That inability is mine." At least until her first death, if it happened. There was no kindness in being able to bear or sire children, when happenstance might mean living centuries beyond them.

"Is it so easy for you?" she asked hoarsely. "To suggest I leave you, that I give up our life together? Our future, however brief it may seem, to you?"

"No." Lorhen bent his head over hers. "No, it's not. I'm a selfish old man, Ghean, and I want to marry you. But there are things I can't give you, and a child is one of them. There are people for whom that is enough, more than enough, to break a marriage contract, and I'm not so selfish as to keep you for myself if bearing a child is one of your heart's true desires. As for the other..." He sighed and spoke into her hair. "The artifacts seem to work. I'm looking for the Crow's artifact. It's supposed to be a book, maybe one that explains how to make the other talismans. It was apparently lost a long time ago." He felt, more than heard, the little sigh of relief that indicated she believed he was not abandoning her to old age. Guilt filtered through him again, and he fell silent, unwilling to betray her secret to her. Muffled against him, she spoke, and he leaned back to hear her better.

"It's supposed to be under the temple," she said. "At least, that's where we always looked for it when we were little. We would stage great hunts every year. There's nothing under there, though, no way to get under it. So we would usually get chased off." She laughed quietly. "The older children tell the younger ones, and it goes down through the years. Nobody's ever found anything under it, though. The temple's the oldest building in Atlantis, and the floor is solid stone."

"I ran into Ertros while I was out, and that's what he said, too. Why didn't any of the scholars tell me that?"

"Because it's a children's story, I suppose. I'm sure that some of them went looking once they reached adulthood and didn't have to hide from the priests anymore. There's nothing there. Everyone would know, if there were."

"Would they?" Lorhen asked. "If someone found the Book of Atlantis under the temple, would they tell everyone? Or anyone? It's supposed to be the city's greatest treasure. Why risk it?"

Ghean's voice became offended. "It is the greatest treasure. Atlanteans aren't brigands or thieves. It would be safe."

"Maybe. But more likely someone would get drunk and mention it to an outsider, and the island would be overrun by armies of men searching for the gift of immortality."

"The gods would protect us," Ghean said confidently. "They have always protected us from outlanders. At any rate, there's no room under the temple. Nobody can hide something so well that thirty generations of children couldn't find it."

Lorhen laughed. "All right. You have a point there."

Ghean looked out the window, considering the rose-colored sky, and then glanced sidelong at Lorhen. "I don't suppose my husband could be persuaded to come to bed for a few hours. I know I'm not as stimulating as intellectual pursuits, but I do try."

Lorhen struggled to keep his voice solemn. "I could use a few hours' sleep," he agreed, and laughed aloud when Ghean caught him in the face with a pillow.

18

Even mortals could go a night without sleep. The Timeless could manage for days, even weeks, without real rest; certainly a single sleepless night wasn't enough to keep Lorhen from being able to coax Ragar into confessing all he knew about the room beneath the temple. He started by plying the other scholar with coffee, not to sharpen his wits but to lull him into complacency, then, as Ragar argued some fine point of history, Lorhen, lazily, said, "How do you get into the room beneath the temple?"

He looked up as he asked the question, watching Ragar's reaction. It was a calculated gambit, one that paid off. Ragar paled, eyes widening as he opened his mouth, on the verge of asking how Lorhen had learned of it. Within a fraction of a second he regained control over his expression, shock panning away to mild perplexity. "What room? The temple is set into the bedrock."

"So Ghean said." Lorhen stood, coming around the table the duo shared to lean on it, studying Ragar from above. "It must have been difficult to carve out, then."

The mortal scholar returned Lorhen's gaze with convincing confusion. "I have no idea what you're talking about, Lorhen."

Lorhen sighed, straightening away from the table to pace

the room with long, idle steps. "You're a very good liar, Ragar, but I'm an even better truth-reader. My guess is that there's a tunnel, probably leading from the Crow's House, probably very deep in the stone, that leads directly to the room. A maze would be more clever, but it would also be a great deal more work, and most people who don't keep slaves tend to be a little more straightforward when it comes to hard labor. Of course, I'm assuming the histories haven't been adapted, and that Atlantis was never a civilization built on the backs of slaves."

"We are the favored of the gods," Ragar said stiffly. "We have no need to enslave other races."

"Ah." Lorhen nodded. "So the tunnel *was* dug by Atlanteans."

"I don't know what you're talking about," Ragar repeated, only narrowly keeping from snapping the words out.

"The stone is soft enough to carve," Lorhen continued thoughtfully. "The small altar in the temple has only the shallow blood bowl, but the larger one outside seems to have a room for pooling blood beneath it. I presume it drains into the waste crevasses that Ghean told me about. How long do you think it would take to break into the other room, if I went into the blood room and started chiseling my way toward the temple?" He reached the far side of the room and began circling back the other way, watching Ragar. "The tunnel probably leads from the Crow," he repeated, "from a room hidden underground itself; the architects of Atlantis are too astute to fail to notice an extra wall or wing on the outside of the house that wasn't available from the inside."

Ragar frowned. Lorhen smiled in response, ticking off his suppositions on his fingers as he continued. "It must have been built at very nearly the same time Atlantis was, I'd think. The room constructed, the temple built on top of it, the tunnel dug and the Book of Atlantis stashed there, safe from prying eyes. Perhaps not even the head of the House knew where it went, so when someone got around to asking, maybe generations later, it really had disappeared. Only a handful of scholars still knew where it was."

Ragar's frown grew deeper. "Where did you come up with these ideas?"

"The priests are going to be very unhappy when I go into their blood room and start chopping a hole under their temple," Lorhen said, almost enjoying himself. "I think Ertros might help me. He seemed enthusiastic about the prospect."

Ragar's eyebrows shot up. "Ertros told you about th—" He broke off, eyes closing at his self-betrayal. "Ertros told you there was a room under the temple?" he asked, much more mildly.

"Ertros told me a children's story about a room under the temple. You just confirmed it. How much of it did I have right?"

Ragar sighed. "I'm going to have to invite that boy into the Bull's House," he muttered. "He's too clever by half."

"He really was talking about chopping a hole in the temple floor," Lorhen warned. "I saw him the other night when I was leaving the temple and the thought struck him to try it in the middle of the night when no priests were around."

"He tried two years ago," Ragar said dryly. "At midday. If he weren't a commoner he'd have found the tunnel by the time he was nine. It's harder to get into the House grounds if you're not a member of one of the Houses."

Lorhen smiled. "Ghean said it was impossible to hide something from thirty generations of children. I realized she was right. Some of the more enterprising children had to have found the tunnel's entrance. Were you one of them?"

Ragar's expression was caught between defeat and the remains of a childhood pride. "I was," he allowed. "There are a few in every generation who do. They're almost all brought into the circle who know and protect the truth, and they virtually all become scholars."

Lorhen's eyes narrowed. "Almost all? What about the ones who aren't?"

"There are always one or two who aren't suited for the task of protecting the Book. Gods, man," Ragar said, staring at the dark look clouding Lorhen's face. "What do you think we do, drown them? They're given a drink that makes them susceptible to believing what they're told. We give them a story about a dead-end tunnel outside the city, and encourage them not to talk about it. They rarely do."

Lorhen relaxed a bit, nodding. "What about the ones who do?"

Ragar shrugged. "There's a dead-end tunnel outside the city." A smile tugged at the corner of his mouth. "How prosaic, hm? It's maintained so it won't be dangerous. They lose interest."

Lorhen brushed the explanation aside, satisfied that the refined Atlantean culture wasn't hiding a barbaric underside. "I want to see the Book, Ragar."

The other man shook his head almost violently. "No one outside of Atlantis has ever read it. They would never let you near it."

"I'm not interested in what 'they' would do. Apprentice me, adopt me into your House; I don't care." The germ of an idea finally focused in Lorhen's mind, the real reason the hidden book was of such interest to him: if it really had the secrets of immortality in its pages, then perhaps the Timeless themselves were explained. Minyah had claimed Atlantis was older than Lorhen; maybe somewhere in the island city's past, those who had held the power to create the artifacts had also crossed paths with the first of the Timeless. Lorhen looked up, eyes intent on Ragar. "Ragar, please. This is very important to me, for reasons I can't explain."

Ragar studied Lorhen shrewdly. "Can't, or won't?" Dismissing the question as he asked it, he added, "It was written in the earliest days of Atlantis, Lorhen. Even I find the language difficult at times, and I've spent my entire life studying it. You wouldn't be able to read it."

Lorhen lowered his eyes, then looked up. "I'll be able to read it," he said with soft confidence. "Just get me to it."

Ragar took on the almost quivering stillness of an animal being hunted. He said nothing, completely absorbed by his examination of Lorhen, as if another moment's study would produce a flash of insight that would explain him. Seconds stretched into a full minute before he broke the pose. "If I do this for you," he said slowly, "you will tell me what it is that you're hiding."

"I'd risk my life by doing that, Ragar."

"I risk mine by smuggling you in to see the Book!" Ragar snapped. "Is it a bargain, Lorhen?"

Lorhen fell silent, once more regarding his companion. In time he inclined his head. "It is a bargain, Ragar. The Book, and then my story. How do we do this?"

As it turned out, the entrance beneath the Crow's House garden was left unguarded, simply to avoid broadcasting the fact there was something worthy of guarding. A significant portion of the afternoon was spent waiting for the head of the household to make his daily journey down into the city. When finally he did, Lorhen and Ragar took the hill up to the House and requested an audience with its lord. His wife apologetically explained his absence, and escorted them out through the garden, glad of the chance to show off the wild flower arrangements. Ragar propped the garden's outermost door open while Lorhen admired the foliage, and they left with promises to visit again soon.

No doubt the mistress of the House didn't expect them to return within the hour, slipping in through the propped-open outer door. Lorhen took the rock away, letting the door close, and followed Ragar through twisting paths to a dead-end wall. Ragar pushed aside a fall of branches to reveal a divot in the wall that could easily have been no more than a flaw in the stone, and with swift confidence employed lock-picking tools that, after a moment's work, caused the dead-end wall to sigh as it popped open. Ragar put his shoulder against it, shoving lightly, and it swung inward, leaving Lorhen studying the width of the walls all around with some curiosity.

"Come on," Ragar hissed, and disappeared down a ladder built into the wall, barely two feet from the door.

Lorhen followed, swinging the door shut again with a faint grating of stone. "I hope that opens again from down here."

"It does," Ragar said. "There's even a remarkably clever device which uses mirrors and allows you to check the surrounding area to be certain no one is there when you come out again."

"Good idea," Lorhen said. "Was it installed before or after someone got caught?"

Ragar struck up a light, lifting it to show off a broad grin. "After. They say there were rather more recruits than usual that year. Someone came out in the middle of a birthday party."

Lorhen laughed. "Poor planning, that." He glanced around. The room they stood in was barely large enough to deserve the name, bleeding into the tunnel only a few feet away. "Tell me, where does a scholar learn the knack of lock-picking?"

Ragar cleared his throat, and turned down the tunnel. Lorhen ducked after him, realizing in dismay that the only reason he'd had head room was to permit the ladder that reached back up to the garden. He rubbed his neck in anticipation of stiff muscles as Ragar said, "There are half a dozen rooms in the library that you can't get into unless you employ somewhat circumspect methods. I learned how to pick locks when I was about twelve." He was silent a while, concentrating on the steep downward slope before the ground leveled out and he followed a sharp twist in the stone. "It's come in surprisingly handy over my life, actually. Not in the least for sneaking in the Crow's back door. Be glad I can. It's an easier way to access the Book than trying to ask permission."

"Are we likely to be caught?"

Ragar shook his head, following another bend. "No. The Book is left alone most of the time. It's fragile. We copy parts we want to study and use the copies down in the room."

"Why not copy the whole thing?"

"Half of it is unintelligible. Besides, the gods told us it needed to be protected. Making copies to distribute isn't a good way to protect something."

"Unless disaster should happen to strike and you should lose the original," Lorhen said.

Ragar stopped abruptly and turned around to stare at him. "Must you point out glaring follies in our logic?"

"Sorry."

Ragar snorted and turned again, following yet another sharp curve.

"This was dug this way on purpose?" Lorhen asked.

"Oh no," Ragar said, lifting the light close to the wall, allowing a reflection. "The first section, the sharp downhill, had been carved out when someone broke through to a chute in the stone. They followed it to its end, or as close to it as they could. It comes out under water, not far from the harbor. After enough surveying, they determined it passed within meters of the temple." He gestured with the little lantern, making light bounce off the walls. "See how smooth the walls are? My teacher thought there had been a river through here once. If you follow it the other way, it comes out in a deep basin outside the city."

"Where the blocked-off tunnel is?" Lorhen guessed.

"Indeed." Ragar continued down the passageway. "There's more than fifty feet of solid packed rock between that blockaded end and open tunnel." He swung the lantern forward, indicating the far end of the tunnel. "They didn't want to risk water damage to the Book, so the other end has also been blocked off. It's one of the things initiates do, repacking and re-filling the stone that's worn or shaken down. Every time there's a major earthquake, someone goes tearing down to check on it. So far, though, nothing has budged the stones we've set in."

"Earthquakes?" Lorhen asked. "Are there a lot of those?"

Ragar nodded, unconcerned. "I'm surprised you haven't felt one. There's usually one or two every moon that are strong enough to feel, but nothing damaging. You get used to it. We don't think much of them."

Lorhen laughed. "I'll try to adopt that cavalier attitude, Ragar. It may take some time."

"There are no earthquakes where you come from?"

Good question. "No, though I've felt them a few times in my travels. Disconcerting, to have the earth shift under your feet."

Ragar laughed, about to respond, but pulled up as the men rounded yet another corner and faced a dead end. Lorhen frowned at it curiously. "Either that's a door or your initiates have been a little too thorough."

"The former." Ragar chuckled, lowering the lantern to inspect a small crevasse in the stone. Two faint clicks sounded as he poked his finger into the niche. The wall swung back silently. "The Book," Ragar said dryly, and gestured Lorhen into the room.

"You first. I insist." Though Lorhen kept his tone light, Ragar glanced at him sharply before stepping through the doorway into the room beneath the temple.

It was only slightly smaller than the temple itself. To Lorhen's relief, it was also carved a smidge higher than the tunnel had been. He straightened, rubbing his neck as he looked around. The top of his head barely missed the ceiling; had his hair been cut short, the ceiling would have bent it.

Ragar circled the room, lighting torches spaced evenly every few feet. A longish table dominated the room, half a dozen chairs scattered around it. The door directly behind Lorhen appeared to be the only exit or entrance. Lorhen squinted at the walls as he followed Ragar around. "You said the initiates worked to fill the tunnel from the other side. I don't see another door."

"You wouldn't see that one if it were closed behind you," Ragar said, completing his circuit. "But there's only the one door into this room. This is all hand carved. We left the river chute a few minutes ago. The other door you're looking for was built between the natural tunnel and the one we created, back where we turned the last time. It's beyond there that they add to the blockade."

"Ah." Lorhen came to a stop in front of the door again, beside Ragar. "I don't mean to be difficult," he said after a moment, "but there are no books in here."

Ragar crossed the room again, locating a chisel in the stone, completely indistinguishable from any other to Lorhen's eyes. The same double-click the door had made sounded, and a wide slab of rock detached itself from the surrounding stone. The scholar lifted another slab out from within it, and set the second on the table, pressing his fingertips against seven different points, in rapid succession. A hairline crack appeared in the box, and he slid the two halves apart.

"Minyah has a box like that," Lorhen said with fascination. "How do they do that?"

"I have no idea. I don't make them." With delicate precision, Ragar lifted a tome from the black stone box. The outside covers were a warm dark wood filled with thin sheets of paper held in place by long leather thongs. The cover was carved with the circle that symbolized the Houses of Atlantis, studs rising from the depressed wood. Within was the triangular star pattern, overlaid with an artist's rendering of a sharp-beaked crow, its wings spread: the symbol of that House. Excluding the covers, the book was nearly five inches thick, by far the largest volume of any sort Lorhen had ever seen. "Gods of earth and heaven," he murmured, reaching a tentative hand toward the book. "It's beautiful."

Ragar set it on the table, holding it in place by way of his fingertips, barely touching the wooden cover. "If you damage it," he said levelly, and Lorhen looked up.

"I won't," he said swiftly, before Ragar had time to complete the threat. "I would sooner die." While the statement was wildly untrue, it soothed Ragar, who lifted his hands to nudge the volume toward Lorhen.

"I would suggest you read and absorb quickly. In time, you may be accepted into the circle of protectorates, but until then, this will be your sole opportunity to study it."

Lorhen was already pulling a chair up, a long leg stretched out to hook the nearest and drag it across the floor. Judging it close enough without looking, he sat down on the very edge, nearly sliding off. Impatiently, he hitched it forward, and carefully drew the book across the table to open it.

Neat handwriting lettered across the page, ancestor to the texts he had already studied. For a moment Lorhen simply examined the scripting, then looked at Ragar. "Atlantis developed a written language like this originally? Not pictography first?"

Ragar settled down in another chair, pulling out a bundle of papers from a bag he'd carried down with him. "Our gods gave us our written language. It's evolved since then, but that's the oldest example we have. When they gave us the Book, they gave us writing. It's over a thousand years old."

Lorhen looked down at the book, hardly breathing. "More than a thousand years?" he asked, all too aware that his wonder would be interpreted as awe of being in the presence of something of such great age. It was partly true, but the hope that the Timeless might be explained in the thin pages struck a deeper chord in him.

"It tells its own history," Ragar said. "Read."

They tell us we are gods, the text began, *and it is somehow easier to not argue.*

> *They tell us we are gods. We are not; we are only men and women. Our godhood lies in an immortality we didn't ask for, and in the knowledge gained over years of study.*

*My name is Lonan. I no longer remember how long I have
been alive. The thirteenth generation of Atlantis is growing
up around me now, and my family and I have been on this
island thousands of years. We came here to avoid the war that
is the way of life beyond Atlantis. Our kind, we Timeless,
fight compulsively, surviving one day to the next by killing
our brothers. We 'gods', my brothers and sisters and I, turned
our back on that path a long time ago, to use our immortality
to better ends. We came to Atlantis, and we have studied here
for uncounted centuries, learning to harness the power within
us, to shape it and to imbue objects with its magic. Even of
those of us who have retreated here, only a few can manipulate
the Blending in this way; there is something in those few, a
creativity or a spark of some kind, that runs deeper than it does
in the rest of us.*

*A thousand years ago, we began to feel weary. It may
be that without constant battle, without the influx of energy
from the Blending, that we pall; it makes little difference. We
formed a plan, to build a civilization here of a people whose
lives were dictated by scholarship, not war. We were never
completely alone on the island; dozens of small fishing villages
litter the coast. We went among them and chose the wisest, the
brightest, the most intuitive of them, and brought them to this
valley in the mountains.*

*We taught them as best we could. After so long apart from
mortals, it came as a shock to us, their brief lifespans. Still,
they were eager to learn, and we taught them. With them we
built the city of Atlantis, and we built the Houses in the hills,
and named them for the constellations in the sky. The symbol of
Atlantis became a circle, never-ending, with points to repre-
sent the Houses. Each House took its sky-sign and rendered it
within the circle, and those signed Houses made the govern-
ment of the city and the island.*

None of this happened quickly. In each new generation,

more people came to the city, and in each generation some of those newcomers joined Houses, to keep fresh blood and fresh ideas circulating. The building, the studying, the creation of a new way of life took hundreds of years, and through it all we guided them.

I suppose it's no wonder they call us gods. We didn't age and we didn't change, mentors to every generation. When they read this book we'll be gone, and I do not know if they will still call us gods. I cannot explain where we came from, any more than they can, and I wonder if it is not easier to simply call us gods, and forget the rest.

Some four hundred years ago there seemed a stabilization, a sudden cohesiveness that had not been there before. Atlantis had reached adulthood, and no longer needed our supervision so much.

Most of our time since then has been spent writing this book, and creating gifts for the Houses. This book, the greatest of the gifts, will go to the Crow, first of the Houses. In it are notes on everything we have learned about science, about the body, and about engineering, in our centuries of study. We have chosen to not write out our learnings in detail for the Houses; mortal man is a violent and vicious creature, and I fear what might happen if we were to offer them our studies wholesale. Instead there are pointers, enough detail to set them on the right path. They will learn, over the years, how to create the things we have left outlines of, in so far as it is possible to do what we have done, without the Blending. Perhaps it won't be possible at all, but I will not be here to see that.

When they reach the point of being able to understand what we offer—assuming that they do—the other gifts may be useful as examples. The horned horses have a panacea in the horn; it's a compound that can be rediscovered with the right knowledge. The cup is of the same material, though it takes specific liquids to trigger the panacea's properties. Half a dozen *of the gifts—all of them that are meant to be worn or carried, including the crystal—prevent the ravages of age and afford a degree of physical protection. The larger the item, the more effective it is in the second half of this; it was a side effect, not our primary goal. If Atlantis reaches the level of technology to be able to replicate the gifts, they should be able to use the ones we left as guidelines.*

My brothers and sisters and I are tired of our long lives. We left the world behind so long ago that I wonder if there are even any more like us still beyond Atlantis. Since we have had no Timeless visitors in many centuries, we think it is likely we are the last.

If that's so, it is time for the last battles, and that, perhaps, explains our weariness. The book is finished, and we've decided who will be the last of us, the one to carry the full power of the Blending, into the future. I will not be that one, and I think in the end I am grateful for that. I've journeyed in this world a very long time, and have helped to create a legacy in Atlantis that should stand through time. It is enough.

Lorhen stared at the last paragraph a long time, rarely blinking. "But it didn't end," he finally whispered. "We're still here."

"Eh?" Ragar looked up from his papers. "What?"

Lorhen lifted his head slowly. "You've read the introduction? Written by Lonan, about how they were not gods at all?"

Ragar smiled. "What else would you call them? They lived thousands of years."

Lorhen shook his head. "What happened?" he asked. "When the gods decided it was time to leave you, what happened?"

"There was a lightning storm," Ragar replied. "Legend tells us that it fell from the sky for hours, and when it finally ceased, the gods were gone and the city was bleached white." He gestured at the book. "The Book actually tells us where the white stone was mined to build the city, centuries ago, but Methuselah swore to the truth of the lightning storm. He was a child then, maybe the last of us to speak with the gods."

Lorhen closed his eyes. "Did he keep any records? Any written stories of what he saw then?"

Ragar frowned thoughtfully. "Not that I've ever seen, but I've never looked for them. There aren't any in the library, certainly. You could ask someone in the Scorpion. That was his House. If there are any papers, they might have them stored away somewhere. Why?"

Lorhen looked back down at the brief history. "Do you believe they lived as long as they did?"

"All of our histories, all of the old tales, agree they did. I know Methuselah lived hundreds of years himself, with the crystal they gave him. I think it's not impossible. What," Ragar smiled, "you want to live forever?"

Lorhen glanced up again. "Don't we all?"

The other scholar smiled again. "Methuselah said he was tired of living, when he gave his stone to Noah. He said mortal man was not meant to live nine hundred years."

Mortal men, perhaps. Voice soft, Lorhen said, "I can't imagine tiring of living."

Ragar laughed. "You're young, Lorhen. Thirty years, perhaps? I've seen more than fifty, a good long life, and there are days when I think I'm ready to lay down this body and join the gods on their mountaintops."

Lorhen lowered his eyes to hide a smile, and turned the next page of the book. The immortal who'd written the introduction had meant what he said: the notes on the fine paper were cryptic, sketches and brief explanations enough to give a hint of the destination, but not enough to see the path clearly. The stories he hoped for were not there. Instead, there were pages detailing the building of ships, of pyramids; the arts of smithery and warfare, medical practices and plumbing. Beyond that the material grew increasingly incomprehensible, discussing the building blocks of life, too small to be seen, and snakes wound through all bodies, determining their make up. Lorhen's head began to hurt, but there were glimpses, here and there, that he almost understood; at the very least, it was clear the Blending could be used for far more than he, or any other Timeless since the ancient Atlanteans, had imagined. Finally he looked up at Ragar, clearing his throat to speak for the first time in hours. "How much of this can you understand?"

Ragar glanced at where Lorhen had the book open to, and shook his head. "Turn back about thirty pages. The first third or so we've been able to follow. It's concrete material, building and surgery, things we can figure out. There's a jump, after the section on surgery, though. It goes into topics we can't even begin to understand, things that seem to have to do with the body, but we're not sure what." He shook his head again. "Eventually we'll get there. The gods didn't want us to have the knowledge until we were ready to figure it out on our own, with only a few hints. I'm not sure how much of the information is theoretical and how much is actually tested."

Lorhen sighed, carefully closing the book. "It's humbling, isn't it? Being presented with so much information we can't fathom."

Ragar nodded, smiling wryly, and tucked his papers away before lifting the Book and replacing it in its black stone box. Sliding it back home into the wall, he asked, "Did you find what you were looking for?"

Lorhen shook his head. "No. I should have expected as much, I suppose. I only ended up with more questions."

"That's the way of things," Ragar agreed philosophically. "Come. It's a long walk back, and you have a story to tell me."

19

Lorhen left Ragar at the foot of the mountains, the mortal scholar making his way back into the city to digest the tale he'd been told. Lorhen watched him go, then, a little weary, made his way up the hillside to the Hunter's House.

He'd had no intention of telling Ragar the truth, until he read the story written by Lonan. *They weren't gods,* he'd chosen to say, in the end. *They weren't gods, and neither am I.* They just had an extraordinary number of years to study in. Almost anyone could discover impossible secrets, given thousands of years of undisturbed study.

And one of them, it seemed, had been chosen to Blend all the others, and go forward. He or she might still be alive, but without so much as a name, Lorhen couldn't imagine how he might find the sole survivor. Perhaps he could see if the Scorpion's House had any of Methuselah's records, assuming the long-lived mortal had kept any.

Minyah greeted him at the door to the house, an amused glint in her eyes. "Ghean has been looking for you," she warned. "Two days until the wedding, and her betrothed nowhere to be found. She has gone down to the city to find you."

Lorhen groaned softly, running his hand back through his hair and loosening the tie that bound it at the nape of his neck.

"I haven't missed anything of importance, have I? No unexpected rituals that the ceremony can't be completed without?"

"No," Minyah said, "but she will want a magnificent apology. You may wish to begin thinking about it."

Lorhen glanced over his shoulder, back down the hill he'd just climbed. "Have you had the evening meal? Maybe we could share dinner and look for her together."

Minyah smiled. "I would enjoy that, but if you think my presence will curb Ghean's tongue, I believe you will be greatly disappointed."

Lorhen offered his arm gallantly. "I can only hope. Meanwhile, I'll practice my apology on you."

Minyah laughed. "A moment." She retreated through the door, re-emerging a few seconds later with a neatly woven satchel slung over her shoulder. A glance inside showed Lorhen a bundle of parchment, bound together at the top of the bag.

"You anticipate my company to be so dull that you bring papers along with you?" he teased as she slipped her arm through his.

"No. I intend to listen to your practiced apologies, and write down the parts that you should keep. Did you find the Book?"

Lorhen blinked. "Am I that transparent? Does Ghean know I went looking for it?"

"Ghean," Minyah said placidly, "is not as much a study of human nature as I. At worst she thinks you are, hm. Engaging in activities only a bachelor might be permitted to do, for the last time. At best, and knowing Ghean, this is probably her thought, she thinks that you are out searching for the perfect gift for the ceremony."

"Oh dear," Lorhen murmured. "And what might the perfect gift be? I only have two days to find it."

"Something symbolic of the House, perhaps. She is very proud to be the last daughter of the Hunter."

"Most of the Houses seem larger," Lorhen said after a moment. "Why is the Hunter so small?"

"We adopted too little new blood," Minyah replied frankly. "Too caught up in our own explorations and studies, I suppose, and perhaps a little surprised to only have one or two children in a generation. I imagined Ghean might be the mother of a large brood, although truthfully I cannot imagine why. And now suddenly we are all but gone. It is the way of the world, that nothing carries on forever." She glanced up at Lorhen and amended, "Almost nothing."

"Not even the Timeless go on forever." The conversation died away as they entered the busy town market. Lorhen peered over heads in search of Ghean, finally chuckling at himself. "She's so small that there could be a single person between us and I wouldn't be able to see her." Only sense her, he thought. Ghean's potential Awakening didn't have the radius of a full Timeless' warning circle, but if they passed by each other, the peculiar tingle would alert him to her presence.

"I would suggest we try the Bull's Tavern, then," Minyah said, turning down a side alley. "It is her favorite place to eat. She and Aroz often go there."

"You couldn't have said that in the first place?" Lorhen demanded, half dancing around the crowd to regain Minyah's side.

She smiled. "I could have, but I would have missed you bobbing around the people like a tall seabird. I deemed the spectacle worthy of a short delay."

Lorhen couldn't stop the laugh that spilled out. "I see where Ghean got her sense of humor."

Minyah inclined her head with a modest smile, then, without warning, stepped to the left, disappearing into a suddenly coalescing group. Lorhen blinked down at the sea of dark hair, recognizing Minyah several seconds later by her satchel. Weaving through the throng a second time to catch up with her, he said, "That's twice you've abandoned me. Am I to take this as a repri—"

Nausea swept over him, a quick rush that left him chilled. Lorhen straightened, momentarily blessing the height that allowed him to scan the mass of people with an easy glance. Karem's head, light among the darkness, moved off to the right toward a table, without looking to see what Timeless approached. Lorhen looked ahead, following Karem's path to its end, and touched Minyah's shoulder. "I've found Ghean. This way."

They circled toward Ghean's table, Minyah using the satchel to swat someone out of the way, and looking wide-eyed with indignation when he frowned down at her. Lorhen laughed as the fellow looked startled, then, with an apologetic and sheepish grin, stepped out of the way. Minyah's eyes danced as she glanced at Lorhen. "The trick," she said, "is making them think it was somehow their fault."

"I think women have been doing that since the dawn of time." Lorhen guided Minyah to a halt at Ghean's table. Hidden in what amounted to a corner of the open tavern, she sat across from both Aroz and Karem, the latter just settling down with three mugs of the sweet ale that the Atlanteans drank almost as much as they did coffee. "I see you're able to entertain yourself in my absence, beloved Ghean."

Ghean came to her feet in surprise, hugging him and stealing a kiss. "There you are! Have you met Karem? And Mother! We've been talking about history. You'll be a great help. Lorhen, Karem is as interested in the House artifacts as you are. Perhaps you should pool your resources and try to find the Book together."

Lorhen struggled to keep dismay off his face. "Perhaps," he agreed, "though Karem claimed to be no scholar, and thus without hope for studying the artifacts. We've met," he added, and inclined his head to Karem in greeting.

"Ghean tells me you've been staying up late reading about

the artifacts," Karem said, words belying the glint of steel in his eyes. "Not holding out on me, old man, are you?"

"What ever would I do that for?" Lorhen asked dryly, swinging a long leg over the bench to sit. "I haven't found anything useful at all."

"You spent half the day missing and found nothing useful?" Karem's skepticism colored his tone, now.

Lorhen arched his eyebrows. "Telling your woes to strangers? The unbearable trauma of a missing betrothed?"

"He's not a stranger." Ghean sat on one side of Lorhen as Minyah took the other. "He's a friend of Aroz's, and Aroz is family." She smiled across the table at the dark man, whose face went bleak.

"Perhaps I should get the newcomers something to drink," he offered, standing. "Minyah?"

"A cup of coffee, please. Lorhen?"

Lorhen, all too aware of how little Aroz desired to bring him anything, hesitated. It had been hours since he'd had anything to eat or drink. "Ale, please," he said after a moment. Aroz, barely refraining from a scowl, nodded and made his way across the busy tavern.

Karem studied the three across from him with open interest. Ghean all but vibrated with life, chattering merrily back and forth with Lorhen and her mother. She was lovely, dark eyes large and long hair swishing over her shoulders as it framed her animated face. Energy poured out of her; the effect was childlike, compounded by her small size and easy trust. He let a smile crease his face and answered a question absently as he watched the young woman.

Even more than the enthusiasm for life that radiated from her, the power of her potential Awakening enthralled Karem. He had met very few women Timeless, and those he had met were vastly different from this woman. They had certainly been bigger. Karem doubted the little Atlantean's ability to wield sword or ax well enough to defend herself against a larger opponent, even with the best of teachers.

Which Lorhen would no doubt be. Karem's eyes narrowed as he turned his regard to the Timeless who had claimed the title of oldest. He looked the part of a scholar, paler than Karem himself and with the long black hair tied in a tail at the base of his neck. An unpleasant grin slid over Karem's features as he considered the exposed neck. So very polite of him to get his hair out of the way for a clean blow, once the heartstrike was made. With the Blended power of a thousand years in him, Karem would hardly need any of the Atlantean artifacts to ensure his own eternal survival.

But the chances of obtaining any of those trinkets—especially the legendary Book—seemed slim, without Lorhen's help. The ancient Timeless had been accepted into Atlantean society in a way Karem had yet to achieve, although the other woman sitting across from him presented an intriguing possibility.

Minyah was more delicate than her daughter, with high cheekbones and a small pointed chin. Torchlight lent a hint of red to her hair, clasped away from her face in curls by a golden headband. She disputed the theories that were put forth about the Book with easy logic, apparently unaware of Karem's eyes on her.

He very much doubted that was the case. Karem suspected she was entirely aware that he watched her, perhaps even flattered by it. She would be far more useful than Lorhen, being long accepted in the halls of Atlantean scholarship. Karem knew from Aroz that Minyah was a widow of more than a decade, and after the shock of Aroz's death—he would have to arrange for it to seem Lorhen had killed him—Minyah would no doubt require comforting. If he couldn't make a grieving mortal desire him, he would be embarrassed to look at his own face in a mirror.

Ghean he would take for himself after Minyah died of old age. It wasn't that he particularly wanted her, although she was pretty enough. It was that Lorhen and Aroz wanted her. The anticipation of their deaths was sweetened that much more by the knowledge that he would possess what they had desired. It would be easy: Ghean would have only adoration for the man who led her beyond her mortal life, and Lorhen was not the man to do it. She'd make an entertaining little prize until it came time to take her head, though the longer he avoided that the more worthwhile the power of her Blending would be; it aged, like wine, gathering in strength.

But most of all, he wanted that Book and its secrets. Immortality was well and good, but any artifact that could offer a mortal endless centuries would surely be that much more effective in the hands of a Timeless. Gods were made of less, and he wanted to be one; why not, when he and his kind were so nearly gods already? Karem shook himself, returning his attention to the conversation. Eventually they would give in to his easy smiles and polite charm, and tell him what he wanted to know. It was only a matter of time, and time he had in abundance.

Aroz returned with the second tray of drinks, still scowling at everyone in general and Lorhen in particular. The Timeless scholar showed none of the respect due the women of the Hunter: he was too familiar with Minyah, arguing back and forth like old companions, equals in a longtime friendship. It was preposterous and insulting for a commoner, no matter his age, to presume such an air with a member of any House. As another commoner, it was not Aroz's place to encourage Minyah to reprimand the ancient Timeless for his audacity, so, bitterly, he held his tongue.

The way Lorhen treated Ghean was worse. Aroz handed the mugs out and regained his seat next to Karem, glowering across the table at Lorhen. A thousand years of living had not taught him how to appreciate Ghean's precious vitality. Lorhen seemed content to share her with the world, watching her actions with no attempt to rein her in. It was as though she was an exotic bird, trying her wings, and he the keeper, too reluctant to clip them. Unless he learned to contain her, Lorhen would lose her to another; lose her to Aroz, who would better keep that vibrancy safe. Aroz had kept Ghean safe her whole lifetime, watching her grow. Her entire life, he had waited patiently for her to grow into a woman, so that he could keep her safe for eternity. The memory of the pale outland scholar would fade.

He glanced Karem's way, over his mug of ale. Karem remained an enigma to Aroz, his single obsession seeming to be the possession of the artifacts. He spoke eagerly of the idea of 'children', those he envisioned handing immortality to as though it were a simple gift, no more than the exchange of words or smiles. There were certainly mortals who should live eternally, including the only one who sat at the table with him, and Aroz had no compunction against picking and choosing which ones should be granted the gift. Karem, though, appeared to have something larger in mind, a kingdom under his own rule, perhaps, and on that one topic, Aroz agreed with Lorhen: mortals, broadly speaking, would not take well to a Timeless king, and more, to anoint himself as such would draw Karem to the attention of other Timeless. Aroz knew the Atlantean artifacts worked, but in the end no magic cloak or crystal would stop a truly determined Timeless from taking Karem's head. It would come down to who was the better swordsman, who wanted most to live, and no artifact could change that. Aroz shrugged at his mug, and looked up to see Ghean smiling at him.

"Don't be such a sourpuss," she said, reaching across the table to touch his hand. "The ceremony is in two days. Won't you be happy for me, old friend? Is there not even one smile within you for me?"

Aroz dredged up a smile, tinged with regret. "I am happy for you, Ghean. I wish you all the joy of many days."

Ghean's answering smile was almost enough to make the lie worth telling, though beside her, Lorhen cast a crooked smile at the table, and Aroz knew that he, at least, wasn't fooled by the platitude. Ghean might never forgive him if he fought Lorhen again and won, but then, neither would she forgive Lorhen if he should take Aroz's own Blending. It would almost be worth it, and Aroz would take the opportunity, if it arose, to try for the heartstrike in combat with Lorhen again.

Too trusting and too kind to think such things herself, Ghean smiled at him. "Thank you, Aroz. That wasn't so bad, was it? You'll stand in place of my father, won't you? I'd like to have all of my family together for the ceremony, and you're a part of it."

Aroz's jaw clenched, but he could say nothing other than, "I would be honored, Ghean."

Ghean beamed, squeezing his hand again. "Thank you. Thank you so much, Aroz."

Aroz muttered, "Of course," and was grateful when Karem, as if blithely unaware, said, "Pleasantries aside, I wonder if I could impose on you, Minyah? Your expertise on the artifacts is clearly far greater than Lorhen's, and I would greatly enjoy learning what you know about them."

If Karem had intended a barb to land, it failed entirely: Lorhen nodded agreement. "You're right, Karem. She's far more likely to be able to determine the location of the Book, if it still exists, than I am. An entire lifetime in Atlantis, versus a few weeks." He shrugged, playfully rueful. "I'm outclassed."

"In that, you are entirely correct," Minyah said serenely, though the smile that shot across her face ruined the effect, and everyone, even Aroz, laughed. "I would be delighted to instruct you in what little I know, Karem. Perhaps Lorhen would like to join us, as he has finally confessed his interest in the artifacts as well?" She lifted an eyebrow at Lorhen curiously.

Lorhen opened his mouth to protest that it wasn't necessary, then stilled the words as he took in Minyah's expression. She was—not afraid; he didn't think Minyah was *afraid* of anyone. But wary. Wary of being alone with Karem. Lorhen couldn't blame her, and changed his sentence while still inhaling to speak it. "I'd be delighted," he admitted, adding a touch of chagrin at having been found out. "I'd no doubt have gotten further myself if I'd had the presence of mind to ask you, Minyah."

"No doubt. Men, however, often seem reluctant to ask the help of a woman." Minyah picked up her coffee mug and smiled over the brim of it at each of the men in turn. "I suspect it is due to the fear that they will confirm that women are far more intelligent than they are."

For a moment, Lorhen, Aroz and Karem became a monument to solidarity, properly offended on the behalf of all men. Ghean laughed, applauding her mother, and Minyah looked smugly pleased. "I trust you will remember that in the future," she said to Lorhen, who gave up his expression of mock offense to join the laughter.

"I'll try," he promised. "Meanwhile, I propose our study sessions don't begin until next week? The ceremony is in two days—"

"A day and a half, now," Ghean interjected.

"A day and a half," Lorhen corrected, smiling, "and most of us here are rather intimately involved with it." He shrugged at Karem. "A few days' delay won't make that much difference."

Karem frowned very slightly, glancing over the others at the table before shrugging. "I suppose not, at that," he agreed with well-feigned pleasantry. "Forgive my eagerness, Minyah. I've never been good at patience."

"Few of the young are," Minyah said in a tone so dry Lorhen shot a sideways glance at her. She arched an eyebrow back at him, elegantly. The corner of her mouth turned up, self-mocking, and she lifted a hand to gesture briefly at her own eyes. It is something in the eyes, she had said when she'd deduced Lorhen's secret; something, apparently, that she could discern in many Timeless. Lorhen sat back, mouth held in a tiny purse as he regarded Minyah.

She could be very, very dangerous to the Timeless, if she chose to be. He wondered how old they had to be, how many lifetimes they had to have lived, before she could see it in their eyes, or if it was the very first death that marked them with something visible to a discerning gaze. Lorhen turned his head to study Ghean, who smiled back up at him curiously.

Nothing but the tingle of potential Awakening marked her as Timeless. Her eyes were bright, full of life and excitement, untouched by the deaths he could see in the faces of his immortal counterparts across the table. Looking at Ghean, Lorhen wondered when those changes would settle into her face, invisible to all but those who knew how to look for them.

Karem was grinning apologetically, unaware his secret was betrayed to the Atlantean scholar sitting across from him. "Perhaps patience will come to me as I age," he agreed. Lorhen could hear the underlying tinge of amusement, so often injected into his own words. Sometimes it was the only way to maintain sanity, to pretend as if immortality and great age were a colossal joke, one only the Timeless were in on.

Except this time, Minyah was also in on it. She smiled, nodded, and said, "Perhaps," with such polite disbelief that Ghean blinked in surprise.

All trace of humor fell away from Karem's face. Coolly, he stood, looking down at Minyah. "And perhaps not," he agreed, acidly. "Maybe you're right. What a pity that would be for you." He turned and stalked away through the thinning crowd.

Lorhen watched him a moment before speaking to Minyah. "That may have been a mistake."

"I do not care to be laughed at," Minyah said irritably. "Particularly by children who think they are my better."

Aroz, voice slightly strangled, said, "He's more than four hundred years old, Minyah."

"And yet my statement stands," she snapped. "He is a child, eager for toys beyond his understanding, and I do not care to be mocked."

Ghean was staring after Karem in dismay. "He's one of you, too?" Her voice rose to a higher pitch. "Is everyone going to live forev—"

Lorhen elbowed Ghean in the stomach, wincing apologetically as he did so. Ghean's expression exploded into outrage. Aroz half lurched to his feet, snatching for his sword, Lorhen echoing the action.

Minyah's voice cracked out: "Stop this!"

Both men froze, eyes locked on each other across the table, hands comfortable on sword hilts, entirely ready to do battle. A circle of quiet washed out from their table, as other patrons turned to watch the commotion. Aroz, finally, snarled, "Later," and slammed his sword fully back into the sheath, regaining his seat.

"Later," Lorhen agreed. "Ghean, I'm sorry," he said as he sat down again. "You were becoming uncomfortably loud. I'm sorry," he repeated. "Are you all right?"

Ghean rubbed her stomach sullenly. "I'm fine. Is everyone going to live forever but me?" she demanded more quietly. "It's not fair."

Lorhen exchanged uneasy glances with Minyah. "Life has never been fair, Ghean," the woman said, "but I am quite certain I will not live forever. Perhaps you will be lucky and will be like them."

Ghean looked up at Lorhen, eyes pleading. "Will I?" she asked. "Could that happen?"

Lorhen closed his eyes, releasing a soft sigh, then looked at

Ghean. "I don't know. I don't know, Ghean. We don't make that decision." He looked over at Aroz, whose face was pinched, though he nodded his head in agreement after a few seconds. Lorhen sighed again, shaking his head, and repeated a third time, "I don't know."

20

How dare she! How dare an upstart of a mortal act as though she was superior to him! Karem stalked though the emptying streets with no heed for passers-by. Most prudently stepped out of his way ahead of time; a few of the less lucky were nearly bowled over as he plowed by with no regard.

Thwarted at every turn! Betrayed by Lorhen—what a gem Ghean was, open and trusting to a fault. It was a pity he hadn't had more time to talk with her alone. He'd have pried every movement Lorhen had made out of her within an hour or two.

Karem had to admit, the ancient Timeless was a good liar. After nearly half a millennium, he wouldn't have imagined anyone could lie to him so successfully, yet he'd genuinely believed that Lorhen had spent no time fussing with the artifacts.

Maybe it was the temple's aura, blinding him to the truth. The thought almost made him laugh, and he slowed his angry rush forward somewhat. No, the truth was that Lorhen was an astonishingly good liar, and Karem arrogant enough to believe he couldn't be lied to. He should have known better. Next time, he would. In the meantime, no irreversible damage had been done. Whatever Lorhen had found out, if anything, Karem would learn from Minyah.

His expression darkened again, thinking of the scholar. She

couldn't possibly know the truth about him, and yet she had targeted her barbs so well. No: it was merely the arrogance of physical maturity that had given Minyah her certainty. She appeared fifteen years older than he. There was no reason for her to believe anything else. That she didn't trust him was quite obvious, but he didn't need her trust. He needed her knowledge, and to gain that, fear was as effective a tool as trust.

Two days, until after the wedding. Karem twisted his mouth as he slowed again, walking by the temple. He could afford a few days.

Just after midnight, Lorhen jerked upright, hand closing on the covers in search of a sword that wasn't there. Ghean pushed herself up on her elbows, blinking in alarm. "What is it?"

Lorhen swung out of bed, shaking his hair back over his shoulders. "A nightmare," he answered. "Go back to sleep. I'm going to get a drink of water. I'll be back soon."

Ghean nodded, eyes already closed again as her head dropped into the pillow. Lorhen watched her for a brief moment, bending to brush the back of his hand across the air above her cheekbone. "I love you," he whispered, and picked up the sword by the bed to go out and meet the Timeless who waited for him.

The moon had faded to a sliver, its light reflecting poorly from the garden walls and making monsters of trees and shadows. Lorhen walked the path cautiously, flat sandals offering little purchase and causing the gravel stones to shift slightly under his weight. Each movement cracked like a ricochet to Lorhen's ears, forcing him to abandon any pretense of silence.

Aroz sat on one of the stone benches, elbows on his knees and hands hanging loosely, head dropped as he studied the ground. He was dressed as Lorhen was, in the lightweight pants that Atlanteans customarily wore to sleep in, shirt left behind in his quarters. His sword lay on the bench beside him, bronze glinting dully in the light. As Lorhen stopped a few yards away, Aroz lifted his head, expression unreadable in the half light. After a few moments he stood, sword gripped loosely in his hand. "I wasn't sure you would come."

"We don't have to do this," Lorhen said tiredly.

Aroz smiled thinly, casting a glance back at the small house Lorhen had come from. "You struck her. I am still her bodyguard. Even if we were not Timeless, her honor would still be at stake."

"She was about to expose us," Lorhen pointed out. "Loudly, and to a sizable group of people. I couldn't allow that."

Aroz shrugged. "Who would have believed her?"

"Someone might have. I didn't live as long as I have by letting people announce to random strangers that I'm immortal. I couldn't take the chance."

"And so you prefer to strike your beloved?"

Lorhen sighed. "I elbowed her. I didn't belt her." A fit of unwise honesty prompted him to add, "And yes. I will stop someone by any means necessary from blurting out our secret."

"Even the woman you are to marry."

Lorhen tilted his head back a little, weariness in the movement. Eyes still on Aroz, he said, "Yes. There will be a time that she understands, Aroz, but it hasn't come yet. She's still mortal."

Aroz looked up at the house again. "How long will you continue to allow her to be unaware of what she is?"

"Allow?" Lorhen straightened his head, staring at Aroz. "I don't allow or disallow anything, Aroz. I'm old, not omnipotent. It's not my choice when or if she Awakens." He, too, glanced back toward the house, and then his shoulders dropped. More softly, he admitted, "I don't think I could bear to lose her to old age, not knowing the potential is in her. A few years, maybe five or six. She'd still be young."

"And if she hates you for keeping it secret? What if you lose her to that?"

Lorhen looked back with a wry smile. "Maybe she'd let me make it up to her in a few hundred years. I don't expect the marriage to last after she learns, truthfully. It wouldn't be fair to her."

Aroz shook his head. "Then why not tell her now? Let her make the choice now?"

"Why not tell her yourself?" Lorhen said shortly, lifting his eyebrows when Aroz looked away uncomfortably. The older Timeless let the silence draw out a few moments before speaking again. "I won't tell her yet because immortality changes us all in a fundamental way, and Ghean is still very young. I don't want to see her vivaciousness fade. Not yet." He closed his eyes, calling the image of Ghean's smile to mind. "Let her enjoy that passion while she can. It might not survive the first death." Lorhen could hear the sorrow in his own voice, and smiled sardonically at it. When he opened his eyes a moment later, it was to find Aroz staring at him, a quizzical frown wrinkling his forehead.

"You really do love her."

Lorhen groaned. "Of course I do. You think I want to marry her so you can't have her? Don't be stupid, Aroz. I haven't kept my head a thousand years by courting that sort of idiocy."

Aroz stood quietly a few minutes, eyebrows still drawn down as he examined Lorhen. "I don't understand you," he said eventually.

Lorhen snorted, a sound of amusement that shook his body. "You're not the first, and you won't be the last. Does your lack of understanding go so far that it requires us to fight, Aroz? Because whether it does or doesn't, I'd like to get it over with so I can go back to bed."

Aroz's expression darkened again, and for the third time he looked toward the house where Ghean slept. "I have protected her all her life, at any cost. Will you do the same?"

At any cost except my own life. Lorhen nodded slowly, the caveat remaining unspoken. "I will."

Aroz nodded once. "Then we have no real quarrel. Much as I would like to stand in your place, I haven't got the heart to deprive Ghean of her groom mere hours before the ceremony." He lifted his sword, leveling it at Lorhen. "Do not betray her," he said flatly.

Lorhen smirked. "I'll expect to find you waiting, if I do." He took two steps backwards, effectively dismissing the other Timeless. Aroz nodded again, and turned his back, walking swiftly from the gardens.

Lorhen waited until Aroz was entirely out of sight before releasing a slow breath. Some day he wouldn't be able to avoid that battle, and it might be better to force it now, when he knew he could beat Aroz. But he would no more divest Ghean of Aroz's presence at the wedding than Aroz would deprive her of Lorhen's own, and so they would remain at a stalemate a while longer. With a sigh, Lorhen turned back to the house. He'd taken only a step or two when an indistinct tingle shivered down his backbone. He lifted the bared sword blade instinctively, searching the darkness for the Timeless whose presence he'd been warned of.

"It's only me." Ghean stepped out from behind a tree barely two feet away from him, a blanket clutched around her shoulders. "I thought I was being quiet."

Lorhen lowered the sword, slipping an arm around Ghean's shoulders. "You were. How long have you been out here?" The awareness of her potential Awakening thudded at the back of his head, a headache timed to match his heartbeat.

"Just a few minutes," she answered, snuggling against his side. "You'd been gone too long to get water, so I got up to look for you."

Lorhen encouraged her to begin walking with a brief squeeze. "I didn't think you'd really woken up at all." Hesitantly, he asked, "You were listening to us?"

Ghean nodded against his ribs. "I'm glad you didn't have to fight him," she said softly. "I love you both."

"I know," Lorhen said, equally gently. "I'm glad too." He pushed the door open, escorting Ghean inside. She padded back into the bedroom, dragging the blanket up onto the bed with her, and curling into a small lump in the center of the bed. Lorhen laughed quietly, leaving his sandals by the side of the bed as he climbed in with her. She rolled over sleepily, looking up at him with half-lidded eyes.

"You won't fight him?" she asked drowsily.

Lorhen laid his hand along her cheek, smiling down at her. "I will try not to," he promised. "Someday I might have to, but I'll try not to."

Ghean smiled contentedly, eyes drifting fully closed as sleep claimed her again.

She hadn't heard, Lorhen concluded. Had she heard the debate of whether or not to end her mortal life, he was quite sure Ghean would be entirely awake and full of angry questions. He wrapped an arm around her, pulling her against his chest, and let sleep find him again, as well.

Twenty-four hours later, at just past daybreak, Ghean kissed his cheek and told him to find something to keep busy for the morning. Thus far, Lorhen's method of entertainment had been nervously pacing the outer wall of the temple, repeatedly dismissing the urge to peek through the windows. A quick glance at the sun told him he'd been at this task for almost four hours. He was relatively certain he would wear a path in the stone tier the temple sat on before the sun reached its zenith and it was time for the ceremony.

A burst of giggles from inside nearly forced him to break his vow to not spy on the women inside. They had been doing that all morning, and Lorhen's curiosity was eating him alive. He slowed next to a window, then fixed his gaze on his toes, finally smiling at himself. He would think hundreds of years of practice would reduce the apprehension of getting married, but then, he might also think that hundreds of years of warfare would numb someone enough that each new battle wouldn't send a surge of adrenaline through the body. He would be wrong about that, too, and, Lorhen decided, he should probably not pursue the comparisons of marriage and warfare any further. Grinning, he resumed his methodical walk around the building.

Minyah appeared from within the temple, hazel eyes merry. "Ghean tells me that it is time for you to bathe and dress for the ceremony," she announced.

Lorhen shot another glance at the sky, eyebrows lifting. "It's not for almost two hours," he protested.

Minyah nodded solemnly. "True," she agreed, "but Ghean is certain that you are wearing a path in the stone and that you will trip in the groove when you enter the temple. Such an ignominious entrance would be an insult to the Hunter." The words were delivered with utter sincerity, the smile developing across her face completely at odds with her tone. "Had she realized you would occupy yourself by carving a new riverbed with your feet, she would have given you specific tasks to do." Minyah's voice gave way to the laughter showing on her face. "I told her men never know what to do with themselves on the day of the ceremony. I see that age makes no difference, and I was correct." Minyah looked distinctly pleased. "That is always satisfying."

Lorhen threw his head back and laughed. "Minyah, are you ever wrong?"

The scholar grinned. "Rarely, and on those occasions that I am, I do not admit it. Go and bathe, Lorhen. Here." Minyah stepped forward, holding her hand out, palm up. "This is for you."

Curious, Lorhen lifted the package out of Minyah's hand,

raising an eyebrow for permission to open it. She nodded, stepping back again with a small smile.

The box was not unlike the one the Book was kept in, though simpler in design. Lorhen studied it a moment, finding the pressure points that slid it open—three of them, not seven like the Book's box had—by the faint indented marks in the wood. It popped open, revealing a length of soft leather slipped through a silver pendant. Lorhen picked it up, turning it over in his hand to examine the delicate replica of the Hunter's symbol. Sunlight bounced off tiny stones set into the hourglass' four corners and across its glittering belt, and silver studs that represented the Houses gleamed around an encompassing circle.

"It is a hair tie," Minyah explained, gesturing at the short leather strip. "Our House laws only allow necklaces to be worn by those born or adopted to the House, but there are no laws against other versions of the symbols being worn as jewelry. I hoped it might welcome you to the House properly. Your hair is quite long enough to wear it."

Minyah sounded anxious for the first time since Lorhen had met her. Smiling, he offered an extended hand. "Thank you, Minyah. This is the first time I've ever received a gift from a parent who knew the truth. It means a great deal to me." Lorhen closed his hand protectively over the piece. "Thank you," he repeated. "I will treasure it."

Minyah clapped her hands together, dismissing sentimentality with the sharp sound. "Excellent," she said, clearly pleased. "Now you must go and bathe. Take your time," she advised. "I am not certain the priests would appreciate you returning to wear a rut around their temple."

A little while later, Lorhen closed his eyes, sinking into the bath until only his hair floated on top of the water, a black spider's web hovering above him. Heat seeped into him slowly, and he drifted in the darkness, listening to the sound of his blood coursing in his ears. Tension ebbed out of his shoulders, and he smiled sleepily into the water. One of the overlooked advantages of immortality—at least, Timeless immortality—was the ability to submerge himself until all his cares filtered away in the peculiar silence of underwater, without ever having to come up for air. The Atlanteans were the only people he'd ever met who bathed with at least weekly frequency, a habit he found blissfully luxurious. The cleverly-laid pipes that carried both hot and cold water from the mountain springs made private, heated bathing extraordinarily easy, and Lorhen wholeheartedly approved. Perhaps he could stay in Atlantis until the rest of the world caught up to their level of civilization. The thought made him laugh, and he surged out of the water, hair streaming over his face.

"I thought you were never going to come up."

"Yagh!" Lorhen leapt backwards, half scrambling out of the bath in a frantic search for a blade before the voice settled into a familiar place in his mind. Edgily pushing wet hair out of his face, Lorhen glared at Ragar, who laughed openly.

"I'm sorry," the portly scholar said, not sounding the least bit repentant. "I've been sitting here for at least ten minutes. If I hadn't believed you before, I'd have to now."

Lorhen settled back into the hot water, ducking his head under to smooth hair back from his face before muttering, "You scared me."

Ragar laughed again. "Evidently. I really didn't mean to, but I must say it was worth it. I've never seen anyone levitate out of a bathtub before. I got your note. I can't decide if you're astonishingly arrogant or painfully humble."

"Probably arrogant," Lorhen said. "Why?"

"Because after telling me a story which is outrageous and difficult to believe, and after I've abandoned you to think seriously about this absurd story and try to draw conclusions about it, you send me a note asking me to stand for you in your wedding. The day before the wedding. That is not usual, my friend."

"Oh." Lorhen took a handful of soap, scrubbing it through his hair. "I didn't know I was supposed to have someone stand as a witness for me until yesterday morning. You were the only one who came to mind. I don't make friends particularly easily, Ragar, but I'd consider you a friend."

"Would you?" Ragar asked curiously. "Can a thousand year old man make a mortal friend that quickly?"

Lorhen smiled wistfully. "A thousand year old man has to, Ragar. Taking time to make up my mind could too easily take the rest of your life. I have to decide very quickly if I want to be friends with someone." He ducked his head again, rinsing his hair. When he sat up, he added, "If I didn't consider you a friend, and trustworthy, you can be sure I wouldn't have told you about myself."

"How can you be certain I'm trustworthy?"

Lorhen shrugged. "Nobody's pointed at me and started telling stories yet. If you tell people about me, I'd have to run, and then you'd never learn the stories I have to tell."

Ragar pulled a face. "Sometimes being a scholar is too transparent a calling. You're right: your secret is safe. But this wedding thing—"

Lorhen leaned forward. "I'd be honored if you'd stand as my witness, Ragar. I know it's presumptuous to ask, given we've only known each other a month and I only asked yesterday, but I would very much appreciate it. It would be the first, and probably the last time that nearly everyone intimately involved with the ceremony would know who and what I really was. That's something I'd like very much."

Ragar pursed his lips as Lorhen spoke. "It's all about you, isn't it?" he asked curiously. "Nothing else really matters."

"Other things matter," Lorhen said stiffly.

"Just not as much."

Lorhen was silent a moment, mouth flattening as he looked

for a way around an honest answer. After a moment he shrugged. "Just not as much."

"Mmm." Ragar folded his arms, thinking. "I'll stand for you," he said after deliberation, "but I want to ask something equally greedy."

Lorhen twisted a grin. "And what's that?"

"Remember me," the mortal scholar said. "In your journal, or however it is that you keep the days and years and centuries straight in your mind. I would like someone, a thousand years from now, to remember Ragar the scholar, even if he never did anything particularly spectacular with his life."

"You earned the trust of a thousand year old man," Lorhen said dryly. "That's not something that happens every day."

Ragar shook his head, not to be put off. "That's what I want in exchange, Lorhen. Remember me, and live, so that I will have made some small mark on history, even if it's through just one man."

"I will remember you," Lorhen promised softly. He glanced at the water, a small smile reflecting back at him. Out of all the promises he'd made over the last weeks, it was the only one he was sure he could keep.

Ragar nodded, satisfied, then stood energetically. "Well, get out of the water," he ordered. "You have a wedding to dress for. It's only an hour away!"

Butterflies rattled Lorhen's stomach, swinging the pendulum into an iron-cast nervousness. *You're ten centuries old*, he scolded himself. *You should be able to handle this.*

"Five more minutes," he mumbled pleadingly to Ragar, and sank underwater again to the sound of laughter.

21

Minutes before noon, Lorhen stepped into the temple, flexing his fingers restlessly. His hair, only just dried, was smoothed back from his face, bound neatly at the base of his neck with Minyah's gift, the silver glinting under the direct sunlight as he entered the temple. The tail of hair hung to his shoulder blades, falling over bare skin. A golden sash held cream pants tightly at his waist, a thin double-belt of leather buckled over it, hanging down one hip slightly to hold the steel sword he had gained from Aroz.

The sword had caused some hours of debate. Atlantean men traditionally went unarmed to their wedding ceremonies, though the other men in the ceremony were expected to wear theirs, to fight off potential invaders. Lorhen flatly refused to go unarmed when others would bear weapons, holy ground or not. Ghean eventually relented, her revenge being a six hour modeling session while the women squabbled over how best to arrange the ceremonial robe over an inconvenient sword. Lorhen stood through it stoically, preferring the wait to being caught without a blade. Eventually a discreet slit was decided upon, and Lorhen given strict instruction on how to move to make certain the sword wouldn't cause his robe to fall in ungainly folds.

The floor was warm under his bare feet. For a moment he

frowned at his toes, then glanced to the side to see if others were unshod as well.

Minyah was, at least. Standing to the side of the temple with a gentle smile, she wore a sleeveless dress the same cream as Lorhen's pants, belted at the waist with an identical golden sash. Her heavy silver pendant hung to below her breastbone, on a silver chain for the ceremony instead of its usual leather strap. A gold cloak, a few shades lighter than the belt, fell from her shoulders, and her hair was bound up in a delicate golden headdress, curls falling loose down her back. Lorhen shot her a quick smile, glancing away before his attention snapped back to the slender woman. The cloak she wore was mid-length, lightweight, and he suddenly suspected he'd seen it before. His eyebrows rose questioningly, and Minyah winked, very deliberately, before looking away again.

Lorhen nearly laughed aloud, scanning the temple for the Timeless he knew Ghean had invited. Karem stood across the room, arms folded over his chest. Out of all the occupants of the temple, he was the only one not wearing the deep gold of the Hunter. His tunic and pants were dark green, emphasizing his eyes, and the only belt he wore was to support the blade at his hip. Lorhen nodded a greeting, letting the excitement of the day be the reason for the smile he couldn't stop. One of the precious immortality artifacts was right under Karem's nose, and he would never know. Lorhen's smile grew wider as he finished looking around the room.

Ragar and Aroz stood side by side, the stout scholar with a pleased grin plastered across his face. Aroz, on the other hand, looked much as though he were trying very hard to look pleasant, the result being a somewhat alarming glower, confused by his mouth turning up when he remembered to smile. Dressed in the cream of the wedding party, his robe already over his shoulders, he made a striking contrast to the smaller man beside him. Like Lorhen, he wore a sword, though his was sheathed across his back, the dark leather of the harness a black streak across the golden robe and all but blending in against his bare chest. He looked decidedly dangerous. For a moment, Lorhen cast his eyes to the pillars that supported the temple dome, offering brief and remarkably sincere thanks to the gods represented that he stood on holy ground.

He was left grinning at the temple gods. Someone had climbed up among them and left wreathes of wildflowers tangled about the heads and shoulders and tops of the creatures portrayed. The Hunter was littered in the gold worn by all the House members, flowers rakishly dangling from his staff and barely kept in place by tumbling over his shoulder. It gave the sculpture a gentle air, and Lorhen smiled again before examining the rest of the temple.

Sunlight spilled between the pillars, highlighting the flower-braided ropes that held in place sheets of brilliantly colored wildflowers which cascaded down the temple's inner walls. Woven with unfathomable patience, the symbols of Atlantis were splashed in white against the vivid rainbow of flowers. Each was minutely detailed with a myriad of tiny, pale flowers, different shades picking out eyes and nostrils on the animals, or shading the curve of a shoulder to render the illusion of three dimensions. Lorhen rocked back on bare heels, inspecting the weavings with admiration. It was absolutely impossible that Minyah and Ghean had done it all themselves. He would have to ask, later, who had done them, and seek the artists out to compliment the crafting that went into them.

Aroz cleared his throat. Lorhen spun, eyebrows elevated, and went still as Ghean padded into the temple from the glare of the noonday sun. For a few brief seconds, the dazzling light back-lit the tiny woman, creating a halo that glowed warmly before fading as she stepped away from the temple entrance. Her steps were dainty, the dress brushing the floor so nearly that a more normal stride would cause her to step on the hem. Bare toes peeked out from under the gown as she came forward.

Unlike any of the others, Ghean wore red, the gown dyed a deep crimson, darker than blood. The sash at her waist was Hunter gold, and trailed down the back to blend with a wide slash of gold inset into the skirt. The back of the dress was cowled, crimson warm against the smooth olive tones of her skin. Ghean's waist-length hair was bound up in a perfectly smooth bun, surrounded by a delicate tiara of gold, the symbol of the Hunter worked into the metal at the crown of her head. A length of the thick black hair was left to swing free, washing down over the back of the tiara, creating a glittering mark where the gold suddenly appeared. Smiling shyly, Ghean offered her hand to Lorhen, over-full sleeves of the dress falling away to expose her fingertips.

"You are positively radiant," Lorhen whispered as he took her hand. Ghean's smile exploded with pride. Together, they knelt before the altar as the priest circled around to stand in front of them. Dressed in pristine white embroidered with the symbols of all the Houses, he beamed genially down at the couple, gesturing Ragar and Minyah forward.

"Do you have the robe this man is to wear?" the priest boomed, and Lorhen fought the urge to look back over his shoulder. Aside from the wedding party, only a dozen or so guests actually attended the ceremony; the mass of people remained outside to greet the couple as they exited, a welcoming from all of Atlantis to their new lives together. The priest was evidently an expert at making certain the crowd outside got to hear what was going on.

Ragar began to unfold the robe as he and Minyah came forward. "We do," he replied, not quite as loudly, but equally formally.

For a moment, Lorhen thought the sharp crack was the sound of the robe being shaken out. The violent shake that followed nearly before he could register the sound corrected the belief. As the walls groaned and shuddered, he jumped to his feet, pulling Ghean against his chest protectively.

"Earthquake," Minyah explained, voice astonishingly calm next to the alarm Lorhen felt. "It will pass in a moment."

For long seconds the rumbles continued, settling into an almost rhythmic pattern before they began to fade away. Lorhen let out a slow breath, and Ragar grinned at him.

"I told you you'd feel one sooner or later. They're not so bad—" The round scholar broke off as a second jolt shook the temple, far harder than the first. Unable to keep his balance at the unexpected second shock, Ragar dropped to his knees, surprise clear on his face.

At the same time Minyah gave a sharp cry, and Lorhen whirled, reaching a hand out to catch her an instant too late. She fell backwards, reaching back to catch herself. Lorhen winced at the motion, able to see before she hit that the angle would shatter her wrist.

As the floor danced beneath their feet, Minyah bounced off the stone slabs, unharmed. Struggling to sit up, she lifted her arm, staring at it in astonishment before tentatively prodding at it with her other hand. Her eyes widened, and she looked up at Lorhen, touching the uninjured hand to the shoulder of the golden cloak she wore.

Karem's shout of outraged realization overpowered the dull, insistent rattle of the earthquake. "You bitch! You're wearing one of the artifacts!" He surged forward, lifting his blade to strike at the woman on the floor. "You lying bitch!"

"No!" Ghean's scream cut thorough Karem's voice as she flung herself forward, blocking the man's path to her mother. Karem's expression dropped into feral delight.

"You first, then," he snarled. "I always wanted to taste the power of an unAwakened." The sword swung down to the sound of Ghean's screaming. The tiny woman threw her arms up, twisting away from the falling sword, her cries silenced abruptly as the blow cut her nearly in half. She fell, silent with shock, and the blood that flowed from her was indistinguishable, at first, from the crimson gown she wore. Karem kicked her silent, still form out of the way, raising his sword a second time to strike at Minyah.

"Ghean!" Aroz crossed the intervening space impossibly fast, knocking Karem's blade aside and pressing an attack. Sweat beaded on his face instantly, skin turning ashy with effort, and even Lorhen felt the gut-twisting sickness that wracked the other Timeless.

"Holy ground!" Lorhen's scream was all but lost in the cacophony of battle. "You can't do this! We're on *holy ground*!" The earth lurched again, sending him sprawling on the floor next to Minyah. Above him, Karem's sword clashed against Aroz's in an angry ring of metal. "You can't do this!" Lorhen screamed again. "Can't you feel it?"

As he shouted, the sun went out. Lorhen shot a frantic look through the pillars that supported the dome to see black clouds boiling in the sky, clouds that had appeared out of nowhere. Blindly, he reached for Minyah's wrist, clamping his fingers around it. "Run!" he yelled above a suddenly shrieking wind, pushing Minyah to her feet as he struggled to stand himself. "*Run!*" he bellowed again, and shoved her toward the door. Ragar, only a step or two away, remained on his hands and knees, unable to regain his feet. Lorhen grabbed his collar, hauling him upward, and nearly threw the other man at the door, then followed, herding the two mortals along in front of him.

Ragar bolted toward the square, but Minyah stopped just outside the door, whipping to face Lorhen, curls lashing her face in the black wind. "Ghean!"

Lorhen grabbed the front of Minyah's cloak, pulling her centimeters from his face. "Ghean is dead!" he shouted. "Keep that cloak on, Minyah, and run!" For a heartbeat he looked over his shoulder at the battle being fought in the temple walls. Aroz had the advantage for the moment, but Lorhen could see grief blinding him, and knew it would be mere minutes, at best, before the fight was ended.

"What's happening?" Minyah lunged toward the temple.

Lorhen snatched her wrist again, hauling her the other way. "The penalty for fighting on holy ground." He turned from the temple and ran, dragging Minyah behind him. The earth buckled and bent beneath their feet, sending the Timeless leaping from point to point, pulling Minyah with him.

At once, as if orchestrated, the pillars shattered, sending the temple's dome crashing down against its thick walls. Aroz flinched at the implosion of sound, staggering to keep his feet as the ground twisted violently again. Lightning smashed outside the temple, blackening the ground and sending acrid smoke into the flower-scented room. He met another blow from Karem, silently cursing the inferior bronze blade he carried. Had he still had the steel sword Lorhen had taken from him, the battle would already be over.

Karem leaped onto the altar, beckoning with one hand as he tracked Aroz's movements with his sword. "First you," Karem growled, "and then your precious Ghean and all her sweet untapped Awakening. And then that bastard Lorhen, and then that lying bitch Minyah. And then the cloak is mine, and the world with it." He grinned, vaulting off the altar again, and moved to attack.

Aroz backed up, fury blinding his defense. "Over my dead body," he grated, and Karem laughed.

"Exactly."

Across the room, Ghean inhaled sharply, the sound entirely lost in the crash of swords and shaking earth. Disbelieving, her fingers crept down to feel her ribs, where the sword had struck. There was blood, blending with the crimson gown, and a wound, but far smaller than it seemed it should have been. As she pulled the dress away from the gash, the bloody injury inexplicably knitted itself before her eyes. She pushed to her feet in confusion, reaching up to touch her head. The golden crown was crooked, nearly falling off her head. With a rough movement, she pulled it off, throwing it on the floor to roll toward the door. Just beyond the opening, it curved to roll in a circle, clinking against the outer wall of the temple. As if the tiny sound were a catalyst in the raging storm, the doors were moved by winds, slamming shut with a boom only slightly less loud than the falling ceiling had been minutes before.

"Aroz?" Ghean whispered as the opponents in the battle before her became clear. Although he couldn't have heard her, Aroz suddenly looked her way, breaking off the fight to run toward her.

"Ghean! Stay out of the way—it will be all right—"

Karem's laughter followed him, harsh over the sounds of the storm, as he crossed the temple behind Aroz. "Enjoy this, Ghean," he advised. "Aroz's death is going to be the last thing you ever see. Except, of course, your own. How does it feel, knowing your pathetic beloved preferred keeping his own neck whole to saving yours? Betrayal is a bitter dish, mmm?" Karem's expression became perfectly even, his voice flat. "Now, Aroz."

Aroz wheeled, sword at the ready. "Now," he agreed. Ghean slid to her knees, tears draining down her cheeks as she watched in silent, miserable confusion. The wind outside suddenly stopped, as though a wailing woman had lost all the air in her lungs to sob with. The earth's rumblings shuddered and came to a stop, leaving the collapsing temple unbearably quiet.

Half a dozen blows were exchanged, rapid and loud in the eerie silence. Karem threw a series of strikes at Aroz's head, each parried with unbelievable speed. The fourth time, Karem jerked his sword around halfway through the blow, an awkward, ugly motion that Aroz didn't expect. Before he could rework his defense, Karem slammed his blade into Aroz's side, the same motion that had felled Ghean only minutes before. His knife finally came free from its belt, a flash of motion with his quick hands as he flipped it forward, burying it in Aroz's heart.

Aroz slid to his knees, defeat etched in his face, more colored with regret than despair. Very calmly, he turned his head to smile gently at Ghean. "I love you," he said clearly. The words were left hanging in the air as Karem's sword swept down to behead him.

Ghean screamed.

Outside, the wind began its howling again. The temple stone roared out as the earth convulsed again, and lightning bombarded into Karem through the temple roof and windows.

The Timeless flung his head back in a shout of triumph, feeling the first wash of the Blending dance through him. *Something's not right.* The thought had barely formed when the Blending exploded into agony, a thousand times worse than any Karem had ever felt. Pain fogged his mind, scoring his throat raw with screams. Dimly, the warning Lorhen had shouted out came back to him: *holy ground.*

He'd felt it, the roiling churn in his gut, the shakiness of his hands, but he hadn't thought anything of it. All battles carried a certain fear of that nature in them, and if it had felt worse than usual, then he had thought it was only his rage at having been within grasping distance of one of the immortality artifacts, and having lost it. But Lorhen had cried out about it, had asked if they couldn't feel it, and now he understood what the ancient Timeless had meant. It had been the power of the Blending inside him, warning him that they stood on holy ground. Warning of the price to be paid for fighting on holy ground, when everything in Timeless nature told them not to. He hadn't—couldn't have—imagined that the price was cataclysm, or annihilation. They should be warned about that, he thought with child-like offense, and then thought no more.

The blade fell from Karem's hand, only inches from where Aroz's lay. Lightning turned to pure fire, hammering into the blades, leaping from bronze to stone to flesh. It burned hotter than open fire could, melting the temple's stone floor into smoothness, and Aroz's body into a grease patch on the floor, charcoaled bones shattering into dust. Karem disintegrated more slowly before Ghean's horrified eyes, collapsing in pieces to the floor, his screams echoing above the fire's roar.

The stone boiled. Frantic, Ghean ran to the altar, perching on it as she sobbed a supplication to the gods. "Please, please, please. Save me, please. Please." The litany gave her no release as the fire swept up the walls, melting away the fractures in the stone, rendering imperfections invisible. The door faded into obscurity, the windows reduced to smooth curves in the walls.

The air was too hot to breathe. Under her, the altar slipped, stone beginning to reform into the liquid that the rest of the floor already seemed to be. Ghean closed her eyes and screamed until her lungs could take in no more oxygen from the broiling temple air. She was unconscious before the flames reached her.

22

In the moment that the winds stopped and the earth ceased its shaking, Lorhen skidded to a halt, jerking around to stare back through the fractured city toward the temple.

"What?" Minyah gasped. "What is it?"

"I don't know," Lorhen answered. "Maybe they've stopped."

"Stopped?" Minyah demanded breathlessly. "Then Ghean…?"

"Maybe," Lorhen said again. *Stop*, he prayed. *Don't let them do this. Stop while we're all still alive.*

The wind screamed anew. Lorhen swore, yanking Minyah back around. "Dead," he grated, and began to run again. The earth's shaking redoubled, stone crashing in pieces down into fractures as they split open around the runners.

"Lorhen!" Ragar's bellow came from above as he waved wildly. "This way!" He turned and continued up the hill. Lorhen glanced around in search of a better path before shrugging and giving chase, still hauling Minyah behind him. It was the road leading out of the city, down to the harbor, and it seemed as good a choice as any.

Ragar, panting, stopped to wait for the duo following him. "There are boats," he puffed, "if we can get to them we should be safer—" Beneath his feet, the earth split open. Ragar fell, silent with surprise, flinging a hand up in a cry for help at the last moment. Lorhen sprang forward, reaching, only narrowly snatching his hand back in time as the earth slammed shut again centimeters from his fingers.

"Damn!" For a few futile seconds, the Timeless beat his hand against the stone. "Damn!"

This time, it was Minyah who grabbed Lorhen by the arm, pulling him to his feet. "Run," she whispered in near exhaustion. "We have to run."

Lorhen nodded silently. They darted forward again. Screams punctuated the sounds of grinding rock as others tried to survive the maze of randomly opening stone. The road to the harbor was frighteningly empty, given the numbers of people in Atlantis. Lorhen cast one more rapid look over his shoulder at the black sky swallowing the city whole, wondering how many had already died there.

He tripped, crashing onto his face as he looked back toward the road, pulling Minyah down on top of him. A boulder broke off from the cliff wall above them, falling too rapidly to roll out of the way. Its silent fall ended with a soft bump as it bounced off Minyah's cloak, rolling a few yards away harmlessly. Lorhen lay on his belly, breathless for several seconds, watching the boulder settle, before blurting, "Thanks for thinking to wear that today."

Minyah's laugh was tinged with hysteria. She clambered to her feet without answering, once more tugging Lorhen up as well. They ran, intent on avoiding the opening fissures, jumping madly over those that appeared.

The ground fell away as they leapt. Minyah screamed, watching the black stone of the mountain road drop fifteen feet as she plummeted toward it. She expelled a hard gasp of shock as she landed, unharmed, and began running again, pulling Lorhen behind her.

Again and again the land fell away, until an abrupt drop

plunged them into the salt water of the bay instead of onto stone. "Keep the cloak!" Lorhen yelled frantically. Minyah clutched one hand to the throat of it, the other still clinging tightly to Lorhen's. "Boat boat boat boat boat," Lorhen raved, kicking madly to keep his head above the water. "Look for a boat!"

"Forget the boat!" Minyah screamed. "Swim!" She released his hand and struck out through the grey waves, intent on putting as much distance between herself and Atlantis as possible. Lorhen stared for a split second, then set out after her, less agile but equally enthusiastic.

The shriek of stone minutes later made them both turn, almost against their will, to look at the drowning island. Stone continued to shatter as Atlantis dropped in surges, yards at a time, visible to their panicked eyes. "Swim!" Lorhen shouted back at her. "The undertow!"

Minyah blanched, setting off again with a stronger, more steady stroke. The waters around them roiled, each new breaking wave bringing with it the bodies of drowned Atlanteans. Unexpectedly, Minyah came up short, cutting off a choked cry. A boy's body floated in front of her, expression peculiarly content in the chaos. Lorhen stopped beside her to glance at the body, and closed his eyes. The child was Ertros, who'd had a crush on Ghean and whose stories had led Lorhen to the Book of Atlantis. "Come," Lorhen said softly, unhappily, to Minyah. "We can't help him." It hurt to speak, his throat rough from screaming. He began swimming again, putting the image of the dead boy out of his mind.

"Lorhen." The weak plea came several minutes later. Lorhen turned in the water just in time to see Minyah disappear under a wave. Cursing, he dove, searching the murky waters for her, fighting against the pull of the waters back toward the sinking island. An impossible amount of time seemed to pass, as he snatched at bodies, drawing them close to study their faces in the greyness. A strong current pulled him back the way he'd come, and he swore again, kicking to the surface. He cast about in a frenzy, shouting Minyah's name as the water drew him back toward Atlantis.

"Damn," he whispered once more, and put his energy into escaping the determined pull of the drowning civilization.

Hours later, as the skies began to clear, Lorhen righted himself to search the slowly calming water for the remains of Atlantis. As far as he could see, the water was unbroken by any land mass. On the wind, he could smell the faint scent of blood as sharks found the meal left for them by the drownings. He drifted a while, weary, then began to swim again.

Methuselah's grandson had been right, he thought an indeterminable time later. The world had ended. He wondered if the grandson's boat had made it away safely.

He wondered, very distantly, why Minyah had decided to wear the Hunter's cloak that day, and hated, with brief intensity, that it had not been enough to save her.

Ghean, he could not even let his thoughts touch on. Not then. Perhaps not ever.

Two or three days later the sea washed him ashore. He lay in the sand, trembling with exhaustion and staring at a flawless sky, until even his Timeless body objected to the sea water he'd ingested and he had to roll, suddenly, to vomit on the wet sand. The motion knocked his hair over his shoulder, and the tie Minyah had given him slipped free, falling to the ground. He folded it into his palm, shaking with the effort, and felt its symbol with astonished fingers: he'd known, vaguely, that his hair hadn't gotten in his face as he swam, but he hadn't thought clearly enough to realize it meant the tie hadn't been lost.

Neither had Aroz's sword, still belted at his hip. There'd been no point in getting rid of that: it didn't impede his swimming enough to bother, and even if it had, the idea of coming ashore without a weapon was worse than being slowed down by keeping it. He curled onto his side, the hair tie in one hand and his other hand on the blade's hilt, hanging on to them like they were precious legacies of Atlantis as he waited for his body to regain some strength.

Long before that strength returned, the painful throb of another Timeless approaching slammed through him. His fingers clenched around the Hunter's symbol until it cut into his palm. It would be a stupid way to die, lying helpless on a beach somewhere. Using the pain in his hand to goad himself, he got to his feet, barely able to keep his balance, and waited to see if he would have to fight.

The other Timeless stopped some feet away from Lorhen, an unpleasant smile creeping across his face. Not quite as tall as Lorhen, he was slimmer and warmly colored, tones of dark mahogany in his skin and eyes, and in the highlights of his black hair. The side of his face was badly scarred, an ugly twist pulling at his eye and mouth. "Hello, brother."

"Am I your brother?" Lorhen asked with light-headed curiosity.

The slim man folded his arms across his chest and jerked his head out at the water. "Ships say a whole island sank out there. Did you have anything to do with that?"

Lorhen, slowly, said, "In a manner of speaking."

"And you're half dead now." An unpleasant smile fixed itself firmly on the scarred man's face. "Way I see it, you have two choices."

Lorhen lowered his head, staring through falling hair at the man. "Do I?"

"You could be my brother, or you could be dead." The scarred Timeless let the words hang a moment, then added, "I could use a man who can sink an island."

Lorhen turned his head slowly to look out over the water, beyond the horizon where Atlantis had been. If he had killed

Aroz, none of this would have happened. He would never have lost Ghean. If he had told her what she was, he wouldn't have lost her. If. If. *If.* He shied away from those thoughts, still unable to face them, and returned his bleary regard to the scarred man. "I've never had a brother."

The smile turned to a grin, no more pleasant as it split the scarred man's face. "You do now," he said. "My name is Yama, and we are going to rule the world, brother."

23

Silence lay heavy over the living room a few long moments, as Lorhen and Ghean's combined story came to an end. Emma looked away from the pair, scanning the room for something less unsettling to rest her eyes on. Instead, her gaze landed on a scarred white stone at the end of the bookcases, so out of place with the other elegant decorations. For an instant she stared at it, then turned horrified eyes back toward Ghean.

Ghean followed Emma's look, and turned a smile on her, full of bitter resignation and betrayal. Over her years as a Keeper, Emma had become accustomed to the world-weary expressions that would settle in the eyes of her Timeless charge. Mortals were all dying; from a Timeless perspective, they were *all* dying. Lorhen had said that to her once, an unusually cruel comment from a man who prided himself on not seeming to care. Devane cared enough to be gentle about his immortality compared to Emma's mortal span, but Lorhen, Emma thought, cared even more deeply. Deeply enough to say that to her, to show that vulnerability, his impotent rage at the brief years mortals had to see and experience the world.

Emma glanced at Lorhen, sunk deep in his chair, elbows propped at awkward angles against its arms so he could steeple his fingers against his mouth. He regarded Ghean as if no one else was in the room, changeable eyes black with memory. He looked contained, apart, even sitting with three others who knew his most basic secrets, and Emma shivered. He remembered Ragar, after all these centuries, a single mortal scholar whom he'd known for little more than a heartbeat in his long life. He would remember her, too, when death took her, and like Ragar, she thought that might be enough. More than enough, which made it hard to stay angry. She would probably have to forgive him, and soon, for having lied to her about who and what he was.

Not, though, for hiding the First Keeper's records. Anger sparked in her again after all, conflicting and wearying. Emma sighed and brought her attention back to Ghean, whose acrid smile had left her mouth, but remained deep-set in her eyes. Hers had been a hell worse than the other Timeless had suffered, even with the pain of lost friends. Eternal life and eternal death, in eternal captivity. The hairs on the back of her neck stood again, and Emma glanced at the stone on the bookshelf once more.

"Yes," Ghean said to the unspoken question. "It's the same stone. I kept it as if it were a precious talisman, a piece of jewelry so valuable it couldn't be parted with." Her faintly accented voice was self-mocking.

Emma shook her head. "It is. It bought you your freedom, didn't it?"

Ghean looked at her curiously. "I suppose it did. I hadn't thought of it that way."

Emma half smiled. "Mortals do have the occasional insight."

"Occasionally," Ghean said with an equally brief smile, then turned her attention back to Lorhen, a serene calmness settling over her face. Emma imagined she could see Minyah looking out from her daughter's face, in that steady contemplation. "Tell me what happened to my mother," Ghean said imperiously.

"I thought she'd died," Lorhen answered, fingers still against his lips. "After I couldn't find her, I assumed the cloak had been torn off her in the water and that she'd drowned."

"And you did not look further." Ghean's voice was soft.

Lorhen ignored the question. "I didn't see her for a thousand years." His glance ran to Cathal and Emma, and slid off them again. "Not until after the Unending disbanded."

Heat rose in heavy waves from the desert floor, warping the air so greatly that Lorhen made a habit of looking twice before feeling any assurance that objects were real, and not figments of a heat-strained imagination. More than weeks had passed since he'd last seen a traveler through the wasteland; months, at least, had gone by, and perhaps more. After a thousand years of warfare, the silence was welcome, even in the inhospitable desert.

His oasis was a tiny one, a patch of green in the desert so small that passing nomad tribes stayed only long enough to water themselves and their animals before moving on, unwilling to encroach on the little home Lorhen had dug himself out of the sand. It couldn't possibly be him, he thought; surely his demeanor was pleasant and welcoming, despite what the reflection in the still water showed him.

Truthfully, if he could escape his own face, he would; he could hardly blame visitors for moving along as quickly as possible. The changeable eyes had gone to black, a fathomless darkness whose first and most easily read expression was rage, seconded by hatred. The features, always sharp, were chiseled thin with an everlasting anger that fed in his belly, churning and boiling. Hair framed his face, unkempt, the top once chopped short and finally growing out. Left to its ragged path, it completed the aura of complete disdain for humanity that radiated from his slender form.

The approaching traveler was either real or a remarkably persistent hallucination. Lorhen turned from his perch at the

edge of the oasis, flinging a loose length of fabric over his face
and shoulder to cut down the sun's glare. The waterhole was
easily enough found, and without an offer of hospitality, perhaps
whomever it was would move on. A millennium of battle was
hard to set aside, and the more Lorhen could avoid mortals who
provoked his temper, the better. In a decade—or a century—or
two he would rejoin the world. Until then, the solitude suited
his need to reconstruct himself from what relentless death had
left him.

Some of the passion for killing had left him already. Had
he gods, Lorhen would have thanked them, as he settled to
his knees in the sand under a slim tree, the scarf falling away
from his face again. A thousand years had gone by since Yama
had found him on the beach in Atlantis' wake. He had killed
where he wanted, fought whom he chose, and hunted with his
brothers, sharing spoils and graciously offering Blendings back
and forth, the unfortunate victims left to listen while four murderous Timeless debated whose turn it was to indulge in the
heartstrike. The power had been heady, but in time it grew sour.
Mortals were little sport, and only his brothers equaled his skill
with a blade. Even the rush of the Blending seemed dulled, when
he never doubted he would be the victor in Timeless combat.

Then came Cassandra. Laden with power even before Awakening, she'd been able to wield the Blending unlike anyone Lorhen had ever met: well enough to bring him back to himself,
and to remember, at least faintly, the long-buried memories of
Atlantis and its gods. Her beauty and fire had been his, for a
little while, but in the end, Yama had wanted her. Yama, the
ringleader, the most vicious and the best with the sword.

Lorhen had never been the strongest, only the smartest. He
let Yama take Cassandra, and then watched her run away into
the night, and didn't stop her.

The thousand-year reign of the Unending began to falter,

after that. It had not been easy, spreading the seeds of dissent so carefully and subtly that the blame rested on no one, least of all Lorhen. He'd clasped arms with Yama, the last of the four to part ways, and promised, "Someday. Someday, we'll ride together again, you and I. Until then, brother."

And then he ran like hell into the desert, to an insignificant oasis that had once been someone's holy ground, and there he stayed, in search of sanity. It was long in coming, but at least the killing rage was fading.

The traveler's camel was slurping noisily at the water. Lorhen closed his eyes, willing the newcomer away, only to open them again almost immediately. He was safe enough from Timeless, here on the ancient holy ground, but holy ground wouldn't prevent a bloodthirsty mortal from taking his head. Then his power would be dispersed to the ether, just as happened to any Timeless who died from a beheading without the heartstrike, and that, frankly, would be a waste of two millennia or more of life. The very idea that some random child, or children, could inherit scraps of his power, of his memories, rather than the whole of what he was being taken as one by some lucky Timeless, offended him on a personal level. Better to be vigilant in the face of mortals than cast to the winds by unfortunate happenstance.

The faint shift of sand underfoot made him turn his head, looking to the approaching stranger. Slight, and wrapped in the loose robes that kept the desert heat from killing, the interloper stopped a few yards from where Lorhen knelt. After half a minute's silence, Lorhen heard a language he had not heard in ten centuries, spoken by a voice he thought dead those many years.

"They told me that I would find a madman alone in the desert if I passed this way," Minyah said, and pulled her scarf from around her face. "Never did I imagine he might be a friend from a thousand years gone by."

For long seconds, Lorhen stared up at the Atlantean scholar, speechless, and when he found his voice, it was raw with disuse and disbelief. "A friend? Is that what I am?"

"You saved my life," Minyah answered evenly. "Had you not dragged me out of the temple, I would have died as certainly as Ghean did. I do not think any of the House artifacts are remarkable enough to compensate for fires as hot as the earth's core itself. I saw the sea boil in places where Atlantis' stone fell from the island as it melted. I would not have wished to die in those fires."

"I thought you drowned."

"I waited to." Minyah knelt gracefully, still a few meters away. "I waited to. The water's pull dragged me under, but in time it released me again. When I finally reached the surface, you were gone."

"I looked for you," Lorhen said eventually. "Until the water came too close to pulling me back to Atlantis."

Minyah crooked a smile. "And so you left, and so you would again, if it were to happen again. For a long time I was angry at you. It took centuries before I was able to understand the need that compelled you to run from the temple, to abandon those who fought or died there. The desire for survival in itself, that is understandable. But for you, it is more, is it not? It was not something I understood well enough to see, in Atlantis. Only retrospect gave me that wisdom. It is not only survival, for you. It is survival at any cost."

"I betrayed that instinct once," Lorhen grated as Minyah's words ceased. "I let Ghean stop me from killing Aroz in Kemet, and in the end it cost us everything." The chill of death settled over his face, the cold lines comforting. "Love's lessons can be hard. It's not a mistake I'll make again."

Minyah came to her feet in a smooth motion, crossing the sands with a few steps, and resting her fingers atop Lorhen's head. "My dear Lorhen," she murmured after a moment, "what has happened to you this thousand years?"

Lorhen broke off his narrative to frown uncomfortably at Ghean. "She stayed a while," he said. "Years. Decades, maybe. My sense of time was...not good. I told her about the Unending, and she, in turn, told me about the Keepers. We parted as very close friends. Over the years we met up again, now and then, and exchanged tales. Her files on me were frighteningly complete."

"It's good you were friends," Ghean said softly. Lorhen closed his eyes, exhaling gently, and looking at the petite woman again when she spoke again. "But what happened to her, in the end? I want to know."

"She died," Lorhen said tiredly. "Isn't that enough, Ghean?"

Ghean, insistently, said, "No. She was my mother, Lorhen. I want to know."

Lorhen lowered his face against his steepled hands, sliding his fingers along the bridge of his nose to press at the inner corners of his eyes. He held the posture so long that Ghean glanced uncertainly at Cathal and Emma. Just as she pulled in a breath to speak, Lorhen's voice broke the silence. "All right."

"Yours?" The twins were just in their teens, both tall and slender, and madly running through the surf, soaked to the skin. Lorhen stared openly, first at the children, and then at the unaging mortal beside him.

"Not by birth," Minyah said, amused. "For all the artifacts' wonders, they do not turn back the years, only hold them at bay. My child-bearing days were over while Atlantis still stood." She stood, looking out over the blue water. "I miss it sometimes," she said. "I hardly recognize myself, from my oldest journals. I knew so little, then. Is that how it always must be?"

Lorhen shook his head. "You were always knowledgeable,

Minyah. The world has changed, and you've watched it happen. It's that way for all of us."

She folded her arms under her breasts, pushing the cloak back over a shoulder. "I was proud of my knowledge, then. I knew there was always more to be learned, but I was proud of what I had." A hand drifted up to touch the cloak's hem. "Were my gods wise or foolish, Lorhen, to give us these gifts? Mortal life is so short, but the world has so much potential. Part of me wants everyone to share in it. The greater part fears what might happen if all people were given this gift."

Lorhen rested his chin on his knees, watching the water and the children playing in it below. "Your gods were well-meaning," he said. "I don't know whether they were wise or foolish, but they meant well. And if more people knew about the artifacts, or if there were more of them, it would make war. There's always war. Artifacts would be hoarded, and only the rich would be able to afford them. For most people, it would be the same as it is now. For the dangerous ones, the ambitious ones, there'd be no way to stop them." He glanced up, eyes hazel in the sunlight. "My kind of immortality is less dangerous. I can die. I don't know if you can."

Minyah laughed, settling down beside him on the rock again. "Can you? Three thousand years, my old friend, and you still think you can die?"

"I wouldn't keep my head if I didn't know I could lose it," Lorhen said, then nodded at the children. "Where did they come from?"

"Nephele, the first wife of Athamas the king. He lost interest in her, and left her. He remarried when the children were small, but his new wife does not like them very much. I have played nursemaid, and helped to raise them. I have missed children, over the years."

Lorhen nodded again. "What will you do?"

Minyah glanced away from the children to look at Lorhen. "What do you mean, what will I do?"

"Our kind were not meant to have children, Minyah." Lorhen smiled faintly down at the water. "I forget," he said after a moment, "that you and I are different. Despite there being no warning at your approach, I think of you as one like me. Even we old ones categorize things in the most familiar manner, whether or not we know better. But that aside, Minyah, they'll grow old and die, while you go on eternally. Watching it happen to friends is bad enough. Can you stand to watch it happen to your children?"

Minyah sat silent a long time. "The war-horses drowned with Atlantis," she said eventually. "They tell stories about them, did you know? They call them unicorns. Noah took Methuselah's crystal away with him on his ship. I have the cloak. Did you ever wonder what had happened to the rest of the artifacts, Lorhen?"

Lorhen glanced at her. "I'd assume they'd all sank with the island."

Minyah shook her head. "I have searched out fabulous stories about magical items over the years. The cauldron, the sword and scabbard, the grail; I've found them. Even the ring, which is so small I would have thought it lost forever." She lifted her hand, showing a simple gold ring on her right middle finger. Lorhen took her hand, folding her fingers over his. Barely visible even in the bright sunlight remained the faint lines of an etching that had once scarred the ring more noticeably. "The Lion," he guessed from the lay of the still-lasting marks.

Minyah nodded. "I only found it a few months ago. I tracked it nearly two centuries. A rumor here and there about a magic ring, a half-remembered tale about an ancient man who wore it—eventually I found the man who wore it."

"And how did you get it from him?"

Minyah gave a sideways smile. "I stole it."

Lorhen's eyebrows shot up. "You?"

"It is not much like me, is it? He was a small man, black of heart. He'd woven a tale of woe, and gained it from the last owner, before killing him. He was a warlord, not well loved. I became his lover, and slipped it off his finger one night. I understand he died not long after." There was no sympathy in her voice, and Lorhen's mouth curled.

"Judging who lives and who dies?"

Minyah lifted a shoulder, let it fall again. "We all die, in the end. You have just reminded me of that. I judged him unworthy of special protection. I cannot find distress in that."

"Do you think you need the protection of both the ring and cloak?"

"No." Minyah shook her head. "I will wear the ring, and put the cloak away. Although after so long I fear I will feel unclothed, without the cloak on my shoulders. I have slept in it, even, for all these years."

"You'd have to, or the hours you spent sleeping would be hours you aged. Your life would only have been two or three times the normal span."

"So long, and yet so little time." Minyah nodded down the beach at the children. "When they are older, unless they are as you are, I will give them the artifacts, or have them sip from the cup if I have discovered how it works."

Lorhen's eyebrows went up again. "You don't know how it works?"

"No," Minyah said in a voice full of chagrin. "Neither water nor wine drunk from it brings eternal life." She laughed suddenly. "And for two thousand years, there has been no coffee to try it with. I miss coffee."

Lorhen grinned, thinking back to the bitter drink. "So do I, now that you've brought it to mind. Have you tried blood?"

"Blood tastes nothing like coffee," Minyah said primly.

Lorhen laughed. "In the chalice, Minyah, in the chalice. Have you tried sipping blood from it?" Curiously, he added, "How did you determine water and wine didn't work?"

"Mice," Minyah answered, "pet mice. They died in the usual time." She looked thoughtful. "I have not tried blood. Perhaps I should."

"Will the cup work on mice?"

Minyah looked up at Lorhen solemnly. "It has not, so far."

Lorhen grinned. "Well, where is it? We'll try it, with blood."

"Kemet," Minyah replied. "Somewhere safe," she added evasively, and Lorhen laughed.

"What is it about old age that inspires such a lack of trust?" he teased. "Eventually you'll have to go get it, and we'll see if blood works."

"What made you think of it?"

A skull, silver hammered into the inner curve and glinting over the eyes, flashed through Lorhen's mind. Yama, toasting his brothers. Thick, cooling blood dribbling crimson over the whitened bone as the skull was passed from one Unending to another, each draining some of the blood away. Lorhen could no longer recall who the enemy whom they'd 'honored' so had been. "You don't want to know."

Minyah's eyes narrowed. "Do not credit me with overly delicate sensibilities, Lorhen," she warned, before allowing, "You are most probably correct. It is likely I do not want to know."

Lorhen stayed nearby, watching Phrixus and Helle grow, mildly horrified at the rate they aged. "Is it this way for mortals?" he asked Minyah one morning, watching the twins tear out of their father's palace for a day of riding.

"Ghean grew fast," Minyah said, "though not this fast. The days and years shorter, now. They do not need our supervision today, Lorhen. Come back in and I will make you breakfast."

"You made breakfast yesterday," Lorhen said idly, returning.

"I'll do it today. Then we can sit around in the sunshine and tell each other how much better the old days were."

Minyah laughed. "As you wish." She glanced toward the clear skies. "Truly, rain would be better. The drought has gone on a long time. The queen sent to the Oracle at Delphi for advice on how to end it."

"It'll eventually rain no matter what her majesty does. I don't suppose I could go tell her that?"

Minyah chuckled. "No, Lorhen. She is the Queen. Friends of the nanny, no matter how close a friend he is, do not tell the Queen that the weather is beyond her control."

"Friends of the nanny," Lorhen replied, "have a bad feeling about this, Minyah. Take your twins away from here and out of Ino's grasp before the messenger returns from Delphi."

"Their father would never allow it," Minyah said, "and Ino would not dare."

"You underestimate the hatred in the human heart, Minyah."

Four days later the messenger from Delphi arrived, bearing the news that to end the drought, young Phrixus and his twin sister Helle must be sacrificed. Minyah went into a silent rage, certain either Oracle or messenger had been bribed to bring the requirements back by a queen determined to rid her life of the reminders of her husband's first wife.

Phrixus accepted the news readily enough, willing to sacrifice himself for his people. Helle, always the quieter of the twins, agreed without argument when Phrixus did.

Noon, three days hence, would see the sacrifice. The hour was not traditional for sacrifices, but the queen argued that the sun would be best able to see the able-bodied youths at that time, and the drought would therefore end that much more quickly. The gods would be pleased, and rain would come again.

Lorhen wasn't surprised, but neither was he happy, when at dawn on the day of sacrifice, Minyah rose and began to gird herself for a battle that was none of her business. She looked at him, not asking, but he answered anyway, his voice flat. "No. No, Minyah. They're mortal. They'd die anyway. I won't risk my head for them. The reward for disrupting a sacrifice is to become one yourself, and I don't want to find out if I can survive having my heart cut out. Walk away from it, Minyah. They're not worth your life."

She regarded him coolly. "Perhaps they are not worth yours, Lorhen. My life is my own to dictate, and I choose this risk."

"Minyah, they'll take the cloak from you, and the ring. You'll have no protection. Underneath this," and he fingered the edge of the cloak, "you're human. You won't stand up again from a mortal blow."

"If that happens," Minyah said evenly, "you will take the artifacts if they can be found, and hide them somewhere safe." She hesitated, her hand over her breast, and then she lifted her Hunter's necklace off for the first time since Lorhen had known her. "Take this," she said quietly. "You know where my papers are, the Keeper records. There is a box among them, one of the stone boxes the artists used to make, in Atlantis. There are letters there, for Ghean." She lifted a hand to ward off his protests. "I know she is dead. They were written by a fanciful mother, when I was very young, long before I knew I would survive down through the centuries. Put this with them, and seal the box again, and leave it in the archives, somewhere hidden, if I do not come back."

Lorhen slowly folded his hand over the necklace. "I don't want to lose you, too," he said distantly, and Minyah smiled.

"We all die, Lorhen. If it goes badly, perhaps I will see you again in the mountaintops of Atlantis."

"I hope there are gods, and that they are so kind," Lorhen said softly, and at noon, watched from a cliff above the waters as the scene far below unfolded in silence.

The children walked forward, unafraid, to the altar by the sea. Helle glanced skyward, to the sun almost at its zenith, and smiled at her brother. Phrixus took her hand, returning the smile, and both faced the sacrificial priest.

Down the beach, sand flew under hoof. A chariot, well-crafted and sure, was driven by the dark-haired mortal woman, her golden cloak snapping out behind her in the wind. Another curve, and she would be there.

Helle stepped forward. Lorhen's muscles tensed, judging the distance that Minyah had left. She would be too late by mere seconds. The knife glittered down, and blood flowed from the suddenly limp child, while behind her body chaos broke loose.

Minyah's sword cut down two guards in an instant, the momentum of the chariot bringing strength to her blows. Lorhen had not known her to ever carry a weapon, much less that she knew how to use one, and for a moment he regretted his decision to not join her on the rescue. Only for a moment: he had left regret behind with Atlantis, and it could barely touch him now. Still, his fingers closed tightly around Minyah's necklace, the silver imprinting a mark on his palm, and he prayed to gods he knew had never existed.

Phrixus was in the chariot now, bodily hauled there by the small Keeper. Settled crookedly over his shoulders was the Hunter's cloak, and a blade shattered against it as someone scrambled into the chariot. An arrow, fired from only a few feet away, split its tip and fell backwards from Minyah's upper arm. Even from the distance, Lorhen could see the horror washing over the priest's face and the panicked gestures that determined Minyah as the enemy. The chariot wheeled, and sped away through the surf.

Ten hours later, Phrixus returned to the palace rooms Lorhen shared with Minyah. Silent, the boy held out his hand, curled around something. Lorhen extended his own hand, and the golden Lion's ring fell into his palm.

"She asked me to give this to you," Phrixus said, and then, in the face of Lorhen's silence, blurted, "She died to end the drought. A sacrifice was needed. She offered herself, and I did as the priests wished."

Lorhen looked behind himself, out the windows. A fine rain drizzled down, discoloring the beach sands. "She raised you," he said. "Helle was already dead. They both had to die?"

"The priests would never have allowed Minyah to live."

Lorhen looked back at the boy. "You know so little," he said, tired rage filling his voice. "Go away, Phrixus. Live your little life, and remember that you chose death for the two women who were your family." He brushed past the boy, then stopped. "Where is the cloak?"

"Gone away on a ship to be hidden beyond the edge of the world. It has a dark god's magic in it."

"You know so little," Lorhen whispered again, and walked away from the palace by the sea.

"It was almost a century before I heard the myth of the Golden Fleece. I hardly recognized it. She chose her death, Ghean. I'll never understand why." For the first time since he'd begun the story of Minyah's fate, Lorhen opened his eyes, looking over templed fingers at the tiny Atlantean woman.

Ghean returned his regard, expression steady. "You hid the box in the archives in the Paris offices. For her. For me."

Lorhen shrugged a shoulder. "'The things we do for old lovers.' I didn't for a moment imagine you had survived, Ghean, but leaving the letters, the box...call it a way of remembering, at least."

"Not atoning?"

"I've never been much of one for guilt or absolution. I left them because your mother asked me to. They were in Atlantean. I never thought anyone would translate them. I certainly never dreamed you'd be alive to find them."

"I'm full of surprises," Ghean murmured, and then stood.

"Gentlemen, Emma, much as I have enjoyed your company, it is a quarter to four in the morning, and I'm to catch a plane in seven hours. Perhaps our paths will cross again someday."

"Oh, I imagine so," Lorhen answered, standing. "Ghean, it has been positively fascinating to see you again." He bent to brush a kiss against the diminutive woman's cheek. "We'll have to do it again."

"Perhaps a little sooner than four and a half thousand years," Ghean suggested, and smiled as she accepted handshakes from Emma and Cathal. "Good night, my friends." She escorted them to the door, leaning in the frame as they went down the steps into the rain. "Good night, Lorhen."

24

Lorhen jogged down the steps, hands shoved in his pockets and shoulders hunched against the rain. "Anybody fancy a trip to Greece?"

Cathal turned the collar of his coat up and belted the waist as he went down the steps in front of Emma. "Greece?"

"It's the most convenient hopping-off place on the way to Atlantis."

Emma followed the men down the steps, casting a tired glance at heavy clouds lit orange by streetlights, and the steady rain. "Weren't you the one telling us Atlantis was better left drowned?"

"That was before Ghean turned up alive, Em. It was better left drowned, but it's not going to stay that way and I don't want to be caught out when she starts revealing whatever it is she's got up her sleeve."

"You may be the most contrary man I've ever known, Lorhen, and I'm from a notoriously contrary people. At least you're not boring."

Lorhen snorted. "I was boring for centuries before I met you, Devane. Boring is good. Boring doesn't draw attention. You're a bad influence."

"You two can stand out here in the rain arguing about this all night," Emma muttered. "Some of us come down with colds if we do that. I'm hailing a cab and going back to the hotel."

Lorhen frowned up at Ghean's apartment, where the lights were already off. "Thoughtful of her to call one for us, yes. All right, Emma. Your wisdom prevails." He hurried down the street toward the main thoroughfare, the other two in his wake. His literal wake, he thought with a glance at his feet and the troughs of water spilling around his shoes.

By the time he and Emma caught up with Lorhen, Cathal had shed his long coat and wrapped it around Emma, whose own jacket was inadequate against the rain. She looked ridiculous, overwhelmed by its size, but amused gratitude danced across her face, too. "Always the gentleman, Cathal."

"I won't catch cold," Cathal said with a smile, and Lorhen, rolling his eyes so hard it was nearly painful, said, "And never mind that you're now standing around in the rain with silk and denim plastered attractively to your body like some kind of expensive ad campaign. Who do you think is going to admire you?"

"I will," Emma offered. "Only out of politeness, of course."

"Of course."

Cathal grinned at Emma. "We won't mention to him that he noticed, too."

"Of course I noticed, Devane. I'm old, not dead. Is that a taxi? No. It might be faster to walk."

"It's certainly warmer to walk while we're looking for one." Emma folded Cathal's coat up so it didn't drag in the puddles and struck out at a brisk walk that had the men scurrying to catch up with her. Under the sounds of their splashing feet, Cathal asked, "What difference does it make if Ghean's alive or not? I'd think you'd be glad to see her."

Lorhen clicked his tongue. "There you go again, Devane. Thinking. Atlantean was an obscure tongue, Cathal." He rubbed water off his nose and scowled as it began to drip again.

"I'm sure you have a point," Emma said.

"Patience, Emma. Don't I always get to the point?"

Emma and Cathal exchanged glances, chorused, "No," and Cathal nodded as Emma said, "Actually, you seem to take great pleasure in being cryptic and avoiding the point altogether."

"It's part of my mystery. The point is, until Ghean turned up alive, I was the only one who could translate any Atlantean texts, and I wasn't about to do that. I wanted to leave the whole place alone under the sea." He kicked rain, scattering the ballerina-skirts of raindrops into larger ripples as headlights flashed in the distance. "Is that a cab? I think it's a cab. The real point, Emma, is that Atlantis—it is a cab." He stepped down off the curb to hail the oncoming vehicle.

"Lousy night for it," the cabbie said as they climbed in. "What're you doing out in the rain?"

"Getting wet," Lorhen muttered, and remained stubbornly silent for the remainder of the trip to the hotel. Once there, Cathal paid, as Lorhen protested, wide-eyed, "What? You think I have money?"

"I can't afford to keep you, Lorhen," Cathal said as they entered the hotel. "You're going to have to go mooch off someone else soon."

"At least I mooched the plane tickets off the Keepers' expense account." Lorhen shook rain out of his hair and crossed the lobby with long strides, shoes squeaking on the tile. A tired bellboy stood to attention and Lorhen dug a ten dollar bill out of his pocket to hand the kid, then waved him back to sitting as he pressed the elevator button and said, "If they hadn't agreed I would have had to ask you to buy them," to Cathal, who waited until they were safely in the elevator to ask, "Have you been freeloading for six thousand years, old man?"

"As much as possible, yes. Don't worry. I'll get out of your hair for a while after I get myself killed."

Emma groaned. "I'll shoot you myself, and I won't doctor the records, if you don't get back to the point about Atlantis soon."

Lorhen turned an alarmed look on her. "You wouldn't."

"Try me." The elevator doors opened on a heavily silent hall, thick carpet muffling the lift's bell, and Lorhen held up his hands in mock defeat. "Fine. The point is...why is Cathal the only one with a key?"

"Because Cathal is the one paying for a penthouse suite," Cathal said dryly as he opened the door.

Emma laughed as they came in. "You don't go to half measures, do you, Cathal?"

He smiled at her. "I try not to."

Lorhen gave them both a look that suggested they were lacking in taste and stopped a few steps inside the door to survey the space with an air of disdain. Armchairs and a deep couch surrounded a coffee table near a well-stocked bar on one side of the room, windows with privacy curtains drawn let city lights glitter through, and a bed broader than Lorhen was tall dominated the room's other half. "Who gets the big bed?"

"Emma," Cathal said, helping her untangle from his coat. "That way she can double up the duvet if she gets cold, which she probably will after being out in the rain."

Lorhen muttered, "I shouldn't have asked," and passed the king-sized bed to drip his way into the second room, which was nearly as large as the first and had two double-sized beds in it. "You'd better not snore, Devane."

"You should know by now if I do." Cathal followed him to hang up both his own coat and Emma's in the closet, then opened his hand to take Lorhen's as well. Lorhen shrugged out of it and went to turn the heat up as Cathal concluded, "Even if I did, try to remember we're a couple of nice young men having a night out with Mammy. She deserves to not have to sleep with squirming youngsters."

"*Never* call me that again. Besides, most people wouldn't believe I'm your mother anyway. You're both too pasty." Emma waggled dark brown fingers at them from the bedroom's doorway. She'd already gotten a towel, though instead of applying it to her hair she wrapped it around her shoulders like a cape. "I'll be telling my friends I spent a weekend in Chicago with my two much younger lovers. I probably won't mention the second bedroom, just the king-sized bed." She affected a shiver and put on an alarmingly convincing damsel-in-distress expression. "After all, I'm chilled to the bone. Surely you two big strong handsome boys wouldn't let a lady huddle in bed alone and half frozen, would you?"

"Oh my God," Lorhen said, and went into the bathroom to get his own towel as Cathal laughed and promised something in a rumble that Lorhen was just as glad he didn't overhear. "You two should have gotten a room of your own."

"Lorhen!" Emma sounded almost genuinely shocked. "Do you really think I'd sleep with my assignment?"

Lorhen came out of the bathroom to throw a towel at Cathal and eye Emma before deciding it was better to pretend he hadn't heard that, either. Cathal laughed again and toweled his hair, dark curls sticking up every which way, as Lorhen blotted his own face dry. "Does anybody have anything to eat?"

"I'll order room service," Emma said. "You'll never tell us what your problem is with Ghean and Atlantis if we go down to the restaurant."

"You know they charge a thirty percent premium on room service," Cathal said dryly.

"I've seen your bank accounts, Devane. You can afford the premium. Start talking, Lorhen, or I'm going to start drafting my entry about how I shot you. 'It was fine, I'd known for months that he was actually Lorhen, the oldest Timeless, and I was tired of him not getting to the point. The record has now been set straight.' They'll probably run me out for not telling the truth in the first place, but nobody ever actually asked me....'"

"The Book," Lorhen finally burst out impatiently. "That

book was two-thirds full of things I couldn't understand, five thousand years ago. Information science is just now getting to, Emma, only they were doing it with magic, not science. They were—" He took a handful of long, frustrated strides, pushing past Cathal into the suite's main room, where he could pace. "You don't know anything," he said in a low, snarling voice. "About the Blending, about the power we can manipulate. None of you do. You're all children and you don't understand what power you have."

"You can dampen your presence," Cathal interrupted quietly. "I know that much, Lorhen. You can mute it entirely, can't you?"

Lorhen reared back, turning to stare at Cathal a moment, and when he spoke most of the passion had left him. "So you do pay attention."

Emma, behind them both, said, "Wait, what? You didn't—neither of you told me this!"

"Why would I?" Lorhen said, still watching Cathal. "Someday I'll let you experience what I really feel like, Cathal. What it's like if I don't hold the power back."

"Like Yama," Cathal said, but Lorhen shook his head.

"He was never as good as I was. You wouldn't still be alive, if he was."

"What," Emma said through her teeth, "the hell are you two talking about? How do you mute yourself, Lorhen? There's nothing in the records—"

Lorhen snapped his gaze to her, then turned abruptly and went to the bar, pouring himself first one drink, then a second before trusting himself to speak. Even then he had to put the tumbler down and brace himself against the counter, head lowered and hands tight on the granite surface. "Of course there's nothing in the records, Em. Only a handful of us can do it, and mortals can't feel it anyway. But I can. I do. Of course I do. It's part of how I hide. It's part of how I've stayed alive this long. I stopped muting it when I met Cathal, because I wanted him to know who I was, but even then, you were as close as across the room, weren't you, Devane, before you knew I was Timeless. And now I keep it at about the same range he has, so I don't draw attention to myself. But he could stand beside me in a crowd and never know I was Timeless, if I wanted it." Lorhen glanced over his shoulder at Emma, and said, softly, "You could stand a city block away and know it, if I wanted."

"Me? But I'm—" Emma swallowed. "I'm mortal."

"And I'm very old, and very strong." Lorhen wet his lips, then turned to lean his backside against the bar counter and turned his hands palm-up. "One time offer, Emma. The truth is, I don't know what it feels like to mortals."

Emma crossed the room to him and put her hands on top of his with such certainty that Lorhen chuckled despite himself. "I doubt I deserve your confidence." He slid his hands under hers until he grasped her forearms, and she wrapped her fingers around his in turn. Cathal, without being asked, came to stand a step or two behind Emma, prepared to offer support.

To Lorhen, it felt like cautiously opening a carefully wrapped package: loosening a bit of tape here, lifting a flap of paper, folding back another piece, all as if what lay within was explosive and could react unpredictably to the incoming light. It wasn't so far from true, that description; the power wanted out, to absorb or be absorbed. The Blending itself drove their fights, its need for expansion the price of their immortality.

Cathal's dark eyes turned black as Lorhen unfurled his power, and his hand flexed at his hip, where a sword would normally hang. A corner of Lorhen's mouth turned up, acknowledging the other Timeless' discomfort, but he kept his eyes on Emma, who, as a mortal, was much slower to react. The hotel suite became the walls of Lorhen's world, the space beyond which he refused to allow his power to travel. Almost no one could do that; almost no one was old enough, or had the training, but he certainly had no intention of announcing his presence to all of

Chicago, especially when Ghean, five thousand years old and primed to him anyway, was out there, and not all that far away.

Even he could tell that the suite's air changed, took on a crystalline shine, like it was filling with more than it could hold; the light felt sharper, like it could cut, like it had brightened to an unfathomable degree. The sounds of their breathing clarified, and the blood rushing in their veins, and the subtle brush of eyelashes closing and opening again. Lorhen's grip on Emma's arm turned razor-sensitive, not only the sound but the heat and speed of her blood coming alive under his fingers.

Her eyes dilated suddenly, the pulse in her throat leaping as color scalded her cheeks. Her head and shoulders surged back, but to her credit, her hands tightened around his forearms, refusing to let go or escape the sudden onslaught of Timeless power even when sweat beaded on her lip and at her hairline. For a suspended heartbeat, Lorhen didn't just look at her; he looked *in* to her, gliding through solitary humanity to forge a brief connection, to see, whether she willed it or not, the things that to her mind, defined her.

They came in rushes, no especial order to them: the desert war she'd fought in, the guitar lessons taken as a child. A dog pulling her into a creek and her fear; her induction into the Keepers. A birthday party that ran late into the night with friends. The Timeless who died in front of her in the war, and his resurrection. Cathal Devane, and most lately, Logan Adams, who had been her mortal friend and was Lorhen, a conflict she still struggled with, but overriding that, a sense of forgiveness. More came on, but that was enough, too much, already. Lorhen released her arms and pulled the power back inside himself, wondering already how badly he had damaged her.

A shudder ran through Emma. She fell back a step, and Cathal caught her, offering support. She stayed in his arms for less than a breath, forcing herself straight without ever breaking Lorhen's gaze. "That was…" Her voice cracked and Cathal stepped around her and Lorhen both, swiftly, to pour her a generous finger of whiskey into the tumbler Lorhen had used. She took it and swallowed it in a gulp, still fixated on Lorhen, and said, "That was what you feel when another Timeless comes near?"

Lorhen shook his head, a bare motion. "What did you feel?"

"Nausea. Headache. The things described in the records. But—" Emma glanced quickly at Cathal, then back to Lorhen. "More than that. M—memories."

Cathal took a sharp breath of surprise, but Lorhen nodded, still watching Emma. "That was—that was more like the heart-strike, the actual Blending experience. Less violent, but—and it doesn't go both ways, the Blending. Only the victor is empowered, enlightened, that way." Another smile pulled at the corner of his mouth, and his voice dropped. "Congratulations, Keeper. You've just given a six thousand year old man a wholly new experience. That...hasn't happened in a very long time."

"What did you see in me?" Her voice was steady, but there was caution in her eyes.

Lorhen glanced at her, then at Cathal. "Perhaps that's for another time. What did you feel, Devane?"

"An eruption waiting to happen. An almost irresistible need to fight." Cathal looked as cautious as Emma. "I've never felt anything like that, either, Lorhen. I fought Yama, but—"

"I told you. He was never as good as I am. Later." Lorhen hunched his shoulders, knowing it for a defensive posture. "All of this, later. I can't right now. It's too—" *Vulnerable*, but he would no more say that aloud than he might go on the news and announce his presence to the world. Nor did he need to; the other two dropped their gazes, then lifted them again with uncomfortably understanding expressions. Lorhen flared his nostrils and turned away to find another tumbler and pour himself another drink. "The point I was trying to reach before all of this nonsense is that the ancient Atlanteans, the group of Timeless who settled that island, didn't just develop technology far past what anybody else in the world was using at the time. They harnessed the Blending, or the power of it, at least, to create artifacts and healing agents that are beyond even what modern science has managed. I had a thousand years of power and knowledge behind me then, and I didn't even know where to start. I'm afraid today somebody, some human, might be able to translate the concepts into modern science and…" He shook his head.

Emma poured herself another drink and retreated to one of the couches. "You're talking about the Book? Lorhen, Atlantis sank nearly five thousand years ago. What makes you think it still exists?"

"Ghean does." Lorhen took his drink and the bottle and dropped into a chair across from Emma. "At this moment, I'm reluctant to discount anything."

Cathal forewent a drink and got the room service menus instead, handing them to the other two before he sat down. "Why are you so angry that she's alive, old man?"

Emma, beneath Cathal's question, said, "You said you didn't know what was in the Book."

"I didn't, when you asked."

Emma and Cathal exchanged glances and Lorhen's lip curled. "I'm impossibly old, Em. I don't remember most of my life. Not actively. That's why my journals are so important to me. So when you asked, I didn't know. It started coming back when I saw Ghean. By the time we got to that part of the story, I knew again. I'd remembered. Hell of a thing to forget," he added softly, more to himself than the other two, and then to them, again, knowing he was repeating himself, "That's why I keep the journals."

Emma examined him a moment before shrugging and nodding all at once. "All right. And Ghean? Why are you so angry she's alive?"

Lorhen closed his eyes. "Why don't you spit it out?"

"He's touchy, for someone who dances around the point all the time," Cathal murmured to Emma, then lifted his voice again. "She was trapped for four and a half millennia, Lorhen. You sure it's not guilt that's making you angry?"

Lorhen opened his eyes to regard Cathal. "Yes. They were fighting on holy ground, Devane. I had no idea what was going to happen, but I was certain no one at ground zero was going to survive it. I believed she was dead as soon as Karem cut her down. It appears I was wrong."

"She was Timeless," Emma said over the edge of her whiskey glass. "But you left her body."

"Do you think I haven't thought that a hundred times in the last few hours? A thousand times in the last forty-five hundred years? Do you think I haven't 'what-iffed' the situation to death?" He slammed his glass down on the table beside him. "The goddamned world looked like it was ending, and I made a judgment call. Karem and Aroz were fighting between me and her body, and she'd been damned near cut in half. I did not have the time to scoop up the pieces and run. The world is a very simple place, Emma. If it comes down to me or the other guy, I'm always going to chose me. Always. You're thousands of years too late to make me feel guilty for choosing my life over hers."

"And yet you saved Minyah." Emma's voice was soft, the words almost a question.

Lorhen sighed, anger draining away. "She was mobile. She was also in front of me. I had to get her out of the way so I could move, and no, I am not pretending that only my own best interests motivated me. I am not a heartless monster, and I was not a heartless monster then." A smile drifted across Lorhen's face, without humor, without touching his eyes. "That came immediately after. I would have saved Ghean, if I'd thought I could, and still get out of there alive. Now, knowing what happened to her, knowing that she survived all those centuries in that prison," Lorhen shrugged, "I would do the exact same thing."

"Is it really that easy for you, Lorhen?" Cathal asked, his voice tinged with a sort of faint, horrified admiration.

"After six thousand years? Yes. It really is. Death before dishonor, come home with your shield or on it: they're concepts that don't belong in my world, Cathal. I can live with dishonor. I can't live without my head."

Cathal quirked a curious smile. "Does dishonor mean anything to you at all?"

"No. Someone else might perceive my actions as dishonorable, but my own judgment is the only one I'll accept. There are a few people whose opinion is important enough that I'll alter my habitual behavior for them, but ultimately I'm the only one who gets to judge me."

Cathal's mouth curved more broadly. "You've risked your head for me and Emma both."

"So you're two of the ones whose opinion matters. Can we stop this line of conversation before anyone gets embarrassed by the gushing sentimentality?"

Cathal chuckled. "It might be worth pursuing, someday. The oldest man's perspective on what makes a worthy human being."

Lorhen snorted. "You should have tried that back in Atlantis, Cathal. I was a lot more introspective in those days."

"I wasn't there."

"I guess you've missed your chance, then."

"Lorhen," Emma asked slowly, "how do you know that what's in the Book shouldn't be messed with? You said yourself that it was over your head, when you read it. It might prove incredibly useful today."

"Sure," Lorhen said, "and the Unending might have advanced civilization a thousand years by uniting everyone in fear against them, but we didn't. Whatever's in there, Emma, we're just now beginning to understand. I'm not at all enthusiastic at handing over the secrets of eternal life to the masses, not any more now than I was then."

"But you went after the Lazarus crystal."

Lorhen gave her a sharp look. "To keep it out of anybody else's hands. If it hadn't been shattered, if I could pick and choose who got to use it, without ever risking my own head, sure, I'd do it. But I can't, and what I said then still stands: people with immortality at their fingertips are eventually going to notice us. Whether it's because we survived a mortal blow while not wearing one of their precious artifacts, or if it's because someone realizes we're not filling ourselves with the cocktail of drugs that keeps everyone supple and youthful, eventually the top's going to be blown off the whole mess. I want no part in furthering that. It'll happen sooner or later. It doesn't need my help, or the Book of Atlantis' help. If the Book is still in one piece, I want it contained, and I'm the only one I trust to contain it."

"Maybe Ghean doesn't want it," Emma suggested.

"I don't know what Ghean wants, and that makes me nervous. She knows where it is now, though, and I'd just as soon I was the first one who got to it."

"How?" Cathal demanded. "Do you have a submarine stored somewhere?"

Lorhen pressed his lips together. "Unfortunately, no. I suspect there's going to have to be a rather large donation to the Atlantis research fund by a historian who would like to join the team on their dives."

Cathal eyed Lorhen suspiciously. "And just who is providing this rather large donation?"

"Aren't you the skeptical one?" Lorhen chuckled softly. "It'd be a lot more in keeping with Logan Adams if you provided it. I can transfer the money into your account."

Cathal glowered at Lorhen. "Are you saying you actually have money?"

"I'm six thousand years old, Devane. I have more money than God. Logan Adams is usually broke, though. I wouldn't borrow really significant amounts of cash from you, but one must keep up pretenses."

Cathal turned an incredulous look on Emma. "Did you know about this?"

"I didn't." Emma finished the last of her drink and regarded Lorhen over the edge of the tumbler. "I haven't done any digging into Logan Adams' history. Maybe I should have."

"You wouldn't find much. I'm good at building lives, Em, and I'm very careful about not overlapping. Come on, Cathal. You'll get a chance to see the ruins of the world's greatest ancient civilization. You joining us, Emma?"

"I joined the Army for a reason, Lorhen. I like keeping my feet on dry land. You can tell me all about it if your submarine doesn't implode."

"We'll tell you all about it anyway," Cathal said. "Wouldn't that be a nicely dramatic way to die, Lorhen? Sudden compression? You could burst to the surface in agonized awe, trembling with relief to be alive."

"It's not polite to make fun of your elders."

"Would I do that?" Cathal grinned. "Then I could go back and tell Emma how you handled your first death, and how proud I was of you, and how I planned to walk you through those first uncertain days while you became accustomed to being more than mortal."

Lorhen hid his face in one hand. Cathal's grin grew wider as he warmed to his topic. "We could invite Emma, the old friend of the mortal Logan Adams, to your first sword lesson. She could write up a lengthy tribute to my astonishing skills and your childlike awkwardness. She could comment on my never-ending patience, and your clumsy attempts to emulate me. 'If only Logan will turn out like Cathal,' she'll write. 'The world would be a better place to have two such men.' And I, modestly, will share my meager knowledge, and send you out in the cruel world to fend for yourself against men and women a hundred times your youthful years—"

"Enough! I don't think I've ever heard you accolade yourself so outrageously, Cathal. With any luck, I never will again. Shut up, man, and go to sleep."

Emma grinned suddenly. "I think I'll put a passage in it about how I've always thought of Logan as a son, and how it gladdens my soul to see that this child of mine will endure through the centuries. How does that sound, Cathal?"

Cathal nodded solemnly. "Very good. Very touching. We'll have to add something about how his boyish charm is tainted by the sudden cynicism of death, and how we hope a few years will give him the acceptance he needs for that roguish sense of humor to re-emerge."

"Maybe comment about how he often seemed alone, and how we're afraid that this new difference in him will set him further apart from his fellow man—" Emma broke off with a burst of laughter.

Lorhen staggered out of his chair toward the second bedroom, hands pressed over his ears. "I'm not hearing this. I'm actually not hearing this. Good night, you two…" Six thousand years, and he couldn't think of a decent rejoinder to end the sentence on. More amused than disgusted, he retreated into the second room, and pretended he couldn't hear the other two laughing into the early morning hours.

25

We're falling, the frightened one whispered.

Ghean took a deliberately deep breath, leaning her head against the window and looking down six miles to the feature-less ocean below. A yawn cracked her jaw, and she passed a hand over her eyes, trying to rub away weariness. She'd learned, over the last decades, to sleep in cars and trains, allowing the gentle motion to lull her into rest, despite the speed at which they traveled. Planes were a different matter. *Falling*, the frightened one whimpered again. *The sky can't hold us up. We're falling.*

We are not *falling*, she thought impatiently, but shivered anyway. Traveling so far above the earth's surface, at a nearly unfathomable rate, still seemed unnatural. The roar of the jet engines sounded, even after almost a century, like the sheering scream of stone crashing apart as Atlantis fell.

The sound of the world ending, the patient one said. *It is not ending. We're safe.*

I know, she told it.

Falling, the frightened one repeated, softly. The plane bumped into an air pocket, and Ghean stiffened, fingers clenched around the arm rests. *You see!* screamed the frightened one, and Ghean set her jaw, denying the voice.

At least the seat next to her was empty. Too many concerned

colleagues had asked after her welfare in the past, their concern distracting Ghean from squelching the panicked little voice in her mind. After several flights, she simply made the habit of purchasing not only her own seat, but the one next to her, assuring privacy in her personal terror. She'd learned to meet extended turbulence with a calm exterior. The war with the frightened voice actually made it easier. The struggle to keep from shouting its fears aloud excluded the outside world almost enough to ignore bumps and rattles entirely.

Airplanes are an astonishing invention, the patient one insisted. *It takes only hours to fly from Chicago to Greece. Such a journey would have been undertaken only with great care and nerve, from Atlantis, and would have taken many, many months.*

I appreciate that, Ghean grated silently, *on an intellectual level. They used to make the trip, to South America, to get the beans for chocolate.*

Yes, the patient one said smugly. *They would have embraced flight, the scholars and scientists of Atlantis. So should we.*

"I'm on the plane, aren't I?" she growled, and wished for a book. Though she had shed the habit of mentally translating written work into Atlantean in the early thirties, she was still a slow reader. Fiction held little interest for her, and scientific texts were frequently written in a prose too uninspiring to take her mind off the miles of air beneath the airplane. On the rare occasions that a technical piece of literature captured her attention, she would devour the article or book in her slow, intensive way, and then read every other piece by the author she could locate. These infrequent happenings made air travel almost pleasant: it was the only time she could spend uninterrupted hours deeply involved in reading.

Mostly, though, Ghean spent entire flights with her forehead pressed against the window, waiting in dread for the plane to fall out of the sky. That she was guaranteed survival from even the most horrific wreck—barring the unlikely event that shrapnel would separate her head from her shoulders—did not reassure her in any way. It was the falling that frightened her, the uncontrollable plunge to the earth. There seemed so little difference between free fall in the air and the weightlessness of the temple, and she feared it all the more for its familiarity. Idle fingers twisted her ring around on her thumb. When she noticed the nervous movement, Ghean stopped it deliberately, placing her hands neatly in her lap. The bright, hard light of the tiny overhead lightbulb leeched their color, rendering them pasty. The scars on her fingertips were more visible, the ruined pads bouncing a different quality of light back at her. Ghean lifted one hand, propping her elbow on the armrest, and stared at her fingers, trying to remember how they had looked before her captivity.

"What happened?" Michelle's soft voice, behind her, made Ghean flinch violently and reach for the blade she had tucked away, wrapped in her coat, in the storage compartment above her seat. "To your fingers," Michelle added, coming around the seats to take the one next to Ghean. "I always wanted to ask, but it seemed terribly invasive."

Ghean closed her hands into loose fists, hiding the scars. "A chainsaw. I tried picking one up by the blade when I was very small, and somehow the power switch got knocked on. It shredded my fingers."

"My God," Michelle said. "You're lucky your hands weren't cut to pieces entirely."

"So I've been told," Ghean agreed. "Why are you awake?"

"Guilty conscience." Michelle smiled, then shook her head. "I woke up a while ago, and just called back to the University. Apparently we've had a windfall."

Ghean's eyebrows lifted a little. "We won the lottery?"

Michelle laughed. "Very nearly. Evidently someone at the lecture last night was quite taken with the topic. A gentleman called in at the University this morning with a cashier's check for five million dollars, for the Atlantis excavation fund."

Ghean's eyebrows went higher. "How extraordinarily generous. And what did he want in return?"

"So young, yet so cynical. He wanted to join us, along with a friend of his, on the explorations. Apparently one is a historical scholar of some repute, and the other—the donor, in fact—owns an antique shop."

Ghean's eyebrows lowered, something of a respectful smile playing around her mouth. It was a good tactic, not one she'd expected. "Did these distinguished gentlemen have names?"

"The donor is a fellow called Cathal Devane. Apparently he's more along for the ride; it's his friend who's chomping at the bit for the opportunity to see Atlantis. He may imagine there's a paper or a book in it somewhere, though I'll be damned if I'm giving away those rights to the first fellow who comes along. You'll be writing one first, and if I'm lucky, I'll be second."

Ghean pursed her lips, lifting a hand to tap her thumb against her mouth as she searched for the name Lorhen had asked her to call him. "Logan," she said after a moment. "Logan Adams, is he your scholar?"

"Good Lord," Michelle's eyebrows sailed up from behind her glasses. "You know him?"

"I have known Logan," Ghean said, rolling the words in her mouth with a certain delight, "a very long time."

"Well!" Michelle sat back, pleased. "The University's slavering over the check, of course, but they wanted to check in with us before actually accepting it." She paused, thoughtful. "I imagine they'd tell us to go straight to hell if we declined, but since Dr. Adams is an old friend of yours, I'll let them know it won't be a problem at all for them to accompany us."

"Just Adams," Ghean interjected. "The research sub is tiny enough, and Devane's a big man."

Michelle looked at her, startled. "Mr. Devane is the man with the money, Mary."

"Logan," Ghean said firmly, "is the one who wants this. Just him, or neither of them go. Cathal will accept it."

"You know him, too?" Michelle asked in surprise.

Ghean smiled faintly. "I met him last night, in fact. Logan introduced me. Logan was the friend I saw in the audience after the lecture. He…studies myths." Certainly that had been Lorhen's task in the Keepers. Ghean grinned at the irony and stretched her toes out under the seat in front of her. "I'm sure he'll make a fascinating addition to our team. His knowledge of the ancient world is unparalleled."

"Really," Michelle said with interest. "I don't think I've ever heard of him."

"Oh, he's very withdrawn," Ghean said blithely. "I don't know if he's taught anywhere except in private institutions, and I don't think he's published anything in years, if ever. He's the sort of person who likes knowledge for its own sake, although he adores lecturing people." She narrowed her eyes at the seat back in front of her, idly following the folds in the leather as she considered her options.

We may as well paint him impossibly bright, the patient one advised. *Our own knowledge can only be pressed so far under the guise of inspiration. If we can use Lorhen to crack the secrets of Atlantis, so much the better.*

We'll be caught, the frightened one whispered dismally.

Ghean ignored the second voice. "I would hazard a guess that he knows more about the Atlantis legends and possibilities than anyone else on the planet."

"Excepting you," Michelle half teased.

Ghean shot a smile at the other woman. "Except me. Really, though. His knowledge on the ancient world is extraordinary. I'd wager money on him being able to make a good stab at translating Atlantean text, if we find any. If there's any ancient language it resembles, he'll be able to construct some sense out of it."

"Mary Kostani," Michelle said, amused, "I don't think I've

ever heard you wax quite so lyrical about anyone's talents before. Just how good of friends were you?"

"We were...very good friends," Ghean said, with half a smile. Something about the phrase bothered her, and she fell silent a moment, the smile fading to a frown before she shook her head. "But it was a long time ago. Things have changed."

"Ah. A falling out? Well, I'll restrain my curiosity. So shall I give the U a call back and tell them we'd be glad to accept Mr. Devane's generosity and we'd be delighted to invite Dr. Adams along on the exploratory vessel? How old is this fellow, anyway? He can't be too much older than you if you were, ah. Such good friends. But if he's as widely read as you suggest..." Michelle trailed off with a frown.

Ghean brushed the concern aside with a wave of her hand. "I don't look old enough for my credentials, do I? Logan and I both began studying the ancient world when we were very young." A faint smile curved her lips. "Perhaps past lives haunt us, somewhere deep in our souls, and cannot be put to rest until we have settled their accounts for them."

Michelle started to smile, but it faltered. "Sometimes, Mary, I can't quite tell when you're joking."

Ghean's smile grew. "Isn't it more interesting that way?" She pressed her head against the seat back, tilting it toward the crack between the seats. "Go call the University back and make noises about how flattered we are that such a distinguished scholar would be interested in our little project. It's a drop in the hat compared to what we'll ultimately need, but it's a nice gesture and it certainly won't hurt the coffer. External support is bound to beget more external support, and we're going to sink an awful lot of money into the Mediterranean over the next decade."

Michelle grinned, standing to return to her own seat. "You don't think in the short-term, do you, Mary?"

Ghean turned her head to rest her forehead against the window again. "You have no idea."

Lorhen is going to be a complication, the patient one said thoughtfully. *He'll be convenient for a time. We can use him to further our findings, but in time he'll grow bothersome.*

At least I know where he is now, Ghean retorted. *I know he's alive*. She'd never really doubted he was, of course. Even finding his notes to her in the Keeper files had only been a confirmation of what she'd always believed. After forty-five centuries, another hundred and fifty years couldn't have been enough to kill him. It was a conviction Lorhen would no doubt appreciate and encourage.

But the numbers made her shiver. They were meaningless, really, incomprehensible. The world had changed radically in the time she'd been gone, but the actual time had simply been dark and terrifying, beyond understanding.

We don't need to understand, the patient one broke in, firmly. *Number the years or don't, but we don't need to dwell on it. We're a part of the world again now.*

She nodded against the window, drawing her thoughts away from the years and focusing instead on what mattered: that 'immortal' or not, the Timeless could die. Some were easier to kill than others, and Lorhen would not be at all easy to take. It could be done, though. He was the superior swordsman, of that there was no doubt, but Ghean had passion on her side. She noticed again she was fiddling with her ring, and painstakingly folded her fingers together in her lap.

She'd thought Atlantis might cause the ancient Timeless to surface eventually, but she hadn't imagined it would be so easy. For a moment she let herself wonder what she would have done if he'd never come forward, or if he'd been dead, but shook the thoughts away. Illogical as it was, Lorhen had to have been alive. Ghean needed that to go forward with her life; needed the potential reuniting as a focus, however fuzzy. With billions of people in the world, it was impossible to imagine she might find one extraordinarily old man. It was equally impossible to imagine she would not: she had forever to look. And now not only had she found him, but he had invited himself along on her quest. A quest with far greater scope, now: had he thought about it more carefully, Ghean was certain Lorhen wouldn't have revealed the location of the Book of Atlantis. It was a treasure she'd barely considered, its status legendary even in her mind, and yet she had its resting place now. The temple had been so nearly utterly destroyed. Would the room beneath it have survived the sinking, or the fire that melted the temple's structure? Lorhen had mentioned the blocked-up tunnel leading out to the harbor. Ghean wavered between guesses, imagining first that the tunnel had been crushed by the settling stone, leaving the room unflooded, then supposing that the water had burst through the blockade, drowning the room beneath the temple as well as the temple itself.

She rejected out of hand the idea that the room and Book had been destroyed together. It wasn't that it was impossible or even unlikely; it merely didn't fit into her plans. Thus far everything, including Lorhen's appearance, fit at least loosely into the groundwork she had mentally laid out. The Book would also do so.

The Book. Ghean nestled back into the airplane seat. Her diminutive size was enough to make coach seating nearly comfortable; the roomy first class seats were luxurious. She tapped the call button for a flight attendant. A tall young man appeared moments later, smiling. "What can I do for you, ma'am?"

"Gin and tonic, please," she requested, and smiled as it was delivered in under a minute. "Thank you." Lifting the glass to her mouth, she looked out the window again, almost content despite the flight.

The original plan had been to search out the remaining artifacts. Atlantis' ruins were secondary, more a bitter reminder of a childhood lost than the archaeological find of the century. Somewhere in the drowned city there would be items of remarkable power. The century she'd been reborn into was nearly advanced enough to unravel their secrets.

So many of the artifacts had been lost to time. The Hunter's cloak had apparently been gone since the days of Jason and the Argonauts. For an instant Ghean's expression darkened as she dwelled on the legend. If Lorhen had been telling the truth, Minyah had only been dead a few decades, or perhaps a century, when that adventure happened. Two millennia of life ended by a child's selfishness; two thousand years while Ghean lived and died in a lightless prison beneath the sea. She shivered, and pulled her thoughts away before she spiraled down into pointless rage at the wasted centuries.

Good, the patient one whispered approvingly.

The chalice, found and lost again in Christ's time; the cauldron destroyed, according to Welsh legend, when a living man climbed in it to end the evil of raising men from the dead. Ghean thought it curious that three of the artifacts appeared in the islands of Britain, when the others were so widely scattered. The other two, the sword lost to a lake and the scabbard to battle, were almost the last to be lost, by legend and history's tales. Arthur, who bore the magical blade, had lived only fifteen centuries ago. Ghean wondered if Lorhen had been there, and if he'd recognized the blade as Atlantean work from a life he'd left behind long ago. She sighed, closing her eyes as she sipped at the gin.

The unicorns died with the island, and Methuselah's stone had been broken into pieces, the crystals scattered. The Keepers had collected some of them, storing them in a safehouse, but too many were missing; it would never work again. And both Greek and Chinese legends told tales of stones cast to the ground to sprout undead warriors, and so it seemed safe to believe those gifts—they were called the Dragon's Teeth now, surprisingly close to their Atlantean name; it had been the Dragon's House who held them, then—were irretrievable as well.

There were others, though, House artifacts that had never appeared in legend or history. The Lion's ring had been one. The Book had been another. A girdle had been spoken about when the artifacts were mentioned, and a helmet, both reputed to protect their wearers from danger. They must still be somewhere beneath the waves, and they could be studied, perhaps replicated, but the Book would be the ultimate treasure.

Ghean swirled her drink slowly, studying the pattern of flowing liquid. The hole in the temple would have to be expanded, but it might be possible to pump the water out, leaving the floor empty of most of the water, making excavating down beneath it possible, without flooding the room below if it remained dry.

She took a sip of the gin and frowned, wondering briefly if the temple would be able to take the pressure of the water outside without it being equalized from within. No matter; it was a task she didn't have to worry about today. If Lorhen was right, the Book was sealed in a box like the one that had held her mother's papers. Short of physically cracking it open, it wouldn't leak, and so was safe even if they had to let water in to the secret room.

The idea of the Book was still too new: Ghean could barely imagine what she might do with the knowledge kept in the pages. The dearest thought to her at the moment was to use it to rebuild Atlantis, though it could never be the same. Still, to bring its science and magic back into the world seemed a fitting tribute to the city that had died in such an untimely fashion.

Lorhen wouldn't approve, with his unwillingness to share immortality with the world. Fortunately, Lorhen would only be part of the equation as long as he was useful. Ghean turned her attention out the window again, lifting her gin and tonic to her lips to sip at it. The light bounced off her ring, catching in the engraved lion's head that marked the surface of gold.

26

Lorhen stood on the Mediterranean shore, hands shoved deeply in his pockets. Despite the heat, he wore his greatcoat, the heavy black wool stirring slightly in the breeze off the water. The wind had more success with his hair, ruffling it in slightly varying patterns, leaving a few black strands to stand up straight when it faded away. Khaki pants and a white polo shirt, open at the throat, were something of a concession to the temperature. The sandals that left his toes bared were the greatest indication that he'd left the chillier climate of Chicago thousands of miles behind.

He stood with his eyes closed, tasting the salt and fish in the air. A hundred miles off the coast, drowned beneath the sea, lay the city that had been Ghean's prison for so long. It had never occurred to him to go back and look; of all the possibilities of what might have been that he'd considered, that had simply never crossed his mind. And now they were going back, Ghean and himself, in a race that neither would acknowledge: a race to find the Book, to control it. To hide it, if Lorhen had his way, although Cathal would never approve.

Lorhen smiled thinly at the waves. Cathal had changed him. Less than a decade ago, Lorhen wouldn't have stopped to consider what another's actions might be, or whether his own were right or wrong in the eyes of another. Now at least he thought about it. It generally took Cathal's actual presence to make Lorhen go against his base instincts, but it was a remarkable change to have affected in such a short period of time.

Cathal was back in St Louis, at any rate, and unable to translate the Book anyway. He was welcome to hand it over to science; they could puzzle over it together. Lorhen didn't necessarily object to the knowledge being available, and was admittedly curious to re-read it himself. The authors of the Book had had both science and magic beyond his grasp, nearly five millennia earlier. Now he could more easily map the symbolism they'd used for medical knowledge—the twisting snakes that built the body were DNA, of course, but he'd had no concept of such a thing, in Atlantis.

That the Timeless who had settled the island had, was astonishing. That they'd been steeped in magic so deep it became—Lorhen laughed and tipped an imaginary hat toward the hidden stars, saying, "So deep it became indistinguishable from science," aloud, before letting the spill of waves and wind take the place of words again—it fascinated and frightened him. He simply didn't want the kind of knowledge available in the Book to be misused, and he was far too old a student of humanity to believe anything else would happen. The answer, then, was to either destroy it, or control it.

Or, he supposed, make it open source. Give it not to the scientific and medical establishments, but the internet, although it would still require resources—gods knew what kind—to pursue its secrets, and the resources, as always, remained mostly in the hands of the obscenely wealthy. So perhaps it came back to destroy or control, and he would infinitely prefer to control it. He certainly wouldn't willingly destroy the Book, any more than he would have agreed to torch the libraries at Alexandria or Nalanda. It was possible humanity would someday reach the point where his kind and mortals could live together; it was possible that the day would come that immortality would be parceled out to everyone, not just the rich.

It was possible that pigs would sprout wings and fly away. Until all of those things came to pass, Lorhen wanted to be the one with the Book. He didn't trust anyone else. He angled up the beach, heading back to where he'd parked. The sharp cries of seagulls slowed him, and he looked back out over the water, pain tightening his features. Guilt he'd left behind a long time ago, but regret, it seemed, was unavoidable.

Lorhen turned his back on the water, and finished the climb to his car.

He was almost surprised that Ghean wasn't waiting for him at the car. She knew he'd come to Greece; the University of Chicago had returned Cathal's call, politely falling all over itself in its eagerness to accept the donation to the Atlantis fund. They were almost rabidly apologetic at Dr. Kostani's insistence that only Dr. Adams accompany her in the undersea explorations, although, the harried woman on the other end of the line assured Cathal, he was most definitely welcome if he wished to stay at the land base. Cathal had looked at Lorhen, and demurred with such speed that Lorhen was fairly certain the Irishman had decided he would be a third wheel in an absurdly romantic storyline. He'd rolled his eyes as he'd hung up the phone, but Cathal had only smiled.

It wasn't that the idea was unappealing. *Love alters not with his brief hours and weeks, but bears it out even to the edge of doom.* Certainly no one was more qualified than Lorhen to pass judgment on love's ability to pass through the centuries, not that dead lovers often returned to life. Not often, but sometimes; Ghean wasn't actually the first, and probably wouldn't be the last. Her reappearance had a gut-wrenching effect, a sick, thudding disbelief in the pit of the stomach that somehow brought all of the good moments to mind.

Ghean still had her intensity, the dark-eyed focus that made the rest of the universe fade away. Watching her, as they'd exchanged stories, filling in what had happened in Atlantis and after, had been breathtaking. The short haircut that hit at her cheekbones highlighted her eyes in a way the hip-length style she'd worn in Atlantis never could have. The innocence had been lost, as he'd feared. Whether it was the first death, or the ensuing thousands of years of captivity that had broken naivete away from her was irrelevant. Replacing it was anger, a fire that burned a little too near the surface. It was, in its own way, equally compelling, perhaps even more so, for the danger inherent within.

It was also what kept the idea of rekindled romance nothing more than a charming and idle thought. He thrived on passion, other people's passion; his own was too hard to kindle, after so many millennia. It was one reason Cathal, and even Emma and Lisse, had come to matter to Lorhen. They each had an astonishing passion in life—Cathal for his rigid code of right and wrong, Emma for her belief in the Keepers, and Lisse in her sheer joy in going beyond the borders of legality. Lorhen had his own passions, more tempered; scholarship, the practice of medicine, and, above all else, survival.

Ghean had passion in her anger, but no visible focus. It wasn't, Lorhen was certain, that the focus wasn't there, only that he couldn't see it. Far too many years separated them to be able to intuitively guess what she might be thinking or plotting. Until he knew, Lorhen couldn't let sentimentality cloud his judgment.

And yet he'd expected her to be waiting for him at the car. Even he could see the humor, and the arrogance, in that, and smiled at himself.

It wasn't impossible that she might have been waiting. The

University had offered him a room in the small complex they were renting for their land base, but Lorhen had declined. The key word in their description seemed to be 'small'. Lorhen was uncomfortable with placing himself so near to another Timeless, particularly one he didn't entirely trust. Though he'd never slept through the tingling headache that announced another Timeless arrival, the warning wasn't a constant: once a Timeless entered the range of sensitivity, the feeling faded away. Lorhen preferred not to risk the proximity being so close that the warning would be useless, and had rented himself a room in a bed and breakfast. The University had the name and room number, and Ghean could have learned from the proprietor that Dr. Adams had asked directions to the beach that morning.

Lorhen pulled the car up to the B&B, shaking his head at himself. All of that would be a great deal of effort on Ghean's part, and for a man who'd just sworn off revitalized romances, he was spending a lot of time imagining how Ghean might 'just happen' to come across him. He glanced around the car, decided there was nothing worth stealing, and left it without locking the doors, to take the stairs up to the second floor of the B&B two at a time.

Halfway up, the chill of warning slashed through him. Glancing over his shoulder to assure himself there were no mortals lurking, Lorhen drew his shorter blade, taking the last steps more cautiously. At the head of the stairs, he craned his neck around the corner, peering down the hallway.

Ghean stepped out of his room, hands spread deliberately wide and open at her sides. "They let me in," she called. "I explained I was a work colleague. I don't," she added, a smile crossing her face, "think they believed me."

Lorhen sighed, coming around the corner and down the hall without resheathing his knife. "Don't do that. I behave badly when surprised."

"Only when you're surprised? You seem to have displayed bad

behavior extensively since we've become reacquainted." Ghean went back into his room, Lorhen a step behind her.

The room was pink. The walls themselves were an inoffensive pale rose, just enough color to them to warm the room. Alone, it would have been pleasant. Unfortunately, the decorator hadn't stopped there. A fuzzy carpet, a few shades off fuchsia and with loops coming out of the weave, reflected off the walls, leaving both floor and walls brighter than they'd originally been. The curtains over the small window almost defied putting a name to the color; Lorhen had reluctantly decided they were closer to magenta than anything else. The bedclothes were not only pink, but were embroidered with heavy red roses. The effect was overwhelming. Lorhen had literally taken a step backwards when shown into the room, dismay on his features. The proprietor had shrugged helplessly. "It is late in the season. We are redecorating rooms. This is the only one not torn up."

It didn't get better with repeated exposure. Lorhen considered buying a pair of sunglasses just to deal with the glare of the room, although he loathed wearing them outside. Ghean was grinning at the decor. "It's very you, Lor—"

"Logan," he corrected before she finished the word.

After an audible pause, she continued, "Logan. I think they call this being in touch with your feminine side?"

"I make a terrible woman. Too flat-chested, and I just can't disguise the adam's apple. I have," he added, "been surprised a lot since your reappearance."

"Isn't life more exciting that way?" Ghean sat down on the bed, leaving the chair—covered with a pink plush—for Lorhen. He eyed it distastefully, but sat, kicking his feet up on the dresser. He hadn't examined it, but it was probably made of rosewood, to keep in theme.

"No, it's more unpredictable. I don't like unpredictable. Speaking of which, what are you doing here?"

Ghean's eyebrows rose, disappearing beneath her bangs. "Is my appearance unpredictable?"

Lorhen cast a glance at her, then chuckled despite himself. "I was expecting you while I was down at the beach."

"I see. I'll have to work on my timing, then." Ghean folded her arms, leaning against the headboard. "I've painted a glowing review of you, Lorhen. Michelle's expecting a venerable old man, or a child genius beyond compare."

Lorhen leaned backwards in the plush-covered chair, tilting it precariously far and snagging the door with his fingertips to swing it closed as Ghean used his real name again. Her eyebrows lifted a second time, curious. "You're going to have to learn to call me Logan."

"Why? We're behind closed doors now."

"Don't be difficult."

Ghean dimpled, a mockingly apologetic smile. "I'm terribly sorry, Logan. But since we *are* behind closed doors, can't I use your true name?"

Goosebumps ran over Lorhen's arms, even under the greatcoat he hadn't shed. A true name was, in stories, a thing of power and he, despite knowing better, seemed to be a superstitious old man. "You can call me Lorhen," he agreed. "But watch it in public, Ghean. Legends are confirmed by chance encounters and eavesdropping, and I much prefer my status to be legendary instead of confirmed."

Ghean lifted a hand to her lips, pursing them and tapping her thumb against them idly. "Were you this paranoid in Atlantis, Lorhen?"

"No," he said shortly. "but I was a lot younger then, too."

Ghean was silent a moment, folding her arms again. "Tell me about your life, Lorhen," she asked quietly. "Tell me about the life I might have lived."

Lorhen studied her a few seconds. She wore a white silk tank-top tucked into an above-the-knee black skirt. The tank left her arms bared, and there was more muscle in them than Lorhen remembered from Atlantis. She'd left her shoes, black pumps, on the floor, and had her ankles crossed in front of her on the bed. The Hunter's necklace was caught in her arms, silver chain loose against her neck. Her hair was held back by a white head-band, leaving her bangs down. She looked kitten-like, brown eyes tempered with curiosity. Lorhen shut his eyes against the image, and stood to pull his coat off and drape it over the back of his chair. "You read the chronicles. That's a lot of what your life might have been like, and I'll tell you the rest another time. Right now I need to know about this role I'm supposed to play."

"You sound like I've assigned it to you." Ghean's face lost the odd youthfulness and settled into more determined lines. "It was your idea to tag along on my exploration."

"Yes, but you told your Dr. Powers that I was inutterably clever. While I'd never disagree, I need to know how far my supposed boundaries stretch."

"She's known me for years," Ghean defended herself. "I can only push my own apparent knowledge so far, before it starts to look suspicious. You wanted to come along. The least I could do was make you useful to me."

"I live to serve," Lorhen said dryly. "What do I know, Ghean, or shall I just make it up as I go along?" He steepled his fingers, listening intently as Ghean outlined the history she'd sketched for Michelle. "Good God," he burst out when she was done. "You told her I could translate Atlantean?"

"Don't be silly," she said smoothly. "I merely suggested that if anyone could, you could. Besides, there may be nothing left. The papyrus and scrolls won't have survived."

"Unless they're encapsulated like the Book was," Lorhen said.

"Even so, the room might have been destroyed, Those boxes won't hold up under being crushed into a pulp, no matter how well made they were." Ghean took a pillow and switched ends of the bed, rolling onto her stomach and folding the pillow under her chin to she could keep watching Lorhen.

Lorhen arched an eyebrow. "Do you think it was destroyed?"

Ghean hesitated. "I don't want it to have been. There isn't a great deal left to the city, Lorhen. Without something like the Book, I'll never prove that Atlantis really *was* the great advanced civilization of legend. I want it to be there."

"How were you going to do that before I told you about the Book's location?"

Ghean shrugged a shoulder. "Dig up the sewer systems, rebuild the art that I could. Hope for the miraculous preservation of texts. The Book would make it much easier."

"Papyrus was heavy. It might have survived underwater, if it was in anything sealed or partially sealed. Is that what you're looking for, Ghean? Ease of fame and fortune?"

Ghean's eyes glittered as she looked up at Lorhen. "No," she said softly. "I want Atlantis back."

Lorhen shook his head. "It's gone. It's been gone for thousands of years. The past doesn't come back."

"I did," Ghean said. "You did. All we need is the island, now."

"I doubt you're going to be able to raise it from the sea floor, Ghean. Somebody doesn't like it when Timeless fight on holy ground. Atlantis is drowned for good."

Ghean shifted again, sitting up cross-legged with the pillow hugged across her middle. "How did you know?" she asked. "How did you know that something terrible would happen?"

Lorhen spread his hands. "Not much revulses me, Ghean. Even then, not much did, but the idea of fighting on holy ground made my skin crawl. It's as powerful a feeling as the urge to fight when we meet. I didn't know what would happen, and I didn't want to stay to find out. I don't remember ever being in a similar situation before that. The idea just scared the hell out of me, so I ran."

"A lot of people would call you a coward," Ghean observed softly.

"A lot of people," Lorhen said, "would be dead. What do you want me to say, Ghean? Do you want me to say I'm sorry? I'm sorry you were caught in an oubliette for four and a half millennia. Does that help? Does it make it better, or make it all go away?"

Ghean's shoulders tensed as she looked at Lorhen. "Are you sorry you didn't try to rescue me?"

"No," Lorhen said, and watched everything gentle drain from Ghean's face. "You're asking me to be sorry for putting my survival first, and I won't do that, Ghean."

She stood up, putting her shoes on and placing the pillow very carefully back at the head of the bed. "The first expedition leaves at seven, Tuesday morning. We'll be meeting a ship anchored out in the Mediterranean, and we'll go out to the site from there. Please be on time." She brushed past him, stopping just inside the door to look over her shoulder. "You could have lied."

Lorhen listened to the staccato clip of her heels going down the hallway, standing to go to the window when the sound faded entirely. Pushing the curtain aside, he looked down into the parking lot. Ghean came out a moment later, climbing into her car and slamming the door with a hard dull thud. Seconds later the car disappeared down the road. She hadn't been an enemy when she came in, but Lorhen was not certain she wasn't one as she left.

Poorly, if honestly, handled, he thought mockingly, and turned away from the window, letting the curtain drop.

27

The research vessel was a made-over fishing boat, and called *Retribution*. Lorhen scowled at the peeling letters on the prow, waiting for the gangplank to be lowered to the dock. "You couldn't possibly have named it that deliberately," he said to Ghean, who stood a few feet away.

She glanced up at the ship and laughed. "It was donated by an oceanographer about fifteen years ago. He was going through an ugly divorce and got rid of the ship as a tax write-off. His only stipulation was that it be named *Retribution*."

Lorhen glanced back at the ship with a little more approval. "I like his sense of humor."

"The University liked his donation. We rebuilt it from the inside out for this project. The equipment's not quite as modern as I'd like, but funding doesn't keep up with technology."

"I'd ask if there have been funding problems, but I spent the last decade in research."

Ghean shot Lorhen an amused look. "Have they gotten stingy?" she asked, deliberately not naming the Keepers aloud. "When I worked with them, they were remarkably generous."

"You probably fluttered your eyelashes at the bureaucrats. I didn't even recognize my own boss. Funding wasn't a particular concern of his, not for someone who insisted on chasing wild goose tales without any sort of verification over centuries at a time. Really, I don't know how skeptics like that get into the organization."

Michelle Powers, flushed pink with heat, joined the pair as Lorhen finished speaking. "Dr. Adams?"

"The same," Lorhen agreed, and offered his hand. "Dr. Powers, I presume."

"A pleasure. You're younger than I expected." She took his hand and offered him a cursory smile, the kind that women put on in order to prevent male coworkers from considering them bitchy. A genuine smile tugged the corner of Lorhen's mouth in return, and it warmed Powers' smile considerably.

"I'm older than I look," Lorhen promised her. "No one wants to take me seriously because my face doesn't seem to want to age. I expect I'll be grateful for that in a few decades. In the meantime—well, Mary told you I'm something of a recluse. An inability to look properly old and stuffy is part of why I am." Out of the corner of his eye, he watched Ghean lift a hand to cover a broad smile.

"Well, that's a trait you share with Mary. I've known her six years and I swear she hasn't aged a day."

Ghean let her smile come through. "I'm short and exceptionally good at applying makeup. It creates a facade."

"*I'm* good at applying makeup," Powers said dryly. "If I'm good, you must be a wizard. Mary said you two were old friends, Dr. Adams. Was she always this modest?"

"Mmm," Lorhen said thoughtfully, then shook his head. "No. It wasn't that she thought the sun rose and set on her, mind you." He warded off Ghean's pretense of a blow with mock alarm, cringing back with a smile before straightening. She folded her arms, deliberately pouting, and Lorhen couldn't help another smile. "The sun did rise and set on her," he said, watching the tiny woman. "She just never knew how much light she brought with her."

Ghean's expression softened a little, and Lorhen looked away to catch Powers' look of amusement. If he was getting sentimental, at least there was an audience to enjoy it. The tense exchange at the B&B seemed to have blown over. Lorhen was relieved; he'd handled it inelegantly, and had no desire to spend several days cooped up with an edgy Timeless.

"I'm sorry you weren't able to join us at Saturday's dinner party. It was something of a fundraiser, but there were a number of ancient-world scholars there. I'm sure your input would have been fascinating. Mary said you weren't feeling well after the long flight."

Lorhen's eyebrows went up a little. "A little of that, and a little terminal shyness, I think it was. I've never thought my social skills were my strongest point." He looked over Powers' head at Ghean, one eyebrow lifting higher. Ghean shrugged, failing to look even slightly apologetic. Lorhen grinned in spite of himself. The conversation hadn't blown over. Ghean had deliberately failed to mention the dinner in retaliation for his honesty. It made him something of a boor in the eyes of his new colleagues, and that, evidently, leveled the playing field. "Touché," he mouthed at Ghean, and her lips twitched in acknowledgment.

"...you specialized in ancient languages? Is that correct, Dr. Adams?"

Lorhen blinked, turning his focus onto Dr. Powers again. "Logan," he said absently. "We're going to be working together, after all. No need for such formality. Myths and languages, yes. They tend to go hand in hand. It's difficult to decipher old texts if you know nothing of the language. I like to think of myself as a purist, translating as accurately as possible."

"It's a pity we'll never know how accurate any of our translations are," Powers said. "There are moments when I reel with the arrogance of trying to choose the best words for languages dead thousands of years."

"Oh? Are you a translator, Dr. Powers?"

"Michelle," Powers corrected, "if I'm supposed to call you Logan. No," she added hastily, "not myself. Man in general, I meant."

Lorhen twisted half a smile. "From the myths and legends we do have, I think it's safe to say that arrogance is a failing mankind has had since history began, and no doubt long before."

Ghean eyed Lorhen, murmuring, "You would know," before saying, more audibly, "They've finally got the gangplank down. Shall we board?"

The ship managed to be bigger inside than it was outside, though it wasn't small from the outside. They were conspicuously abandoned on deck by Dr. Powers, so Ghean showed Lorhen down to the tiny cabin that was his quarters. "It's a little isolated," she said, navigating the narrow passageways, "but I thought you might prefer that. Michelle's cabin is down on the other end, next to mine. She tried very hard to exchange yours for hers."

Lorhen smirked. "She and Cathal should talk," he said softly, and glanced into the cabin. He had no more than two inches of clearance above his head. The decor was compact, unattractive, and extremely functional. A hard-looking bed with a blanket turned at military corners filled one wall; a shelf above it with webbing across the opening allowed a place to store luggage. Lorhen dropped his small suitcase on the bed for the moment, turning to survey the rest of the room. A desk and a closet took up the other long wall; if he stood in the middle and stretched his arms, he could touch both walls.

"Small," Ghean said dryly, "but you weren't expected."

"Why do I have the feeling you insisted that I would be content with standard quarters, despite having handed over an obscene amount of money to your excavation fund?"

Ghean flashed a smile. "Because it wouldn't make any sense

to donate all that money and then use it to fix up a room so you could live in indulgent comfort while joining us on the explorations."

Lorhen snorted. "Of course. Well, it's fine. I've lived in worse."

"Besides." Ghean's smile was abruptly underscored by a veneer of steel. "It's my party, and I don't want anyone to forget that. Including you."

For a moment Lorhen was captivated by the zeal in her eyes. Reflected in the excitement there was a girl anticipating a journey home, her wedding day, a lifetime with her beloved. The motion of lowering his head to kiss her was checked just as the muscles began to tense; instead, Lorhen lifted a hand to flick a salute at her. "Aye, aye, ma'am."

She ignored him. "There are reports in the conference room, or what we call the conference room, anyway. It's actually the mess hall. You may wish to look at them. They detail what we've found so far. You'll probably want the information so you don't overstep the limits of our current knowledge."

Lorhen nodded. Leaving his coat behind, he followed Ghean through the narrow halls to the galley. As she opened the door, he laughed. "Where do you actually eat?"

There wasn't a flat surface in the room, including the floor, that wasn't stacked with in-boxes clamped, screwed, and occasionally tied in place, all filled with files, papers, and maps. Some of the boxes were more precariously balanced than others—more than one was bungee-corded onto a chair that had been bolted or tied to the floor—and the only way to find a seat was to judge which box was least likely to capsize if moved, and how to anchor it once it was set aside. Fluorescent light glared down on the papers, reflecting brilliantly off the grey walls. Without the masses of paperwork, the room would be extraordinarily dull; with them, Lorhen had to squint briefly while his eyes adjusted to the peculiar light level.

"Usually frantically running down the hallways. Mealtime seems to signal either a disaster or a discovery, around here." Ghean rifled through a stack of plastic boxes to find what she wanted. "This," she said, and laid out a fat pamphlet on the table, "and this and this." She planted two more texts, of increasing thickness, on top of the first. "Geologic history of the Mediterranean," she said, tapping the top one, then bumping it aside half an inch to prod the second. "A history of the project," and she pushed it away to get to the third. "And a location record and theories on use of the artifacts we've found. Some of them are painfully wrong. Worse than watching the floodlights ghosting over houses I once visited is hearing the wildly inaccurate hypotheses the other archaeologists are coming up with. Don't you want to shake them and yell until they listen, sometimes?"

"I tend to bury that desire in my own best self-interest," Lorhen said, "but there are moments, yes. These days, I go rant at Devane when a particularly disastrous interpretation makes the news." He frowned at the stack Ghean had set aside for him. "Actually, that's how I ended up here. I was going to poke fun at the poor fool who thought he'd found Atlantis." He looked up at Ghean, expression wry. "Goodness, wasn't I surprised."

Ghean laughed, and moved an eighteen-inch pile of papers off a chair, depositing them neatly into a box on the floor instead. "Sit," she said, "and read. I'll make a concerted effort to not surprise you again for at least fifteen minutes. You're much more pleasant when you think you're in control." She walked past him, then stopped with her hand on the doorknob, looking at him curiously. After a moment she shook her had and stepped out, letting the door latch behind her.

Lorhen frowned after her. "Everybody's more pleasant when they think they're in control. It's a very nice illusion," he muttered, and sat, turning the frown on the pile Ghean had left him. Then the lure of research seized him, and he pulled the first report toward himself, beginning to read.

❧

Ghean tapped a forefinger against her thigh as she walked back down the hall from the ship's mess. *It's obvious, now that we've hit on it,* the patient one murmured. *Lorhen's security blanket is control.*

She mumbled, "Mmm," aloud. "He was in control all the time in Atlantis, wasn't he?"

He had the time to anticipate his options, the patient one agreed. *The circumstances may have changed from moment to moment, but never too drastically. There was always time to think and choose.*

Never enough time, the frightened one muttered. *Can't choose that fast.*

For once the patient one listened to the frightened one, considering. *Perhaps it's more likely he played out potential confrontations and events well ahead of time,* it suggested. *Factoring in what he knew of human behavior to determine the most likely course of events and how to deal with them.*

"Gods, that would be exhausting," Ghean protested.

We do not know him at all, the patient one said severely. *We had no appreciation of how little we could understand him, in Atlantis. Our childhood experiences with him were less than a single facet of the man.*

"He tried," Ghean said. "He tried to show us more when he told us about being Timeless."

We lacked in sophistication. The patient one brushed aside Ghean's argument. *That lack thwarted his ability to expose himself to us, as much as his own habits of privacy did. In time, with maturity, we would have understood him better.*

But we had no time, the frightened one hissed. *We only had darkness and the sea, forever and ever. When will we go home?*

Time should have been ours, the patient one said soothingly. *We'll regain it when we we take his Blending. It won't be quite the same, but it will be deeply satisfying. The centuries we missed will be ours, and we will rebuild Atlantis. Patience. All we need is patience.*

Ghean rubbed her fingertip against the gold of her ring, feeling the smooth surface bump slightly over the scars. "He was in control until the earthquake," she suggested. "That's when he panicked, that's when he ran. Even some Atlanteans kept their fear of earthquakes all their lives." A smile flitted across her face. "I might be able to forgive him for panicking."

'*You're asking me to be sorry for putting my survival first, and I won't do that,*' the patient one reminded her with a snap. *His words. It wasn't panic. He chose to run. He knew we would be resurrected from the blow that felled us, and still he ran. He was so certain that choice was right that he would offer neither apology for it nor lie to spare us. He was in control. We shouldn't doubt that. We shouldn't forgive him for that choice.*

Ghean made her way up to deck, leaning on the railing. Wind pushed hair back from her face, and she bared her teeth into it. *You're right*, she acknowledged the patient one silently.

There won't be any more surprises, then, the patient one said. *We'll allow him apparent control over our relationship with him, tenuous as it is. It will make betraying him in the end that much more satisfying, watching him grasp at threads he thought he'd woven as they come unraveled around him.*

Betrayal, the frightened one whispered hungrily.

Down in the galley, Lorhen leaned back, rubbing his eyes with one hand. It was no wonder new archaeological treasures kept being discovered on the Mediterranean floor, despite it being well-explored. A history of the seabed activity detailed earthquakes of a 4.0 magnitude or higher occurring at least yearly for most of the last century, and sometimes there were many in a year. While not enough to do much more than rumble on land,

and knock a few jars off their shelves, every quake did resettle the sea floor a little. Eventually it made a difference, exposing new land and what it carried for explorers to find. It seemed almost inevitable that Atlantis would have been found. Ghean's knowledge of where her ancient home had been merely made it easier.

The report actually traced the seabed's history back several thousand years, citing quakes that had rocked the Mediterranean area more than three thousand years ago. One or two had been significant enough that Lorhen actually remembered them; his own journals cited the volcanic eruptions and earthquakes when Pompeii was buried and preserved forever in a fall of ash. Much earlier, while Lorhen rode with the Unending, had been the destruction of Minoan Crete. Both disasters had made Lorhen curious as to whether or not they'd been triggered by Timeless fighting on holy ground. It had only been a year or two since Emma Hickman had confirmed that the eruption at Pompeii, at least, had been. *So I was right*, Lorhen thought, deliberately shaping the words as a remembrance to Minyah. *That is always satisfying.*

He picked up the earthquake report again, flipping through it to the early twentieth century. Ghean had broken free from her prison in the early months of World War I, she'd said. From the report, Lorhen guessed an earthquake in October of 1914 was the one that had finally twisted the temple stone enough to give way a little. Its epicenter had been considerably north of Atlantis' location, but it had measured a 7.7, enough to do damage over a widespread area.

Lorhen looked through the other reports perfunctorily. Had he not known the truth, the history of the development of the Atlantis Project would have been fascinating. As it was, Lorhen had a difficult time reading it as anything other than a cover story. It was a good one: young Mary Kostani's remarkable education and passion for finding the lost civilization could and had inspired research and funding on a cause most scholars would prefer to leave alone for fear of ridicule. The report was liberally scattered with instances of 'genius' and 'prodigy' by Ghean's colleagues. Lorhen grinned every time he came across them. 'Astonishing leaps of intuition leading to daring precepts about the day-to-day lives of ancient citizens'. Ghean must love the accolades; he certainly would. He was surprised she didn't have to go through a door sideways to accommodate the ego the report must have given her. Of course, he thought with a smirk, she was short.

The final report dealt with what they'd found and what they thought of it. Halfway through a minutely detailed description of a mug inscribed with a bull, Lorhen let the papers fall to his lap and frowned at the far wall. Someone was going to find the Hunter House's symbol, sooner or later. Michelle Powers, at the very least, was going to recognize it as matching Ghean's necklace. Lorhen looked at the description again, glancing over the accounting of the circle and the points within it that circled the bull's head. Save for the object inside the circle, Ghean's necklace was identical. Somebody should have noticed that already. Maybe Ghean had confessed her immortality to Powers.

Lorhen rejected the thought out of hand. Powers wouldn't have made a joke about Ghean's apparent failure to age if she'd known she was Timeless. Perhaps Ghean simply had a prepared explanation already, because she certainly couldn't be that clumsy. Or perhaps she could be. For a woman who had survived well over four millennia, Ghean was still very young.

A warning rush of nausea swept through him. Lorhen stood, reaching for his sword, and then let his hand fall away, on the chance that Ghean was not alone. He did, however, step around the table, so it was between him and the door when it opened a moment later. Ghean leaned on the doorknob, brown eyes dancing. After a quick look over her shoulder to be certain no one had followed her, she smiled at Lorhen. "We're almost there. The ship will be anchoring in a few minutes, and we'll drop down for a preliminary dive this afternoon to decide what area we want to begin in. Well, Lorhen. Are you ready to go back to Atlantis?"

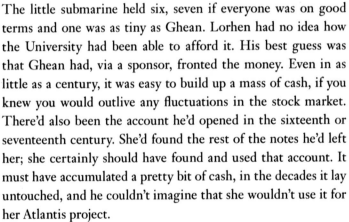

28

The little submarine held six, seven if everyone was on good terms and one was as tiny as Ghean. Lorhen had no idea how the University had been able to afford it. His best guess was that Ghean had, via a sponsor, fronted the money. Even in as little as a century, it was easy to build up a mass of cash, if you knew you would outlive any fluctuations in the stock market. There'd also been the account he'd opened in the sixteenth or seventeenth century. She'd found the rest of the notes he'd left her; she certainly should have found and used that account. It must have accumulated a pretty bit of cash, in the decades it lay untouched, and he couldn't imagine that she wouldn't use it for her Atlantis project.

Because unlike the *Retribution*, the sub's equipment was state of the art. It didn't look more than fifteen feet from end to end, and a significant portion of the walls were filled with computer screens. The pilot's seat and array covered most of the front end, tiny windows of information beeping quietly as they displayed and redisplayed data, updating it every few seconds. Immediately behind and to the left of the cockpit, an alarming-looking armed waldo was set up in front of the largest screen, which flickered grey. Opposite it was a camera, set up at an angle to look out a porthole, and next to that, a seat. The back of another terminal setup made a back for the seat at exactly the wrong height to provide comfort. The rest of the submarine's interior essentially reflected the layout of the camera and seat, with an extraneous porthole at the tail end. In front of both, sturdy black metal boxes, one with 'electrical equipment' stenciled on the outside, had been stacked up to make haphazard chairs.

Lorhen, too tall to stand comfortably in the compact tube, laughed as he stepped in. "I feel like I'm watching *Titanic* again," he said to Ghean.

She grinned. "Only ours isn't a set. Since you're here, Logan, let's put you to good use. Know anything about mapping software?" She lead him through the tangle of seats and terminals, stepping over boxes on the floor.

"I forgot to brush up," Lorhen said. "Too bad I missed the dinner party. Someone could have reminded me." Once seated, it wasn't too uncomfortable. There was a porthole behind his left shoulder that he could see through if he twisted at the proper angle, and he had head room. To make up for it, there was no leg room. Lorhen decided wisdom was the better part of valor, and didn't complain.

Ghean shrugged deprecatingly. "I could always hope. Luckily for you, the computer does all the work. If this goes off," and she flicked a finger at an unlit light, "call him." Ghean pointed over her shoulder with her thumb as a long-haired young man, taller than Lorhen, crawled into the sub.

"What about me?" he asked, ducking toward the duo.

"Logan, this is Jerry. Jerry, Dr. Adams, one of our sponsors. Jerry keeps the computer systems running."

"I'm the resident geek," Jerry agreed, and stuck out his hand. "Michelle mentioned you at the party Saturday, but said you couldn't make it. Too bad. Mary actually put on a party dress. It was worth seeing."

Lorhen grinned. "Hi, Jerry. I'm sorry I missed it. It's been a while since I've seen her dressed up."

Ghean leveled an icy stare at Lorhen. He widened his eyes, saved from having to defend himself by Michelle's arrival with two others. "Mary Jerry Logan," Michelle said without looking at any of the three as she took her seat. She had a video camera in one hand, a battery case in the other, and went to prod at the camera behind the pilot's seat.

Behind her came a woman in her mid forties, her hair cut military-short. "Afternoon," she said pleasantly, offering her hand to Lorhen. "Dana Franks. I'm the pilot. Presumably you're the honored guest. This is my wife, Anne." She stepped aside to present a blonde woman in her late thirties.

"Hi," she said, "no relation."

Lorhen blinked, then laughed. "No, I don't imagine there is. Logan Adams. It's a pleasure." He shook hands as they were offered, then watched curiously as Anne seated herself in front of the waldo. "I gather you drive the robot?"

Anne glanced over and nodded. "Handy. I volunteered for this job because I get to stare dreamily out the window and imagine life in Atlantis when I'm not working." She grinned. "It's quite the sight, Dr. Adams. You're in for the experience of a lifetime."

Lorhen looked up momentarily to meet Ghean's eyes. "I'm sure I am."

Ghean smiled, more an expression of acknowledgment than humor. She dropped into her seat, just in front of Lorhen, and turned to look at the pale water outside.

"Finished the systems check fifteen minutes ago," Dana announced. "Unless anybody forgot to stop by the bathroom, we're ready to go." She waited ten seconds, then nodded. "Seal up the hatch, would you, Adams? Anne, check it."

Lorhen stood to do as he was told, then found himself engaged in an awkward little dance with Anne as he tried to regain his seat while she went to check the seal. They ended up grinning broadly at one another, and Lorhen backed up with exaggerated steps to get out of her way. Fortune, more than skill, prevented him from setting his foot down on a box, and he wavered briefly, regaining his balance more solidly after Anne stepped back again. "Nice and tight," she reported. "You all right there, Logan?"

"Fine," he answered, returning to his seat. "Just working through a lifelong desire to be Charlie Chaplin. I just don't have his knack for physical schtick."

"Charlie Chaplin never had to work under these conditions," Jerry pointed out.

The sub broke loose from the *Retribution*, sinking into the Mediterranean waters. Lorhen looked out a porthole, watching bubbles rise rapidly by. "You're certainly right about that."

The light change was gradual as the submarine sank into the sea. Fifty feet down, Lorhen noticed the sub's internal lights for the first time; by fifty meters the light from the water outside was of a peculiar, ethereal quality. Aside from the occasional school of startled fish, the outside scenery was not particularly captivating. The others bantered back and forth lightly, and Lorhen listened with half an ear for a few moments, watching as the submarine descended into darkness. Within minutes it was too dark to make out more than vague shapes. Lorhen took his gaze from the porthole, glancing instead at Ghean, wondering suddenly how well she handled the submersions, considering her history.

She stared fixedly out a porthole. Lorhen could see tiny tense muscles along her jaw, though her shoulders appeared relaxed. Her breathing was deliberately even, long slow breaths through her nostrils. Her posture was rigid, but for her shoulders; Lorhen imagined the stiff muscles along her spine, and for a moment considered reaching out to comfort her. Probably not a good idea, all things considered.

He was nearly certain he hadn't spoken aloud, but Ghean turned her head to look at him as if she'd heard him. Her eyes were black, expressionless in the off-colored lighting of the submarine. She watched him for several seconds, silent and stony-faced, before returning her attention to the growing darkness outside the porthole.

Michelle finally succeeded in the arcane adjustments she was making to her cameras, and sat back, satisfied. She caught Lorhen's intent study of Ghean, and grinned broadly, gesturing at the pair with a tilt of her head as she murmured to Anne. The blonde woman looked over her shoulder to smile as well, and Lorhen lifted his eyebrows quizzically at the two. Anne pulled an innocent moue, and Michelle averted her eyes, chuckling.

They were surrounded by matchmakers. Lorhen, knowing it would add fuel to the fire, still couldn't help grinning. He leaned forward, murmuring, "Didn't you tell them we were just friends?" to Ghean.

Her gaze snapped back to him. "Yes," she replied, "I said we were very g..." Color drained from her face. "Very good friends," she repeated, barely more than a breath. Her chin moved fractionally, as if a blow had been taken and almost entirely absorbed. "Just like you said you and my mother were."

Oh, shit, Lorhen thought with perfect clarity.

"You utter bastard," Ghean said precisely, out loud, and in a tongue dead for forty-five hundred years. Every head in the submarine snapped around to stare in open interest at the petite woman.

Briefly, unpleasantly, Lorhen wondered what happened if there was a Blending underwater, but shut the thought down as hard as he could. They couldn't fight here, even if they'd brought their weapons on board: there just wasn't enough room, and it would certainly end badly for the mortals. "Ghean," he said, in the softest, most reasonable tone he could command, and in the same language she'd spoken in, "you'd been dead for a thousand years. I thought *she'd* been dead that long, for gods' sake."

"She was my mother!"

Lorhen winced. "Ghean, after that long, what difference does that sort of relationship make? We were both at hard places in our lives and we found an old friend when we needed one. It's not unusual for Timeless to become lovers—"

Ghean erupted out of her seat, an explosion of movement startling and effective despite her diminutive size. "My mother, Lorhen! She was my mother! You were about to be my husband! 'You were at hard places'. Don't try that, you son of a bitch. She was my mother. You slept with my *mother*!"

Lorhen grimaced. "Dammit, Ghean. That relationship, Minyah being your mother, was a thousand years dead. She was a friend when I needed one. Old friends become lovers—"

"Oh, clearly. I was your lover, Lorhen, and I don't see you trying that tack with me!"

Astonishment slammed through Lorhen, half powered by disbelief and half by relief. Her offense offered a way to handle the situation, at least, and if he chose not to think too deeply about whether his words were true, he was all right with that. "When have I had time?" he demanded. "Do you think you're not still beautiful? Do you think I don't want you? Gods above, Ghean, I loved you. I mourned for a thousand years. I became someone else entirely to walk away from the pain. It took that long to put away the grief. And then you show up out of the deep blue sea," Lorhen flinched mentally at the unfortunately accurate phrase, "and I find out that loving you didn't go away with the pain. What do you think I'm doing here?"

Ghean's eyes and mouth vied for a winning position in roundness. Lorhen didn't dare look at the rest of the sub's crew to see their expressions. The absolute silence was more than enough to suggest what was on their faces, and it was only broken by Ghean's faltering, "The...Book...?"

Lorhen's shoulders dropped and he looked away a moment.

"What was I supposed to say? Especially after the story you told us about your captivity. Why would you forgive me, why would you even look at me? But a book isn't worth five million dollars, Ghean. I want to know you again. Who you've become."

Ghean dropped back into her seat, still staring at Lorhen. "You said…you said you weren't sorry."

Lorhen spread his hands helplessly. "I'm not sorry I've survived. I can't be sorry for the choices that have kept me alive, Ghean. They're what make me who I am. I can regret the consequences of those choices." A sad smile pulled at his mouth. "You're the only Timeless woman I ever wanted to marry."

"Oh." Ghean turned away abruptly to resume staring out the porthole. Lorhen let out a long, slow breath, eyes closing. When he opened them again a moment later, it was to find the four other crew members gaping at him.

"What," Michelle, the first to regain her voice, demanded, "the hell was that?"

"An old quarrel," Lorhen answered softly. "I apologize for subjecting you to that." He closed his eyes against the audibly restrained silence. After several seconds, he heard Dana turn her chair back around to being piloting again. A few minutes later, conversation picked up, giving Lorhen the privacy he needed to sort through what he'd said. Enough of what he'd said had been true, or true enough, to lend credence to the rest. At the least, that his relationship with Minyah had grown out of friendship, and that he had indeed become someone else for a thousand years after Ghean's death was true. Riding with the Unending hadn't been a time for healing, though. The pain of Ghean's death had faded in time, as it always did, but the Unending had been about reveling in bloodlust and power, not mourning loss. Only the first choice, to join Yama, had been spurred by bitterness at death—and, Lorhen reminded himself, the desire to keep his head. He shouldn't flatter himself, lest he grow too fond of a more noble self-image than belonged to him.

Still, a thousand years of mourning made a good dramatic statement, and Ghean seemed to have been taken by it. It was unlikely that mere seduction would be enough to calm her fury, but it had obviously been a step in the right direction. And technically he *hadn't* had the time or opportunity to try resuming an ancient romance; the fact that he hadn't wanted or planned to, either, was—at the moment—beside the point. And the Book was worth millions, was priceless, but Ghean clearly didn't need to hear him say that right now.

Mostly, though, he couldn't pretend that he didn't still have strong feelings for the Atlantean woman. Perhaps not the feelings Ghean herself wanted him to have, although she certainly still stirred passion in him, albeit tempered with disbelief and distrust. Nor was he so old as to be inured to curiosity about whether they might have some kind of relationship. That had nothing to do with his decision to bribe the University into allowing him passage on the ship to Atlantis, but apparently the idea could be used to appeal to Ghean's more romantic nature.

Ghean was a romantic. Lorhen's eyes popped open suddenly, and he caught Anne staring frankly across the sub at him. Caught, she blushed and looked away, and Lorhen closed his eyes again. It was foolish to judge Ghean by his own standards. She wasn't as old as his memory told him she had to be, and she had been—effectively—the princess locked in the tower, for aeons. Maybe an almost-insane clinging to hope was the only way to deal with eternal captivity.

He would, he concluded, make a lousy prince in a tower. Hope was rarely his stock in trade; betting on human nature served him more reliably, but that cynical attitude probably wouldn't see him through four and a half thousand years of captivity.

Ghean *had* been the only Timeless woman he'd ever wanted to marry. The disaster surrounding that was more than enough to put him off the idea permanently. Lorhen noticed he was holding his breath, and let it out in a long exhalation. The goal, ultimately, was possession of the Book, preferably to hide it away somewhere as inaccessible as it had been for the last several millennia. If romance was the easiest way to reach that goal, so be it. Lorhen twisted half a smile. He'd had more unpleasant tasks. Just as long as he didn't get carried away.

Ghean stared at the blackness beyond the porthole, barely hearing Lorhen as he explained the outburst to the other crew members. His words were still ringing in her ears. It was just barely possible she had misjudged his motives. She struggled with the idea, caught between worried suspicion and wanting to believe.

The belief was beginning to win out. It was the question of control that brought Ghean down that path. Lorhen had been careful with his description of his relationship with her mother. Had she not used the same phrase to characterize her own relationship with him, she wouldn't have hit on the truth. Lorhen couldn't have anticipated the random chain of events to prepare the lie in advance. It gave credence to his words.

So did the language. Unlike Ghean, who still thought in Atlantean at times, Lorhen would have had no reason to speak the language in at least three thousand years. Translating lies into a tongue long put out of mind on an instant's notice wouldn't be an easy undertaking. It was possible, perhaps even likely, that he had been telling the truth. He was still in love with her.

For a moment, Ghean tried to examine her own feelings toward Lorhen. Prominent was betrayal, and that wound was made even deeper by her new knowledge. The union between her mother and Lorhen made a certain sense, though, once Ghean thought on it. Lorhen would have believed that Minyah was his only access to the girl he'd loved, to Ghean herself. Being with Minyah was not so much seeking comfort in the arms of an old friend, but searching desperately for what he had lost, in the person who had been closest to Ghean. Ghean shivered lightly.

To have used Minyah in that way was not only reprehensible, but pathetic. Ghean could almost feel sorry for Lorhen.

Pity, then, was another aspect. Anger, though, was greater, and bound up irrevocably with betrayal. She could still see him as attractive, however, and he obviously still loved her. Ghean would allow him in her bed, if that was what he desired. There would be physical pleasure, at the least, and in the end the treachery of taking his head would be that much more satisfying.

Ghean glanced over her shoulder quickly, to half smile at Lorhen. His eyes were closed, a small smile on his own lips. Imagining them together, Ghean guessed, and her smile widened. The elaborate plans of revenge she'd built over the years to occupy herself were crumbling beneath the vastly more satisfying reality that was playing out. She hadn't imagined she'd have so much power over the ancient Timeless. With one hand, she would give him the world, and with the other, take it away when he least expected it.

Everything will be ours, the patient one crowed. *His power, our revenge, and the memories that he made over thousands of years. Years that should have been ours to live. Everything will finally be ours.*

And then we'll go home to Atlantis, Ghean promised the frightened voice, and closed her eyes, sleeping as the submarine continued its way to the ocean bottom.

29

Half an hour later, the sea lit up in a sudden flood of light. "Water's nice and clear down here, long as there haven't been any quakes," Dana said. "We're about fifty meters from the bottom. Take a peek, Logan. You'll be able to see the city any minute now."

Lorhen, instead, leaned his head against the porthole's rim and closed his eyes, a queer thrill of anticipation running through him. Forty-five hundred years ago his first look at Atlantis had been from above, looking down the mountain slope to the glistening metropolis. Today, the water still hid the vista, but Lorhen rebuilt the image in his mind.

It wouldn't be the same, of course; nothing was ever the same. *You can't go home again*, the saying went, although it wasn't true. Lorhen had long since learned to recognize the changes taking place around him, or to ignore them without finding them a betrayal when he looked back to see they'd taken root. And Atlantis had been drowned for millennia; it was surprising there was anything left to return to. In the frantic minutes while he and Minyah ran from the epicenter at the temple, he'd seen buildings crumble and be swallowed whole into the crust. The old city must have been well-built indeed, for anything to have survived.

"There we go," Michelle breathed, "Atlantis."

Lorhen opened his eyes to look through the light-stained water. "Jesus," he said inadvertently, and clamped his teeth together to prevent further commentary.

Even in the light's rapidly fading radius, it was obvious far more of the city had survived than he could have imagined. Streets were still visible, only a few feet below the submarine. Loosely collected sediment stirred into a fine film as the sub's engines disturbed the water. Shattered buildings lined the streets, walls crumpled in, leaving enough foundation to make vivid the separation of boulevards and buildings. Lorhen leaned forward, not quite pressing his nose against the glass to look as far to the sides as he could. They were too far from the city's center for the temple to be visible, and from the width of the street below, he suspected they were on one of the narrow cross-streets that sliced through the major roads.

"There isn't a lot of crusting on the buildings," he wondered aloud.

Michelle nodded. "We're not sure why. The seabed is pretty active. We've been trying to figure out if there was some sort of protective layer over the city that's been knocked loose recently, maybe a slick residue or a heavy layer of dirt that settled after the city sank. Something that corrosion couldn't quite get a grip on."

"Favored of the gods," Lorhen murmured, looking back out the window. "Maybe they protected it." *Until all its children had left it*, he finished silently.

Michelle chuckled. "Maybe. The amount of buildup is what we'd normally see on something that'd been underwater a century or so, maybe a little less. Their gods must be favoring *us*. More than they did the people who lived here, at any rate."

As the submarine moved slowly forward, Lorhen could see that there were huge chunks of land that had been left smooth by the quake. A building in front of them had been sheared in two, one side still standing, a small plain of black rock where the other half had once been. Lorhen closed his eyes a moment, contrasting the absolute stillness of the drowned city to its last panicked minutes. Memories of voices echoed in his ears, terrorized screams and calls for help. The sound of rock, tearing apart and resealing itself without rhythm, ground out the voices, and was in turn replaced by the boiling of water as it drank the city down into the ocean.

Lorhen could feel the pulse in his throat, throbbing nearly as hard as memory swept him up as it had those many millennia ago. The sheer, stark stab of hope that had jolted through him in the moment that everything had fallen silent ripped into him again, making his heart lurch with a sickening double-beat. Devastation replaced it a breath later, as it had then, as his thoughts reeled through the next seconds, the redoubling of the quake that sent Atlantis to the sea bed. His muscles felt again the stretch as he reached for Ragar's hand, an instant too late, and memory jarred his feet with the falls from one broken piece of road to another.

There was a hand on his shoulder. Lorhen jerked back, eyes flying open to see Ghean leaning toward him. "I actually think it's taking you harder than it did me," she said in quiet astonishment.

Lorhen pushed the heel of his hand against his forehead, wiping away beaded sweat. *I was there*, he thought. *You were dead.*

Michelle gave him a sympathetic smile, across the sub. "It's hit us all pretty hard," she said. "Can you imagine how terrifying it must have been?"

Through a dry throat, Lorhen answered, "I think I was." He inhaled sharply, feeling the lack of air in his lungs.

"There are ghosts here," Anne said, in all apparent seriousness. "I've driven a lot of waldos through a lot of wrecks, but I've never seen anything like Atlantis. Something happened here, something that shouldn't have."

Lorhen and Ghean locked eyes, neither willing to look away. "I think you're right," Lorhen agreed softly, and shook himself, willing himself toward steadiness. "You're sure this is Atlantis?" The question was meant for Michelle; Ghean knew, and Lorhen had never doubted her.

"The carbon dating completely fails to match any of the legends," Michelle said slowly. "At least, what we've found doesn't. We've found artifacts dating back six thousand years. From the stories out of Egypt, they should be either twice that, or only four thousand years old."

"Thera," Lorhen guessed.

Michelle nodded. "It exploded in 1627BC, drowning Crete. I have to admit that I was a believer, not that long ago, that Crete had been Atlantis, I mean. When Mary pinpointed this location as the city, I assumed anything we found here would date back to then, that the quakes set off by Thera's eruption had perhaps sunk another town, too." She shook her head. "The youngest material we've found is a little more than forty-five centuries old. Whatever sank this place, it wasn't Thera. Not the eruption that drowned Crete." She looked out the porthole, shaking her head again. "This is Atlantis," she said. "I can feel it in my gut." She glanced back at Lorhen with a self-deprecating grin. "Nicely scientific, eh?"

"Careers have been made on less." Lorhen returned his gaze to the city they drifted through.

Beneath the crust of sea grime that roughened the once clean lines of the city, the stone was still white, untarnished by its centuries beneath the sea. Under the sub's flood lights, they glowed an unnerving pale blue, the color of moon shadows on snow. Dana changed directions, turning down a wider street; within seconds, Lorhen saw it as one of the main avenues. There was no way to determine if they were heading into town or out, and he frowned in frustration out the window.

Ghean reached over the back of the ledge in front of him, and tapped the terminal window at his elbow. "It's mapping," she reminded him, "figure out where we are."

Lorhen blinked at the screen, then nodded. "Jerry? Can I make it tell me what's been mapped previously?"

"Sure. Here." Jerry came over, tapping out a sequence. A smaller window opened lower in the screen, covering a quarter of the original image. He said, "Navigate with the arrow keys," and returned to his seat.

"How many dives have there been?" Lorhen asked absently, studying what Jerry had brought up.

"This is the fifth," Ghean answered. "We went back to the States to try to get more money to fund more."

"It worked," Lorhen said dryly. Ghean grinned.

Lorhen studied the screen intently, trying to overlay his memories of the city onto the map. After several minutes, he concluded memory was making it more difficult than it would be to study it fresh; he was expecting streets and buildings where the map showed only empty stretches of rock. Still, four of the streets spidered inward, and the additions from the new mapping the computer did indicated they were traveling toward the city center. "Did you find the temple?" he asked thoughtlessly.

Michelle looked away from her camera to lift an eyebrow at him. "Temple?"

Lorhen kicked himself silently, but tapped the smaller window in his screen. "Look at the layout. There's obviously a central point. Governments and religious institutions go at the center of almost any city."

Michelle nodded. "There's a building there. Except for one obvious point where the rock was broken, there are no entrances, no decorations, nothing that might indicate it was a temple."

Lorhen closed his eyes, building the image in his mind. Three daises, the temple centered on the last one. The House symbols, holding the temple roof above its thick walls. And, carved on the outer walls, artistry of the gods coming down out of the mountains to share their gifts with the citizens of the fishing village that became the legendary city. Opening his eyes, he studied Ghean's profile. Could the fire have melted all that away? If so, what had happened to the room below, and the Book? "Is it higher than the city around it?" he asked aloud.

"Yeah," Michelle said, "but who would build a temple without doors?"

"Someone who didn't want their gods disturbed," Jerry said to his computer, and looked up defensively when Michelle spun to stare at him with interest. "What? Doesn't the geek get to be esoteric and wise sometimes too?"

"You seem a little grounded in this century for that, Jerry, that's all," Anne grinned.

"Hey, I've got a degree in philosophy."

Anne's eyebrows shot up. "You do? What are you doing here?"

"Philosophy doesn't pay very well." Jerry shrugged.

"You may be on to something there, though," Michelle said slowly. "We call our churches the houses of God. An ancient civilization may have taken that idea more literally."

Lorhen and Ghean exchanged glances, Ghean visibly biting her tongue as a debate ensued. The worst of it was, Lorhen knew, that the mortals' deductions weren't unreasonable. A doorless temple was more likely than the truth, certainly. Lorhen returned his attention to the map, glancing occasionally at Ghean, whose face held more tightness than just the debate could account for.

He couldn't blame her: the ghost city disturbed him, and its former beauty was far more deeply imprinted on Ghean than it had been on Lorhen. If the temple's features were melted away, there was no real way to tell what direction anything lay in; he, certainly, wouldn't trust what had once been north and south to have remained the same as the island twisted and sank. He badly wanted a sense of perspective, and if *he* wanted one, Ghean's sense of being unmoored had to be much more dramatic.

"Care to explore, Logan?" Michelle asked suddenly.

Lorhen and Ghean both looked up, equally startled out of their respective musings. "Explore? Perhaps I'm a little narrow-minded, Michelle, but somehow the idea of popping out of the sub for a quick jaunt through the streets doesn't entirely appeal to me."

Michelle laughed. "Look, practicality dictates we take this in a pretty methodical manner, mapping out the city and then focusing on what we think will be the biggest motherlode of information. If we can find a place with access to the sewer system, that'll be our number one stopping place. Sewers tend to have more information about a culture than anything else."

Lorhen shot Ghean a glance, thinking of Atlantis' advanced, tidy sewer system, and forbore to tell Dr. Powers that she was bound to be disappointed by what would usually be a safe archaeologist bet. Powers, however, didn't notice the glance, and went on, "The thing is, we've been given an unexpected donation by an extraordinarily generous fellow, and it seemed like we ought to bend to his whim today. You won't get another chance, Logan, so what would you like to look for?"

"Buried treasure!" Lorhen said promptly. "Pirate's gold!"

Anne laughed. "All men are little boys," she said, "and little boys always want pirate treasure."

"It doesn't seem very likely," Lorhen admitted. "What if we took a spin around the outer edge of the city?" He nodded at his screen. "It looks like you've found some boundaries. I wonder if there's anything beyond them."

Ghean glanced at him, an eyebrow arched. "I thought you'd want to look at your so-called temple."

He did, but he hadn't thought of a way to get the submarine into it, and then into the room beneath. It seemed more likely he would have to go swimming, and he couldn't exactly step out of the sub without drowning the lot of them, so: "I do, but I was looking at the symbols on that cup you found, the one with the bull's head. There are points outside it. I have a hunch that the city's laid out like that. The central point is that temple, and maybe there's something in the outlying area that might be of interest." Lorhen widened his eyes, shrugging. "Who knows?"

Ghean's grin was slow and approving. "Who knows?" she repeated. "Shall we, Dana?"

"Sure. The readings say we're in sort of a valley here, maybe the original structure of the island, who knows," she said, deliberately echoing the other two. "I'm going to go up a ways, maybe halfway up the valley wall, and we'll buzz around about there. How's that sound?" Dana looked over her shoulder too briefly to obtain approval, and pulled the submarine up through the water.

Lorhen met Ghean's eyes again, half smiling. The gods lived on the mountaintops; the Houses had been built halfway up, between the gods and the people they'd been raised from. "Sounds like a plan," Lorhen agreed. "Let's see if we can follow the path of one of these wider roads up. Maybe it'll lead to something."

"Sure." Dana nodded.

"Don't get your hopes up too high," Anne advised. "I'd hate to see you disappointed on your first dive."

Lorhen quirked a smile at the blonde woman. "You'd hate to see me put a stop on that check," he teased.

"Too late," Michelle said cheerfully. "The University called me yesterday morning to say it'd been cashed in and credited to our fund."

"Ah well." Lorhen spread his hands. "If I'm disappointed, I'll have to just live with it, then. I've been disappointed before."

"Wise man," Jerry said, without looking up from what he was doing. "You could be a philosopher too."

Lorhen grinned. "I don't know enough about computers."

Jerry looked up with a laugh, touching a finger to his nose. "On the nose, buddy," he grinned, "you got it on the nose."

"Mountains coming up," Dana reported. "Keep your eyes peeled. We'll see if Logan's feeling lucky today."

"Do ya feel lucky, punk?" Ghean grated in a singularly terrible imitation of Clint Eastwood. "Well? Do ya?" Anne shot her a grin as Lorhen focused out the window.

Barely two minutes later, he murmured, "Yes, I believe I do. Mary." He nodded out the porthole.

"What?" Michelle demanded sharply, jumping to her feet to step across the sub and look out Lorhen's porthole. "Did you find—oh, my God. Anne, Anne, give me the camera, Anne." She held out her hand, fingers beckoning impatiently as she leaned over Lorhen's shoulder. Anne handed it to her, switching sides of the submarine to look out Ghean's porthole with her.

One of the Houses, at least, had survived the fall of Atlantis almost entirely intact. The outer wall nearest the submarine had been partially shattered, and the sub's flood lights cast light into a home unvisited for forty-five centuries. Unlike the guest house Lorhen had lived in, this was a part of the permanent structure, and even the furniture within was designed with eternity in mind. A stone table still stood, cracks at the bases of the legs where it once had melded with the floor. Fragmented pottery lay across the floor in pieces, the sediment in the alcove so low that from their vantage the patterns were still visible, though not decipherable. Slender pieces of stone lay in lengths around the floor; chairs with broken legs and backrests suggested where they had come from.

"Handy Handy Handy," Michelle was chanting, "get Handy in there, Anne." She had the camera up on her shoulder, filming. "My God, Logan, you're a genius."

"Just lucky," Lorhen demurred, and lifted his hand to block the camera's lens as Michelle swung it to face him. "I'd rather not be filmed, please."

Jerry finally untangled himself from his computer to lean over and stare out an unoccupied porthole. "Are you nuts? This is the find of a lifetime, and you don't want on-film credit for it? Damn, can I have it, then?"

Lorhen kept his hand up, a determined smile of apology fixed on his face. "Please, Michelle." He genuinely didn't want to have to wipe the project's data drives, but he was too fond of his head to risk having it displayed anywhere along with other five thousand year old treasures.

Michelle shook her head, turning the camera back to the apparent dining room setting. "You're not much of a glory hound, are you, Adams? Anne, have you got Handy ready yet?"

"I'm really not," Lorhen murmured.

"One more minute," Anne promised. "All right, I'm launching him now." Arms in the waldo, she reached up, twisting her hands. The submarine shook a little as the two-fisted robot detached itself from the bottom and dropped into the water. "Okay, Michelle, here's your eyes." Her screen flickered, light changing as the headlamps on Handy added to the wash of light. "In we go...." The little robot swam up to the break in the wall, looking absurdly slow to the watchers inside the sub. A few seconds later, as the camera perched on its top sent back detailed images of the pottery on the floor, everyone scrambled for a good look at Anne's screen. A plate, nearly whole, was a few feet in front of the robot. Anne carefully extended a hand, clasping with the waldo. A moment later, the plate was held directly in front of the camera. "Damn," Anne said. "That's pretty."

A shallow, curved groove had been carved into the outer rim of the plate. Below it, baked into the clay, ran a pattern of dancers and bulls; each quarter of the plate had a different step in the dance. In the center of the plate, only a few shades darker than the clay itself, was a representation of the Bull.

"They must have been bull worshipers," Michelle proclaimed in a hushed voice. "The pattern, the bull's head—it's the second time we've seen that. Look, it even has the bullets around it like the cup did." She made a quick circle above the screen, pointing out the faded detail. "It's beautiful. Anne, can we bring it in?"

"Sure." Anne lowered the plate away from Handy's eyes, tucking it away out of sight, apparently under the robot.

"He's got a pouch down there," Ghean explained quietly to Lorhen. "Not much can fit in it, but it means we can bring more than one thing up at a time."

"Go on, go on," Michelle said excitedly. "Let's see what else there is. Go look behind the table."

"Wow," Jerry said a moment later.

A fourth chair lay behind the table, completely intact. Handy hovered above it, focusing on the legs—less slender than they'd appeared lying on the floor, but elegantly carved to maintain the illusion of slimness. The back was squared off, but open, the symbol of the Bull carved into the stone.

"How the hell did that survive falling over?" Anne demanded. "Want me to pick it up?"

"Look at that," Michelle whispered. "Hardly any damage, very little crusting, nothing. I wonder why. Maybe it's the stone. This is going to make everybody very, very happy." Still filming, she looked at Lorhen, leaving the camera pointed at the window. "Maybe you should choose all our destinations for us, Adams. Looks like you're a lucky charm."

Lorhen chuckled, moving back to his seat. "Maybe. Maybe I just got lucky this time. Let Mary decide the next one. It's her project." And she would have a much better idea of where to find artifacts than Lorhen would, now that she was situated. "I'll just sit in the corner and look modest about this find, and let the rest of you do all the work."

Anne *tsk*ed, grinning. "Just like a man. All right. Shall I see if I can get that beauty?"

"Wait," Lorhen said. "How far can Handy go looking?"

Anne looked over her shoulder at him. "About forty meters, why?"

Lorhen nodded. "There's that door," he said, half smiling. "Don't you want to know what's on the other side?"

30

The sound of the sub's engines filled the silence for a few seconds. "Wow," Jerry said, "did anybody else get a feeling of impending doom when he said that?"

Anne exhaled. "I admit I sort of expected a kraken to burst out the door."

"There's no such thing," Dana said under her breath.

Lorhen smiled. "Atlantis is only a legend, too," he reminded the pilot. "Michelle, do we have time? Can we explore the house?"

Michelle looked wryly at Lorhen. "You're a better archaeologist than I am. I make one good find—well, *you* do!—and I want to haul it topside so we can get a good look at it. Sure, we can go exploring. There's a little room left, right, Anne?"

Anne gave her a brief, sour look. "Says the woman not driving the robot. Yeah, I can get another little thing or two, and if we find something really spectacular I can always leave the chair behind."

"If this room is intact, maybe others are," Ghean said quietly. "Logan seems to be having a good day. We may as well cash in on it."

"All right, all right," Anne said. At her command, Handy rose away from the chair and puttered up over the half wall, into the next room. It was almost half again as long as the dining room, with stone counters built against the walls. Above them was shelving, all of it stone, much of it emptied. Endless broken pottery on the floor pointed to where the material that belonged on the shelves had gone. Some of the counters had collapsed, leaving piles of rubble on the floor, but a few still stood, one with a bowl sitting on it.

"Go look at it!" Michelle nearly bounced in her seat. Anne laughed, and Handy swam toward the bowl, which sat as if it had been left there only yesterday. It was considerably less elegant than the plate they'd found, plain and undecorated, but still whole. "A kitchen?" Michelle hazarded. "A mixing bowl. Let's see if we can find any utensils. If we're lucky they'll have used stone, not wood."

Dana chuckled. "What, you don't think we're going to find any stainless steel? Over there, Anne, to the right. I thought I saw something on the floor."

"There's a lot on the floor," Anne pointed out. "Mostly broken. Must have been one hell of a quake." Still, Handy dropped away from the bowl to veer to the right, exploring the floor a few feet at a time. "Good eye," she added admiringly a moment later, and used one of Handy's claws to carefully push away debris from a long spoon and a stone knife that still visibly held an edge. The end of the spoon was broken off, but Michelle crowed with delight anyway.

"Mary, you should have brought Dr. Adams on board for this project a long time ago. At this moment I'd say he's worth his weight in gold. Anne, can we do a quick perimeter sweep before we look at the floor any more? I want to see how big the room is."

"Sure." Handy bobbled back up, working his way down the wall they'd begun on, over the bowl.

Lorhen glanced at Ghean, who mouthed 'servant's quarters'. He nodded, looking back at Handy's screen. The Atlantean

Houses had been run by servants, still part of the House, but not the noble blood who ruled the city and island. The kitchen almost invariably was in their quarters, set off a little from the rest of the House. The dining room they'd come in through wasn't the main one, then. There would be another one, larger, somewhere else.

Lorhen straightened abruptly, almost cracking his head on the top of the submarine. *Servants, scholars and housekeepers,* Ragar had said to him one afternoon as he and Lorhen had made their way through the gardens toward the Bull's House. *We all live in this part of the House, not quite part of the nobility, but too useful to keep further away.* "Ghean," he said out loud, and she looked at him sharply.

"Afraid so," Michelle said. "Half the back wall is gone, in fact." Handy lit up what had once been part of a door, the left side of it broken away, along with most of the corner of the kitchen. Michelle leaned forward, as if she could bring Handy closer to the wreckage by doing so. "It doesn't look like there's anything past that. No more walls."

Anne pushed Handy up to the remains of the door, shedding light on the ground outside. "Looks like this had floor laid here, though. Out, or do you want to look at the rest of the kitchen?"

"The kitchen," Michelle said.

Ghean stepped back to lift her eyebrows at Lorhen. "And you were admonishing *me* to be careful?" she asked very softly. "What is it?"

Lorhen pulled an apologetic face, lowering his head to speak quietly into her ear. "Ragar's room is the next one over, just off the terrace there. He kept a journal in one of those boxes."

Ghean's face lit up. "Do you think—" she began, still very softly.

"God damn!" Michelle clapped her hands together, shouting with delight. "You *are* worth your weight in gold, Adams!"

Lorhen leaned around her to look at Anne's screen. Handy

was in front of a set of cupboards in the back corner of the room, and had pulled one of the doors open. Unbroken pots and utensils lined the shelves. "Well, aren't I clever," he grinned. "There's your motherlode, Michelle."

"They used a lot of stone," Jerry said. "I don't get the impression these people thought in the short-term."

Ghean smiled crookedly. "Perhaps when you're the most advanced civilization of the time, you want to make a good impression on the neighbors."

"Apparently so. All right, Logan. We've struck gold twice in a row here. Do you have another inspiration as to where we should take a look next? You've given us a fine show of their architecture and pottery. I don't suppose you could point us at a perfectly preserved body or a closet full of undamaged clothes so we could see what they wore and ate? Maybe some murals to give us an idea of the level of art in their culture? Although," Michelle added, musing, "that plate with the dancers is a pretty good showing of that. Well?" She lifted her eyebrows at Lorhen.

A perfectly preserved Atlantean body. Lorhen deliberately didn't look at Ghean, afraid of her expression. "You don't ask for much, do you?" He frowned, running a hand over his mouth. "Finish the other wall of the kitchen, anyway, and let's go through the door back on the other end of the kitchen. There's got to be more to the house over there, right?"

"How practical of you," Anne said. "You don't want to go surging blindly into the night? You're no fun at all." She grinned over her shoulder, then sent Handy back along the kitchen's other wall, stopping to examine shattered fragments of pottery. A few minutes later she directed him through the kitchen door, and let him hover there. "Left or right?" she asked. "Which wall do you want to follow? All I can see is floor, right now."

"Left," Lorhen said, at the same time Michelle said, "Right." They grinned at each other, and Michelle waved a hand. "Left," she agreed. "I'd hate to jinx this now."

"I don't think you can jinx it," Dana said. "I figure about the only thing that'd lose us this is if there was an earthquake that brought it all down around our ears right now."

Silence filled the sub as everyone stared at her. After long seconds, she cleared her throat and mumbled, "Sorry."

"God, Dana," Anne said disapprovingly, and then shook herself, passing it off. "Don't do that! Left it is, then." Handy began his exploration along the wall, and the blonde woman added, "Really, Logan, I know I gave you a hard time, but I don't know if you realize this is the right way to explore, methodically like this. We're far less likely to miss something. Have you ever been on a dig before?"

Not since the twenties. Lorhen shook his head. "No, just read about them. Being systematic makes sense, that's all. Although this isn't a very interesting wall, is it?" There had been a wood-framed painting on it once, a brilliantly colored rendition of a god taming one of the unicorns, with the city gleaming behind it. Lorhen straightened again, this time cracking his head on the top of the sub. He rubbed his head, muttering, "Ow," as he watched Handy follow the wall. It was the Bull's House, at that. Taurus, he told himself absently. They would certainly call it Taurus, and Ghean's House, Orion. He might as well start thinking in those terms. But Taurus had kept the war-horses. The stables might have survived, and—maybe, if not probably—a unicorn skeleton. Emma would be all bent out of shape. Lorhen grinned at the thought.

"Door," Anne announced as Handy rounded the corner. "In or not?"

"In," Lorhen said. No one argued as the robot swam into the next room. Barely damaged at all, it was also almost empty. Lorhen had expected that. Ragar's furniture was of wood, as most of the Houses' furniture had been, despite the stone table in the dining room. Time and water had dissolved them, leaving the more durable belongings littered on the floor. An ink pot and stylus lay where a desk had once been, the ink pot overturned. A small knife lay with them, used for sharpening charcoal. Anne collected the items without asking, tucking them away into Handy's pouch.

"They wrote," Michelle murmured, as the stylus was lifted and examined before being put away. "That's an incredible find, right there. I wonder why there's no furniture."

"Rotted away," Ghean said. "It must have been wooden."

"Either that or they liked sleeping on stone floors," Lorhen said innocently, and fought off a laugh as Ghean glared sideways at him.

Dana leaned forward, squinting at Handy's screen. "What's that? Can you move Handy to the left, Annie?"

"It's just a box," she said dubiously. "Not all that interesting, and it's kind of big. I'm not going to be able to get anything else, if I take it."

Lorhen caught his breath, and Ghean's hand crept into his, tightening in anticipation. Ragar had kept his journal in that box, and although Ghean couldn't know that, she would know that Atlanteans kept all sorts of treasures in those boxes. He squeezed her hand back, trying to keep his voice casual. "I have a feeling."

Michelle grinned. "Careers," she said, "have been made on less. Go on, Anne. Worst that can happen is that Logan's feeling is wrong and we'll get to give him hell."

"How quickly you turn against me," Lorhen sniffed. Ghean's grip on his arm loosened as Anne maneuvered Handy's claws around the box and lifted it into his pouch. Lorhen looked down at her, and she smiled, excitement coloring her cheeks. "Now only if it's undamaged," he murmured, and she nodded.

Anne brought Handy out of Ragar's room, exploring the other rooms in the servant's quarters. The common area, much larger than any of the other rooms, had a wide door, still closed, that led into the rest of the house. After prodding at the door a minute or two, Anne shook her head. "I could probably open it," she said, "with some patience and maybe a wedge of some sort, but we're about full up already. Let's go get that chair and head topside to look at our treasures. If I'd known Logan was going to bring us to a gold mine, I'd have used a bigger pouch for Handy."

Lorhen returned to his seat, smiling. "Next time you'll know better."

"Hey," Dana said, "if you want to choose all our sites for us, at this point I'm for it. I don't know if we'd have ever checked out here."

"Eventually you would have, I'm sure," Lorhen said smoothly. Anne shook her head as she moved Handy back out to the dining room, and nudged a claw under the chair back. The claw closed gently around the carved bull in the center, and she carefully closed another one around the chair's upper leg.

"Maybe we would have," she muttered, concentrating, then exhaled, "Moment of truth," and lifted the chair.

It remained intact. Dana let out a cheer, narrowly stopping herself from clapping Anne on the back. She grinned, biting her lower lip in concentration as she reversed Handy's engines and backed out of the room, chair in her grasp.

"Nicely done," Michelle said. "Let's get out of here. We're gonna be famous."

Jerry flashed a grin. "Boy howdy do I like the sound of that."

"Are you sure it's a box?" Michelle leaned over the drying stone dubiously. Lorhen scraped buildup off the sides with a piece of sandpaper, nodding.

"It's too light to be solid," he explained, "and I think this is a seam." He rubbed a finger over the slightest flaw in the stone, then glanced up at Michelle. "I can't believe you're hovering over me fussing over this with all *that*." He nodded toward the buzz of activity that had been going on since the sub resurfaced.

The chair had survived the journey to the top unscathed, and more than a dozen people were crowded around it, inspecting and filming it, everyone talking at the same time.

Each of the individual pieces they'd brought up garnered the same attention. The apparently impenetrable box Lorhen was cleaning up was the focus of the least interest. Michelle glanced at the crew examining the chair, but shook her head. "I'm as interested as they are, but I guess I'm kind of counting on your hunch, here. I want to be paying attention when you get that thing open."

"Your confidence is flattering." Lorhen looked down at the box, then frowned, glancing around again. "Where's Mary?"

"Being drowned in champagne, I think. She was going to bring some back for all of us."

"Into the lab?" Lorhen asked, horrified. "What if it gets spilled?"

"In the hall," Michelle assured him. "Not in here. Don't worry. How do you think it opens?"

"With a chisel, failing all else." Lorhen smiled at Michelle's expression, turning the box on its side. "No, there's a little indentation," he said, running his finger over it. "I found a couple of others. One of them, maybe. I'll figure it out. But I need to get the rest of this crap off it before I can. I think I'm missing some of them." He scraped more of the salty buildup away, concentrating on the task at hand to the exclusion of the world around him.

The box was almost clean when the chill of Ghean's arrival swept over him. Lorhen looked up, popping his neck as she entered with an empty champagne flute in hand and dropped into the chair beside his. "Well? Have you cracked the secrets of the universe yet?"

"I didn't know that was in my job description. Does cleaning up a stone box count?"

"Only if you get it opened." Ghean reached out to touch one

scarred fingertip against the side of the box and *tsk*ed. "You scratched it."

Lorhen set the box on the table, finding the pressure points on the sides. "It's been underwater for aeons. The scratches were already there. I was careful, Mary. I could only find four indentations. I hope there aren't any more." The box the Book was in had seven.

Ghean shook her head. "Probably not." Michelle was across the room, examining the stylus, leaving Lorhen and Ghean more or less alone for the moment. "Three or four were average," she murmured. "The more points, the more secure the box. Even the ones in the library only had six. I never saw one with seven."

"Seven what?" Michelle asked, returning to their table.

"Dwarves," Ghean said lightly. "You should have some champagne, Michelle."

"No, thanks. It tickles my nose."

Ghean clicked her tongue in disappointment. The sound masked the low hiss as Lorhen found the right pattern and the stone box slid open, a hairline fracture appearing in the stone. For a few seconds, he stared at the break in the white stone, then he lifted his head, looking at Ghean, whose whole body had gone rigid with anticipation. His own hands were suddenly cold as he pushed the box a few inches toward her. "Would you like the pleasure, Doctor Kostani?"

She put the champagne flute down and rested her fingertips on the box's lid, whispering, "It could be empty."

"It could be." Lorhen's voice rose and he struggled not to laugh with excitement. "Devoid of all but hope."

"This is not Pandora's box, Lor—Logan."

"Schroedinger's, then," Lorhen whispered. "The box is neither empty nor full until it's opened."

"If a cat jumps out of here," Ghean said severely, "I'm going to scream."

"If you don't open it, *I'm* going to scream." Michelle stood on the other side of the table, fists held so tightly her knuckles gleamed white. Ghean shot her a maniacal smile, then bit her lower lip, holding her breath as she slid the box halfway open. For a few seconds they all stared into the box, speechless, until Michelle whispered, "Holy shit. Holy shit."

It was as if she'd broken a spell. Ghean suddenly shrieked, flinging her hands in the air, and launched herself into Lorhen's arms. "Yes! Yes! Yes!"

Lorhen spun her, laughing with triumph. Heads snapped around and people turned to their table, watching them whirl as he crowed, "There's your proof, Mary. There's your civilization!"

"Put me down, put me down!" she shouted, laughing. "I want to look at it! I can't believe it!"

Lorhen laughed, setting the tiny woman back on her feet, and leaned behind her to grin down at the neatly stacked papers. Ragar's handwriting filled the top page in small, fine print. Michelle sat down hard in her chair, staring incredulously at the papers. "Writing," she said wonderingly. "My God, look at the paper. Look how fine it is. Just look at it."

"We are," Ghean beamed. Anne pushed her way through the gathering crowd to gape down at the tightly packed papers.

"Jesus Christ, that survived? My God. What's that?" she asked as Ghean opened the box the rest of the way.

Nestled at the end of the box was a thin piece of stone, sectioning off a narrow length of space. Metal glinted there, and Ghean worked it out of its resting place, tipping a bone handle up and pulling the knife out of the box. Under age-induced tarnish, the blade glinted dull silver, and Ghean's eyes widened. "Steel," she whispered. "He had a steel knife."

"It can't be," Michelle said, disbelieving, and snatched up a soft cloth to place the knife on as Ghean handed it over and took a little step backward, hand pressed against her mouth.

Lorhen caught her as she swayed. "There's your civilization," he repeated, into her hair, voice soft. "You did it. There's your proof." Someone pushed in front of Ghean, looking wonderingly at the discovery. The noise level rose dramatically as the knife was carefully handed around. Ghean caught Lorhen's hand and pulled him away from the find, out into the hall, letting the door bump closed behind her.

"*You* did it," she corrected, falling into her native tongue. "Lorhen, you did it. You found it. Writing, a journal, and a knife! A steel knife!"

Lorhen smiled at the ceiling, then back down at Ghean. "For you. For you, Ghean. You deserve it. Gods above, I had no idea he had a steel knife in there."

"Whose was it?"

"Ragar's. The Taurian scholar, do you re—"

"Taurian?"

"Oh, come on, you know that's what they'll be calling him. Taurus, Orion, Aquarius—"

"It's a crow's head, not a jug of water—!" Ghean flung her head back again, shouting with laughter. "But you're right, you're right. Oh, I can't believe it!" As she had thousands of years ago, she flung herself at Lorhen, confident he'd catch her as readily as he'd often done in Atlantis. He did, laughing, making a small 'ooof' as she knocked him back a step.

"There's your proof," he said again, and thought, *damned if you do*, and kissed her. *Don't get carried away, old man*, he ordered himself, and still whispered, "You are so beautiful, Ghean. I'd forgotten how beautiful you are when you're happy."

Ghean's smile was slow and delighted as she curled her arms around Lorhen's neck. "I haven't been happy in a long time." She rolled her eyes at the door, and murmured, "Do you think they'll miss us?"

Lorhen shot a glance at the door, eyebrows rising. "Probably, but I think Michelle would stop them from looking right away. And maybe they won't miss us at all." He lowered his head, kissing her again, then rather dramatically swept her up in his arms. "Carrying brides over thresholds wasn't exactly an Atlantean tradition, but perhaps a little new with the old?"

Ghean laughed, kicking her feet. "My cabin's closer," she whispered into his neck. "That way." She pointed imperiously with her toes.

31

Michelle did an admirable job of looking like Lorhen had hardly been missed, when he returned a few hours later. "There you are. We've stored the paper in mylar sheets. It's very delicate, so we're going to get some stiffer supports for it as soon as we can, but no one expected us to find paper of any sort. It's a wonder we had any mylar around at all." She cleared her throat, trying very hard not to grin as she asked, "Where's Mary?"

Lorhen looked at her sideways and chuckled. "Showering and getting some dinner. Have you made any sense out of anything yet? Is any of it recognizable?"

Michelle turned to the neat stacks of mylar-encased paper. "They're pretty clearly in chronological order. It looks like a journal of some sort. We kept them in order. This," she said, touching the first pile, "was on the top. I don't know if it's the newest entry or the oldest. I'd guess the newest, and that they get older as they go deeper—they won't fit in the box anymore, I'm afraid—but until we figure out a dating system of some sort we won't know. You're the one Mary thought might be able to find some kind of basis in some other language to help us translate."

Lorhen leaned on the table, hands turned out. Michelle stared at the inside of his left wrist with interest. "That's like Mary's necklace."

I should have worn long sleeves. Lorhen turned his wrist up to look at the tattoo, rubbing his thumb over it. "We were going to be married," he said slowly. "A long time ago. I got the tattoo then. Her mother gave her the necklace."

"Mary doesn't strike me as the type you'd tattoo yourself for. Come to think of it, you don't seem like the sort who'd get one."

"I was a lot younger then," Lorhen said dryly. "People do strange things for love." He frowned at the papers, lifting the first one up by its mylar encasing. The date was ten years before Lorhen had come to Atlantis. He set it down again and went to the last pile, taking the last sheet or two out from the bottom. His own name leapt out at him, partway down the final page.

> *Lorhen has told me the most incredible story. I'm reluctant to even write it down, to keep his secret. He trusted me with it, not a choice he made easily, I think, and so I'm left to be circumspect even in my own journals. So many of our journals end up in the library, though, and I think Lorhen ought not be undone by my clumsiness.*
>
> *I've been up most of the night thinking on the tale he told. I find I believe it, though I can't say exactly why. Perhaps because it's so outrageous that no one would bother making it up. He said Minyah knows the truth. I may talk to her about him. If it really is true, dear gods, the stories he could tell! No wonder he's so well-learned. I admit, I was jealous, when I first met him. He seemed so young, and knew so much. Now that I understand him a little more fully, I wonder at his ability to deal with pompous asses like myself.*

"You look like you're reading it," Michelle observed. Lorhen looked up, blinking, and shook his head.

"Most people staring intently at a piece of paper look like they're reading it. Wondering about the person who wrote it, I suppose." *Not only do I remember you, Ragar, but if they manage to translate this, you'll become one of the most famous men in history. I hope that pleases you, my friend. You were a good man. You deserve to be remembered.* Lorhen smiled, shaking his head. *You weren't a pompous ass,* he added silently. *Far from it.*

A chill ran through him as Ghean came down the hall. Lorhen lifted his head, waiting for the door to open, a little nervous. If she'd decided in the last half hour that making love had been an error, the next several days were going to be awkward.

She smiled as she came through the door, licking the last bites of dinner off her fingers. "Hello," she said cheerfully. "Have you translated everything yet?"

Lorhen grinned, relaxing a little. "Not yet," he said. "Give me another fifteen or twenty minutes."

Ghean laughed, coming to his side. Lorhen caught Michelle eying them surreptitiously and lifted his eyebrows at the mortal woman. Michelle smiled and shook her head, looking like the proverbial canary-catching cat. Ghean clucked her tongue. "You're getting lazy," she said to Lorhen. "Slipping. I mean, you were useful this morning, but if you haven't gotten the translations done, well, what have you done for me lately?"

She blinked as Michelle burst into laughter, then tried hopelessly not to grin. "What?" she demanded of Michelle. "*What?*" The grin got away from her, and she laughed as well.

Lorhen looked at both of them through his eyebrows, shaking his head and smiling. "Are you quite finished?" he asked without rancor, and Michelle dropped into a chair to laugh again.

"I'm sorry," the archaeologist eventually said, wiping at her eyes, "but you two make a really wonderful couple. You're so tall," she said to Lorhen, and laughed again.

"I'm not that tall," Lorhen protested. Not anymore, anyway. Once he'd towered over almost everyone, but that had been centuries ago. Aeons, even.

"Next to Mary you are."

"Next to Mary, Napoleon was tall, Michelle."

Chortling, Michelle leaned forward in her chair, trying to get down to business. "Look, I know it's completely unreasonable to ask, but do you want to take a look at these and see if you can make heads or tails out of it? We probably won't go down for another three days, with all the loot we brought up today. Do you know that knife looks like it might really be steel? Can you imagine? Forty-five centuries ago someone had the ability to make steel? At any rate, we'll be doing photography and reports and tests and maybe we'll even get the press out here to admire us. My God," Michelle said, standing up, "has anyone called the University?"

"It's four in the morning there," Ghean said.

"Oh. Yes, of course. They're planning a party tomorrow night, you missed the talk about that."

"Why not tonight?" Lorhen asked.

Michelle shrugged. "Tonight the general consensus is studying the artifacts. Tomorrow we'll celebrate. Everyone's eating right now, but this place is going to fill up again. You'll have company, Logan, if you decide to work on these at all tonight."

Lorhen looked at the papers he still held. "I think I can do that," he agreed. "Put in a few hours' work, anyway. I'm not sure I have anything else to do." He looked sideways at Ghean, who elbowed him.

"Like I said, what have you done for me lately?" she asked, and tilted her head at Michelle. "Come on, let's let our boy wonder here get some work done."

"You're the boss," Michelle said. "Logan, that laptop over there is mine. Feel free to use it."

"Mmm," Lorhen said. "Thanks." He put the papers down and went to get the computer, setting up as the other pair left the room.

Michelle walked Ghean up to the deck, leaning on the railing. "I want to know what's going on," she said eventually.

She knows! the frightened one shrieked. *She knows, she's found us out! We're caught, we'll die, Atlantis will never return!*

Quiet, Ghean ordered sharply. "What?" she asked aloud.

"I want to know what the hell is going on," Michelle repeated, tipping her head toward where they'd left Lorhen. "With you and Logan."

Ghean smiled slowly, lazily. "What do you think?"

"Not that." Michelle looked exasperated. "That's pretty obvious. No, I'm talking about that fight you had in the sub, Mary. That was no made-up kid's language. I've been thinking about it all day. There was structure to it, even to an ear that doesn't know it. Kids don't do that. I remember. What the hell was it?"

Tell the truth, the patient one hissed. *Parts of it. It will make the lie more plausible.*

"It was my native language," Ghean answered. "What does it matter?" She reached for her ring to play with, only to remember she'd taken it off while Lorhen undressed her earlier. She tugged her necklace instead, the pendant in the palm of her hand.

"I've never heard anything like it. What is it?" Michelle frowned at Ghean as she played with the necklace. "He's got a tattoo of that necklace. He said he got it when you two were going to be married. When was that?"

"A long time ago," Ghean answered. "We were a lot younger then."

"He also said your mother gave it to you."

Ghean frowned. "She did. What's wrong, Michelle?"

"You told me you were adopted."

"I was." Ghean sighed. "So?"

"So you have a picture on your bookcase in Chicago. From

your grandmother. Who looks exactly like you. And she's wearing that necklace. Which has bullets around the outside, just like those bull decorations we found."

Ghean closed her eyes momentarily, constructing a story, then, impatiently, said, "I found my birth mother. The picture of my grandmother was from when she was young, in the twenties. Mother gave it to me because we looked so much alike. Michelle, why are you grilling me like this?"

Good, the patient one whispered. *Put her on the defensive. She's noticing too much.*

Rather than answer, Michelle studied her face intently. "You're not wearing makeup now," she said after a moment. "You haven't gotten older, have you, Mary?"

"Michelle." Ghean opened her eyes, irked. "Everyone gets older. It's dark out, for goodness sake. The light's just kind to me right now."

"It's not your grandmother," Michelle continued, as if Ghean hadn't spoken. "It's you. It looks exactly like you. *Exactly* like you. And Logan Adams is just like you, isn't he? It's why you both know so much even when you don't look old enough to. How do you do it? What was that language?"

She knows, the frightened one gasped.

She's guessing, the patient one snapped.

Ghean pressed her eyes shut. "It was Atlantean," she said, forcing as much sarcasm into the words as she could. "Logan and I are both really five thousand years old and we were there when Atlantis sank. Is that the kind of story you want to hear, Michelle? I can make some more up if you want."

Don't tell her! the frightened one shrieked. The patient one was, for once, stunned into silence. Ghean opened her eyes to see Michelle staring down at her, shocked belief in her eyes.

"Gods of earth and heaven," Ghean said wearily, and stepped away from the railing. "I suppose you'd better come down to my room and hear the whole thing."

It took nearly three hours to tell Michelle an abbreviated version of the tale. Over the objections of the voices, she explained the artifacts, and the very different immortality that kept her alive. Through the entire telling, Michelle sat in numb silence, examining her face, as if she was trying to find the years Ghean had lived somewhere hidden in her eyes.

"So they're all lost?" Michelle asked, when Ghean finished. "The House artifacts?"

Ghean shook her head, picking up the lion's-head ring and tossing it to her. "This is one of them," she said. "I didn't even know it until a few days ago. I just thought it was something my mother had left me, a reminder of Atlantis. You can keep it, after I'm done with Lorhen. I won't need it then, and if I regain the Book, I should be able to learn how to make them. I'd make one for you anyway, but wouldn't it be more fun to have one of the originals? I think there are two more, still in Atlantis somewhere. We won't find one at the House we've found. It's the Bull's House, and they had the unicorns."

"Unicorns?" Michelle asked, incredulously.

For one brief moment Ghean understood how Lorhen felt, and rubbed a hand over her eyes. "Unicorns. You believed the rest of this but you don't believe in unicorns?"

"Unicorns aren't real, Mary," Michelle said, as if she was talking to a small child. Ghean stared at her until she flushed, looking away. "All right," she mumbled uncomfortably. "Unicorns. Right."

"I think I should have told you a long time ago," Ghean said. "When I'm finished with Logan, and you have the ring, well, call it a repayment for the deception."

"Thank you," Michelle finally managed, handing the ring back to her. "After you're done with Logan?"

Ghean smiled, putting the ring down beside the bed before standing to pull her rapier down from above the bed. Despite the story she'd told, Michelle stood up, taking a step or two backwards.

"Christ Almighty, you actually use a sword?"

"It would take a very long time to remove someone's head with a Swiss Army knife, Michelle." Despite that, Ghean put the rapier back where it belonged and drew her heartstrike knife from the small of her back. "We use these, too, though."

Prove it to her, the patient one said dourly. *Like Lorhen did for us. Then she'll believe.*

Don't! She knows too much already! Don't show her anything else, the frightened one begged.

"For what?"

"We take power from one another when we kill each other. It only works if there's been a heartstrike first, though. I could take Lorhen's head—"

"Lorhen?"

"Logan," Ghean said after a moment. "It's the name I knew him by, in Atlantis." She leveled the heartstrike knife across her hand, then folded her fingers around it, drawing the blade sideways. She winced as skin and flesh separated, and released the blade, turning her hand up to show Michelle the gashes. Horror warped the other woman's features, slowly turning to amazement as the wounds healed before her eyes.

That, Ghean thought, *must have been what I looked like when Lorhen showed me this, the first time.* "I am Timeless," she said softly, and cleaned the blood off the blade, replacing it in its sheath at the small of her back. "And I'm going to take Logan's head, and his power. He heals the same way you just saw me do. The ring is my buffer. In fair combat, I'd never beat him. He's got too much experience, and a reach I can't possibly match." Ghean gestured briefly, indicating her height. "The ring will counter it. If I can't be hurt, eventually I'll be able to take his head."

"You really only die if someone takes your head," Michelle breathed.

Ghean nodded. "Anything short of that and I'll survive. I can be killed, but unless my head leaves my shoulders, within a few minutes I'll be back on my feet again."

Michelle asked, uncertainly, "You have to kill him?"

Ghean glanced up at the sword again as she regained her seat on the bed. "He's less use to me now that you know the truth," she said. "You can have your share of epiphanies about the site now. I'll tell you what we're dealing with. I think we should stick with the House findings for several dives, before going back to the city and the temple. We've obviously found a site worthy of excavating. It would look strange to go back to the temple right now. Lorhen would wonder why you agreed to it."

"I thought you were lovers," Michelle said slowly. "And you'd still kill him?"

Ghean shrugged. "We were, and we are again. He's still in love with me, even after all this time, and since that's the case, I thought I might as well enjoy myself while he was useful to me. I have you, now, though, and I'd rather work with you than him. I imagine Logan will meet with a fatal accident in the next few days."

She hesitated, watching Michelle's face. "Understand, Michelle," she said quietly. "Even if this wasn't personal, my kind have a need to fight one another. It's something in the power that heals us and keeps us alive. I won't lie to you. I'm motivated by revenge. But you lose a certain sentimentality as you get older, and you learn to do what you must to survive. With Logan's power combined with my own years, I should be undefeatable." She lifted the golden leonine ring between two fingers. "And as soon as I'm done with this, you'll gain immortality, Michelle. Wouldn't it be a pity to lose me now?"

Michelle glanced at the ring, then at Ghean before speaking slowly. "I suppose you're the old hand at this. It's just a little much to take in all at once."

"I know," Ghean said wryly. "You're doing better than I did. It'll get easier, in a few days. Just try to stay steady until then.

It's probably best if Logan doesn't find out you know the truth." She lifted her head as a chill shuddered through her, and stood. "Speaking of which, here he comes. It's about bedtime anyway, hm?"

Michelle's eyebrows lifted. "It's been quite a day," she said in agreement.

Ghean nodded. "I'll take a look at the papers and tell you what they say, tomorrow. For now, good night, Michelle." She opened the door as Lorhen was about to knock and smiled up at the tall immortal. "There you are," she said. "Michelle was keeping me company. Any luck?"

"Conjecture," Lorhen said, rubbing his eyes. "Frequently repeated words that could be articles, theorized letter-to-letter translations. I just came by to say good night, Mary." He smiled tiredly. "And Michelle," he added, as Michelle stepped past him out the door and opened her own door just down the hall. As Michelle's door closed, Lorhen smiled down at Ghean. "These beds are too small for two people to actually sleep in."

"Sleep?" Ghean asked. "Who said anything about sleep?" She caught his hand, drawing him into the room. "You can go back to your own room later."

32

He didn't, in fact, go back to his own room later. Not with Ragar's journal waiting. He got a cup of coffee instead, and settled back down with the ancient papers. It was too easy to forget himself, and simply turn the pages, reading the journal of the last decade of Ragar's life, instead of painstakingly noting out letters and acting out the deciphering of the text. Lorhen caught himself reading for the fourth time in an hour and pushed the pages away, looking for a clock. People had been in and out of the galley several times, eating and drinking, but he'd been mostly left undisturbed, and had no sense of the time.

"You've been at it all day, Logan," Anne said, poking her head in the door. "Come have a drink with the rest of us. The party's started."

Lorhen looked up, around the emptied-out room. "I didn't even notice everyone had gone," he said, rubbing his eyes. "What time is it?"

"About seven thirty. You look tired."

Lorhen smiled, straightening the papers before standing. "I am," he admitted. "I think it's going to be an early night, party or not."

Anne laughed. "You'd better be able to sleep through a

ruckus, then. I don't think anybody else is planning on going to bed until the sun comes up."

Lorhen came to the door, switching out the light as he followed Anne out. "I'm wearing my brain out, looking at all that writing. I keep staring at it and expecting it to suddenly make sense."

Anne shook her head. "I'll just drive a robot," she said. "You can do the hard part."

"Without you and your robot I wouldn't have any work to do," Lorhen pointed out. "Funny how it all kind of works together, isn't it?" The shiver of Ghean's presence ran through him as they approached the conference room that had been emptied out for the party. She waited inside the door, and slid her arm through Lorhen's possessively.

"I thought you'd run out on me," she said. "Jerry wants to get a picture of all of us with our pretty stone chair."

"Not me," Lorhen said. "Someone kept me up all night, and I've been thinking all day. That sort of activity makes for tired researchers. Call it vanity, if you want. It'd be an unflattering picture."

"Smile and bear it, Logan," Ghean said. "They already think you're crazy for not letting Michelle film you."

"You painted me as the eccentric scholar," Lorhen muttered, as Jerry, armed with a DSLR, waved them over to pose with the stone chair and the rest of the submarine team. "Couldn't you have mentioned I thought cameras stole souls, or something?"

Once the shot was taken, Lorhen gallantly insisted he be allowed to take a picture with Jerry in it, switched places with the young man, deleted the photo with himself in it, and took a photo of Jerry and the crew before handing the camera back. "Can't wait to see them, but everybody's taking their phones out for pictures now, and I really don't like being caught on film."

"Pixels," Jerry said, and Lorhen shrugged agreeably. "What is it, a privacy thing? Personal privacy is so last century, Logan."

"I know. I'm the last bastion against the inevitable future." It was a pity that being Timeless didn't have a more exotic side to it, like vampires were supposed to: no reflections, and pictures couldn't be taken of them. Although that would no doubt cause its own problems, not the least of which would be getting a decent haircut. Lorhen escaped from the crowd as quickly as he could, sharing a glass of champagne with Ghean. Then, pleading mental exhaustion, he kissed Ghean's cheek and took his leave, catching Michelle's amused glance on his way out the door.

"'Mental' exhaustion?" she asked quietly, and Lorhen laughed as softly.

"I have to sleep *sometime*. Good night, Michelle." The door closed behind him, and for a moment Lorhen stood in the relative silence of the hallway, sighing with relief. The *Retribution* was extraordinarily quiet, virtually all of the crew cheering their success at the party. It was as good a time as any, Lorhen decided. Striking while the iron was hot, no time like the present, and mostly, clichés aside, he would have all night. He went to his cabin, glancing out the window as he unzipped the suitcase that still lay on his bed. The sun had almost set, vivid colors fading to grey. Within a few more minutes, it would be dark. With the party below, it was unlikely anyone would notice him creeping around on deck.

Lorhen piled clothes from the case onto the bed and smiled faintly at what was left. Just as well no one had inspected his luggage; explaining a wetsuit without SCUBA equipment might have been a handful. The wetsuit went onto the bed, and a loosely packed backpack came out of the suitcase, leaving it empty. He'd been worried about how to go overboard without anyone noticing, but the party would help that enormously. Lorhen stripped down to pull the wetsuit on, thinking that he should have brought Lisse along for the caper. Except that probably would have cost another five million, and she would have wanted to stay at the party anyway. It was fully dark by the time he'd finished dressing. Lorhen slung the backpack on, poked his head out of the cabin, checked the hall, and scurried up to the deck.

There wasn't as much as a close call. Minutes later, he slid into the submarine tank, kicking down several yards beneath the bottom of the ship. Drifting, he pulled the backpack off to take flippers, goggles and a headlamp out of it. A compass and a watch were already secured around his wrists, but he pulled the flippers and headlamp on, then snugged the goggles on, taking a few minutes to clear them. The headlamp's battery was guaranteed for twelve hours of use without recharging, and although with luck he wouldn't need it for anything like that long, he still didn't turn it on, not this close to the surface. Instead he pulled the backpack on again, then exhaled grimly and took a deep breath of water, letting pressure equalize inside and out. Even immortals didn't like that: the impulse was to cough and hack, spitting water out, for several horrible minutes until he adjusted. Then, finally, he began kicking downward.

The Mediterranean at its deepest was around forty-five hundred feet. Where Atlantis had sank, it was only—*only*, he thought with a shudder—about three thousand feet deep. Lorhen thought it shouldn't take more than an hour, even with the currents, to make it to the bottom. The pressure would not be comfortable, but neither, he thought dryly, would it be killing. Ghean had survived in it without pulverized bones or ruptured organs for centuries, and he knew how to acclimatize himself as best he could. Lorhen glanced at the watch's depth gauge: two hundred meters. He switched on the headlamp, turned the watch to a compass reading, and began the swim into the depths.

It took longer than he anticipated. The currents pulled him off course, and he spent more time swimming laterally than he'd expected. Every few feet he cleared his ears, hearing the faint internal squeal as the tubes tried to adjust to the rising pressure. Eventually his eardrums burst, sending him into a convulsive ball, clutching his head at the pain. Blood tinged the water around him and swept away in seconds. The continuing pressure would probably prevent them from healing, which was just as well.

He could feel his body adjusting to the pressure in other ways, what little gaseous air he had left forcing its way out to equalize the pressures within and without. He grew lightheaded as the fine adjustments were made, and slowed his descent. Whatever element of his Timeless body allowed him to survive in the water, it required time to condition him to it. The lightheadedness passed as he slowed, and he maintained the new swimming pace, no new bouts of dizziness hampering him.

Once the internal adaptations were made, the water's pressure became an uncomfortable inconvenience, weighing his movements. It stopped just shy of pain, a pervading discomfort that was the price for daring the dive. Lorhen focused on the task of reaching the sea floor, aware that too much acknowledgment of the water's pressure would only make it worse.

Eventually the sea bed came into the range of his headlamp. Situating himself to find the city and locate recognizable sections took more time, and navigating his way to the ancient temple took longer still.

Disconcerting as exploring sunken Atlantis in the sub had been, the sensations were measurably more disturbing without the protective walls separating Lorhen from the sea. Anne was more than right. Atlantis had ghosts, and too many of them had faded faces and voices in Lorhen's memory. He kicked up a side alley, broken walls on either side of him sullen reminders of the past. Ahead and to his left was an open area, city floor broken up, but largely intact; the layout suggested the area had never been walled. Lorhen hesitated there, swimming toward a wall shattered at half its height at the back of the empty stretch. Grime coated the wall, and he reached out to brush some of it away, leaving streaked lines against the wall. A few more swipes cleared much of the sediment away, and exposed the lower half of a carving in the stone.

Memory, rather than intuition, completed the image. Another bull's head, though not encompassed in the circle of the Houses. Lorhen turned in the undisturbed water, looking across the floor again. The outer perimeter of his headlight brushed the back corner of the Bull's Head Tavern. A tabletop, broken in two, lay on the ground, wooden legs long since rotted away. For an instant, the activity of the pub the last time he'd seen it passed over him: voices, raised in general pleasantry; close-pressed bodies maneuvering around each other; Minyah, just outside the tavern, making someone apologize for something she'd done. Sour-faced Aroz, reluctant to greet him, and Karem, calculating how best to use him. Most vividly, Ghean, laughing in delight to see him, her brown eyes bright and excited, leaping up to hug him. Lorhen clamped his eyes shut, shaking his head to dislodge the images, and shoved violently off the floor. From here he could find the temple, if he could let memory guide him without overwhelming him.

It was easier than he thought it might be. Beyond the strangeness of swimming over streets he'd walked, he could almost make himself imagine that it was the quiet, moonlit night that he'd spoken to Karem in the temple. Keeping the illusion in mind helped keep other memories at bay, until he found the temple, and crouched on top of it, just above the hole Ghean had chopped in her escape.

It was impossibly small. Lorhen ran a finger around the edge of it. She couldn't have been much more than skin and bones. And hair, he thought with a shudder, remembering her parts of the story. He took the backpack off again, opening it to pull out a small hammer and chisel. They weren't the most effective tools, but they would insure the temple roof wouldn't crumble inward and bury the floor entirely, and they'd do the job. Lorhen pulled the backpack on again, more to keep it out of the way than anything else, and began diligently breaking away a larger hole in the stone. It was fast work, made easier by not needing to make room for an oxygen tank to pass through. A glance at his watch told him he'd been in the water for nearly four hours, much longer than he'd hoped. He estimated he had only another four to return to the surface, if he wanted to be sure to get back on the *Retribution* before daylight. Perhaps going up wouldn't take as long as going down had. He didn't believe that, but it was a little late to abort now.

Less than twenty minutes later he kicked down into the temple, struggling against the memory of Ghean's story. It took all his willpower to not swim back out of the temple and away from Atlantis. He hovered in the water for a moment, staring around the smoothed temple walls, then, with a kind of sick fascination, he reached up and turned the headlamp off.

The blackness was absolute. Even knowing an escape route existed, Lorhen flinched violently back from the darkness, as if it had come alive. *More than four thousand years,* he thought, horrified. *In this silence, in this blackness. Gods up above. It's a wonder Ghean isn't stark raving mad.* Swallowing a scream, anything that would at least break the utter silence, Lorhen switched the headlight back on, unspeakably relieved when light flooded the temple again. He remained where he was, trying to regain his equilibrium before he was able to circle the temple.

The altar had once been more than three feet high, in the center of the temple. There was no suggestion it had ever existed at all. The floor was perfectly smooth, other than the small stones that had fallen away as Ghean chipped her way loose. Looking around once more, Lorhen again quelled the desire to retreat, then knelt, sliding out of the backpack a final time. Chisel and hammer still in hand, he cracked a wedge out of the floor, then abandoned the tools for the backpack.

Two dozen shaped explosives lay in the bottom of the pack, waterproofed and set off by an electrical charge. Not entirely certain how much of a hole it would blow under the conditions, Lorhen set the first into the wedge he'd dug out, then collected the backpack and swam toward the opening in the ceiling again. As he reached it, a thought struck him, and he turned, watching the floor shimmer as the light ran over it. The texture changed twice, two strips near each other, where the stone turned to metal slag, boiled into the floor. Lorhen stared down at the legacy of the fight and shook his head. He'd warned them it was holy ground. Then he kicked through the ceiling to the comparative safety of the Mediterranean, and set off the charge.

Sediment-filled water roiled out of the hole behind him in a rather satisfying manner. Lorhen waited for it to settle before going in to inspect the damage he'd done. An opening perhaps two feet wide and half a foot deep was gouged in the temple floor. Lorhen cleared the rubble out of it, set another charge, tamped it with some of the excess stone from the first explosion, and swam outside again. He went through the sequence another nine times, drifting in the water outside as the explosions tore holes in the temple floor: wash, rinse, repeat, Lorhen thought as he set another charge. His shoulders brushed the ragged edges of the tunnel he was creating, but there was enough room for passage.

After the dozenth explosion, there was no rubble to be cleared away. Lorhen kicked down through the roof slowly, catching himself on the rough walls he'd made to look around the room below the temple.

It was water-filled, of course, but the walls were whole. The water, Lorhen suspected, rushed in as the charge blew away the last of the ceiling. Rock scattered around the table directly below his head supported the theory. Lorhen kicked down into the room, righting himself.

Aside from the hole in the ceiling, it looked exactly as it had the last time Lorhen saw it, more than four and a half thousand years ago. The table and its chairs were undamaged, except for a few scars on the table, which looked new. Stone and the rush of seawater had almost certainly caused them. Lorhen sat in the center of the table, closing his eyes to reconstruct the scene from the past.

Ragar had crossed the room to the left of the table from the door. The door, Lorhen recalled, which he wouldn't be able to see if it were closed. He opened his eyes and inspected the walls.

Forty-five hundred years ago, Ragar had been right. The stresses of the earthquake and sinking had changed the dynamics of the room slightly, though, and there was a visible line in the wall where the door sat. Had he not known it was there, Lorhen would not have seen it for perhaps days, perhaps weeks. He closed his eyes again, trying to remember the angle Ragar had passed the table at.

Standing, he echoed the movement as best he could, coming to stop at a point a third of the way around the room from the door. The release had been at waist height on the Atlantean scholar. Eyes closed again, Lorhen began exploring the chinks in the wall with his fingertips. Patience, he thought: this was the part that would take patience.

More than two hours passed before the soft double-click signaled that the right catch had been found. As smoothly as it had thousands of years earlier, a slab of stone slid out from the wall. Lorhen opened his eyes, half disbelieving that the gamble had paid off. Stone in stone, the Book's heavy protective case sat within the extended rock. With something close to awe, he lifted the stone box out. Cradled protectively across his chest, he brought it back to the table and his backpack, emptying the remaining charges out of the latter. He packed the Book carefully into the backpack. The charges he left scattered on the table; he wouldn't need them again, and it would perplex Ghean for a few seconds before she realized what he'd done.

Lorhen looked around the room once more, then pushed up through the tunnel, and the temple, to leave Atlantis with his buried treasure on his back.

33

A few hundred feet below the surface, Lorhen abandoned the flippers, headlight and goggles. The last was an unspeakable relief. Lorhen rubbed his eyes, feeling circulation restore as the pressure from the goggles was eased. He watched the flippers rotate heel-down into the water and sink into the darkness, and wrapped the goggles around the headlamp, letting them go as well. He could feel pressure against his eardrums again, indicating they'd healed sometime in the journey back to the air.

He broke the surface with a relieved gasp, pulling air back into his lungs. Much of an advantage as not needing to breathe underwater was, he still preferred inhaling and exhaling. Shocked at his own exhaustion, Lorhen lay on the surface of the water, fatigue sending trembles through his body. The sky grew marginally lighter, and he groaned, turning in the water to search for the ship.

It took a few minutes to pick it out of the still-dull light, the grey of the ocean blending with the distant clouds meeting the horizon. The *Retribution* was nearly a half mile away. Lorhen sighed and sank underwater again, swimming a few yards beneath the surface. It wouldn't do to have someone notice him swimming up to the ship at this point. It had been an incredibly long night, and all he wanted was a few hours' sleep.

At least he had the Book. A thrill of triumph washed away his weariness for a moment. He hoped it hadn't been damaged or destroyed by the sudden onslaught of water he'd let into the secret room, but the relevant fact was that it was in his possession, not an unknown. If it was damaged, so be it. At least it wasn't a factor to worry about anymore.

Lorhen dove under the *Retribution*, turning on his back to look for the submarine dock. He broke the surface silently when he found it, then pulled himself up the ladder, hiding behind the sub to peeked out of the dock and watching for passers-by. After several seconds of silence, he hurried across the deck, glancing west to the horizon. The sky was beginning to color scarlet and gold with the rising sun, with clouds bundling together to make grey shadows in the warm colors. *Sailors take warning*, Lorhen thought, slipping through the door that led eventually to his cabin. As it closed, he let out a soft breath. *Almost there*.

With the thought came the gut-wrenching warning of an approaching Timeless. Lorhen looked over his shoulder to see Ghean, only a few meters down the hall, open the door he'd just come through, a rapier sheathed at her hip. For an instant, neither of them moved, as Ghean took in Lorhen's wetsuit and the backpack slung over his shoulders. Then her eyes widened as she deduced the meaning of the costume, and she started forward.

Lorhen ran.

He had the advantage of longer legs, a short head start, and the impetus of running for his life, while Ghean was only running for his head. He didn't bother with the first set of stairs at all: a long, low leap sent him to the foot of the steps, wet feet slipping in a hard landing. He scrambled forward before he'd really regained his footing, tearing down the hall to barge into his cabin before Ghean reached the head of the stairs.

So close. He'd been *so close* to getting away with it, and he was not, dammit, fighting to the death in a wetsuit. With one hand Lorhen slammed the door shut and the lock closed on it, and with the other, flung the soaking wet backpack onto the bed. The wetsuit clung, ripping at his nails and fingertips as he struggled to free himself of it, but the material had not been designed to come off quickly. Lorhen cursed, yanking the zipper down and jerking the rubbery outfit off, leaving his arms clammy. He hopped up and down on one foot, pulling the suit down while trying to reach for his sword with the other. After two futile attempts, he fell sideways on the bed, kicked the wetsuit off, and struggled into the jeans he'd left on the floor the night before.

He heard Ghean try the door, and opted for his sword instead of his shirt. He barely managed to button the jeans, and stuck a knife into the back of them just as a sharp crack fragmented the door frame around the lock. Ghean kicked it open a fraction of a second later. Lorhen flung the sheath from his sword and brought the blade up to a defensive position. "Witnesses," he rasped. "We can't fight here, Ghean." More to the point, *he* couldn't fight there; the room was to her advantage, both for her size and her blade.

"Everyone's asleep," she snarled. "We most certainly can."

Without taking his eyes off her, Lorhen reached for the backpack. "I'll destroy it."

Her eyes flickered to the pack. "You're bluffing. You want it as much as I do."

"I assure you," Lorhen said through his teeth, "I want it far less than I want my head." He threw the pack full force at her face. Ghean stumbled backwards, sword dropping as she tried to catch the heavy backpack. Lorhen rocketed past her, back the way he'd come, up the stairs and tearing back out onto the deck. He could hear Ghean's curse, and a pause before her footsteps followed him: she had the Book, too precious to pass up. He slid across the deck on wet, bare feet, spinning to face the door as she came charging out.

She was far better prepared for the fight than he was, clad in battle colors, even: a crimson blouse tucked into smooth black pants that met soft black boots which clearly had traction, from the ease with which she moved on the slick deck. Her eyes were bright, with both anticipation and the light of the coming dawn reflected in them, and her color was high from the dash between decks. The Hunter's necklace glittered against the blouse, and as she dropped into a guard position, Lorhen saw the Lion's ring bounce the early sunlight. She'd come prepared, all right; she'd been planning, he expected, to murder him in his sleep, if she could.

And what an easy target he'd have made, or at least, knew he looked like he would have made: bedraggled, barefoot, jeans half buttoned and clinging uncomfortably to the salt water left on his skin. Goosebumps were collecting where water didn't roll down his bare arms and chest, and he could feel his hair drying in random spikes where it was escaping from the slicking back that the sea had given it. Despite himself, the opposing images made him twist a smile, and Ghean's expression blackened. She threw the backpack across the deck and fell into a guard stance. The pack cracked against a bulwark, settling into a heap, an enigmatic prize for the winner to collect.

"No!" Lorhen backed up hastily, lifting his blade. "I'm not laughing at you. Ghean, we don't have to do this. All I want is the Book. Go live your life. God knows you deserve the chance."

She advanced without breaking form, scooting easily across the deck. "We do have to do this," she corrected. "All I want is your head. The Book is just an extraordinary second prize." She smiled tightly. "All you came here for is the Book? That's not what you said two days ago."

Lorhen made an apologetic little gesture with his free hand. "I lied."

Ghean's eyes went darker. "You're a very good liar, Lorhen. We even believed you." She lunged forward with the words, making first contact with the blades, nothing more than a faint scrape of metal.

Lorhen knocked her blade away with a tap, shaking his head. "Ghean, let it go. What possible good will killing me do? The years are never going to come back to you."

"What good will it do?" Ghean lunged again, another quick attack. "It'll make us feel a hell of a lot better, that's what."

"Us?" Lorhen danced back, stepping around a heavy pile of chain on the deck. "I assure you, it won't make me feel any better. Forgive me my selfishness, but I'd really rather you didn't feel better at the expense of my head."

Ghean drew herself up momentarily, looking at Lorhen down the length of her blade. "Your selfishness," she said precisely, "is exactly what we cannot forgive."

Sometimes, Lorhen thought, he had a real talent for finding the one irrevocably wrong thing to say. He suggested, "Try," anyway. "You'd be surprised how much easier life is if you can forgive people their little faults."

Ghean surged forward again, keeping her attack on a low line. The tactic was sound for a woman of her height; a high attack would bring her opponent's sword into play at a level uncomfortably near her neck, and the lower attacks kept anyone of greater height slightly off-balance in meeting them. "Little faults," she snarled, in time to the clash of blades. "Failing to mention our immortality. Refusing to fight for us on our wedding day. Leaving us for dead when you knew we would waken again. Abandoning us to hell for five thousand years. Saving our mother. *Sleeping* with our mother. Which of those, Lorhen, is a *little* fault? We'll be happy to forgive you for it." Each sentence was highlighted by a swift attack, less designed for blood than eventual weariness.

"I would have mentioned the immortality," Lorhen protested. "I thought we had time." He no longer backed up, but nor did he go on the offensive, merely answering the attacks in a steady pattern. "Ghean, this could go on all day. People are eventually going to wake up."

She smiled, a flash of teeth in the early light. The sun broke the horizon, shooting spires of red through the clouds above them, and it began to rain. "Our healing will be your death. So much fun, we thought, to pretend we still loved you, to use you and then to kill you. And you even proved Atlantis for us. You did very well, Lorhen. Now it's time to die. They won't wake up if it's over soon." She shifted her attack, moving from low to high in a smooth, rapid sequence, then dropping it again.

"Dammit, Ghean! I'm better than you are, and we're in the middle of the ocean on a metal ship full of mortals. If you press this, don't you think it's probably going to end badly for them? Never mind you?"

Ghean straightened again, falling back out of his reach. "You won't even take us seriously," she said quietly. "Fight us, Lorhen. The challenge has been made. You can't walk away from it."

"Us," he echoed again, softly this time. "We. What are you talking about, Ghean? *Who* are you talking about?"

"We haven't been whole in a long time," she whispered in a voice not quite her own. "So patient. So frightened. Holding her together in the darkness. In the silence. We could do nothing else. She had to stop screaming somehow."

"Ghean." Her name sounded helpless on his lips. "Ghean, you need help, not a Blending."

"A Blending, *your* Blending, will set us right! All the years we should have lived, all the memories and all the power that should have been ours, we will have it, Lorhen! We will have it."

"Ghean." Lorhen closed his eyes, then spread his free hand upward, meeting her gaze again. "All right. Have it your way."

Ghean's jaw set, and she nodded, satisfied. Her next lunge Lorhen met with no more enthusiasm, but greater dedication. He could see the surprise in her eyes at the power behind the blow. Then something else colored her expression: pleasure. Lorhen took the fight to high ground, throwing a blow at her shoulder with the two-handed sword he used. Ghean tangled her rapier in the other sword, thrusting it away, and retreated.

They tossed offensive and defensive back and forth, blades sparking as they smashed together, bleeding red with the rising sun. The ring of metal on metal was loud to Lorhen's ears, but the mortals on the ship continued to sleep, protected from the sounds of battle by the heavy steel floor and walls.

Wind picked up, knocking Ghean's hair into her eyes a moment. She brushed it back, a fighting grin growing wider as none of Lorhen's blows hit home. He remained serious, scowling as they fought in the rain. Ghean's moment came as they whirled around each other, Lorhen's footing bad on the wet deck. A thin ray of sunlight broke through to bounce off Lorhen's own sword, reflecting brilliantly off steel and water alike to blind him momentarily. Ghean lunged forward, scoring a thin red line across his belly before he could knock the rapier off course. He fell back, touching his fingers to the cut to test its depth. It stung, but it would heal within the minute.

"We can draw your blood," she said into the abrupt silence, "but you'll never take ours." Secret delight crackled in Ghean's brown eyes. "We're surprised you didn't recognize it." She lifted her sword hand to display the ring she wore around her thumb. "The ring of the Lion, Lorhen. It protects us. You're going to die." The words were a sing-song, mocking and light.

Lorhen looked at the blood on his fingers, diluted by the pouring rain, then raised his eyes to Ghean. She split a grin of triumph at the horror on his face, and laughed as he whispered, "Oh, Ghean," very quietly. "I did love you."

Ghean laughed, throwing her arms wide to the sky, embracing the morning sun. "Too late!" she crowed. "Today you pay—"

The blow that sent her to her knees was identical to the one that brought her the first death aeons ago. Lorhen's sword came down in a wide arc, half gutting the tiny woman. Her rapier fell from numb fingers as she crashed to her knees, one hand wrapping disbelievingly around her midsection. Incredulous, she lifted her head, brown eyes staring as life drained from them. "How—?"

Another voice, thin and terrified, broke from her lips: "We never tested it."

And another, deeper, calm, even through shock: "He told us himself. 'An arrow embedded itself in Minyah's arm.' She wore the ring that day. He told us and we didn't hear, we never thought—"

"The larger the artifact is, the more effective it is in providing physical protection," Lorhen said, still softly. "The ring offers eternal life, not protection from external harm. I did love you once, Ghean," he repeated, his voice gentle. "I'm so, so sorry. For everything. And I wish I could just let you go, my love. I wish I could let your Blending go free, so you could be reborn and start over, and over, and over. But you're mad, Ghean, my poor beloved. I can't release that, I can't poison so many potential Timeless with your insanity. I'm so very, very sorry."

"No." He could hear it in her voice now, threads of panic and notes of calm, making resonances that had never been there before. "No, we would rather die, die forever, die for good, than be part of you for eternity!"

"You won't be," Lorhen whispered. "You'll be gone, Ghean. I'm that much stronger than you. There will be nothing left, I promise. I'm so sorry."

Ghean whispered, "Lorhen," and he moved swiftly, first drawing and driving the heartstrike blade home. Without taking his eyes from hers, he swung the sword up and over, the weight and speed of nearly a full circle racing down to sever her head from her neck.

I did love you.

The thought burned through Lorhen's mind, and for an eternal heartbeat he stood in the sudden stillness, letting grief be his companion. Then necessity spurred him into motion: the

Retribution would conduct the Blending's electric power. Ghean would bring the ship down with her, unless—

Lorhen turned and ran for the edge of the ship, vaulting one-handed to the waist-high railing. He took one deep breath as the sky began to boil, and launched himself from the railing out into the sunrise.

The lightning caught him as he hit the water. Already colored golden-red by the rising sun, the Mediterranean added blue fire to its palette, flashes of electricity slicing through Lorhen as he fell deeper through the sea.

Memory sent a scream of panic and pain through him, out into the water, as Ghean's life pounded into him with her Blending. The terror of the water closing over her head in the temple made him scream again, reaching for the grey skies above the surface. Waves pushed him further down, pain rocketing through his body as lightning struck again and again, bringing with it thousands of years of solitude and fear, whispering voices and mindless despair. Lorhen held on to himself, on to his own memories of those many centuries, forcing what Ghean had been deeper into himself, acknowledging it, accepting it, but not surrendering to it.

The sea seethed, flinging him back out on an outburst of water, to meet lightning falling from the stormy sky. It danced down around him, a ragged pattern of rapid-fire shocks that surged into the water and back up through it, up through the soles of his feet and through his body, building toward the nerve-wrecking threshold between absolute pain and excruciating pleasure. Lorhen flung his head back in a wordless shout of pain and grief and release, the only release the Blending ever allowed. Time ceased, a few seconds lasting forever, before the Blending cast him back into the ocean, spent.

For long minutes Lorhen remained in the sea's cradle, choppy waves made by natural winds rocking him as the sky brought forth the storm that the red dawn warned of. Dazed, he opened his eyes, finding his sword still clutched in his hand. The hilt left dimples marked deep in his palm, and he loosened his grip on it a little, trying to right himself in the waves, energy drained. After a moment he oriented himself, turning wearily toward the ship.

Michelle Powers stood on the deck, hands light on the railing. She watched, silent, as Lorhen swam weakly back to the ship, and dove under to search out the submarine dock again. One-handed, he pulled himself up the ladder. Powers, still wordless, offered him a hand; after a moment's hesitation, Lorhen accepted it, letting the mortal help him onto the deck. The two stared at each other, Lorhen marked with exhaustion, Michelle with unhappy understanding.

"She told you what we were," Lorhen said when the silence drew out too long.

"Her ring didn't work," Michelle replied.

Lorhen shook his head. "No," he said, "it didn't." He glanced at the body, then back at Michelle. "There was a winter storm this morning," he suggested quietly.

Michelle licked her lips, and nodded, swallowing hard.

"Thank you," Lorhen said, and went to pick up Ghean's sword, pausing at the *Retribution*'s rail. "Do you want it?"

Michelle shook her head mutely. Lorhen nodded, and dropped the rapier over the side. It made a tiny ripple in the choppy sea as it sank. "You don't want to watch the rest of this," Lorhen advised the mortal. Without responding, Michelle turned away, walking below-decks.

Lorhen closed his eyes momentarily, then crouched beside Ghean's body, hands steepled in front of his mouth. Wrapping his hand around the Hunter's pendant, he took it from her body, and then slid the golden ring off her thumb, putting the ring on the chain with the pendant. He stood, slipping the necklace into his jeans pocket, and found a length of chain to weight Ghean's body with, sending it after her sword into the Mediterranean.

The storm did a fair job of washing blood away, but he found a bucket and filled it with seawater, splashing it over the deck. The deck was scored black under the blood, a long trail of charred steel where lightning had followed his leap off the ship's railing. Lorhen toed at the burned metal, and then, still soaking wet, he went below to get the sheath for his sword. He took the wetsuit as well, finding another length of chain to weight it with before dropping it over the side of the ship. Sword strapped to his back, he returned to the submarine port, looking down into the pale water.

The Book. Lorhen looked up. It lay where Ghean had tossed it, crumpled against the edge of the bulwark. He smiled without humor, and went to collect it, retying the sword to the outside of the backpack. He glanced at the submarine port, but instead vaulted once again over the side of the *Retribution*, following the same path he'd sent Ghean on.

Seconds later he resurfaced and began, for the second time in his life, swimming through a storm, away from Atlantis toward the safety of shore.

34

A newspaper spun twice as it was thrown down the counter, landing with the text upside-down at Emma's elbow. A gold ring bounced after it, rattling to a stop a foot or two away from where Emma polished the bar. Emma glanced up to see who'd tossed them, then muttered, "An actual newspaper. How retro. I'll put it up on the wall to go with the decor," as she picked the paper up.

"The decor already looks good. You've tarted the place up a bit since I was here last." Lorhen sat down across from Emma, glancing over the club. A stage with vintage footlights and a velvet backdrop dominated one end of the room, with a couple dozen small round tables with two or three chairs each facing it. Booths lined two of the walls, and the bar curved down the length of the last, all of it done in a style now pressing a hundred years old. "It looks good," he repeated. "And throwing a tablet down the bar just seemed too expensive and not really the same effect," he said with a nod at the paper. "Read the article. I like the part where it says I saved a lot of lives."

"I'm reading, Logan. Shut up and let me."

WINTER STORM CLAIMS LIVES
A brief lightning storm on the Mediterranean Sea claimed the lives of two research doctors last week. Mary Kostani of

the University of Chicago, recently acclaimed for finding the legendary city of Atlantis, and unaffiliated researcher Logan Adams, died Wednesday morning when a winter storm came up. The two were the only ones on the deck of the research vessel Retribution, *thanks to a late-night party the evening before. Dr. Michelle Powers, head of the exploration and a friend of both the deceased, said she came up from below decks just as the storm was ending. No bodies have been found. Neither Kostani nor Adams have next of kin; Kostani's assets were left to the University.*

"We're usually a crew that's up early," Powers said in a subdued interview Thursday afternoon. "We had a fantastic find the day before, and we were celebrating until late. I guess we were lucky, if you can call it that. Mary was the mover behind this project. I'd like to see it go forward, in her memory."

When asked about Adams, Powers said she had only met him recently, and that he was, to the best of her knowledge, a recluse, and that it was Adams' discovery that the crew had been celebrating the night before. "We owe him a strange debt of gratitude," she said, "as a lot more of us might have been on deck that morning if he hadn't found materials worth celebrating."

The article went on about the Atlantis Project, but Emma reached for the ring, turning it in her fingertips, and lifted her eyebrows at Lorhen. "This was Ghean's."

"It was." Lorhen sat on a stool, watching the Keeper. "Call it a legacy of Atlantis. A gift."

"Hell of a gift, Logan." Emma tilted the ring until light sank into the lion's head etching, then looked up with a brief smile. "You couldn't have brought me a unicorn, huh?"

A smile twitch Lorhen's mouth, too. "Everybody knows there's no such thing as unicorns, Em."

Emma laughed. "Of course." She glanced at the ring again, folding it into her palm. "Hope you don't mind if I'm not sure I want to wear it. That kind of choice takes some thought."

"As long as you're lucky enough to have the choice."

"Why me? There are a lot of people you could give this to. More you couldn't. Wouldn't."

"You're right. There are." Lorhen turned his head as a shiver of awareness ran over him. "Company."

Emma, softly, said, "I'm going to want answers from you sooner rather than later, Lorhen," but let it go as Cathal strode into the club and asked, "What happened?" before the door closed all the way.

"I saved a lot of lives," Lorhen said immediately. "Says so right there in the paper. Aren't you proud of me? And Logan Adams turned out to be Timeless. He'll need a Keeper, Emma. Make it somebody we can trust."

Emma poured drinks for herself and the two Timeless men. "Way the Keepers figure it, Adams survived because he knew what to do. It's happened a couple of times in the past, a Keeper has turned out to be Timeless and survived her first fight because she had insider knowledge. But we reckon Adams is going to need some training with a sword, and we all know Cathal Devane's been palling around with Adams for a while now. Probably been waiting for Adams to get himself killed, so he can be his teacher." Emma lifted a shot of whiskey at Cathal. "Devane's like that, you know."

Cathal picked up his own shot glass and touched it to Emma's. "He is," he agreed with something of a smile. "And will his Keeper be keeping an eye on Logan Adams, too?"

"She will be. No point in wasting resources, and besides, the three of them have this complicated relationship anyway, the way I understand it. Devane knows he's got a Keeper, Adams was a Keeper…they figure it'll all work out, one way or another."

"They're probably right." Cathal looked at Lorhen again, eyebrows lifted. "Lorhen? What happened?"

Lorhen lifted his glass to look at the amber liquid. After a brief silence, he touched his glass against his friends', and shrugged. "I survived."

Lorhen's story (and history) continues in
PROMETHEUS BOUND and AVALON RISING,
coming soon....

Acknowledgments

This book has been, in some ways, a very long time coming. Particular thanks to Carl, Bryant, Michelle, Mikaela and Sarah for encouraging me with this project, as well as to Ted, who listened patiently while I world-built at him.

Karina Sumner-Smith and Patricia Burroughs are due a particular hat-tip thanks to their efforts in helping me brainstorm the series' titles. Early readers Elizabeth Glover, Thirzah Brown, Marjorie Taylor, Laura Hobbs and Catherine Sharp offered insightful feedback, and Tara O'Shea not only provided a brilliant cover but also (irritatingly, in a good way) invaluable commentary on the manuscript; this would literally be a different book without her questions and thoughts on it.

Special thanks

to the Atlantis Fallen Patrons

Amelinda Webb, Amy Stromquist, Anne Burner, Arysani, Auntie Makeel, Axisor, Barbara Field White, Barbara Hasebe, Barbara Stephenson, Beverly Lee, Blue Haired Angie, Brian J. Showers, Brian Nisbet, Bryant Durrell, Cari Goldfine, Carl Rigney, Cat (the Mystical Divinity of Unashamed Felinity), Catherine Sharp, Cathy Schwartz, Christine Swendseid, Chrysoula Tzavelas, Claire Vaughan, Coby Haas, Cori May, Danielle Ingber, Deanna Zinn, Debbie Ochsner, Deirdre "Wyvernfriend" Murphy, Diane Dupey, Dino Hicks, Donna Gaudet, Earl Miles, Elektra Hammond, Elena Barrick, Elizabeth, Elizabeth Belden Handler, Ella Peabody, Emily Poole, Erlinda Sustaita, G. Stewart, Gadgetman!, Gareth Kavanagh, Gemma Tapscott, Georgina Scott, Heather Fagan, James Shields, Jennifer Cabbage, Jennifer Canova, Jessica Bay, Jessica Godfrey, Jim Hameister, Joliene McAnly, Judy Glaser, K. Gavenman, Karl Kloeden, Karyl Fulkerson, Kat Bonson, Kate Malloy, Kathleen Hanrahan, Kathy Rogers, Katie Hynes, Katrina Lehto, Kellie, Kelly Babcock, Kelsey Kumpula, Kerry Kuhn, Kerry Malone, Kris Zieska, Laura Wallace,

Leading Edge, Leah Moore, Limugurl, Lisa J. Pegg, Louise
Löwenspets, Mandie "Baca" Forgue, Maresa Welke, Margaret
A. Menzies, Marjorie Taylor, Mary Anne Walker, Mary
Garner, Mary Rodgers, Melinda Skye, Michael Bernardi,
Michael Feldhusen, Michelle C., Michelle Carlson, Naasaw
Nayts, Paul-Gabriel Wiener, Pete Kreitchet, Rachel Gollub,
Rachel Narow, Rick McKnight, Rob Donoghue, Robert
Lynch, Roisin McCormac, Sam Dailey, Sara Harville, Sarah
Brooks, Shannon Long, Sharon Sayegh, Shawn Tumey,
Shelley Kennon, Shiver Carr, Sonia (and Kate), Stacey Hill,
Stephanie Boose, Stephanie Fischer, Stormraider, Sue Carlson,
Susan L. Johnston, Susan Simko, Tara Lynch (The Ninja
Hedgehog), Tennille, The Perfectly Magnificent E!, Tina
Chopee, Todd Nagengast, Valentine Lewis, Wolf SilverOak

About the Author

CE Murphy was born and raised in Alaska, now lives in Ireland, and can be found on social media at @ce_murphy & fb.com/cemurphywriter.

Lightning Source UK Ltd.
Milton Keynes UK
UKOW02f2143210317
297166UK00002B/27/P